More Praise For
The Woman Who Fell from the Sky

"In the gifted hands of Barbara Riefe, the ancient nations of the eastern forests come vividly to life. She knows those Indian people; how they thought, what they believed, their strengths and vulnerabilities. Her story of a white woman among the Indians is compelling and soul-touching. By all means, buy and enjoy *The Woman Who Fell from the Sky*. It will draw you into A BREATHTAKING WORLD YOU NEVER KNEW EXISTED."

—Richard S. Wheeler,
Golden Spur Award-winning author of *Badlands*

"SUPERB NOVEL and a classy example of the 'Eastern Western.' I especially like Riefe's crackling dialogue, especially that between Margaret Addison and Two Eagles. The Iroquois lore is wonderful stuff: patching the canoe with the stomach fat from the slain trapper, making canoes, wilderness Indian medicine, folkways of the Oneidas, and making fire. *THE WOMAN WHO FELL FROM THE SKY* IS FILLED WITH SEARING SCENES AND POWERFUL EMOTIONS."

—Dale L. Walker, columnist,
Rocky Mountain News

"A strong novel. . . . Her heroine is one of the most fascinating characters in modern literature and the Oneidas rival and surpass any American Indian created by James Fenimore Cooper. This is a gripping story, full of twists and turns, rich in history, packed with accurate Indian lore."

—Jory Sherman,
author of GRASS KINGDOM

BARBARA RIEFE

THE WOMAN WHO FELL FROM THE SKY

A TOM DOHERTY ASSOCIATES BOOK
NEW YORK

This is a work of fiction. All the characters and events portrayed in this book are fictitious, and any resemblance to real people or events is purely coincidental.

THE WOMAN WHO FELL FROM THE SKY

Copyright © 1994 by Barbara Riefe

All rights reserved, including the right to reproduce this book, or portions thereof, in any form.

Cover art by Brad Schmehl

A Forge Book
Published by Tom Doherty Associates, Inc.
175 Fifth Avenue
New York, N.Y. 10010

Forge® is a registered trademark of Tom Doherty Associates, Inc.

ISBN: 0-812-52377-6
Library of Congress Catalog Card Number: 94-2980

First edition: July 1994
First mass market edition: August 1995

Printed in the United States of America

0 9 8 7 6 5 4 3 2 1

This book is dedicated to
my great-grandmother,
who bore ten children,
smoked a pipe and was
a full-blooded Mohican Indian.

CONTENTS

Place Names

Ganawagehas—*Catskill Mountains*
Green Mountains—*Adirondacks*
Shaw-na-taw-ty—*Hudson River*
Te-uge´-ga—*Mohawk River*
Kanawage—*St. Lawrence River*
O-chog-wä—*Richelieu River and Falls*
O-jik´-ha-dä-ge´-ga—*the Wide Water—Atlantic Ocean*
Schoharie Creek
Osh-we-geh—*Oswego River*
Onekahoncka—*Mohawk castle*
Schandisse—*Mohawk castle*
Tenotoge—*Mohawk castle*
Onneyuttahage—*Oneida castle*
Massowaganine—*Onondaga castle—peace conference site*
Da-yä´-hoo-wä´-quat—*Carrying Place, rendezvous area
   for the* coureurs de bois
Ne-ah´-gä-te-car-ne-o-di—*Lake Ontario*
Cataraqui—*Fort Frontenac*
Gananoque—*French settlement on the St. Lawrence River*
Hochelga—*Montreal*
Stadacona—*Quebec*
O-ne-ä-da´-lote—*Lake Champlain*
Andia-ta-roc-te—*Lake St. Sacrement*
Lake Oneida

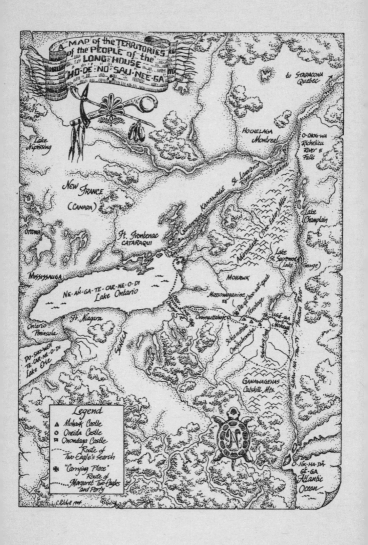

Cast of Characters

Oneidas

Do-wa-sku-ta *(Thrown-in-bear's-den)*—Thrown Bear, warrior

Tékni-ska-je-a-nah *(Two Eagles)*—Pine Tree *(war)* chief

Tyagohuens *(Splitting Moon)*—Warrior

Bone *(formerly Black Wolf)*—Mohican adoptee of the Oneidas, warrior

Sa-ga-na-qua-de *(He-who-makes-everyone-angry)*—Anger Maker, warrior

O-kwen-cha *(Red Paint)*—warrior

Sku-nak-su *(Fox)*—warrior

Swift Doe—wife of Long Feather and Two Eagles' sister-in-law

Téklq?-eyo *(Eight Minks)*—Two Eagles' aunt

Ataentsic—Iroquois spirit credited with creating the earth—The Woman Who Fell from the Sky

Taouscaron
Jouskeha } *grandsons of Atatentsic*

So-hat-tis—Long Feather, Two Eagles' brother

Graywind—Two Eagles' wife

Sho-non-ses *(His Longhouse)*—chief of Bear Clan

To-na-oh-ge-na *(Two-branches-of-water)*—chief of the Turtle Clan

Hat-ya-tone-nent-ha *(He-who-swallows-his-body-from-the-foot)*—chief of the Wolf Clan

Kah-nah-chi-wah-ne *(He-big-kettle)*—Oneida sachem and representative to the peace conference at Massowaganine

Agreskoue—Iroquois sun god

Moon Dancer—wife of Thrown Bear

Hi-sen *(Red Squirrel)*—tribal elder

Mohawks (Maquen)

Ho-ka-ah-ta-ken *(Burnt Eye)*—chief of the Mohawks at Onekahoncka Castle

Dreamer—*his wife*

Joshú-we-agoochsa *(Hole Face)*—tribal sachem, friend and advisor to Burnt Eye

Cahonsye-rú-kwe *(Black)*—Burnt Eye's cousin

Onondagans

To-do-da-ho *(He-great-wizard)—sachem-orator*
Ta-ha-nah-gai-eh-ne *(Two-horns-lying-down)—tribal chief*
Willow Song—*granddaughter of He-great-wizard*
Gä-de-a-yo *(Lobster)—Sgt. Gordon Duncan, Onondaga adoptee*

Aboard the *Aventurier*

Margaret Addison Lacroix
Celestine—*her maid*
Captain Jurieu—*captain of the vessel*

On the St. Lawrence

Father Gilbert—*Sulpician priest*

In Quebec

Lorette Hurons

Little Cloud—*Two Buttons*
Winter Heart—*tribal elder*

French

Pvt. Emile Campeau *(Nez)—orderly to Capt. Pierre Lacroix*
Capt. Pierre Lacroix—*captain of dragoons, aide-de-camp to Governor General Frontenac*
Corp. Claude Lemieux
Maj. Hertel Boulanger
Mme. Jeanette Boulanger
Louis de Baude, *comte de Palluau et de Frontenac— Governor general of New France*
Gen. Eugene LaFleur
Gen. Philip Desmaines
Dr. Blaise—*physician at Fort St-Louis*
Lieutenant Girard—*wharf officer*
Police Sergeant Bordagary
Jacques, *coureur de bois—translator*

league—*a distance approximating 3 miles*
nyoh—*yes*
neh—*no*

═══ **PROLOGUE** ═══

About the year 1450 five sovereign nations whose people were of the same stock formed a confederacy. They destroyed, dispersed or assimilated all the tribes surrounding their territories. Europeans later exploited them shamelessly and depleted their numbers to near extinction, and yet in the power struggle between England and France to determine which nation would ultimately dominate North America, history was to invest the five nations with the pivotal role.

Their confederacy survives to this day.

They are the League of the Iroquois.

I

SAVAGE REALM

1

Rain battered the grounded ship and sluiced off the deck in torrents through the larboard scuppers. Below, Margaret Addison Lacroix sat seething amidst tumbled trunks and portmanteaus. Lightning bleached the disarray, thunder shook the musty little cabin like a dice box. A pelisse pulled over her night shift protected against the chill air. Margaret had been tying up her hair for bed when the ship shuddered to a stop, tilting, nearly falling on its side. Above her, the storm hammered the decks furiously, she half-expected kindling to rain down on them. Cowering in a corner clutching her rosary beads sat her maid Celestine, wailing, starting with each new thunderclap, her eyes threatening to pop from her head. Margaret's little white poodle raced about yapping.

"We'll all be killed!" cried Celestine, "struck by lightning, drowned, buried in the mud! Sweet blessed Saint Anne save us, I beseech you!"

Again and again she crossed herself, kissed her beads and cowered.

"Oh, do shut up. Niche, you, too!" Picking her way through the chaos of luggage, Margaret cornered the dog, snatching it up. "Get up, Celestine, help me straighten this place!"

Celestine cringed and flinched as thunder pounded the vessel. Lurching to her feet, she began picking things up.

Margaret set Niche at the foot of the bunk, restored a

small bag to its shelf, and paused. "Listen . . . it's letting up."

"Sweet blessed Saint Anne heard me, she heard!" Celestine's scrawny fingers flew about her bosom in the sign of the cross.

"I'm going up on deck."

"*Non!* You can't." She wrung her talon hands. "Don't leave me, milady, I beseech you!"

"For pity's sake, get hold of yourself!" Margaret turned up the hood of her pelisse. "Hang onto Niche."

Outside, she felt her way toward the companionway, stumbling into the bottom step, barking a shin, damning the dark, slowly ascending to the afterdeck. Captain Jurieu clung to the mainmast, his broad back to her, barking commands to his men working in the water below to free the grounded *Aventurier.* The heavens were silent, the rain had stopped. A mist quilted the river that gently buffeted the ship, snugging around it like batting around packed glass. The shrouds and ratlines dripped silver, masts gleamed like burnished metal in the glow of the deck lanterns. Along both banks massive trees blocked out all but a strip of scowling sky. Behind the *Aventurier* the river meandered south to the burgeoning world of New York City, the Atlantic, places at the moment so remote from this black isolation that they seemed removed to another planet.

Captain Jurieu was frantically shouting orders. Margaret tensed. What if they were unable to free the ship, were forced to abandon it and continue on in the canoes stored in the hold? The original plan had been to travel the Hudson up to above Albany, where the first falls blocked further advance. From that point on they would canoe through the lakes and up the Richelieu River to Quebec. Quebec, where Pierre waited as impatiently as she herself waited to feel his embrace.

But at the moment, Quebec lay even farther distant to the north than did New York behind them. Two crewmen scrambled over the railing to assist their shipmates in loosening the sandbar's grip and Captain Jurieu grew more frustrated by the moment. She was about to start back

down the companionway when out of the gloom whirred
an arrow, thumping into Jurieu's neck above the stiff collar
of his roquelaure.

2

He let go of the mast, pivoting slowly. A bloody arrow
pierced and protruded from his neck. His eyes widened, his knees buckled. Instantly the air was filled with
blood-curdling screams and whooping and arrows flying
toward the crewmen who stood transfixed at the rail and in
the waist-deep water below. Down the companionway
scrambled Margaret, feeling her way back to the cabin, her
pelisse slipping from her shoulders. Celestine still huddled
in a corner. Niche bounced from her lap yapping at his
mistress.

"Get up!" snapped Margaret. "Can't you hear? We're
being attacked. Savages! We must get away!"

"*Mon Dieu!* They will kill us!"

"If we stay down here they will. Move!"

"*Non!*"

Celestine crossed herself and shrank into her corner, her
lower lip protruding stubbornly. Margaret rasped exasperation, snatched up her wedding gown, wound it in a ball,
cradled Niche and ran to the doorway. Turning, she glared.

"Celestine!"

"*Non!*"

"For the last time!"

Celestine appeared bolted to the corner. Margaret waved
her away in disgust. Groping up the passageway, she could
hear the shrill cries overhead, the crack of a pistol, and another. She stumbled over her pelisse and nearly fell. Niche
leaped from her grasp, scampering up the stairs. She
caught him on the top step.

Outside, she could see the men of her escort along with
crew members counterattacking. Six men wielding swords
clambered up the bank. Out of the darkness the screaming
savages poured.

Clutching her wedding gown with one arm, Niche with the other, she slipped over the rail into the frigid, waist-deep water. She waded to the bank, losing both slippers scrambling up it. She had almost reached cover when an arrow came straight at Niche in her arm, piercing the side of his neck. He yelped and wrenched to get free. Flinging the gown ahead of her, she snapped the arrow in two and pulled it loose. Blood spurted. She ripped the hem from her shift, folded half of it into a pad and with the rest tied it snugly around Niche's neck.

She retrieved her gown and slipped behind a tree. To the right, boughs swished and whipped, then came blood-chilling screams: more savages come to join the massacre. The deck swarmed with them. They crowded the companionway, pushing and shoving to get down it. She sighed, nausea finding the pit of her stomach as she pictured them bursting in on Celestine.

Niche whined and shuddered in her arms and off she ran. Ran and ran and ran until she could no longer hear the screaming, the sound of gunfire. Only the dripping from the branches, the wind high overhead setting the trees groaning and Niche's whimper.

And she was alone.

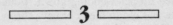 **3**

A plane of sunlight pierced the tree branches to where a she-wolf gorged on a white-tailed buck. While he drank from a pond, she had charged it, sinking her fangs into his rump, bringing him down. Now glutted, she dug a shallow hole and ripped open the buck's belly, peeling from the intestinal membranes long strips of fat. Burying them, covering the hole, she prepared to cache the liver the same way, when a sound above the breeze froze her. She straightened, still rigid, pointing her muzzle upwind. Her eyes slanted as she caught a familiar scent. Off she loped, the liver in her jaws, leaving the carcass to the mosquitoes and humpbacked black flies.

* * *

So strong was the scent of pine it stung Two Eagles' nostrils. A woodpecker's rapping faded. Silence again enveloped the Oneida warrior and his six companions ringing the cookfire. Staring into the fire fingering his bearclaw necklace, Two Eagles recognized the warrior from whom he had taken it. He had trekked 500 miles into hostile Huron Territory to avenge his father, murdered by Huron hunters. The man he saw now in the flames he had fought and killed. Home he had come with the necklace and his enemy's scalp, to be chided for his rashness by his Aunt Eight Minks. But the smile she could not hide confirmed that his courage pleased her. Long Feather, his older brother, had praised him. Two Eagles had departed a boy and returned a man.

Of fourteen.

He stared intently into the fire reflecting on his present dilemma. With his companions he had searched for Long Feather's hunting party for nearly one whole moon. From their castle near Oneida Lake in the west they had ventured southward toward the Ganawagehas, the mountains the Dutch call the Catskills. In time they had turned toward the Shaw-na-taw-ty, the Great River of Iroquois Territory and its eastern boundary. They had searched from before the first pale light of day, while the birds still slept, to when the sun lowered, melting into the rod of gold that seams heaven and earth. So far, to no avail.

A sigh of discouragement vied with the crackling of the fire.

"Are their bones already picked clean by wolves and their spirits on the way to the Village of the Dead?" asked a gloomy-looking, solidly built warrior squatting opposite Two Eagles.

Two Eagles stiffened. "How could that be, Tyagohuens? How could my brother escape death in the war as many times as you have fingers and toes to die on the hunt? From what, snakebite?"

"That or a cut that sucks poison into the blood."

"Or a dead tree falling on him?" Two Eagles scoffed.

"On all of them?" He studied the others' eyes around the fire. All held the same dispirited look. "They are somewhere in these woods and we will find them. And no more talk about wolves and the Village of the Dead!"

The sun's rays fell as straight as the pines, the searchers had assembled for their single daily meal.

"We still have far to go," asserted Do-wa-sku-ta, to Two Eagles' right. "Tékni-ska-je-a-nah is right, Tyagohuens, we will find them."

Tyagohuens—Splitting Moon—grunted. "We have found nothing that says they got even this far."

Two Eagles shot to his feet, towering over the pessimist. "And nothing that says they did not! Why do you always throw your rancid meat in the stew!"

Do-wa-sku-ta's hand gripped his arm, pulling him gently back down. Do-wa-sku-ta—Thrown in Bear's Den—was Two Eagles' childhood friend, whose name had been corrupted to Thrown Bear. His boast was that he had eaten raw the liver of every creature that walked, crawled or swam in the Territory (except that of the dog, which, like the raw meat of the acorn, can kill a man). Thrown Bear had lost his left hand to a Huron tomahawk in the raid on Lachine in the heart of New France early in the seven years of red days between the English-Iroquois alliance and the French and their Indian allies.

"Do not start bickering," said Thrown Bear.

"If you think we won't find them, why stay?" asked Two Eagles of Splitting Moon. "Why waste your time searching for the dead?"

"*Da-neh,*" growled Thrown Bear, "no more words. It is circle talk. My stomach is empty, let us eat."

Again Splitting Moon grunted. Stumpy, powerful, he delighted in crushing enemy skulls like pumpkins with his toothed-ball tomahawk. He had crushed many French and French moccasin skulls in the fighting. He suffered from a chronically weak stomach and was careful what he ate: mainly corn in its various baked forms. Meat, he abhorred. His friend Thrown Bear's fondness for liver repelled him.

On Splitting Moon's right sat Bone, who carried the

smoldering punk fire for the party in a hollow corn cob: grass mixed with fungus wrapped in a tight cylinder. A Mohican, Bone had been adopted by the turtle clan of the Oneidas. He had come to the tribe calling himself Black Wolf but so many of his bones had been broken and poorly reset he was left with a knobby, bumpy appearance so his adoptive family renamed him "Bone."

Next to Bone sat Sa-ga-na-qua-de—He Who Makes Everyone Angry, Anger Maker. He, too, had fought in the war. French greed for Iroquois beaver pelfry had threatened to destroy the tribes' fur trade, there was no choice but to ally with the English against the lace-cuffs and their Huron, Abnaki, Miami and Ottawa allies. Anger furrowed Anger Maker's face; in his hulking shoulders and surly tone it abided. When he bellowed his fury all eyes near him turned upward to summon patience. His temper had driven his wife from their bed.

His disposition aside, he was a tough and fearless warrior, greatly respected for his loyalty. He had once halved the face of a drunken Cayuga bully with his tomahawk, rescuing a friend from the man's abuse.

He smoked incessantly, cramming the bowl of his ash wood pipe with a blend of tobacco, dried sumac leaves and red willow bark. The stench it emitted was as foul as putrid fish but his friends rarely complained. Not to Anger Maker.

Two other volunteers completed the party. The search was exacting its toll. Splitting Moon's pessimism infected everyone's expression, even the eternally cheerful and optimistic Thrown Bear's; prompting Two Eagles to resolve that if he had to do it by himself he would find his brother. Or his bones. Splitting Moon stirred the fire. The flames fashioned the pretty face of Long Feather's wife, Swift Doe, in Two Eagles' eyes. Her belly was rounding with their third child. He saw himself facing her as she bid him goodbye, her voice trembling, eyes brimming with desperate hope. How could he return without her husband?

Anger Maker got out his pipe and began stuffing the bowl, eliciting a chorus of groans.

"Why must you smoke when we are sitting so close?" Thrown Bear asked.

"Back off, One Hand."

He ignited his pipe with Bone's smoldering punk. The others widened the circle, leaving him squatting nearest the fire and puffing contentedly.

They had already consumed their daily allotment of hard cranberry-corn bread spread with deer oil by Anger Maker. Iroquois warriors ate little for it was believed that overeating weakened the capacity to withstand hunger in times of deprivation. The bread was delicious, crumbled readily in the mouth and was filling, but hot food was needed for energy for the afternoon search. Bone had killed an *ochquoha*, a wolf, sleepy from the fullness of her belly, late in the afternoon of the previous day. In cutting her open, he had found undigested chunks of *aque* meat. The venison was washed in a nearby pond to rid it of its sour taste; now the chunks were fixed to pointed sticks to be roasted over the fire and the wolf's ribs thrust into the coals. Thrown Bear hoisted the prize of Bone's efforts: the deer's liver, found between the sleeping wolf's jaws. He announced he would eat half.

"And give you the other half, Tyagohuens."

Splitting Moon made the face of resentment. He growled and compared liver eaters to the Ottawas who, it was claimed, subsisted on dog droppings after a lean harvest or unsuccessful hunt. Thrown Bear laughed. Everyone ate except Splitting Moon. His knees cracked as he rose, waved away the stench of Anger Maker's pipe and walked off.

Two Eagles followed. "You should eat," he said.

"After him. I should shit and bake it for him. Or would he like *it* raw?"

Two Eagles slapped his back and laughed. The others looked their way grinning; his leer gleaming greasily, Thrown Bear held up what was left of the liver. The collective tension seemed to ease.

"We move on after we eat," said Two Eagles. "We should reach the Shaw-na-taw-ty by late this afternoon."

Tite-ti, the yellow-billed cuckoo, sent its familiar Ká-ká-cow-cow through the woodlands, the breeze sang more forcefully; the birds around the Oneidas were feeding lower than earlier on flying insects; Two Eagles' wounds throbbed dully. All of these were signs that, despite the sun's brightness and the blueness of the heavens, a storm was coming. It had rained heavily if briefly the night before.

The sun was starting its downward path when Two Eagles positioned himself second from the north in the wide-spread line, with Thrown Bear to his left. This was Maquen Territory: Mohawk, home of the "Keepers of the Eastern Door of the Lodge"—the Iroquois Confederacy. The Mohawk had come through the war with far fewer casualties than had the Oneida. They occupied three castles while the Oneida, the "People of the Place of the Stone," had been reduced to but one. "Mohawk"—man-eater—was a name ascribed to the tribe by its enemies. The Mohawk *had* practiced cannibalism in the hostilities, but more to increase their enemies' fear of them than any fondness of human flesh. They called themselves the Gä-ne-ă-ga-o-nó-ga—"People of the Place of the Flint."

Voices called loudly as the line moved forward, the echoes ringing through the pines. Two Eagles stooped to pick up a handful of needles, letting them sift through his fingers. Each a man's life. How many had he killed since his first Huron? How many French long knives? French Moccasins: Hurons, Miamis, Ottawas, Abnakis? How many more would sheathe his knife before some stranger—warrior or whiteskin—gave him his own immortality?

Bone approached him. "Your brother So-hat-tis nearly died in the war."

"All of us 'nearly died' too many times," said Two Eagles.

"Do you think it is over for good?"

"*Neh.*"

"Are not both sides preparing to meet in the Council House of the Onondaga to work out a treaty?"

"*Nyoh*, all nine of our sachems will be there." Two Eagles scoffed, his brows drawing together in a frown. "Why they bother I do not know."

"They must talk."

"Why? The lace-cuffs have broken every treaty they have made this side of the O-jik´-ha-dä-ge´-ga, the Wide Water. What makes you think they will keep this one?"

"I do not 'think,' I do not know."

Two Eagles was becoming heated. "Why should we trust any whiteskin when they refuse to trust each other?"

"So you say nothing will come of talking."

"Nothing. It will be words into the wind as usual. Oh, both sides will make many speeches, they will agree on a treaty. And before Gâ´-oh, the north wind, blows across our lands they will break it like a stick."

"I have never fought in a war."

"You are lucky. Sometimes I think that the red days have been most of the days of my life."

A belted kingfisher, with its ragged crest, black bill and harsh rattling call, flew by as Bone resumed his position in the line of searchers. Two Eagles glanced aloft. Through a break in the treetops he glimpsed a familiar dark shape. Resting on rising air, it appeared suspended from the heavens by an invisible cord. The sun's glare painted it black but he recognized it from its distinctive wing tips and knew it to be dark brown with white hood and tailfeathers. Now it circled slowly, vanishing into the glare, reappearing, carving the warm air.

Ska-je-a-nah, the great golden eagle: his óyaron.

He shaded his eyes and watched it wheel. It was a sign. Tonight while the others slept he would consult it. Would it advise him to call off the search and return home? How could he? Only *if* it said to he must do so. One did not defy one's óyaron. He reached up to feel his single feather, *ska-je-a-nah's*, his medicine. Tonight in some secluded place he would hold it at eye level, offer his óyaron tobacco, chant and seek counsel.

Once more he looked upward; the eagle had vanished.

4

Anger Maker called out: "The Shaw-na-taw-ty . . ."
The Oneidas assembled on the riverbank. Those carrying bows and quivers removed them. No longer capable of holding a bow, Thrown Bear avoided looking at Anger Maker taking off his quiver. Before losing his hand, Thrown Bear could shoot an arrow with such force the head drove cleanly through a man's chest and out his back. In the arrow game he could fire six arrows in the air before the first fell to earth. Now his inability to do even simple tasks—tie a knot, climb a tree, pick a hot kettle up by the handles—set him against himself. At times his frustration infuriated him so even Anger Maker backed away from him, for his stump was a ram that could stave a man's forehead or crush his heart behind his ribs.

"*Wah-ah*, we will never find them," lamented Splitting Moon, who could be relied on to find the shadows in even the most promising situation.

Two Eagles said nothing. How could he take exception to anyone's pessimism?

"We have come only halfway," Thrown Bear reminded Splitting Moon. "We will surely find them on the way back. I bet my knife against yours on it."

"I do not want your knife, liver eater," growled Splitting Moon.

"It is English, better than yours."

Anger Maker joined them, nodding agreement, goading. "His knife is better, Tyagohuens, bet him, bet him. I will be witness."

"Go swim," groused Splitting Moon. And turned his attention to removing his corn husk moccasins. Anger Maker persisted in his goading. He delighted in starting an argument between others. Delighted even more in starting an argument himself, involving a third person, stirring the talk until it got hot then walking away from it. Bone ended his goading by pushing him into the water. In seconds all

were splashing about. Managing with one hand, Thrown
Bear could still swim passably well. They dove, swam,
threw mud at each other, ducked each other. The shadows
stretched, blackening the river. The sun glinted through the
trees. Two Eagles climbed the bank and lay back to catch
his breath. Overhead, his visitor had returned, only to glide
away almost immediately.

What would his óyaron tell him tonight? Would it advise him on the quest for Long Feather? In time it would.
He must hold his patience as tightly as the knot in his
heart held his worry.

The enormous, cloudless blue vault overhead, the color
of the asters that flourished near Lake Oneida in autumn,
brought thoughts of home and of Swift Doe. He sighed inwardly.

One by one the others emerged from the water wringing
out their breechclouts. Thrown Bear and O-kwen-cha, Red
Paint, swam upstream. Two Eagles watched them disap-
pear around a bend. Red Paint's face displayed his bravery
and his pride. He was never seen without three angled red
streaks adorning each cheek—color made from mixing the
fruit and root of the sumac with berry juices and bloodroot
to produce a hue more vivid than fresh blood. In a single
battle he had killed fourteen Ottawas and then tortured to
death two French dragoon prisoners, tying them to trees,
drawing out their fingernails with his teeth and pulling the
tendons out of their wrists to make hanging strings for
their scalps, already stretched on hoops to dry.

Bone and Splitting Moon sat on either side of Two Eagles.

"Do-wa-sku-ta is right," said Bone. "We will find So-
hat-tis on the way back to Onneyuttahage."

Two Eagles bunched his lips and frowned. "I wonder."

"What does your óyaron say?"

"I have consulted it only two times since we left. It says
nothing. Yet. A bad sign. Maybe my medicine is worn
out."

Reaching for his scalp lock he took down his feather,
twirling it aimlessly. It was frayed and yellowed with age.

"Useless."

"That could be so," said Splitting Moon.

"Neh, neh," protested Bone. "Keep asking it, it will help guide us."

From behind them came shouting.

"Come see! Come see!"

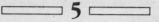

5

Thrown Bear and Red Paint had run back from their swim upriver.

"Come!" Thrown Bear beckoned with his stump.

Upriver around the bend a strange sight met their eyes: the blackened skeleton of a ship. It was charred from bowsprit to rudder. Both masts were intact but the flames had consumed the spars, sails, shrouds and ratlines. Sitting on a sandbar, it looked to Two Eagles like a *gachga*, a giant crow perched on a rock. Anger Maker paced off its length: twenty-four strides.

Blackened corpses stripped of their scalps lay everywhere, many with arrows sticking in them. Charred boxes and chests broken open and emptied were strewn about the deck. Anger Maker descended the blackened companionway, Two Eagles and Splitting Moon following. The cabins had been ransacked. The sickly sweet stench of death mingled with the acrid odor of burnt wood over two corpses in one cabin. In another they found the body of a woman, her head lopped off, charred shreds of her dress clinging to the blackened remains, her rosary beads still in her fist.

They retreated to the bank and surveyed the hulk.

Thrown Bear found an arrow unblackened by the fire. The others crowded around as he examined it. The fletching was fashioned of the tailfeathers of the blue jay. Thrown Bear handed it to Bone.

"Not Mohican," said Bone.

"Maquen," said Two Eagles.

They resumed the search for Long Feather and his com-

panions, following the Shaw-na-taw-ty north before turning westward into the descending coppery disk. They
would continue searching until the stars fired and the dark
blanket that touched the earth was hung behind them. Two
Eagles' mind raced ahead to his next rendezvous with his
óyaron. If it advised him to give up the search, so be it.
They would obtain canoes from the nearest Mohawk castle
and travel a good part of the way home by the Te-ugé-ga,
the Mohawk River.

Swift Doe would be waiting. Closing his eyes, he could
see tears glistening in hers. But why assume Long Feather
was already dead? Why give up halfway?

To his left he heard shouting. It was Sku-nak-su—
Fox—Red Paint's cousin and best friend, who fought like
a cornered fox and chased women old enough to be his
grandmother. From his belt dangled a dried and shrunken
scalp; around his neck he wore a crucifix taken from a
black robe. Some thought his brain was upside down in
his head, made so in the war, but he did not act crazy
when not fighting. Instead he was as gentle and harmless
as a child.

Fox shouted, waving both hands wildly, his eyes round
with fear, "*Nah-kweh, nah-kweh*! Ataentsic! Ataentsic!"

They ran to join him at the far side of a tree struck by
lightning, the trunk snapped off at about twice the height
of a man. Huddled in a rotted out opening, knees drawn
up, a ball of white cloth at her feet, in her lap a small dog,
its neck matted with dried blood, slept a whiteskin woman.

6

Two Eagles poked her shoulder. She woke, blanched,
screamed so loudly birds took flight, and he stepped
back, clapping his hands over his ears.

Fox continued pointing at her, shouting over her screams.
"Ataentsic!"

Two Eagles pulled her upright, the dog slipping from

her lap. He shook her. She stopped screaming and jerked free, glaring at him. "Don't touch me!"

"Ataentsic," Fox repeated, his voice now almost reverent. She retrieved the dog and held it close, petting it, talking soothingly to it. Two Eagles pulled it from her. "It is dead."

"No! He's alive. Niche!"

He threw it aside. She flew at him, pounding his chest. He gripped her wrists. Anger Maker went to where the dog lay. He raised his tomahawk to behead it then hesitated and looked toward her. Fear filled his eyes.

"Dead," said Two Eagles. "Cover it."

Anger Maker heaped pine needles over the dog.

"Filthy savages!" she shrilled. "How dare you?" Uttering the words brought a change, as if triggering awareness of the danger she was in. "You stay away from me. I'm warning you . . ."

Two Eagles towered over her, his arms folded, head cocked, appraising her. Picking up one end of the cloth at her feet, he let it unroll.

"That's my wedding gown. Leave it alone!" She snatched it from him.

"Wed . . . ding . . . gown," repeated Bone.

Fox had gotten control of himself. He moved closer to her, like a small boy daring to approach a motionless snake. He gazed wonderingly at her, as did the others, except for Two Eagles and Bone. Fox pushed his face close to hers. She recoiled, glowering. Two Eagles had noticed that first sight of them had frightened her, but now she had no fear.

"You speak English?" she said.

"Who are you?" he asked.

She drew herself up, tilting her head back, eyeing him down her nose.

"My name is Margaret Addison La . . ."

She had raised a hand to her forehead, teetered and fainted. He caught her as she fell and lay her down. Splitting Moon spread the gown over her.

"Ataentsic," murmured Fox.

The others nodded solemnly. Bone looked confused, his eyes shifting from one face to the next.

"At . . .?!" he began. "Who?"

"Nothing," said Two Eagles.

"What is she doing here?" asked Fox. "Where did she come from?"

"The ship," replied Two Eagles. "Where else?"

"Neh!" snapped Thrown Bear.

"Nyoh!" Two Eagles softened his tone. "Somehow she got away from the Maquens."

He studied the unconscious Margaret. Her skin gleamed like snow. Before Splitting Moon covered her with the wedding gown he had seen her large, firm breasts, only partially concealed by her shift. Her waist was slender, her little feet bare, scratched and red-welted. Her lips were full, nose small. Her face was long, her cheekbones unusually high for a whiteskin, although he had never seen a whiteskin woman before. The color of her eyes he had not noticed. Red Paint, kneeling beside her, brought her to. Her eyes opened as blue as bellflowers, narrowing, glaring.

She had fainted not from fear but exhaustion; she felt no fear. On first sight of them, she'd been terrified by their nakedness and weapons; her first thought was that the attacking savages had caught up with her. But these did not look like victorious captors, did not leer or gloat, nor had they touched her, other than the tall one to quiet her screaming. Was she unafraid because of how they gaped at her, as if she was a saint or an angel descended from heaven? All of them gaping except for the one with the knobby face. And the tall one, who seemed unimpressed and was evidently their leader. He towered over the others and looked powerful enough to uproot the tree she had been sitting in. And despite his brooding look, his cold surliness and arrogance, he was not bad looking. Except for his hair, the scalp shaven around a lock the size of a shilling piece. Handsome, actually, even sensitive looking when he wasn't barking. A sensitive savage? What was she thinking? She must be delirious!

She sat up, snatching the gown to cover herself, then got to her feet, shaking off the bony one's helping hand. She looked over at the mound of needles.

"Niche!"

Two Eagles toed the dog, rolling it over to reveal the covering long since come loose and dried blood half-girdling its neck.

"Niche, Niche, you're not dead, no!"

Kneeling, she began stroking it, murmuring soothingly to it.

Two Eagles looked puzzled. " 'Niche'?"

"It's French for trick, prank . . ."

"You are French?"

"English."

"So why give your dog a French name?"

"Because it pleases me to, poor, poor little love. . . . My husband is French."

"Why?"

"Why?"

"You are English," he said. "Why marry a French? Are there no English good enough for you? No French good enough for him?"

He obviously wouldn't understand. Their gawking was making her uncomfortable. Was it more than respect? Was it awe? Were they afraid of her? Was it the first time they'd seen blonde hair? She sat back down and massaged her sore feet. One heel was becoming black and blue. They watched her in silence as she got up, turned her back on them and put on her wedding gown. And assumed the most imperious expression she could muster. If they were in awe of her, it made sense to keep them that way.

"Our ship was coming up the river," she explained to Two Eagles.

"The Shaw-na-taw-ty."

"The Hudson."

"Shaw-na-taw-ty."

"We ran onto a sandbar. It was all so stupid. The man at the wheel was probably drunk."

"You were attacked. They set fire to your ship."

"No, there was no fire . . . !"

"Everyone was killed but you. How did you get away?"

"*Everyone* killed? Dear Lord, poor Celestine. How ghastly?"

"Where was your ship heading?"

"As far upriver as possible. Then we were to travel by canoe to Quebec. My husband is stationed there. He's a captain of dragoons, chief aide to Governor-general Frontenac. Captain Pierre Lacroix. Pierre's father and Daddy do business. Silk."

"Silk." Two Eagles turned to Bone. "Silk."

"Pierre and I were married by proxy in London but when I get to Quebec we'll have a proper ceremony. Which is why I'm bringing my wedding gown, you see. You don't understand a word."

She had noticed their expressions of sullen disdain at mention of Frontenac's name.

"The governor general we know," muttered Two Eagles. "He steals our furs and burns our castles. His men drink the blood of our children."

"The war's over . . ."

"It is stopped. It will start again. They will start it."

"They won't, never, but that's not important. See here, you absolutely must help me get to Quebec. I shall need at least ten men, preferably armed with muskets. I'm sure you can find some, trade for them or something. You'll be in command. Do you know how to get there? You must . . ."

"No." He turned from her.

"Oh, don't worry, you'll be paid handsomely. Pierre has oodles of money. Besides the silk business, his family owns acres and acres of vineyards."

"We do not go near New France," said Two Eagles. "They would kill us."

"Fiddlesticks and rot, you'll be under my protection. No one will harm you. The war's over."

"Not in their hearts, not in ours. We do not go near Quebec. You do not. No more talk about it."

"See here!"

"Stop! You talk too much, too loud. You hurt my ears. We are wasting what is left of the sun. You will come with us."

"I demand you escort me to Quebec!"

"The chiefs will decide what to do with her," he said to Thrown Bear.

"Ataentsic," murmured Fox. The others nodded solemnly.

"What did he say?" she asked.

"Nothing," said Two Eagles. "Will you come or do we tie you and carry you on a pole?"

The others gasped. She was right, they *had* mistaken her for someone important, perhaps a goddess or spirit. She confronted them. "Are you going to stand there and let him bullyrag me?"

"Two Eagles . . ." began Thrown Bear.

"Enough. O-kwen-cha, your feet are the smallest. Give her your spare moccasins." Two Eagles lowered his face to within an inch of hers. He spoke softly but there was no mistaking the menace in his tone. "Put them on and be quick. We will go on until the sun takes its rest."

She glared defiantly. "I'm hungry. I'm not budging until I get something to eat."

Anger Maker offered her bread.

"What's that?"

"*Gagai-te-ta-a-kwa,*" said Two Eagles. "Bread."

"Keep it, I prefer fruit."

"Eat the bread."

She fingered it hesitantly. "It's hard as a rock."

"Eat."

Anger Maker pulled his knife. She started. He grinned and spread deer oil on the bread. She continued to eye it contemptuously.

"Eat!" snapped Two Eagles.

With difficulty, she finally managed to soften it in her mouth. She ate every crumb. "It tastes of cranberry. I'm still hungry, I'm famished."

Bone got out some of the venison roasted the day before. She sniffed it and made a face.

"It's rancid."

"It is fresh," said Bone.

"Fresh from *ochquoha's* belly," said Thrown Bear. The others laughed.

"From a wolf," said Two Eagles.

She shook her head. "Venison comes from a deer, not a wolf."

"If you are so hungry, why so much talk? Eat."

"What else have you?"

"*Ochquoha* meat," said Bone.

"Wolf," said Two Eagles. "Eat one or the other. There is nothing else."

"Tomorrow maybe we get fish from the river," said Fox, seemingly anxious to please, "the fish that shines like the sun and the red one."

Two Eagles nodded. "Breame and mullet."

She crinkled her nose. "I dislike fish intensely."

He shrugged. "Do not eat them."

"I'll have some more of that bread."

"You have had all we can spare for now."

He dismissed her by turning away. She despised him for belittling her in the others' eyes. She thought of Pierre, a gentleman through and through, courteous, considerate. He made her feel a princess. This creature . . . Curious, unlike his friends, he hadn't the least regard for her. She might as well be a bondmaid. Ignorant savage, how could she possibly credit him with so much as a grain of sensitivity?

But she would go with them. There had to be someone in their village willing to escort her to Quebec for a price. Now he was staring at her; for the first time his frown relaxed into a smile. A smirk.

"The devil take you," she rasped.

"The devil take you! Now, decide, do we carry you strung to a pole or do you walk?"

They went on. A damp chill had settled over the woodland. From an overhanging rotting tree limb he plucked a fistful of thick white spines resembling a wig, cramming some in his mouth, offering her the rest. She shook her head. She felt foolish wearing her wedding gown, and the red one's moccasins that kept slipping off, braided corn husks in place of the dainty doeskin pumps from that delightful bootery in London, or the high-heeled slippers that had fallen off during her scrambling up that wretched riverbank. It was a miracle she'd gotten away.

And poor Celestine. Of course, he could be lying about everyone being massacred—although the last time she'd looked back at the ship all she could see were savages running about. By the time these Indians got there, any survivors would have fled. And yet, if that were so, why hadn't any caught up with her? Should she have ventured back this morning to see for herself? Hardly!

Now this naked rabble finding her: cavemen with feathers, no better than the brutes who attacked the ship. Staying with these, to take advantage of their protection, though, made sense. She didn't feel threatened. If they intended to harm her they wouldn't have let her get this far.

She hurried to keep pace with Two Eagles. She nodded toward Thrown Bear, at a distance to their right.

"Why does he wear that disgusting-looking turkey claw around his neck?"

"That is no claw?"

She gasped. "It's not his . . ." Her hand went to her mouth.

"*Nyoh.* It was chopped off in a battle. He killed the man who did it, then rammed his spurting stump into the mud to stop the bleeding."

"How ghastly . . ."

"I sealed the wound with pine pitch. The next day he was back in the thick of the fighting. He lost his hand, he found it."

"Revolting, I can't look."

"Did he ask you to? If it was your hand what would you do, throw it away?"

They went on in silence. Her feet ached furiously but damned if she would show him the least sign of weakness. It was all beastly uncomfortable, but, thank the Lord, only temporary. She had survived. Nothing else mattered at this stage. And she'd show them what Englishwomen were made of!

He stopped to survey the sky. Stars pricked the cobalt darkness. The oncoming night appeared clear. He called out for the others to halt. An owl hooted through the flapping of wings just above their heads. She reacted in alarm, then embarrassment when he snickered. The others approached from both sides.

"We camp here," he said to her. "You will sleep by me."

"I will not!"

"I will not touch you. You do not appeal to me. You are pale like a fish's belly. Your tongue never stops wagging. You argue over everything. You give orders. I do not like you."

"I despise you. You stink of sweat!"

"You stink of rotten flowers."

"Lavender sachets were packed with my wedding gown. Why am I explaining to you? I might as well talk to my foot!"

"Do." He indicated a tree larger than those surrounding it. "Over there. Make us beds of needles. Make them thick. If you want water, ask for it. Do not go wandering off."

"I . . . I have to . . ." Her cheeks colored.

He understood. "Piss, shit. So do it."

"In privacy!"

He pointed off toward the Mohawk River and watched her walk away.

Thrown Bear snickered and shook his head. "She has some mouth. Do you think she will run away?"

"Where would she go? Besides, she thinks when we get back she will get men to escort her up to Quebec."

Thrown Bear grinned. "Through the gate into Fort St-Louis, *nyoh*."

"She has big tits," said Bone.

The others eyed him reprovingly. He withdrew.

"Mohicans do not respect women," said Two Eagles.

"Bones does not understand about Ataentsic," murmured Thrown Bear.

"*Is* she Ataentsic?"

"You do not think so?"

"Ataentsic a white woman? An English?"

"A spirit," murmured Thrown Bear. "Who can assume any form she pleases."

This Two Eagles pondered, biting his forefinger and narrowing one eye characteristically. She was returning. Thrown Bear walked off.

"How far to your village?" she asked.

"Castle."

She showed a puzzled smile. "Is it built of stone, with a moat around it? And a portcullis? Battlements?"

"It is poles stuck upright to form a wall around our longhouses."

"A wooden castle? Fascinating."

"Castle is what we call it, as did the English who were here. Are you sure you are English?"

She drew herself up haughtily. "To the core. Our family traces its ancestry back to King John. My mother has noble blood."

"Good. Your tongue must be as tired as my ears. Fix our beds and go to sleep. We still start out tomorrow before the birds wake." He sniffed. "The air is heavy. It will rain again before morning."

"The sky is clear, you can see stars."

"It will rain."

"Lovely." She indicated Bone. "Why do you call him 'Bone'?"

"Look at his bones, the way they stick out all over. He is an adoptee."

"You adopted him when he was a child?"

"*Neh*, a man. He was adopted by a family of the turtle clan. He was Mohican. *Courieurs de bois* massacred his whole family; he was alone. He came one day to Onneyuttahage."

"Onney . . ."

"Yuttahage, our castle. Asking to be adopted. We adopt

many: Mohicans, Munsees, even Huron snakes and Ottawa dog shit eaters. Bone is a very skilled hunter and trapper. He also has a gift."

"What sort of 'gift'?"

"For seeing through the screens people weave to protect themselves and conceal their true feelings."

"He's perceptive." Two Eagles did not recognize the word. She pointed. "That one . . ."

"Sku-nak-su. Fox."

"What is that dangling from his belt?"

"A scalp."

"Eccch, how disgusting."

"It belonged to a French major."

"Ugh, I'd rather not hear about it. How far to your vill . . . castle?"

"Many sleeps."

"What are you doing out here so far away?"

He flipped a hand, ending the conversation. While he watched her prepare their beds Thrown Bear came over to him.

"She could be Ataentsic," he whispered.

Two Eagles looked dubious. "When Sku-nak-su said her name she did not recognize it."

"Maybe she pretended not to to deceive us. If she *is* Ataentsic, why tell us, *neh*?"

Two Eagles glanced her way. She was down on her knees heaping pine needles into a second bed. "Whoever she is she has *eshucne otschtiénta.*"

Thrown Bear smiled. "A bone in her back, true. She was more afraid of the *gachnichzóho* hooting by overhead than any of us, even Sa-ga-na-qua-de and his stinking pipe, who scares all women. And this one does not complain, not like my woman."

"She is too busy talking: questions, questions. You can see she is spoiled, used to being waited on, getting her own way. Demanding, nosy, annoying, like a gnat that keeps coming back."

"But she can take it," said Thrown Bear.

"*Eshucne otschtiénta*. Are all English whiteskin women like her, I wonder?"

He yawned. Thrown Bear went to his bed. Two Eagles went to the river, kneeling by it. The eye of heaven fixed on him, the wind moaned plaintively, like the sad, endless song of the chanters in the Feather Dance at the Green Corn Festival. He removed his feather, his medicine, and held it with both hands at eye level. Had its power deserted it, gradually seeping from it like the heat from the sun in winter? Was *ska-je-a-ñah* taunting him from on high, would he urge him to accept their failure to find Long Feather? Perhaps tonight would tell.

He set his feather on the ground, placing a quantity of tobacco beside it. Then raised it again and began chanting, invoking his óyaron.

━━━ 7 ━━━

It rained heavily during the night, as Two Eagles predicted. Margaret kept dry under a thick blanket of needles. When he woke her, she opened her eyes to an eerie sight: primeval Erebus. The silent trees stood dripping, not a branch stirring. A mist rose from the river, floating toward them like an advancing phantom legion. It was as if in her sleep she'd been hurtled back in time, to an age before the dawn of history. And these creatures, with their feathers and small aprons, their painted bodies and barbarous ways, were the sole occupants of the earth. She would never get to Quebec for there was no such place, no trace of civilization.

She shivered at the thought, until her stomach growled, reminding her that all she'd eaten in the past two days was her shipboard supper of mutton, cheese, oat clap bread with Spanish marmalade and tea. And yesterday, the cranberry slate they called their bread.

They started out in the usual line, Two Eagles close by her left side. For two hours they walked, the sun unable to penetrate the gray shroud. Gradually, the white pine and

pitch pine forest gave way to hills of oak, interspersed
with hop hornbeam and elm. They came at last to open
grassy flatlands strewn with starry-bloomed milkweed,
jewelweed with its curious golden arms, wild parsnip and
Queen Anne's lace—here one could see for miles in every
direction except to the north, where trees lining the river
blocked sight of the opposite side.

Her feet were toughening. The corn husk moccasins, despite being too big and occasionally slipping off, now felt
comfortable as old slippers. She was famished. Walking
nonstop was draining away what little energy the night's
sleep had restored.

Being married by proxy had been depressing, standing
beside Pierre's brother in the little chapel in Knightsbridge
with her parents and the Anglican and Catholic priests
sharing the ceremony.

Had his own proxy marriage in Quebec been as depressing as hers? To be sure, it did make everything legal and
acceptable in the sight of God. But not beautiful, not like
her heart had promised it would be when he proposed two
years before. Had they known at the time that his orders
would soon send him off to New France, they'd have married then and there in a civil ceremony.

Even so, she wouldn't have been permitted to accompany him abroad, not with the war on. Governor general's
orders. Which made no sense; whatever the situation,
wasn't a wife's place beside her husband? Frontenac
couldn't prevent her from joining him now. Oh, damn this
huggermugger, this infuriating delay! Conscious of being
stared at, she lifted her eyes. Two Eagles stood with arms
folded studying her. Ignoring him, she looked about. The
one they called Anger Maker, puffing endless clouds of
stinking smoke from his pipe, was sidling up to Splitting
Moon and Thrown Bear. In seconds they were shouting
and pushing one another while Anger Maker retreated.
Two Eagles shouted, ordering them to stop. And looked
back at her, as if to remind her he was in charge. As if she
cared.

Thrown Bear came up smiling affably. She kept her eyes from his withered hand.

"Why does he call himself *Two* Eagles?" she asked. "One isn't enough for his majesty?"

"His Aunt Téklq-eyo, Eight Minks, named him. For when he stole a feather from the great golden eagle's mountain aerie, watching it circle at a distance and not seeing its mate come up behind him."

"He climbed a mountain just to steal a feather?"

"When he was thirteen. The Tree-eater Mountains. And nearly lost his life." He lowered his voice. "That is the very feather, his medicine."

"Is he ill?"

"His medicine is his protection. It gives him control over the spirits of nature, over magic. It makes him one with his guardian óyaron, who counsels and protects him."

Thrown Bear told her about Long Feather and more about Two Eagles. that he was a Pine Tree Chief, respected and admired by the tribe; that his father had been killed by Hurons and his oldest brother had fallen from a cliff into Oneida Lake and drowned. Seeming to sense he was being talked about. Two Eagles came over to them. Thrown Bear withdrew.

"Aren't you hungry?" she asked. "I am."

"You should have eaten the meat yesterday when it was offered you."

"It smelled. What about the fish you were to catch this morning?"

"Why bother? You do not like fish."

"That meat was rancid. I'd as soon eat dirt."

"There is plenty of that. Soon we reach Onekahoncka, the first Mohawk castle. We will stop there."

"Will there be food for us?"

"It is the Iroquois custom to feed all visitors."

"Good." Her brow furrowed. "You said Mohawk?"

"Mohawk, Oneida, Cayuga, Onondaga and Seneca, all are Iroquois."

"An alliance."

"Confederacy."

"Whatever." She patted her skirt and clucked discouragingly. "By tomorrow, this'll be absolute rags. Can I get clothes there?"

He grunted. She took it for "yes."

"How far from where we're stopping to your castle?"

"Many sleeps, I told you. Perhaps half a moon."

"Two weeks? That settles that."

"What?"

"I won't have to go all the way to your castle. I can get my escort from the Mohawks or Iroquois, whatever they are. They have to be more obliging than you. They'll give me the men I'll need."

"Perhaps. Are you sure you want their warriors?"

"Why wouldn't I?"

"You have a generous and forgiving heart."

Thrown Bear and Splitting Moon, walking within earshot, chuckled.

"These Mohawks massacred your friends and burned your ship," said Two Eagles. "The people of the two Mohawk castles farther on do not come even this far to hunt."

"It could have been other savages. It didn't have to be Mohawks."

"It was Burnt Eye's warriors who attacked you. If you still want them to escort you, when we get there . . ." He leered. "Ask them."

She stopped, fuming. "Filthy savages! Butchers! I'll not go near them!"

"But you are hungry, you need clothes . . ."

Ignoring her, Splitting Moon addressed Two Eagles. "Did you consult your óyaron?"

"Animals!"

"I did," replied Two Eagles. "We will find my brother."

"Where?"

"At a hill soon after we leave Onekahoncka."

They resumed walking.

"Then why bother to stop there?" Thrown Bear asked.

"Because Ho-ka-ah-ta-ken may have heard something. May even know which hill."

Splitting Moon looked cynical. "There are so many hills between Onekahoncka and Onneyuttahage."

"You're not listening!" she bawled behind them.

"You do not like this Ho-ka-ah-ta-ken, this Burnt Eye," said Bone to Thrown Bear. "Why not? What sort is he?"

Thrown Bear chuckled. "Imagine a snake with legs."

"As easily as you break a stick he breaks his word," said Two Eagles. "He is a drunkard, a thief, a cheat, a liar. At night he lies with little girls while his wife sleeps in another chamber. In battle he is fearless, the bravest warrior I have ever seen."

Bone looked confused. "If he is a liar, how can you believe what he tells you about your brother?"

"If he lies his only eye will show it."

"We're not stopping!" she shrilled. "And that's final!"

They continued discussing Burnt Eye without a glance in her direction.

8

Down to the water's edge came the wary stag, spreading its forelegs, lowering its head and splendid rack. Sitting in the pool bathing, the girl had smelled the creature's musk before she saw it emerge from the cover of the trees. It seemed not to notice her, or did not consider her a threat. It drank, lifted its majestic head, looked about; their beautiful eyes met in mutual appraisal.

The girl was extraordinarily beautiful in her innocence, her copper skin, hair gleaming black as her lovely eyes and bound in braids that hung to her waist. The softly burbling brook feeding the pool, the "sweet-sweet-sweet" of a cardinal vying with the insistent chirping of a redpoll, the tireless buzzing of insects, set music to the scene. Sun-bleached reeds rose in clumps around the pool, their cylindrical heads bobbing, and between them wildflowers displayed their vivid colors. Overhead fluttered a butterfly, the sun beaming down through its black, red and white wings.

Again the stag lowered his head to drink and the girl resumed her bathing. Above her, from the limb of a red maple within easy reach, hung her clothing.

The world exploded.

 **9**

The ball spun straight through the stag's eye into its brain. Its forelegs gave way, one snapping like a dry stick as it fell awkwardly forward. The girl screamed, snatched down her clothes and ran splashing from the pool. Lowering his musket, the officer looked across at the stag now lying on its side, blood issuing from its mouth.

All nature around was suddenly silent. The breeze had stilled, the cattails stood erect. Waving away the smoke from the muzzle of his weapon, he set out around the pond, ignoring his kill, following the path taken by the girl.

He was tall, broad-shouldered, handsome—and aware of it—in his red uniform with blue facing and brass buttons in a single row down the front of his tunic. His black tricorne with gilt piping displayed the requisite silk rose, his gleaming sword dangled at his side. Clutching his musket, he hurried. He could not see her but the path she had taken was the only one in that direction. He smiled. She would stop to dress before entering the castle. He would catch up with her. All of the Huron women were as modest as Puritans, particularly the young ones, unwilling to show their nakedness even to other women. Modest savages.

"An amusing contradiction in terms, dear boy."

Through the trees he caught sight of her. She had dressed and resumed running. About two hundred yards ahead, beyond the woods, was the Lorette Huron castle. The Lorettes were among the few survivors of the once large and widespread Huron tribe. In the past three quarters of a century nearly all had been exterminated by the

Iroquois. Fortunate were these to be protected by the soldiers at Fort St-Louis nearby. And few red-blooded dragoon "protectors" failed to take advantage of the women's
gratitude.

He came into the clearing surrounding the castle just in
time to see her slip through the open gate. Two braves
standing outside stopped talking to watch her pass. The
captain grinned. Savage or Christian gentlemen, every man
appreciated beauty. He approached them and in French and
sign language inquired after her.

The older, broader one, a pitifully homely individual, responded in halting French. "Little Cloud. She granddaughter of Winter Heart, elder." He pointed. "First longhouse
. . . there."

The captain thanked him and entered the castle. A man,
his face deeply furrowed with his years, his braided hair
snow white, came out the deerskin door as the captain prepared to enter.

"A girl, woman, just went in. Bring her out, there's a
good fellow."

The old man's eyes slitted. "What for, sir?"

"Do as I . . ." The captain paused, thought a moment.
"Never mind, not now. But tonight, send her to the fort.
Do you understand?"

"Yes."

"Tell her to ask for Campeau, my orderly. Campeau,
can you remember?"

"Campeau. Tonight." He leered lasciviously. "But you
should know, sir, she, Little Cloud is a flower."

"Ahhh, an answered prayer."

"Sir . . ." The elder licked his lips expectantly.

"All right, all right, how much?"

Winter Heart's eyes wandered to the musket in his hand.
He pointed.

"*Mais non*, the general would have my head if I returned without my musket or my sword."

"Then silver?"

"I've no money on me."

The old man fingered a button. "This is gold?"

"Almost pure. A single one is worth more than my sword and musket together. You have an eye for value, old man."

Winter Heart held up four fingers.

"Two," said Lacroix. With a knife, he snipped off the top and bottom buttons.

Winter Heart eyed them greedily in his hand. "Gold . . ."

Whatever you say, reflected the captain, amused. "Tonight," he said, "before you go to sleep, see that she's brought to the fort to Campeau."

"Campeau."

Lacroix started off.

"Wait," called Winter Heart. "You are not sick, you will not make her sick?"

"No, no, no."

"Good, good. She is my joy. I love her very much. I protect her, you understand." Again he eyed the "gold" in his hand.

The captain walked off. Little Cloud, he had called her. Rather uninspired name. He would call her . . . Two Buttons.

"Yes, yes, delightful, delightful!"

═══════ **10** ═══════

Margaret felt foolish, as if talking to herself. So involved were they in discussing the Mohawk chief that no one even looked her way when she spoke. What had happened to their high esteem for her? Had *he* been criticizing her behind her back? She studied his shoulders, noting how the muscles tightened each time she voiced comment.

"I'm talking to you!" she burst.

He swung around, scowling, and waved her away. They were within sight of Schoharie Creek. It was wide and turbulent, the water kicking high over the stones, as it thrashed its way south. Thrown Bear had warned her that

it was deep in spots and would be "cold as snow" if she
fell in. She stepped gingerly from stone to stone. Two Eagles was behind her. A third of the way across she slipped
and would have fallen had he not caught her. He held her
as lightly as a pillow. She tingled and hated it, avoiding
his eyes, fixing her gaze on the opposite side. She wanted
to pull free, splash the rest of the way across, get soaked
and risk a cold. But, feeling her body rebel, he now held
her so that she could not move. He set her down on the
other side. All eyes were on them. Thrown Bear snickered.
She felt foolish and detested Two Eagles for his conde-
scending manner toward her. Her cheeks burned.

She would leave them, and they wouldn't dare stop her.
She'd keep going until she found a friendly tribe who'd
help her. Now. At once!

"We stop at Onekahoncka," he said coldly. "You will
meet Burnt Eye and his people. You will smile. You will
not show them anger. You will say nothing about the ship,
about what happened. They will give you food and clothing. You will thank them. You will be the fine English lady
and leave them with honey in their hearts for you."

She said nothing. The others looked appalled. Fox murmured their sentiments: It was no way to talk to Ataentsic.

A mile beyond the confluence of Schoharie Creek and
the Mohawk River, where the river disappeared into the
trees, they came within sight of Onekahoncka. It perched
on a rise; a rectangular log stockade more than six hundred feet long and a hundred feet wide; its pointed walls
were over twenty feet tall. The area surrounding had been
cleared. The woods began about thirty yards from the rear
of the castle and extended to the river about two hundred
yards away.

Anger Maker pointed his pipe in that direction. "Warriors . . ."

Two Eagles nodded. "Ho-ka-ah-ta-ken's. They have
been following us since we came onto the flatlands."

Women carrying deer and other game were approaching
the gate. Drawing closer, Margaret spotted one wearing a

familiar black mantle of durant trimmed with bands of gimp, with a hood of black ducape.

"That's Celestine's," she hissed.

"So?" Two Eagles frowned. "You will see many things taken from the ship, even your own. You will say nothing about them to Burnt Eye, to anyone. Not a word."

She stifled objection. In spite of his overbearing insolence toward her, she was beginning to see him through different eyes. He knew what he was doing, in everything. His men did not question his orders. He did not bully them and they respected him. Of first importance, they had brought her this far without harming her, had treated her quite well, actually, all things considered. She shuddered to think of the liberties they could have taken.

The gate loomed before them. Passing through it, she would enter yet another world: alarmingly primitive, possibly hostile. A giant step backward in time. She thought of the ancient Britons, who painted their naked bodies blue, treasured stones and bones and crouched in their caves. These creatures painted themselves black and red, treasured feathers and bear claws and scalps, and skulked about their woodland; and the British and French had come to lift them out of the mire of their backwardness. Or was it, as Two Eagles claimed, to divide and exploit them?

If this was true, why should they help her, an "English," get to Quebec? And without their help, what hope had she of ever again seeing her beloved Pierre? There was no one to get word to him. Quebec seemed suddenly as remote as China.

The thought chilled her. Tears welled. She glanced at Two Eagles. Whatever she might think of him, he was her only hope. Better she suffer in silence than estrange him further.

What was Pierre doing at that moment? He expected her in about three weeks, a month at most. With luck she wouldn't be terribly late, not so late that he'd begin worrying in earnest.

She would get there, eventually. Dear, darling Pierre. It

had been more than a year since she'd watched his ship sail away. Their letters had flown continuously in both directions. His came in bunches, often with as long as two months between. What a delight to receive one, lock herself in her room and read it aloud over and over.

Even Frontenac couldn't prevent her from joining him now that the war was over. Dear God but she missed him: his smile, his sense of humor, his gentleness and devotion. True, he'd been a rake before; what handsome, eligible bachelor wasn't? In the dragoons, especially. But now there'd be no more gallivanting. He had a wife, responsibility, commitments, a promising future in the army. Would he one day be governor of New France? It could happen, Frontenac was well into his seventies. *Was* she destined to be first lady of New France? How exciting!

They had met at a cotillion at his cousin's house in Montmartre. They danced and danced, so taken with each other that neither danced with another soul the whole evening. Scarcely spoke to another. Unforgivably gauche, but once their eyes locked, all else magically vanished. Next day, when they met for lunch at Tour D'Argent on Quai de la Tournelle, he was in uniform. At the time, a sublieutenant, with the strands of gold braid on the Austrian knot over his blue tunic; gold epaulets, gold designs on his sleeve.

She loved him so.

Her daydream dissolved.

Two Eagles. She recalled *his* eyes when they'd first seen each other. While the others looked fearful upon discovering her, in his eyes she had seen apathy.

They had come to within a few yards of the game-retrievers filing through the gate. Somewhere inside a gun went off, the echo bouncing off the wooden walls. The two women nearest the entrance, sharing the burden of a deer tied to a pole, paused, then went in.

"Some of those deer were shot with muskets," said Thrown Bear, gesturing his stump at a buck with a broken rack tied to three poles and being dragged travois-like.

Two Eagles nodded. "Where do you think they got their powder and ball?"

Splitting Moon grunted. "We ran out moons ago."

"So did they." He looked toward Margaret. "Then they found the ship."

The Mohawks following them emerged from the trees and moved toward the gate. Two Eagles signaled his men to stop and turned to her.

"Don't worry," she rasped. "Only I'd like to scratch the eyes out of that one with Celestine's mantle . . ."

They started in. The Mohawks had formed a gauntlet. As she walked it with the Oneidas, she recognized other clothing looted from the ship, including her own: her fur-trimmed velvet samare, an amber satin gown that she loved, a blue petticoat, her cambric cap and a few linen ones. Her wedding gown—with her shift, all she'd been able to bring with her—was stained and would probably never come clean. What a pretty sight for poor Pierre!

The savages had picked the *Aventurier* clean. One warrior looked ridiculous standing in Captain Jurieu's boots: French falls with bucket tops. Anger maker elbowed Two Eagles and pointed out a tall, well-built man, darker than the others, whose face looked carved from oak. On a lanyard around his neck was a small silver medal.

"The English gave your brother a medal like that," whispered Anger Maker to Two Eagles.

"They gave out many such medals," said Red Paint.

Two Eagles' eyes narrowed. "How many with a cut in the edge like that one?"

A woman Margaret's age stood at a mortar two feet tall carved from a tree trunk. She paused in pounding her corn to stare as they passed. She wore a deerskin dress with fringed long sleeves. Margaret could not take her eyes from her. What had prompted fate to bring the woman into this primitive world, while it brought her into a modern, civilized world an ocean away? How was that done? And was there a reason, a purpose?

Women wore stone and animal-claw necklaces and bracelets of wood, bone, beads, even fur. Some wore skirts made of a single large skin wrapped around the waist, secured with a belt, the flap draped over the belt. Many skirts were tailored and fringed and some even ornamented, as were their skirts. All the women stared at her: first at her hair, hanging long and loose and, despite the gray day, as bright as cornsilk; then at her wedding gown. She must look ridiculous but not one even smiled. And their men looked just as serious. Did *they* believe her to be the goddess or angel Fox and the other Oneidas seemed to think she was?

Two women sat scraping hides with bone knives. Another, emerging from the longhouse nearest the front gate, carried a large, heavy basket on one shoulder. Alongside the next house four men were building a canoe. She had seen pictures of birch bark canoes but this bark was too dark and rough to be birch. Heavier and thicker, it looked like the bark on the elms on her grandfather's estate in Staffordshire. She sighed as she thought of Staffordshire and her parents' country house near Bedworth in Warwickshire, where she had been born and reared: the distinctive cornices and pilasters outside the front, the lofty, raftered hall, the broad staircase and landings and elaborately carved baluster; the framed portraits and landscapes and marble sculpture Daddy so treasured; the carpets imported from Turkey and Persia. Her bedroom, her cloudlike tester bed, carved in oak blackened by time with the lace-trimmed canopy and valance. And outside her window the flower garden: tulips, laburnum, the everlasting love-in-a-mist, hosts of perennials and annuals in rectangles, divided by walkways and enclosed by box and lavender hedges. And beyond the garden the orchard, with its orderly ranks of cider pippin trees and lovely green walks shadowed by bowers of honeysuckle.

Tears blurred her sight. Would she ever see Pierre again?

Small boys tossed sticks for yapping dogs to fetch. All activity ceased when they passed, all eyes focused on her. She avoided returning their stares. On the large platforms

mounted inside near the top of the palisades were piles of
stones and large earthenware jars.

"What's in the jars?" she asked Thrown Bear.

"Water, to put out fires from fire arrows."

"Who would attack this place?"

"It is wise to be prepared. If a castle catches fire it can
burn down in minutes. The French are very skilled at
burning down castles."

Two elderly men and a tiny woman, who looked to be
a hundred, sat fashioning fishhooks from the hollow legs
and wing bones of birds. Two crows, their feathers not yet
plucked, lay on the ground nearby. Men chipped stones
with bone tools. She touched Two Eagles' arm.

"Arrowheads," he said.

She could see no cookfires, and, other than the corn being pounded, no food anywhere. They came upon four
bear cubs, each confined in a small, round, cage-like en-
closure. Children poked sticks playfully at them. Two of
the cubs ate noisily from large bowls.

"What's that?" she asked.

"*Sagamité*, boiled corn mush."

"They feed their pets well."

"Until they are half-grown. Then butcher them and eat
them when they celebrate the New Year or some other
feast."

"That's disgusting! How can they kill such cute little
creatures?"

"How can the bear kill such 'cute' little children?"

There were sixteen longhouses set row on row, leaving
room for streets. Varied in size, the largest appeared fully
eighty feet long. All were about twenty feet wide. Sheets
of elm bark, rough side out, covered the frames. On some
of the houses an outer set of poles held the bark siding
firmly in place. The front doors, which could be lifted up,
were either animal hides or hinged bark. Above every entrance were carved wooden images. From a few hung
dried scalps.

Two Eagles saw her eyeing them in disgust. "French,"
he said.

Six men were approaching. Two Eagles signaled a halt. One of the two men at the front of the group was old and decrepit, his face deeply pitted from smallpox. His long hair was as white as cotton. His hair was his only attractive feature, although his eyes—the pupils as dark as jet—were spellbinding. Next to him stood a man half his age, taller, wider, his chest huge, his upper arms bigger than Splitting Moon's. A white scar ran vertically from his left nostril through his lips, down his chin to the base of his jaw. His nose appeared to have been mashed, as by a musket butt, all but sealing his nostrils, so that he breathed with a soft whistling sound. One eye was missing, the socket glistening, pink. The other stared at her breasts, which she covered with her forearm. The tip of his tongue rode across his lower lip to the scar and back.

He had to be the ugliest human she had ever seen. She wanted to look away but Two Eagles' warning came back to her.

He held his hand up in greeting. "*Nyah-weh ska-noh, Ho-ka-ah-ta-ken.*"

"I thank you to know you are strong, Burnt Eye," whispered Thrown Bear to her.

Burnt Eye repeated the greeting.

"*Nyah-weh ska-noh, gayah-da-sey,*" said Two Eagles. "*Doges.*"

"Friend," whispered Thrown Bear. "Truly."

"*Se-go-li,*" continued Two Eagles.

"*Se-go-li,*" repeated Burnt Eye.

"Greetings," whispered Thrown Bear.

Two Eagles addressed the older man in the same manner, calling him Joshu'we-agoochsa.

"Hole Face," whispered Thrown Bear.

"Lovely," she murmured.

Two Eagles introduced his companions. When he came to Bone, Burnt Eye shifted his attention from her to the Mohican. Lifting his hand, he pointed, stepped forward and poked Bone in the chest with each word.

"You are no Mohican. You are Abnaki." He spat contemptuously. "Abnakis tied my wrists behind me, poked a burning stick in my eyes. You are Abnaki!"

"Mohican," said Two Eagles. "He was, now he is one of us."

"Abnaki, French moccasin." Again he spat. His hand went to his knife.

Bone stepped back, glancing nervously at Two Eagles. Two Eagles moved between them, his hand flat against Burnt Eye's chest. Burnt Eye looked down at it.

"He is Oneida. If he is not, I lie. Tell me, Ho-ka-ah-ta-ken, am I a liar?"

Burnt Eye tensed. Watching, she could almost hear the Mohawk's fury. She held her breath. Her heart pounded against her upraised forearm.

Slowly, Burnt Eye's look softened. His hand came away from his knife. Onto his face came a sneer. "Mohican . . ." He spat it, like putrid meat. "Mohicans eat frogs and wild garlic and fight like girls." Back came his eye to focus on her. "What is this one?"

"She is At—" began Fox.

"We found her in the pine woods," Two Eagles cut in. "She was on the ship on the Shaw-na-taw-ty that your men looted and burned."

"*My* men?"

"Your men, your affair. It means nothing to us. We have a thing more important to discuss."

Burnt Eye nodded. "First we eat, then we talk. Come into my house. Tékni-ska-je-a-nah. Come, all of you."

Margaret was prepared for assault by all sorts of stenches inside the longhouse but all she could smell was burning wood. Five firepits in a row occupied the center of the passageway; two fires were smoking. The passageway, about six feet wide, ran the length of the house, separating two lines of individual chambers raised a few inches from the dirt floor and open like stalls. Peeking in as Burnt Eye led them to the rear, Margaret could see raised bunks built around the interior walls. The chambers looked tidy and roomy and the entire house benefited from the light through large openings in the roof that could be covered with movable bark sheets. Light and fresh air entered; the smoke and odors escaped. Poles several inches thick were set in the ground, their tops down together and secured with cords to create an arbor-like roof. From it were suspended strings of corn ears braided with husks and strings of squashes, onions and other vegetables. In three of the chambers were stored corn and other food. From what Margaret could see, the Mohawk kept his house cleaner than Captain Jurieu kept his ship.

At the far end of the longhouse was an area large enough to accommodate upward of fifty men. Burnt Eye dispatched one of his men and gestured to the others and the Oneidas to sit. He and his men sat with their backs to the end of the longhouse, with their visitors facing them. Margaret found herself between Two Eagles and Thrown Bear, whom she was becoming fond of, in spite of the grisly memento adorning his chest. He was good-natured and friendlier toward her than any of the others, who still held her in awe and, for the most part, hesitated to come near her.

"*Jori,*" said Burnt Eye.

"The meal is already cooked," translated Thrown Bear.

"Thank God," she muttered.

She sat opposite Burnt Eye and wondered if being face-to-face with him would affect her appetite. The man he'd sent away now returned with four women, two bearing heavy kettles, which they set in front of the chief. The other two women carried two flat pieces of bark piled with what resembled the corn bread given her the afternoon before, but without the tint of cranberries. Burnt Eye gestured to Two Eagles, who dipped his hand in a kettle and brought out a handful of dripping corn mush.

"Isn't that what the bear cubs outside were eating?" she asked Thrown Bear.

"*Sagamité.* Yes, very good, very filling. Eat."

The odor of the mush intensified her hunger. In her turn she dipped her hand in the kettle, bringing up a dripping handful. It was hot and delicious.

"It could use salt," she whispered to Thrown Bear.

All of them ate like animals, letting the mush run down their wrists and plop on their knees. Should that surprise her? She ate three handfuls. Two Eagles offered her a piece of the bread. She bit off a morsel, letting it soften in her mouth before attempting to chew it. It was not as dry as the cranberry bread, and tasty.

"*Odjis' tă mondä,*" whispered Thrown Bear. "Cracked corn. Ripe, not dried."

Burnt Eye addressed her so loudly he startled her. "*Aga' de-koni, E^nsá dě koni.*"

"I eat, you eat," whispered Thrown Bear.

She forced a smile, nodding, holding up what was left of the portion. He seemed unable to tear his eye from her breasts, even covered as they were by her upraised forearm. She wished she could walk out. But she was in no hurry to test Two Eagles' anger. She sensed the animosity between the two chiefs but, apart from mentioning the raid on the *Aventurier* and standing up for Bone, Two Eagles seemed to be avoiding anything that might spark controversy. Burnt Eye, too, was behaving himself. Still, anyone could see they hated each other. Was it jealousy? Were they rivals? Was there a long-standing feud between them? To Two Eagles' credit he didn't gawk at her, nor did his men. Fox and Red Paint did, but in awe, not like Burnt Eye. Now everyone was dipping their mush-coated hands in the other kettle, bringing out meat.

"What is that?" she asked Thrown Bear suspiciously.

"*Sateeni,*" announced Burnt Eye.

"Do not ask everything," rasped Two Eagles. "No one is going to poison you, just eat."

Thrown Bear proffered a chunk of the meat. She chewed it. To her surprise it was boiled mutton. Delicious, tastier than the first two dishes, although a bit tough. She ate her fill, everyone gorged and belched loudly. She fought the urge to belch.

"You like *sateeni,*" said Burnt Eye.

"Delicious. I'm very fond of mutton, but I do like it roasted. In England that's how it's usually served."

"Mut-ton?" He looked questioningly at Two Eagles.

"Mutton?" Two Eagles repeated to her.

"Sheep," she said. "Fully grown, of course, not lamb."

"This tastes like sheep to you?"

"Mutton, that's the proper term."

"This is not sheep."

"It is *sateeni*," said Thrown Bear.

"Dog," said Two Eagles.

11

For an instant it didn't register, was too outrageous; her mind blocked out the word. Everyone stared at her. She blanched and gagged.

"A delicacy to us *savages*," he went on. "As your mutton is to you. Dog. Tell us, do English sheep wag their tails? Bark? Do they suck bones?"

The others laughed. She felt the color drain from her cheeks. She rose unsteadily, quickly covered her mouth, then her stomach.

Two Eagles pulled her back down. Anger fired his eyes. "Sit still, take your hands away from your stomach. Take that look off your face. Smile."

"I have to throw up!" She shot to her feet and started away holding her stomach with one hand, the other over her mouth, stumbling.

He caught up with her. "Come back! He is our host. You insult his food, you insult him."

"Dog meat, I swallowed dog meat!"

"Get hold of yourself and come back or . . ."

"What, you'll kill me?"

He was right of course. She was making a spectacle of herself and embarrassing him. But how was she to keep it down? She took a deep breath, which at least lessened her nausea. They sat back down.

"You do not like *sateeni*?" Burnt Eye asked, holding his leer in check.

"It is new to her," said Thrown Bear.

"To us it *is* a delicacy," said Burnt Eye. "Of course,

some taste better than others. Young dog is best. This one was only four years old."

"Delicious dog," said Two Eagles.

Burnt Eye leaned toward her. "Perhaps you like it better raw? Some do."

"No, no . . ."

"Eat some more."

He selected a chunk from the kettle, examined it, put it back, took another, offered it. Two Eagles took it. All eyes were on her. There was not a sound as he handed it to her. She put it in her mouth and began chewing. She could not swallow it, not if her life depended on it! She could feel Two Eagles' eyes burning into her. From cheek to cheek she shifted the meat. She swallowed, clamping her hand over her mouth. When she opened her eyes and took down her hand, all were smiling approvingly.

Two Eagles asked Burnt Eye if he had any news of Long Feather's whereabouts.

Puzzlement came onto the Mohawk's face. "You sent out men to inquire. One came here. I myself told him." He shook his head. "So-hat-tis and his friends came nowhere near Onekahoncka. You are on your way back to Onneyut-tahage, keep searching . . ."

"Would there be a certain, special hill that your people know of? Ceremonial, or perhaps a meeting place, some-where between here and Onneyuttahage?"

"There are many hills, none unusual or special to us. I wish I could help you. Tékni-ska-je-a-nah, I know how close you and your brother were."

"Are."

"Of course. I am sure you will find him, but not around here."

It appeared to please him to be able to say it. She suspected that he knew something about the situation but preferred to keep it to himself. More important, keep it from Two Eagles who, from his expression, seemed to be thinking the same thing. But clearly, pressing Burnt Eye further on the subject would be useless. Why prolong his pleasure?

"What have you heard of the Grand Council?" Burnt Eye asked. "Is there any progress on a treaty? Have they even begun to talk?"

"Not until the lace cuffs show up." Two Eagles frowned. "What good is a treaty with them? Their word is as brittle as skin ice."

"And the word of our redback 'friends'?"

Two Eagles shrugged. "Both are weasels, only with different colored coats."

Long Feather was no longer the subject of discussion, but Two Eagles' disappointment, which appeared more like resentment in his expression, seemed fastened to his face. He fidgeted. Burnt Eye seemed to enjoy it. They talked further about the French and English, about the lasting effects of the war on all the Iroquois. Thrown Bear whispered translation for her.

"How many Oneida survived?" Burnt Eye asked.

Two Eagles hesitated. Plainly, it was a question he preferred not to answer.

"Your losses were very heavy," Burnt Eye went on. "That is known throughout the Confederacy. Our hearts held stones for you. So then, how many warriors left, fifty, seventy-five?"

"We are still strong."

The lameness of this answer pleased Burnt Eye. He pounded his chest. "If the fighting started up again I could lead three hundred of us into battle. How many Mohican frog-eaters could the Oneida muster? How many Munsee basket weavers?"

"Must I remind you, Ho-ka-ah-ta-ken, whatever the tribe, our blood becomes theirs when we adopt them. The clan mothers teach them well."

"Is what I hear true, that you now have more Pine Tree chiefs than warriors?"

Two Eagles showed a rare smile. "Is what *I* hear true, that the Maquen who left here and settled at the Sault in the north . . ." He paused and leaned forward. *"Fought with the French against their brothers? Some of your finest warriors?"*

The single eye gleamed. Curiosity masked Two Eagles' face.

"So that you are now a tribe divided?" Two Eagles asked.

"We no longer count them as our blood."

"Their blood changes because they leave? Is that possible? Strange. Is it something they eat? Is it magic? And will more be leaving?"

Tension was building. Everyone had eaten their fill. Burnt Eye could not or would not help them find Long Feather, so it was time to leave. But not one Oneida stirred. All sat stiffly, expectantly, eyeing Two Eagles.

Would the knives come out?

Burnt Eye's mounting fury so tightened his body that he trembled. She glanced at Thrown Bear. He looked petrified with worry.

Burnt Eye spoke: one answer to all five questions. "Maquen affairs are no affair of the Oneida."

"Are all of you leaving here?" Two Eagles persisted. Margaret stiffened against the expected explosion. Two Eagles clapped his hands on his knees. "As you say, Maquen troubles are no business of ours. We thank you for your food and hospitality, Ho-ka-ah-ta-ken. Now we will leave."

Burnt Eye stared at him, then appeared to relax slightly. He nodded. "To look for So-hat-tis."

"To find him."

"If he is to be found." Everyone tensed, Margaret sensed that he knew all about Long Feather, despite his denials.

Two Eagles stared but let it pass.

On their way out Margaret noticed a pretty young woman sitting in one of the chambers, staring into space. Stepping outside, Margaret paused to drink in fresh air to dispel her lingering queasiness. The others followed her out, leaving only Two Eagles and Thrown Bear behind.

Splitting Moon was sweating, appeared jumpy, his eyes flashing about, one hand bunching his stomach as if to relieve discomfort.

The sun had come out. A solitary cloud carried gray on

its underside. Small children were crowding around the canoe builders. She and Splitting Moon watched the workers while the other Oneidas talked in low tones. All seemed relieved to be done with Burnt Eye. Presently, Two Eagles, Thrown Bear and the Mohawks came out.

"Come," said Thrown Bear to her.

They made their way down the side of Burnt Eye's longhouse to the one behind it.

Thrown Bear chuckled. "Ho-ka-ah-ta-ken likes you."

"He's disgusting. I can't even look at him!"

"Shhh, I cannot argue that. Still, you should feel flattered. You were all he talked about after you left. He asked Two Eagles to leave you behind for him."

She bristled. "What did he say? Am I to be bartered like so many furs or baskets of corn?"

"Shhh . . . He told him that you are not his to give, that you are married to a French long knife."

"That was gracious of him."

"You do not like Two Eagles, do you?"

"I don't dislike him."

"You do not know him, do not know how lucky you are it was he who found you. He has been kind toward you and protects you because he respects you, Mar-gar-et. He would not give you to anyone, least of all Ho-ka-ah-ta-ken."

"They hate each other. You could cut the air in there with a knife."

"If he got hold of you he would hurt you. You would be his slave. He would enjoy making you suffer. That woman we saw on the way out is his wife Dreamer. He is very cruel to her. Even his own people say so."

He led the way into the second longhouse. One of Burnt Eye's men was already inside, with a woman whose face was deeply wrinkled. She flitted about like a pecking bird. From a pile of clothing, she selected a one-piece deerskin dress, holding it up to Margaret, nodding approvingly and handing it to her. She also gave her a pair of deerskin moccasins, a much better fit than Red Paint's corn husk moccasins which, by now, were practically in shreds. She

was also given a basket in which to carry her wedding
gown. Shown into a nearby chamber, she changed clothes.
When she rejoined Thrown Bear, he raised his hand in approval, beaming broadly.

"Now you are an Iroquois *coenheckti*, but with English
hair."

She assumed *coenheckti* meant "woman." She thanked
the woman and went out. Everyone, except Two Eagles,
nodded approvingly at her new attire. He wasn't interested.

And yet, despite her frustration with him, his traits that
annoyed her, she came away from Onekahoncka impressed
with how he'd conducted himself. He'd refused to turn her
over to Burnt Eye, which he could have done easily. He'd
handled his adversary intelligently, wielding his needle
deftly, giving as good or better than he got. Burnt Eye's
battle with his temper betrayed his insecurity face-to-face
with Two Eagles. They were Whig and Tory in the House
of Lords, dueling for superiority in front of their adherents.
Two Eagles had come away the victor but it was only
words, with no helpful outcome for him. If Burnt Eye
knew Long Feather's whereabouts, Two Eagles would be
the last person he'd tell.

For one thing she could be grateful, that Anger Maker
had held his tongue.

II

TO THE VICTORS

12

Private Campeau was at loose ends this morning, as he usually was in tending to the needs and demands of Captain Lacroix, picking up after him, reminding him of his duties in the daily schedule, conveying messages from the governor general (now, with the war ended, satisfied to be addressed as Governor Frontenac) and striving to live a life of his own, separate and apart from the captain's. All that kept him on the move and in the nervous state that had come to be normal for him since becoming the captain's orderly.

The bedroom was in upheaval, as it always was after a night of drinking and wenching, which averaged about five nights a week. When he first laid eyes on her when she was brought to him the night before, this "guest" had been so timid and inexperienced that he felt a tug of pity for her. And a virgin, to which the condition of the bedsheets testified. Private Campeau was no prude. He could carouse with the wildest hellraisers in the garrison, but he did know where to draw the line. She looked to be barely into her teens. Her age meant nothing to the captain. He'd bedded even younger girls.

She must have slipped away before sunrise, while the new love of her life was still snoring. When Campeau woke the captain at six he was in his foulest mood, grievously hung over, eyes shot with blood, breath disgusting, head pounding like a blacksmith's hammer. His first act

upon arising was to empty his stomach out the window.
Then he fumbled into his uniform, minus the two buttons
he had paid the man for her, and staggered out to the la-
trine.

That was nearly an hour ago and Campeau had not seen
him since. He had left ordering him to "find, wangle or
steal two new buttons. At once!" This he had done before
anything else, wheedling them out of the quartermaster's
assistant, insisting he himself was to blame for their loss
by letting their binding threads become frayed. Sergeant
Depardieu liked him. They were distant cousins and often
drank together. He was sympathetic, though not for a moment did he believe the explanation.

Campeau tossed the buttons in his hand. Having secured
them as ordered, he now had no tunic to sew them to. He
began picking up the room. The bottom sheet was stained
in the center, badly ripped in two places. He whipped it
into a ball to dispose of, got out the extra sheet—he saw
to it that at least one extra was always on hand—and made
a mental note to replace it from supply.

During the night the captain had gotten up and gone to
the washstand and had carelessly dropped the pitcher, shat-
tering it. A fresh sheet, a replacement pitcher.

A tunic to sew the damn buttons on.

The room stank of body odor and stale cognac. Dare he
open the window out which the captain had vomited
earlier? Yes, and the other window as well for fresh air.
There was no unpleasant smell from outside. The early-
morning drizzle, now ended, must have cleansed the
ground.

Campeau surveyed himself in the washstand mirror. He
was twenty-two, tall, thin, sallow, awkward—"all elbows,"
complained the captain. A nose of extraordinary length
and shape spoiled what otherwise would have been a passably handsome face. The bridge angled left, then right
near the tip; hence his nickname: "Nez." But he didn't
mind. No Don Juan, with no promising future in the service of his country, still he was well-liked, good-natured
and content. And comparing his lot with the captain's, he

thought he was far better off. Not for a million *livres*
would he exchange places. Lacroix was his responsibility
as Frontenac was the captain's. The captain was demanding, so was the governor general. To be sure, the captain
was sloppy and unpunctual in carrying out his duties, at
times downright irresponsible. How he held his job was a
mystery to Nez.

But Frontenac made no effort to disguise his affection
for the fellow, who was more like a spoiled son than an
aide. Understandable, since he'd lost his only son when
his wife left him more than forty years before. Uncle
Louis. A situation "Nephew" Pierre took every possible
advantage of—not that anyone could blame him.

"Where in holy hell are you, *mon capitaine*?"

An hour ago he'd told him he'd be right back. He was
done tidying up when a knock rattled the door. It was Corporal Lemieux. His musket by his side, he saluted it
smartly. Nez held a snicker. He didn't like Lemieux, didn't
know anyone who did, other than his superiors. This was
a garrison in the wilds of New France, not a damned military school. The commander tolerated a relatively loose
ship. What was the point in "tightening" it? All out of step
but Claude.

"He wants him, Nez, immediately."

"*Mon Dieu*, I don't know where he is."

"You are supposed to at all times: Article Ten,
Paragraph—"

"Shut up, Claude, don't tell me my job."

Lemieux shrugged. "If you know it, why not perform it
properly?"

"Help me find the son-of-a-bitch."

"*Non*. My duty is to inform you. I have done so. Find
him yourself."

"Thanks a lot."

He slammed the door in the corporal's face. He but-
toned his tunic, slammed on his cap and hurried to headquarters, hoping that the captain would be in his friend
Major Boulanger's office playing backgammon.

In he rushed. The major was sitting at his desk, mirror

in hand, trimming his magnificent mustachios with a little
pair of scissors. Nez managed to get his mouth open but
was unable to deliver a word before Boulanger spoke.

"He just left, on his way to the big chief's."

"Thank God."

"Sit down, Emile, tell me about the Indian princess he
got into his bed last night. As he described her, she sounds
delicious. Was he exaggerating?"

"She was a child, sir."

"I didn't ask that. We both know his motto: the younger,
the tastier." He returned to his mirror and his mustachios.

Campeau was becoming fidgety. "Excuse me, sir, I had
better go. And make sure he gets to the governor's office.
He may get waylaid."

"He may indeed, knowing our boy. What a lucky, lucky
fellow. He's as full of it as he is of himself. Born lucky,
blessed in a hundred ways. The governor dotes on him.
He's got the easiest job in the army, money coming out of
his ears, a face and build women die for, a beautiful wife
on the way to his bed, nothing but luck. Would that a little
sunshine would fall on me. Still, he does abuse it; one day
it may pack up and desert him like a faithful dog that one
kicks too many times. What do you think?"

"Sir?"

"My mustachios, are they even?"

"They're perfect, sir."

13

The spacious Fort St-Louis office of Governor General
Louis de Baude, Comte de Palluau et de Frontenac,
might well have graced a château in the Loire Valley, so
tastefully and expensively furnished it was. The pieces,
however, looked absurdly out of place, encompassed by
bare pine siding and standing on a rough-hewn plank floor.
A superbly crafted escritoire of teak inlaid with ivory
served as his desk. Intricately carved mahogany legs and
back border distinguished the damask-covered sofa. Three

upholstered Louis XIV ovalback chairs were provided for visitors. An elaborately carved side table with marble top, a fifteenth-century Italian armoire and selected other pieces completed the decor. Opposite the armoire hung a large map of eastern Canada and northeastern America from the Great Lakes to the Atlantic Ocean.

Frontenac sprawled on his sofa, one arm outstretched along the back, his chin on his chest, his great, flowing white mustaches as usual in need of trimming, his shoulder-length white wig concealing a naked pate, his richly embroidered coat open, lace dripping from his cuffs, his bib as white as his beard. He was seventy-seven, as vigorous and strong as a man half his years. As Governor of New France from 1672 to 1682, he had ruled with an iron hand and sympathetic heart. He retired to his ancestral home, but in 1689, when the affairs of the colonial empire were in a critical state, the King assigned him to a second term as governor. His nature was turbulent, his temper defied governing, but he was fearless, resourceful and decisive, he had triumphed as few men could have over the difficulties of forging and governing a New France in the wilderness.

His smile of greeting gave way to a quizzical look. "What happened to your buttons, my boy?"

"I warned that donkey of an orderly they were coming loose. I left him just now with strict orders to get new ones from supply."

"Good. Appearances are important. We mustn't march about looking like a gang of ragamuffins. Maybe you need a new orderly?"

"Nez is all right, just tends to be a bit sloppy."

Frontenac clapped his hands. "Now, first off you're to arrange a meeting with Generals LaFleur and Desmaines. We four must discuss the upcoming conference."

"*Peace* conference, sir." Lacroix smirked.

"What's funny? We need a peace desperately. There's been far too much blood spilling for far too long."

"True, Excellency, but let's be realistic. The savages will never honor a treaty."

"Oh? Who says? I've been here eighteen years on and off and I've yet to see them break one. We do, the British do, but when the Iroquois sign a treaty they stick to it."

Frontenac rose and moved to the map, beckoning the captain to join him. With his finger, he drew a straight line southwesterly from Quebec to the heart of Onondaga Territory.

"Over a hundred and fifteen leagues, through wild and hostile country . . ."

"Beg pardon, Excellency, but wouldn't it be easier on the men if we rode the St. Lawrence River up to here and crossed Lake Ontario down to about here?" He indicated the southeastern shore of the lake. "And from there travel overland. Easier, faster, safer."

"Would you believe I was about to suggest that very thing? I think I was interrupted."

"My apologies, Excellency."

"To continue . . ."

"Excellency . . ."

"What?"

"Must we got to them? Why don't we make them come here?"

"I considered that, too, and rejected it. I prefer we show them a good example of our strength in their backyard. Pomp, ceremony, weaponry, might make a lasting impression on them. Also, if the chiefs were to come here, hundreds of hangers-on would come traipsing along with them, into Huron and Ottawa territory. That could be begging trouble. Besides, it's already been agreed upon with their two council military commanders. They will be the hosts. I've been thinking about the Carignon Regiment."

"Fifteen hundred strong. Now there's a show of strength!"

"We'll take one company, ninety men. You select it. We'll also take at least four Huron scouts. You'll be in charge of logistical details. Major Boulanger will arrange for the scouts. Inform him. Oh, he won't be coming." He snickered. "I haven't the heart to separate him from his mirror and that fascinating wife of his." His smile faded as he turned from the map. "The intendant won't be coming, either. And no priests."

"No priests?"

"You will inform the Bishop. We won't be needing God's intervention in the wrangling. And it's neither the time nor the place for converting." He sighed. "Let us hope this won't turn out a wild-goose chase. Paris will be screaming for our scalps if it does. The Crown simply cannot afford continued fighting."

"Thank the saints the war in Europe is over," said Pierre.

"The point is, the cupboard is all but bare these days. So, the orders of our illustrious chief minister, the Marquis de Barbezieux, are to effect a binding treaty with the Iroquois, one that'll stand up at least as long as I'm here."

"Mmmm."

Frontenac waggled a reproving finger. "You sell them short as enemies, Peter; don't. They are superb fighters. I shouldn't have to remind you. Spartans in feathers. Without their help to the British, we'd have sent the redcoats running back to the coast to their ships in six months. The Iroquois fought like demons. Which, I confess, surprised me. They had nothing to gain, and knew it."

"But everything to lose, Excellency." He could not help marveling at this old man about to embark on such an arduous trek, the last leg of which would be through rugged, hostile territory. Most men halfway to eighty would be locked in their easy chairs. His father, just turned sixty, was already thinking about retiring.

Frontenac paced, his head lowered, hands clasped behind his back. "We'll probably be away at least two months, perhaps longer, getting down there, hammering out the terms of the treaty and return. Your bride is on her way here . . ."

"Yes, sir, due in two or three weeks."

"You'll see to it somebody will welcome her, explain the situation, see to her comfort. Colonel Drapeau will be willing, I'm sure. Professional mother hen if there ever was one. Go, get to work."

"Yes, sir."

The captain straightened and saluted, getting a limp wave in response. He started for the door.

"One last thing," said Frontenac. "They're starting on the renovations in the dining room at Château St-Louis. Until we leave, I want you to keep an eye on the work. I don't mean stand around and watch all day, just pop in from time to time so you can keep me posted on the progress."

Anything else, Your Majesty? "I'd be delighted to, Excellency."

"Go. Appraise LaFleur and Desmaines. Tell them sixteen-hundred hours this afternoon here in my office. You come, too. And cross your fingers, Peter, pray we march down there and bring back a lasting peace. I'm an old man. It's high time I hung up my sword."

14

Leaving Onekahoncka, the search resumed. The Oneidas followed the trail westward. Bone walked beside Two Eagles, Margaret behind them. She was getting used to her new moccasins but Two Eagles seemed determined to walk too fast for her. If Burnt Eye was the most repulsive individual she had ever met, Two Eagles was the most exasperating. He and Bone jabbered in Oneida.

"He is a snake, all right," said Bone. "He hates the world for what the Abnakis did to his eye."

"He hated the world long before that. He lied about the hill, about hearing nothing of So-hat-tis. His every other word was a lie . . ."

"How much farther?" she asked, interrupting.

He flared. "We have just started. How many times must you ask? What, do your feet hurt already?"

"Not a bit! I'm just curious."

Patches of blue violets flowed toward them from both sides of the trail. She paused to pick a handful, laying them on her gown in the basket.

"What do you want with them?" he asked.

His tone softened markedly, surprising her. Was he actually initiating a friendly conversation for the first time? Was he grateful that she hadn't thrown up the dog meat? Pleased at how she'd conducted herself under the glare of that gruesome eye?

"They're pretty," she said. "What better reason to pick them? I love violets."

"We use the root to relieve pain. We mash it until it is soft. We use a gob . . ."

"A poultice."

"Che-gasa."

"Che-gasa," she repeated.

"Good. You might want to learn our language."

"Why? I'll be leaving as soon as we get back. I do know one word . . ."

"Sateeni."

They walked on in silence. She smelled the violets and held them for him to smell.

He declined. "I know their smell."

"Do the Oneidas appreciate the flower as well as its root?"

"We may be 'savages' but we appreciate their beauty enough not to pick them so they die."

"I did call you savages, I was angry, I'm sorry."

"That is what your people call all the tribes, even we who are friendly. I am curious: Europeans are considered not savages but civilized and yet the French and English kill each other."

"Only in the war."

"Yes, they need that as their reason. They make war over anything, I think. Over furs and territory and all else that has been ours for hundreds of years. They kill each other, kill us, burn our castles, murder our women and children, but they call themselves civilized. We form our Confederacy and for hundreds of years respect our laws and preserve peace among us. And yet we are the savages."

He smiled. "I know, it is how we look, how we dress.

We put feathers in our hair instead of wearing them on hats. Instead of silk and lace, we wear deerskins. We do not believe in God so we do not quarrel over one and how He should be worshiped."

In all these things he was right. She thought back to the *Aventurier*. By every measure the Mohawks were savages. Was this Oneida? Questioning it to any white man would bring laughter. How could one classify any of them as anything but savages? With their caveman ways, their crude existence, primitive superstitions, childlike naivete.

And yet they did not think so differently from Europeans. They applied logic and common sense to problems. They exercised judgment. They planned their actions. They weren't stupid.

They rejected the true God and Christ but believed in a whole host of spirits. Of rocks and trees and streams and living creatures; these were their saints and angels.

They were entirely dependent upon nature, what it could provide them. Their environment made them what they were, in such marked contrast to Europeans.

What would Two Eagles have become had he been born to wealth and privilege, brought up in a fine manor house or real family castle? Barrister, physician, general?

And who decided to what a new baby should first open its eyes? Two Eagles had opened his to sight of the interior of a longhouse; Pierre, his to his parents' bedchamber in their château in Normandy. Why hadn't Dreamer been born in a country house near Bedworth and she, herself, in Onekahoncka? And why should these people be made pawns in the game of war involving the French and English?

Who determined that one race should be allowed to rule the destiny of another?

Oddly, her fondness for them was real and increasing. Though once she left them she'd surely leave behind all feelings for them.

As Red Paint and Fox joined him, Two Eagles turned, offering his profile. He looked haggard with worry. Not surprising; they'd completed two thirds of their search route and come away from Onekahoncka with no helpful information, not even a guess from Burnt Eye on Long Feather's whereabouts. Worse was the suspicion that the ugly one knew something but refused to divulge it, purely out of spite. Every so often one of the others would look Two Eagles' way and react to his dejected expression with his own gloomy look.

Thrown Bear had told her about Two Eagles' family: his father's murder, his mother's suicide in consequence, his oldest brother's accidental death in a fall from a cliff. Now Long Feather's disappearance.

"Are Two Eagles and Long Feather close?" she asked Thrown Bear.

"After their older brother's death they became close. Each year, at the Green Corn Festival, they renew their bond. They cut the palms of their right hands and bind their hand together for one night, the night of the War Dance that follows the hanging dog sacrifice. Their palms together, their blood mingles, they become one."

"Two Eagles loves his brother."

"I suppose, underneath, in his heart. But you would not think so seeing them together. All they do is argue. They agree on almost nothing. Often they do not speak for weeks, and Two Eagles talks to Long Feather through Swift Doe, his brother's wife. They have fought, drawn each other's blood. Theirs is a strange relationship.

"Friendship binds Two Eagles and me, as it binds all of us to him and to each other. But it is not friendship that he and Long Feather share. It is something else. I myself think it is the memory of their parents and older brother. That is what joins their flesh, making them inseparable while they live, not the blood bond. I am not being very clear . . ."

"I understand."

"Their bond is given them, set on their shoulders, not something they themselves forge," he went on.

"An . . . obligation. Making them responsible for each other, joining them despite their differences."

"*Nyoh, nyoh,* that is it. But there is no feeling, like brothers."

"Maybe what they share is even stronger than affection."

"What is that, af'—?"

"Affection, a feeling you get inside for somebody. Warm. It leads to love."

" 'Love'?" He looked blank. "I know one thing, if we do not find Long Feather it will be very bad. For all of us it will go hard."

"You're saying stay out of his way. How do I do that?"

"How do any of us?"

The pulsing fire in the sky-blanket lowered slowly into their eyes. They passed many hills overgrown with grasses and wildflowers, some studded with trees and shrubbery. Splitting Moon walked far ahead. They were about two hours away from Onekahoncka, still following the same trail that moved progressively farther away from the Mohawk River to the north. Suddenly, Anger Maker called out. Up ahead, Splitting Moon had stopped and turned, waving his arms, calling loudly and indicating a hill on his right. It was small, more a mound than a hill, and barren of vegetation. Two Eagles and the others ran toward it, leaving her to catch up. No more than six feet high at its center, it looked to be recently raised.

"Is it a burial mound?" she asked Thrown Bear.

He nodded somberly. "I am afraid. . . . But we do not bury our dead in such a way, all together in one grave. No Iroquois do. We dig a hole and bury the corpse sitting up, his arms around his knees, with a mooseskin or deerskin around him. Bark is laid over the grave even with the level of the ground, to keep the dirt from touching him. Then the dirt is heaped in a mound and the grave surrounded with short pickets painted red."

"Do you think Long . . . ?"

"Shhhh."

Two Eagles and the others had circled the mound. He looked angry.

"Spread out in all directions. Look for signs of them.

Whatever you find, bring to me. Anything: a moccasin, a lanyard, an arrow, even the head of one."

"Tékni-ska-je-a-nah . . ." began Thrown Bear.

"You, too. Take her, she can help. Put down the basket." He sat down on the mound. "Go!"

They left him holding his medicine, turning it slowly. He appeared in a trance. As still as stone he sat, only the feather slowly revolving.

They combed the area for an hour, she and Thrown Bear concentrating on the ground along the riverbank. They found nothing. When they returned to the mound Two Eagles was still sitting as before, knees drawn up, head down and resting on them. His feather was back in his scalp lock. The others came drifting back empty-handed, showing helpless and apologetic expressions. They stood expectantly.

"Dig," he said without looking up. "They are buried in this mound."

Anger Maker reacted, shocked. "You do not know that," he blurted.

"Do as I say!"

They began digging with knives and tomahawks. The sun lowered to the width of a hand from the horizon, turned a vivid reddish gold, staining the clouds purple. Two Eagles sat motionless as they worked around him, staring stonily at the ground in front of his moccasins.

Fox called out. "Here is something!"

It was a piece of deerskin. Two Eagles got to his feet. For the first time in over an hour she saw his face; it was that of a man slowly dying within himself. Expecting the worst, he would not be disappointed. The first body disinterred was that of Long Feather's best friend, Lokala-káhte—He-has-many-stories. "Stories" was recognizable, even though his nose had been sliced off. His assailants had also scalped him and cut his throat.

Long Feather's corpse was the third to be excavated. Like the others, it had been buried less than a foot deep. He, too, had been mutilated: both eyes gouged from their sockets. She turned away, revolted. Two Eagles looked down at his brother. The others stood unmoving, waiting for him to speak. When he continued silent, Thrown Bear pointed and spoke.

"They stole his nicked medal from around his neck."

"The one we saw at Onekahoncka was nicked," Anger Maker reminded them.

Two Eagles did not appear to hear either of them. He walked off, standing about ten yards distant, his back to them. No one uttered a sound. They waited for him to speak. When he turned around, she swallowed nervously and took a step back. He bristled, was livid; sparks seemed to fly from his narrowed and gleaming eyes. He clenched and unclenched his hands; his jaw muscles jutted forth like angled iron rods; his right eye twitched. His words came from between his locked teeth: softly, measured, edged with fury.

"I am going back."

"*Neh!*" burst Thrown Bear.

"You will come with me Tyagohuens, only you."

"My friend . . ." began Splitting Moon.

"Are you afraid?"

"*Ney,* I will come."

She and the others watched them trot off. Within calling distance, Two Eagles stopped and turned.

"You are in command, Do-wa-sku-ta. Keep going on to Onneyuttahage."

"Wait," called Thrown Bear, waving his stump. He approached them, the others following. Two Eagles came back a ways.

"What about Swift Doe?" Thrown Bear asked. "What do I tell her?"

"*I* will tell her. We will not be long. We will catch up with you before you get there."

Away they ran. They vanished behind a hill, reappearing, vanishing, growing smaller and smaller until the lengthening shadows blotted them from sight.

"We camp here for the night," announced Thrown Bear. "And wait," he added to her.

"It may be a long wait," she murmured.

He said nothing, but his expression agreed. She had retrieved her basket containing her wedding gown. The violets picked earlier had withered and died. She threw them
away. She was the only one who moved. The rest stood
stock still, their eyes still fixed on the distant spot where
the two had vanished from sight.

III

EYE FOR EYE

15

Two Eagles and Splitting Moon came within sight of the huge rectangular crown of Onekahoncka.

In the time it took them Two Eagles had not spoken a single word; the voice of his anger within him held his full attention.

Splitting Moon touched his arm. "You will have to speak to Burnt Eye. How can you when you are so angry?"

"I will control myself."

"And if you cannot?"

Two Eagles stopped short, glaring.

"No matter what lies he tells you," Splitting Moon went on, "you must not go to your knife."

"Do not instruct me! He knew all along and kept it from me and laughed at me." He seized the hilt of his knife. "I should cut him from jaw to bags, dig out his entrails and hang them around his neck."

"He did not kill So-hat-tis."

"He knows who did and he will give him to me."

"He will refuse you, or lie . . ."

"Not when I explain."

"You will not be telling him anything he does not already know. He will not hand you the killer."

"He will not have to. I will take him."

"You would reach into the clacking snake's hole and

jerk it out? And not be bitten and feel its poison mix with your blood?"

"I know what I am doing!"

"I wish that I did."

"If you are afraid to go in, wait out here for me."

"If *I* do not go in *you* may not come out."

"Ho-ka-ah-ta-ken's heart will sheathe my knife before any of the others get close."

Splitting Moon ran his thumb over the tooth set in the ball of his tomahawk. "Lead the way."

Two Eagles did not budge. He pointed to his friend. "I will do the talking."

"What have I to say? Except this, my friend: I share your grief over So-hat-tis. Your anger I do not. Always it is the shortest path to blood."

"Are you coming or not?"

The castle gate was still open at the late hour, though no game retrievers nor anyone else was passing through it. Inside, puzzled expressions met them, eyes asking why they had returned. They looked about for Long Feather's killer, the dark-skinned warrior, but he was nowhere to be seen. Apprised of their return, Burnt Eye came out of his longhouse accompanied by Hole Face and two others.

Two Eagles raised his hand. "*Nyah-weh ska-nah*, Ho-ka-ah-ta-ken."

"*Nyah-weh ska-nah*, Tékni-ska-je-a-nah. Back again so soon? Did you forget something?"

"To take with me the murderer of my brother."

Burnt Eye's head jerked back in surprise. He frowned. "So-hat-tis is dead?"

"Murdered. By one of your warriors."

"That is a strong accusation."

"That is the truth. The one who wears my brother's whiteskin medal around his neck. I ask you to bring him to me, Ho-ka-ah-ta-ken."

Burnt Eye returned his drilling stare in silence. Behind them the front gate was being closed. Splitting Moon held his breath.

"You know the man," added Two Eagles.

Still Burnt Eye stared. Then amusement lifted the corners of his mouth. He spoke to one of his men who went off. "I invite you both into my house, Tékni-ska-je-a-nah. Let us talk about this."

"There is nothing to talk about."

"Indulge me. I wish to know the details. How else can I understand? Come."

They sat where they had eaten, again with the Oneidas' backs to the passageway. The dark-skinned warrior Anger Maker had pointed out earlier was brought in. Burnt Eye gestured for the suspect to sit beside him and placed his arm around his shoulders.

"This is Cahonsye-rú-kwe, one of my bravest men: killer of many French lace-cuffs, many French moccasins. He is the son of my mother's sister, and my favorite cousin. Cahonsye, this is Tékni-ska-je-a-nah, a great and brave Pine Tree chief among our brothers, the Oneida. His brother has been killed. He tells me it was you who took from him his life."

"He has shit in his brain. I have killed no Oneida."

"Onewachten!" snapped Two Eagles.

Everyone stiffened. Splitting Moon sighed.

Burnt Eye looked offended. "Liar? Are you lying, Cousin? This shocks me. I should not need to tell you, Tékni-ska-je-a-nah, the truth is as sacred to my warriors as it is to me."

"He is the one and you know it, or else you would have brought in another. This is all a game to you. You, take off that medal, give it here."

The warrior, Black, hesitated, looking at his chief. Burnt Eye nodded his permission and, taking the medal from him, handed it to Two Eagles.

Two Eagles indicated: "This nick, like a notch near the top, confirms it is my brother's."

Burnt Eye looked doubtful. "The English whiteskins gave out many such medals, like leaves from the trees. Many nicked and scratched. That one I recall seeing around Cahonsye-rú-kwe's neck when he came home a few days before the war ended. *Nyoh*, we all praised him for it. He has worn it since, and he is proud of it, as well he should be. How many Oneidas came back wearing them? A great number, I am sure. Come to think of it, I myself was given one." He leaned forward. "Would you care to see my medal, Tékni-ska-je-a-nah?"

It happened so swiftly that Splitting Moon, even rigidly expecting trouble, could not move to prevent it. Black, sitting beside his chief, smirked at his accuser. Two Eagles roared, jerked out his knife and plunged it hilt-deep into the warrior's heart. Black's jaw dropped, his eyes swelled, an ominous gurgling escaped his throat, over he fell. Everyone leaped up. Like a cat, Two Eagles sprang forward, grabbing Burnt Eye's upper arm and swinging nimbly around behind him, setting the point of the bloodied knife against his throat.

"Everybody out!" snapped Two Eagles.

Burnt Eye hesitated, assessing the situation. "Leave us," he ordered.

His men filed out without looking back. Splitting Moon stood with his hand on the head of his tomahawk. He could not take his eyes from the dead man, could not believe what had happened.

Two Eagles spoke to him. "We are taking this one with us. Pick up the medal, put it around my neck."

"But . . ."

"Do it! It is all I have to give to Swift Doe."

Splitting Moon complied. Tensed, his eye a slit, fear filling his face when he first felt the point against his neck, Burnt Eye now relaxed. And snickered.

"You disappoint me, Tékni-ska-ja-a-nah. How far do you think you will get?"

"Think, Two Eagles," murmured Splitting Moon. "To use him as a shield would be a mistake. Many of his people hate him. They would celebrate his death. Force our hand, kill all three of us."

"Listen to Tyagohuens . . ."

Two Eagles grunted. "You admit your people hate you?"

"What chief does not have a few envious hearts among

his warriors? I have a better idea for you, sheathe your
knife and I give you my word, no harm will come to either
of you. We will talk about this. I want to know everything.
If Cahonsye-rú-kwe is guilty, he deserved your knife.

"It is too late for talk," said Two Eagles. "Move."

"Do you intend to take me as your hostage all the way
to Onneyuttahage? Or cut my throat on the way?"

"You life is worthless to me. What I want is something
of great value to you, something you treasure." He set the
edge of his knife against the bridge of Burnt Eye's nose,
less than an inch from his eye.

"You would not," murmured Burnt Eye. "That would be
the vengeance of a lace-cuff moccasin, not an Oneida warrior."

"Your cousin took both my brother's eyes. I will be
satisfied with only one."

An empty threat. He had no intention of killing or blind-
ing him, or even taking him as far as Onneyuttahage. He
had acted in haste out of ungoverned rage. The meaning-
less prattle, Burnt Eye's suggestion that many such medals
were damaged, his cousin's taunting smirk and all reason
had fled Two Eagles' brain. Long Feather had to be
avenged! Now, with the murderer executed, this one would
serve as hostage for their safe departure.

But what if, on the way out, one of the chief's men was
so rash as to attack them and force them to kill Burnt Eye?
Sacrifice the protection he afforded them? *Could* he kill
him? That would be senseless. There was another side to
it: would his warriors be pleased to see him taken away
and let them leave, without raising a hand? No, that was
worse than wishful thinking, it was stupid.

"What do we do?" Splitting Moon asked.

Two Eagles ignored the question. He lowered his voice
to his hostage. "Walk," he said, "normally and without
stopping for any reason. Tyagohuens, you will walk with
your back to mine. If anyone so much as moves . . ."

"This is wrong," muttered Splitting Moon.

Burnt Eye snickered. "Listen to him, Tékni-ska-je-a-
nah, is the warrior wiser than his chief? Before you set

foot out the door, consider the consequences. What will your clan chiefs make of this? The humiliation of a Maquen chief who has not raised his hand against you, has not even spoken against you? Are the Oneida prepared to return to the path of war? Against the Maquen, your brothers in blood?"

"No one would go to war over you."

"Not over me. Over face. Over the honor of our people—which you are about to kick dust on, spit upon. It is not me you insult, it is my rank and my people's respect for it."

"He is right," said Splitting Moon.

"Think," said Burnt Eye, "take the time . . ."

"*Ogechta!* One more word and I take your eye and dress you in your blood. Your people would rejoice. Dreamer would dance with joy. Now move!"

"How can I walk with your knife at my eye? If either of us missteps . . ."

"Pray to your óyaron that neither of us does. And for forgiveness for your stupidity in sending warriors out to murder So-hat-tis and his men."

"I did not. Think what you please of me but do not take me for a fool. Why would I order such a mission? What would it gain me? It was the rash act of young hotheads become bored with peace, with inactivity. When scalps can no longer be taken, courage and daring give way to frustration and discontent. Tell me that is not so . . ."

"Move!"

They emerged from the longhouse into the twilight. The Mohawks stopped what they were doing to stand motionless and watch.

"It is a long way to the gate," whispered Splitting Moon.

"You will die before you get halfway there," said Burnt Eye.

Two Eagles paid no attention. He looked up; no one was manning the platforms. They moved at a steady pace, the blade set against the bridge of Burnt Eye's nose, his eye unblinking. Two Eagles spied a man fitting an arrow to his bow, raising and aiming it at his head, a clear target.

Burnt Eye saw. "*Neh*, Pana-tawyne!"

Gray Otter held his aim. Two others, on the opposite side of the gauntlet, raised their bows also, and pulled them taut, all three arrows aimed at Two Eagles.

"Lower your bows, I command you!" rasped Burnt Eye.

They were now about forty feet from the gate. It was still closed and the bar in place.

"Tell them to open it," whispered Two Eagles.

Burnt Eye sneered. "You . . ."

"Do it!"

Two Eagles repositioned the blade, holding it with both hands hilt forward, the point within a half-inch of his captive's eye.

"Put down your bows!" screamed Burnt Eye. "Open the gate!"

One of the three warriors lowered his bow. The others held their aim. The Oneidas and their hostage were now within twenty feet of the gate.

"Open the gate!" Burnt Eye repeated.

The men closest to it stood fast. A woman moved forward and prepared to open it. Two other women hurried to help swing it wide.

"No one follows us out," warned Two Eagles. "Tell them." Burnt Eye did so.

"If you do," Two Eagles shouted, "he dies! On the blood of my brother, I swear it!"

Still the two braves held their aims. In the split-second it would take an arrow to fly from the moose sinew of the bow straight into Two Eagles' face he would start his knife through the eye into Burnt Eye's brain.

The braves ahead of them slowly lowered their bows. But two others stepped before the entrance to block their way, raising their pipe-tomahawks.

"Out of the way!" snarled Two Eagles.

"You will not kill him," said one. "You will die before he falls."

"You strike," warned Two Eagles, "he dies." With his

free hand, he pushed the warrior in the chest, sending him
backward. The man made no move to strike. Burnt Eye
passed through the crowd and the gate, then Two Eagles
stopped and turned Burnt Eye to face him.

"No one is to follow us," said Two Eagles loud enough
for all to hear. And brought his knife around, placing the
tip against Burnt Eye's kidney.

He recognized Dreamer pushing to the front of the
crowd. She was even more beautiful than Swift Doe,
whom he thought to be the prettiest of all the Oneida
squaws.

"Do not harm my husband," she said, with a low, sen-
sual voice.

"That is up to him," said Two Eagles.

"He does not dare to, woman," said Burnt Eye. "He
knows better."

"Let us go," said Two Eagles to Splitting Moon.

"Wait," murmured Burnt Eye. "This is your last chance,
Tékni-ska-je-a-nah. Stop this foolishness. What do you
gain by taking me along? Have I not served your purpose?
You are outside and safe. Leave me and go on your way.
No one will follow, I give you my sacred word."

Two Eagles glanced upward. Men were assembling on
the platforms and nocking arrows. Splitting Moon was
right, it was all a calamitous mistake: spawned in anger,
carried out in obstinacy, fueled by hunger for vengeance.

But if they left behind their shield they would not get
fifty yards before a rain of arrows caught up with their
backs.

"Look at my people," said Burnt Eye. "Look at their
eyes asking, what next? Will you release their chief or take
him with you? Look at their faces, Tékni-ska-je-a-nah. My
plight and their helplessness are embarrassing them. Take
me with you as your prisoner and you humiliate them.
Your own people will despise you for bringing them war,
one they do not have the strength to wage. Their anger
with you will be great. They will cast you out, kill you,
before I get the chance to."

"He is right," said Splitting Moon.

"He is dead if he does not shut his mouth! Turn and run, fast as you can, One-eye, while you still have it to see the trail!"

They ran. Burnt Eye kept pace. Splitting Moon ran shaking his head. Within minutes Onekahoncka was reduced in the distance to the size of the blood-bond scar in the palm of Two Eagles' hand.

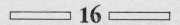

16

Stars swarmed, pricking the gathering darkness. Thrown Bear peered back along the trail toward Onekahoncka. Margaret stood beside him.

"Oh no . . ." he mumbled.

"What is it?"

"*Three* coming."

"I can't see anyone."

Red Paint raised a cry, Fox echoed him. Three men came into her view sprinting along, kicking up clouds of dust that rose behind them. Now she recognized Burnt Eye as the third man. The Oneidas stood motionless as the runners approached.

Two Eagles came up frowning. "Why are you still here?" he asked Thrown Bear, moving his glance to Anger Maker and Bone.

"We stayed to bury the dead in proper graves," replied Thrown Bear. "What happened? Why did you bring him?"

Burnt Eye grinned at Thrown Bear and Anger Maker. "Stump, Quarreler, we meet again."

Two Eagles scanned the dim horizon in the east. There was no sign of pursuit. "Go back to your people."

The Mohawk smirked and shook his head in mock disbelief. "You mean you do not intend to kill me? Mutilate me? How curious. You have gone this far, what stops you now?"

"Get out of here before I change my mind."

"I have a better idea, Tékni-ska-je-a-nah. Let me go with you all the way to Onneyuttahage. I would like to hear you explain all this to Sho-non-ses and your other chiefs."

The last of Two Eagles' patience deserted him. His hand started toward his knife.

"Pull it." Burnt Eye tapped his cheek under his eye. "Use it, show your warriors what a brave Oneida can do to a defenseless hostage."

"Two Eagles . . ." began Thrown Bear.

"Ogechta!"

Burnt Eye was shaking his head and sneering. "How many more blunders will you make before sleep closes your eyes?" Menace supplanted the sarcasm in his tone. His eye slitted. "This is a day both of us will remember, I promise you. So . . . since you refuse my company the rest of your way home, I shall go back."

"Wait." Two Eagles turned to Thrown Bear. "Where is my brother buried now?"

Thrown Bear indicated. They moved to the nearest grave. Two Eagles pushed his face close to the Mohawk's.

"You will see the proof of my accusation," he said, "the reason why my knife found Cahonsye-rú-kwe's heart."

"Your brother's corpse can identify his killer? Will you open his mouth and will Cahonsye-rú-kwe's name be on his tongue?" He shook his head. "I grieve for your loss, Tékni-ska-je-a-nah, but you ask me to stretch my sympathy too far. You have no more 'proof' here than you had back in my longhouse. All you have is your suspicion. In the fire of your anger you confuse one with the other." He jabbed Two Eagles' chest with his finger. "For what you have done to me you will pay dearly. Your Oneidas will see to that. The disgrace you have brought upon yourself today will be a wound that will never heal." His face twisted with hatred. "That you will carry to your grave."

He spat between Two Eagles' feet and ran off. Thrown Bear and the others crowded around Two Eagles. Margaret discreetly kept her distance. Splitting Moon started to speak. Two Eagles cut him off, slashing the air with his hand. "I know, I know, he is right, I am all wrong. Only *I* do not think so."

"What you think does not matter, my friend. What matters now is what is to come of this . . ."

"Nothing. He will return to his people and carry on, bluster and threaten. Joshú-we-agoochsa and the others will calm him and that will be the end of it. How do I know? Because *he* knows in the black stone that he carries for a heart: *his cousin murdered So-hat-tis!* Did he not bring him forward without hesitation? The right man? By now everyone in Onekahoncka knows the truth. Iroquois do not fight to avenge other Iroquois who murder their own. Forget it, it is over."

"I hope . . ."

"Do not 'hope.' Spare me your opinion."

"I will not! You brought me into it. I will speak. I say this, you cannot undo what is done but when we get back you must go straight to the chiefs and explain."

"Of course!" Two Eagles caught himself, lowering his voice. "I will tell them. They will see the justice of my actions and do nothing. There is nothing they can do."

"They may not think with your brain, my friend."

Two Eagles scoffed, but dismissing his private concern was not so easy. Burnt Eye had to return to face his people. The embarrassment they'd seen him put through was enough to goad him to vengeance.

As if he needed goading. But there would be no rush to retribution. He would wait and see what the Oneida leaders would do. His sadistic streak ran deep. He would let the kettle simmer for many moons before taking action to avenge his cousin. And himself.

That night Two Eagles ordered a guard posted should the Mohawks decide to follow.

17

The Mohawk River turned northwest where Otsquago Creek flowed into it. Deserted by the river, the trail to Onneyuttahage continued. It was early in the afternoon of the fifth day since leaving Onekahoncka when Two Ea-

gles, his men and Margaret came within sight of the
Oneida castle. They had seen no Mohawks pursuing.

To Margaret, Onneyuttahage, from this distance, closely
resembled Onekahoncka, although it was larger. Isolated
woods surrounded it. To their left at about a hundred yards
stood a sprawling cornfield, the green stalks grown to the
height of a man. Women were weeding with short hoes.
Some paused to wave as the party passed. Margaret looked
on as Two Eagles approached two young women. They
spoke briefly. When he came back, he was even gloomier
than he had been when he left the burial mound.

"Keep on," he said to Splitting Moon, taking him aside.
"I must go and speak with Swift Doe." He indicated a
stand of trees just beyond the entrance to the castle. "She
is berrypicking on the other side of those woods." He lowered his voice. "See that So-hat-tis' friends are told what
happened. I will speak to them all myself. And pass the
word to the others: There is to be no mention of Ataentsic.
I will handle that, too."

"What about Ho-ka-ah-ta-ken?"

He ignored the question and nodded toward Margaret.
"Tell Do-wa-sku-ta to take her to my longhouse. I will be
there as soon as I can."

"How will you break the news to Swift Doe?"

"She already knows. Women sense these things. It is
their gift." Again he lowered his voice before uttering the
name so that Margaret could not hear. "Remember, not a
word about Ataentsic."

"*Nyoh, nyoh.* Only what will you do with her?"

"Let the chiefs and elders decide, I cannot worry about
it, I have too much else."

Splitting Moon nodded. "You do."

18

Swift Doe had paused in her berrying to play tag with her two sons. Their baskets sat half-filled on a flat rock glittering with mica while the three of them romped happily. Two Eagles stood in the shadows beside a tree watching them. Swift Doe felt his eyes. At sight of him the happiness brightening her face faded. The boys continued playing.

She came over to Two Eagles. "Where did you find his body?"

He hesitated to tell her that Long Feather had been murdered by a Mohawk, knowing it would only aggravate the pain of her loss. Perhaps later. An Iroquois killing a brother Iroquois was considered a terrible crime and very rare. But in withholding the fact he underestimated her. She demanded to know the manner of Long Feather's death.

Two Eagles told her everything, ending by handing her Long Feather's medal. She held it up, eyeing it disdainfully, as if *it* were the cause of the tragedy. In a sense it was, at least the symbol of it. He expected her to fling it away. Instead, she gathered the lanyard and tucked it into her waistband. He still could not see tears in her eyes, nor did he expect to, knowing they were already falling unseen in her heart.

She set her palms on her growing belly. "So," she murmured, "my husband will not get to see his new son after all. And what of his two other sons now without their father to teach them, help them reach manhood, carry his name?"

"They will always carry his name."

"*Nyoh.* And memory. Yet time will fade it as it has your memory of your father."

This he could not deny. And he thought of the coming night and the nights to follow and the empty place beside her in their bed. The days would weigh heavily with sor-

row but the hours of darkness would be torture. He suddenly ached to *do* something for her, touch her comfort-
ingly, offer words of consolation. But nothing would help.
His face was not the face she wanted to see. She was sinking into herself, holding him from her, as she would everyone, so that she might mourn in privacy.

She lifted her tearless eyes to his eyes. She looked
shrunken, vulnerable. "And what will you do about the
ugly one?"

He shrugged. "What will he do about me?"

"He hates you, he always has."

"It will come to a reckoning, I suppose." He sucked a
breath in sharply as he remembered. "I should go and
speak with the chiefs."

"*Nyoh*, they must hear it from your mouth first. Go, I
will be all right. It is painful, but it would be much worse
had I not already made up my mind that I would never see
him again. Go, go."

This was untrue. Her eyes betrayed it: Nothing could
have made her surrender the hope he had seen in them the
last time they talked, before he, Thrown Bear and the others had started out. Her sons had come to stand solemnly
beside her, as if sensing something was wrong. Now she
would have to tell them. He patted their heads, then
touched her cheek. She held his wrist firmly in appreciation.

He left.

I n Two Eagles' family chamber in the longhouse of the
clan members related on his mother's side, sat his wife
Graywind. Behind her the overhead storage shelf was
filled with the couple's extra clothing, moccasins—Two
Eagles wore out twelve pairs annually—weapons and
cooking utensils. Braided strings of corn, dried fish,
squash, apples and other foods and sheaves of tobacco
leaves hung from the poles bracing the roof. Outside the

chamber door to the left of where Graywind sat was a fire
pit, cold at the moment, shared with Swift Doe, who with
her family occupied the chamber down the way toward the
front door. The small hole in the roof directly above the
fire pit was one of many set twenty feet apart and covered
with movable pieces of elm bark that could be opened and
closed with a pole from below. At each end of the longhouse was a door with a bear robe flap. Bunks along the
inside chamber wall served as beds at night, as benches
during the day. A storage closet was accessible outside between their chamber and the one next door, which was un-
occupied. Like all the Oneida longhouses, this one had
many empty chambers.

Graywind sat cross-legged, deep in the valley of her
mind. Her long unbraided black hair parted in the center
hung down below her waist. Her deepset eyes were the intensely dark brown of a deer and displayed at times a glint
of suspicion. A well-shaped, if somewhat broad nose cen-
tered her long face above a determined jaw.

She stared unseeing into space. Knowledge had just
come to her of the events occurring on the trail from
Onekahoncka to Onneyuttahage, not in detail but the gist
of them: the discovery of Long Feather's corpse and the
Mohawk's part in his death. Knowing well her husband's
temper, she worried about his part in the aftermath of the
tragedy, for as surely as the moon displaces the sun in the
heavens the major role would be his.

Graywind had a gift for seeing in her imagination distant events involving individuals she knew. Some of the
Oneida suspected her of being a witch who secretly gathered snakes and roots for concoctions to poison her enemies. It was even rumored that her blood ran back to the
Nanticokes in the south who first founded witchcraft, and
her black gifts were therefore inherited; that she had the
ability to turn into a fox or wolf, and so run very swiftly,
giving off flashes of light in the darkness; she could turn
into a turkey or owl, and fly like the North Wind, and
blow hair and worms into a person. Both husband and
wife vehemently denied these talents, with good reason.

Among the Iroquois, practicing witchcraft was a crime punishable by death. Still, people believed what they wanted to believe. Proof was not required.

Two Eagles considered Graywind's intelligence superior even to Bone's and admired her for it. She was a loyal wife who did not gossip, did not squabble with other women, and the two were deeply fond of each other.

But a raincloud hung over their marriage. Graywind was unable to conceive and it was not easy for Two Eagles to conceal his yearning for a son. Long Feather's death had left Swift Doe with two sons and possibly a third. The thought of never fathering a child pained his heart. He sympathized with his wife, and she had long ago accepted the situation, so it was not a source of contention between them. But they would grow old and leave no heirs, and when Aunt Eight Minks died, only Long Feather's widow and sons would be left to carry on the matrilineal strain.

So it would be preserved, but not by Two Eagles.

Graywind blocked out thoughts of Long Feather's death and the worrisome consequences. Two Eagles had arrived home. She had not yet seen him, but knew he was there; knew as well that he would not come to her right away but instead find Swift Doe to tell her the bad news.

Graywind felt a twinge of pity for her sister-in-law, despite not being overly fond of Swift Doe. Whenever Graywind saw her two nephews she saw her own failure to bear children, and some resentment was natural—not that she ever shared it with Two Eagles, husband and wife found something to agree on about as easily—in Eight Minks' words: "as one finds an arrowhead in Lake Oneida." But they would never disagree again, and Swift Doe was a widow too young, and her sons were fatherless. What had been burnt Eye's part in Long Feather's death?

She heard the end door to the longhouse creak open. Thrown Bear appeared.

"Graywind . . ."

"Do-wa-sku-ta. I knew you were back. And So-hat-tis and the braves with him are dead. What did my husband do when Ho-ka-ah-ta-ken told him?" That Graywind already knew what had happened surprised Thrown Bear, despite knowing of her powers. But he was not prepared to describe in detail what had happened. Something he divulged might stir discussion between husband and wife, raise questions in her mind when Two Eagles overlooked certain events beginning with the death of Burnt Eye's cousin.

Better to change the subject. "We brought a whiteskin back with us."

Her eyes widened. "A slave? For me!"

He shook his head, but it made no impression. He told her how Margaret had a husband waiting for her in Quebec. Still no impression.

"A slave ... Where is she?"

"Outside. She cannot be your slave."

"She must be. Why else would he bring her back?"

He hesitated to argue the point.

Graywind was suddenly babbling like a child anticipating a gift. "What are you waiting for? Bring her in. What does she look like? Young, old, what?"

Thrown Bear sighed. "See for yourself."

He brought her in. "This is Mar-gar-et. This is Graywind, wife of Two Eagles."

"Wife?"

He'd said nothing about being married. Why had he kept it from her? Still, why was she surprised? What did it matter? Graywind got up and walked around her, inspecting her like a side of meat. She fingered her hair. Margaret recoiled. "Don't do that!"

"You shout at me? She shouted at me!"

Graywind slapped her. Margaret swung in retaliation, grazing her shoulder. Thrown Bear pushed between them.

Eight Minks filled the doorway. "What is all the noise?"

"This slave ..." began Graywind.

"Who are you calling 'slave,' vixen!"

"Go out," said Thrown Bear to Margaret.

"Gladly!"

She left, brushing by Eight Minks.

Graywind scowled at Thrown Bear. "Who are you to give orders to my slave?"

"Slave?" Eight Minks looked from one to the other. Thrown Bear explained Margaret's presence.

"Cam down," said the older woman to Graywind. "Tékni-ska-je-a-nah is coming. He will settle it."

"There is nothing to settle." Again she scowled at Thrown Bear. "*You* get out."

He left, catching up with Margaret outside.

"That shrew is his wife? Poor man."

"She is very strong-willed."

She looked around. "Where am I to stay? Not in there, not with her."

"We wait until Two Eagles comes."

"Slave . . . of all the effrontery . . ."

"Captives are kept as slaves."

"I'm no captive. I came with you of my own free will."

"*Nyoh, nyoh*, please, Two Eagles will decide."

"There is nothing to decide. I'll not set foot in there with her. She's a witch! Take me to your chief. I want my escort. I'm leaving!"

 **20**

Two Eagles rolled his eyes impatiently and muttered. He stood with Splitting Moon and Thrown Bear—and Margaret—outside his longhouse.

"Take her back in," he said to Splitting Moon.

"Forget it," she shrilled.

Two Eagles threw up his hands.

Eight Minks emerged from the longhouse, as if she had been listening just inside the door flap.

Two Eagles addressed her, motioned to Margaret. "Keep her with you, Téklq-eyo, out of Graywind's way."

"Don't worry. I shan't set foot in that house!"

"Come . . ." Eight Minks took her by the arm. "We will walk a little, talk, get to know each other."

Margaret set her jaw defiantly, but yielded and joined the older woman to walk away.

"How did Swift Doe take the news?" Thrown Bear asked.

Two Eagles shrugged. "I must go to the chiefs."

Splitting Moon nodded. "Word of what happened must not get to them before you do. We will come with you."

"*Neh,* this is my problem. I will face it alone. But first, I must see my woman."

21

In the longhouse of Sho-non-ses, chief of the bear clan of the People of the Place of the Stone, two parallel benches had been placed on the far side of the fire pit nearest the entrance. The chiefs of the three Oneida clans and the elders of the tribe had assembled at Sho-non-ses' invitation. Sitting facing them, Two Eagles recognized many friends and some not friendly. Seated beside Sho-non-ses, To-na-oh-ge-na—Two-branches-of-water—chief of the turtle clan, scowled at Two Eagles pulled in his heels and rested his hands on his knees.

The two had once been friends but had become estranged over an incident at the Midwinter Rite that marked the beginning of the new year, shortly before the war. The Midwinter Rite was held in early February and lasted several days. It was the custom of clan chiefs to make the rounds of the longhouses for the stirring of the ashes ceremony, which symbolized the new beginning. With the two other chiefs, Two Branches had come to Eight Minks' longhouse to stir the fires for her and her two nephews. Neither was married at the time. As Two Branches moved his stick in the ashes, he compared their coldness to that of Eight Minks' bed and the fact that she slept alone. His sympathy was gratuitous and shocked Eight Minks, erasing her smile and bringing color to her cheeks. It infuriated Two Eagles. Tempers erupted. He attacked Two Branches—who was nearly three times his age—and they

had to be separated. Two Eagles demanded that Two
Branches apologize to Eight Minks. Instead, the turtle clan
chief compounded the insult with a wholly irrelevant re-
mark, citing Two Eagles' reluctance to marry or even be-
friend a woman his age. The implication was clear to all.
Two Eagles went wild, smashing Two Branches in the jaw,
seizing him by the throat. He would have strangled him
had not others intervened.

Even after tempers cooled, neither saw fit to apologize.
From then on they avoided each other. Now in his mid-
sixties, Two Branches had become afflicted with the
wringing pain that invades aging joints. His spitefulness
worsened, his tongue sharpened. He hated everyone, everything.

Sho-non-ses, chief of the bear clan, was twenty years
younger than Two Branches and resembled him not at all
in temperament and personality. Like his fellow chiefs,
Sho-non-ses—His Longhouse—was chosen by the matrons, who were empowered to appoint and depose any
chief in their clan. These women were entrusted with the
keeping of the white wampum belts that carried the hereditary names of the chiefs. A friend of Eight Minks kept
His Longhouse's belt. When a chief died, his title did not
pass on to his son, for titles were hereditary only within
the clan and sons belonged to their mother's clan, not their
fathers. Therefore, the chief's title could be inherited only
by a brother, a sister's son or another male member of the
chief's clan's matron's lineage.

In His Longhouse, Two Eagles had a valuable ally at
this meeting, a voice of reason, one he desperately needed.
He justified his treatment of Burnt Eye to himself but he
suspected that others, some facing him now, would share
Splitting Moon's disapproval of it. He could depend upon
Two Branches to do so.

Despite the differences in their ages and personalities,
Two Branches and His Longhouse were the best of friends.
His Longhouse was popular among his people: patient,
considerate of others, understanding—attributes of character Two Branches conspicuously lacked. His Longhouse

did not have one serious failing: his gleaming eye roamed freely, although his lechery did not approach Burnt Eye's. He did not pursue children or other men's wives, but his dissolute ways were well known and his wife had left his bed because of them.

The third chief, Hat-ya-tone-nent-ha—He-swallows-his-own-body-from-the-foot—was beloved by everyone. Despite his age and chronic infirmities, he had led the warriors of the wolf clan in the war with honor and distinction, nearly losing his life in the final days. Two Eagles admired He Swallows and suspected the feeling was mutual, but they did not really know each other, not nearly as well as Two Eagles knew the other two chiefs.

He Swallows' once lean and muscular frame had withered to that of a scrawny wraith; his bones protruded, his flesh hung, his claw-hands trembled. His feet ached and his rotted teeth distressed him greatly, as much as Two Branches' afflicted joints troubled him. But, unlike the turtle clan chief, He Swallows did not let his discomfort affect his cheerful disposition. He was considered the Oneidas' ablest mediator. After Two Eagles' and Two Branches' bitter clash at the stirring of the fires, he had tried to make peace between them. The effort was one of his few failures.

The others in attendance were elders of the tribe, none titled but all respected—for their longevity, if nothing else.

His Longhouse nodded greeting to Two Eagles and called for silence. "Before we begin," he said, "He Swallows has important news. Let us listen."

He Swallows appeared uncharacteristically dour as he cleared his throat. "What we have long feared has come to pass: The English have deserted us."

A chorus of groans arose from the elders. Two Eagles' heart sank. From their expressions, the other two chiefs had already heard. He Swallows went on to explain that Sir William Phips had sent word to the sachems assembled for the upcoming peace conference in Onondaga Territory, informing them that the English colonies could no longer supply material support to the Five Nations or help defend their lands against the French and their Indian allies.

So now, instead of preparing to negotiate a peace at the pending meeting with Frontenac, the Confederacy would be obliged to sue for one.

"But all fifty sachems agree," continued He Swallows, "that our people have not been pushed so low as to accept any and all terms offered by the French. We will come out of this holding up our heads."

Would the fighting resume? Would the ranks of Oneida warriors, already reduced by nearly two thirds, be further thinned? To Two Eagles, his friction with Burnt Eye suddenly seemed inconsequential, even trivial. The English abandoning the tribes would be uppermost in everyone's mine as they listened to him recount what had happened at Onekahoncka. Why even bring it up? Yet how could he avoid it? Having requested the meeting, he had to tell them what had happened. Even postponing disclosure would cast him in a bad light. He Swallows finished what he had to say. His Longhouse invited Two Eagles to speak. He related what had happened honestly and accurately. From the assembly, quiet gasps, soft groans and angry sharp sucking through clenched teeth punctuated his words.

"The Maquen Cayonsye-rú-kwe murdered my brother without provocation. He displayed the proof of his crime around his neck. My men know and will back me on that."

"Of course they will," said Two Branches. "Why wouldn't they? Friends are loyal to friends. I do not believe this. He actually took Ho-ka-ah-ta-ken hostage! Their chief? Threatened his life? Humiliated him in front of his warriors? Their women and children?"

"We had to get out of there," said Two Eagles. "I admit I may have acted hastily."

"Crazy, you mean, your brain upside-down in your head. What were you thinking? Did you bother to think?"

"Let us hold our tempers," cautioned His Longhouse.

Two Branches threw up his hands and rolled his eyes at

the square of blue sky in the roof. "By all means, side with him . . ."

"I am not 'siding.' I merely wish to hear the whole story."

"What more is there?" Two Branches riveted Two Eagles with his glare. "You realize this could force us into war. Did that even cross your mind? Do you *ever* consider the consequences before you go wild?" He touched his throat with his fingertips where Two Eagles had tried to strangle him years before. "Never!"

"I did act in anger," said Two Eagles. "But if I did not avenge my brother then and there his murderer would have gone unpunished. Ho-ka-ah-ta-ken would have done nothing to him."

"How do you know that?" He Swallows asked.

"Because from then on he denied it. Ask Tyagohuens. He ignored the proof of the English medal with the cut in the edge. So-hat-tis' medal. When I tried to explain to Ho-ka-ah-ta-ken, he all but laughed in my face!"

He could feel his temper rising. "His cousin killed my brother. I killed his cousin. It is that simple."

"It is that simple?" Again Two Branches addressed the others. "Is it that he does not understand or does not want to? Tell us, while you were abducting Ho-ka-ah-ta-ken, why did you not take his woman along and rape her? You might as well have. You could not make matters any worse."

"That is stupid talk," said He Swallows. "And does not help solve the thing."

Two Branches shifted his glare to the wolf clan chief. "And how do we do that?"

"Reparations can be made, a formal apology . . ."

"Now *that* is stupid," rasped Two Branches. "We are talking about Ho-ka-ah-ta-ken, the snake that walks, the child raper who would rather fight than eat, whose hatred for this one runs deeper than our hatred for the French. Will reparations and apologies erase his embarrassment? Cool his anger?"

Two Eagles lifted a hand. "May I speak?"

His Longhouse nodded.

"I cannot deny that Ho-ka-ah-ta-ken and I hate each other. And I agree that anything I might say or do to make amends he will reject . . ."

"That is the heart of it," burst Two Branches. "If you did not hate him so intensely the snake might listen to reason. Can you blame his cousin for *your* hatred? If he was not Ho-ka-ah-ta-ken's blood, would you have been in such a hurry to take his life? You and your temper! What have they done to us? He will attack us, we must prepare!"

His Longhouse shook his head. *"Neh."* He frowned at Two Eagles. "Ho-ka-ah-ta-ken is no fool. To attack us in reprisal would be to compound one foolish act with another. Nor would our brothers, the Seneca and Onondaga, tolerate such rashness. We all stand to suffer greatly because of the English defection. This is no time for quarreling among ourselves."

His frown softened. "If we are to believe you, Ho-ka-ah-ta-ken knows you had every right to avenge your brother's murder. And his people know it. It is not *what* you did but *how* that has created the problem. You embarrassed and demeaned him and that is very bad. But it is personal and has nothing to do with our people or the Maquen."

"He has caused their chief to lose face," said Two Branches. "His face is the face of his people. Are they to overlook that? Pretend it did not happen?"

Two Eagles sighed. He had heard it all before from Splitting Moon and the others. But not with such vehemence. Two Branches was in his glory. Could the others control him?

His Longhouse responded. "We must ask ourselves this, for this is the heart of it: do the Maquen want war? I think not."

From Two Branches came a hollow laugh. "You hope not."

"Let us settle it," said He Swallows. "To-na-oh-ge-na, what would you have Two Eagles do in reparation?"

"What can he?" rasped Two Branches. "Whatever he proposes will be unacceptable to Ho-ka-ah-ta-ken."

He Swallows and His Longhouse both nodded. He Swallows turned to pondering the situation, gnawing his lower lip, his brow deeply furrowed. All eyes fastened on him. Two Eagles expected that Burnt Eye would make him wait and sweat before taking any action in reprisal, but thought it best here to say nothing further; anything added would only elicit sarcasm from Two Branches. The decision was in He Swallows' hands. The mood hung like a pending storm as everyone waited.

He Swallows sucked a rotted tooth, then spoke. "We wait," he began.

"For what?" rasped Two Branches. "An attack?"

"For Ho-ka-ah-ta-ken to come forward with his demands," replied He Swallows. "He will." He smiled grimly at Two Eagles. "Be prepared to be humiliated as you humiliated him. Prepare to pay in blood, if it is his wish."

"*Nyoh.*"

"Still, with the passage of time it is possible his anger will abate. Possibly an apology, abject and sincere and uttered in front of his people, will satisfy him."

Two Eagles could see that He Swallows did not believe this and only said it to lift his spirits. Two Branches greeted it with a scoff and would have commented had not He Swallows gone on.

"You will do whatever he demands of you. You are in no position to protest or bargain."

"*Nyoh.*"

"Ahhh . . ." Two Branches flung a hand in disgust. "For now, we will consider the matter closed."

"One last thing," said He Swallows. "However justified you believe your actions to be when you found your brother's body, you should not have gone back to Onekahoncka. You should have brought your anger home with you and appealed to us for redress. That would have been right and proper." He leaned forward. "And you know it. Now go."

Two Eagles withdrew, thinking as he came out into the sunlight that it could have turned out far worse. They could have sent him back to Onekahoncka unaccompanied, unarmed, for Burnt Eye to punish as he saw fit. Were it up to Two Branches, he would be on his way now. Obviously, there was no solution to the problem at this end.

It was all up to Burnt Eye. Whatever he demanded, however outrageous and unfair, Two Eagles would have no choice but to comply. The chiefs were honor-bound to see to it.

He bit his knuckle and reduced one eye to a slit as he pondered. Perhaps his biggest mistake was letting Burnt Eye go with his life. But no sooner did this cross his mind than his common sense spoke: *Have you learned nothing from what you were just put through?*

22

In a chamber twelve chambers removed from Graywind's and Two Eagles', Margaret sat massaging her swollen feet, wincing. Opposite sat Eight Minks, smiling out of her moon face framed by stone-gray braids. On the wall behind her—painted half red, half black—hung a scalp so old it had shriveled to the size of a hand. Margaret could not resist an occasional look at it. On the wall opposite it was a crucifix skillfully carved from black walnut. Eight Minks proffered a clay dish of a gray cream. Margaret dipped her fingers in it and rubbed it liberally on the sole of her foot.

"It helps?" asked Eight Minks.

"It's very soothing. What is it?"

"*Okases*, ground and boiled in its juices. A weed. I do not know which one in your language."

"You speak very good English."

"I made Tékni-je-a-nah teach me."

"Two Eagles."

"Ah, you speak Oneida!" She laughed merrily.

Again Margaret's glance strayed to the scalp. "Is that French?"

"Huron." Eight Minks turned to look at it and stirred to rise. "Would you like to look at it closely?"

"No thank you."

"A gift from my nephew." Her smile faded. "Now I have only one nephew. Poor Swift Doe."

An uncomfortable silence fell.

Margaret broke it. "Is Two Eagles' wife always so nasty?"

"*Neh*, she can be very sweet. But she is too much inside herself."

"I don't understand."

"She sees things other cannot. Visions, things that happen far away. Her gift makes her proud."

"Overbearing." She paused and studied the older woman. "I have something terribly important to tell you. I need your help. Desperately." She told her about Pierre, the ship's grounding, the massacre and her escape.

Eight Minks pursed her lips, nodding. "Not easy to travel up there," said Eight Minks finally. Margaret sighed. "I did not say impossible."

"Can you help me? Talk to somebody with authority?"

"My nephew must have already told you it would be very dangerous for any of our warriors to venture into New France."

"It doesn't have to be Iroquois warriors. If I could get men from a tribe that sided with the French . . ."

"If you could trust them. They know no English. You would not be able to converse with them. Traveling in their company could be dangerous. You are a woman, you know what I mean."

"Then that settles it."

"What?"

"I'll just have to go by myself."

"You do not seem that foolish to me. Perhaps there is another way. Perhaps word could be sent to your husband, and he could come down from Quebec and take you back."

This possibility had not occurred to her. At first it did make sense. But the more she thought about it the less attractive it became. Even escorted, any French soldier would be in constant danger from roving Iroquois hunters.

Ironically, here in their very midst, she herself felt in no danger. But to put Pierre at peril, with hotheads like Burnt Eye and his cutthroats roaming about, would be as rash as it was unfair. Besides, how would she get word to him of her whereabouts? And would Frontenac risk lives to fetch her? She'd hate to end up with some poor soldier's death on her conscience.

"No, I must go to him."

"I would speak to the sachems for you," said Eight Minks. "With Kah-nah-chi-wah-ne—He-big-kettle. But all are in Onondaga Territory preparing for the peace conference."

"Haven't you a chief?"

"We have three."

"Isn't Two Eagles one?"

"A Pine Tree chief, 'war' chief. Those we have many of. They do not direct the affairs of the clans."

"I must see all three clan chiefs right away, today. Can you arrange it?"

"Perhaps, but not today. Be patient."

"The sooner I get to see them the sooner I get to leave. Two Eagles would be delighted with that. With or without their help, I intend to get to Quebec."

She returned to massaging her feet. Her eyes drifted to the crucifix. "Are you a Christian? Or is that a war trophy?"

"A gift from So-hat-tis. Some Hurons and Ottawas are Christians, but our people are not. Except those that moved up to the St. Lawrence, the Caughnawagas. We have our own belief, our own spirits. Tarenyowagon, Taounyawathat, whom some call Hiawatha, the spirits' messenger; Ataentsic . . ."

"Wait, wait, At—"

"At-a-ent-sic."

"That's the name they kept repeating on the way here! Ataentsic, yes, that was the name. What is she, a goddess?"

"A female spirit."

"Tell me about her."

"Why?"

"Please."

"Very well. But first, you are a Christian?"

"Of course."

Eight Minks eyed the crucifix. "*He* came from heaven to earth, correct?"

"Yes. And was crucified and returned to heaven. We believe He will some day be resurrected and return."

"*You* believe that?"

"All Christians do."

"Interesting. Ataentsic is very like that."

"Tell me."

"We believe that she lived in heaven when the earth was only a waste of waters. In heaven were lakes, streams, plains and forests inhabited by animals and spirits. Ataentsic was out one day gathering medicine leaves for her sick husband. She had her dog with her."

"Like Niche, yes . . ."

"While she was gathering leaves her dog slipped through a hole and fell to earth. She tried to save it but she fell through the hole too. Down below, the animals swimming in the water that covered the earth saw her fall and met in council to decide what to do. The beaver was asked. He asked the turtle, who called upon the other animals to dive, bring up mud and place it on his back. A floating island was formed and Ataentsic landed on it. She was with child and soon gave birth to a daughter. In time her daughter bore two sons."

"How? Who was the father?"

"Gâ´-oh."

"Who?"

"The North Wind."

"Oh."

"The boys names were Taouscaron and Jouskeha. Jouskeha killed his brother with a stag horn."

"Cain and Abel."

"What?"

"Nothing, go on."

"The turtle's back grew into the world. Jouskeha and his

grandmother Ataentsic rule over its destinies. He is the Sun, she is the Moon. He is good, she is evil. Together they live in a longhouse at the end of the earth."

"And she is your spirit of spirits."

"Our first spirit. She created the world. Why so interested in Ataentsic?"

"No special reason, just curious."

"Who is Niche?"

"My dog. He was killed by the Mohawks."

"So they took you for the woman who fell from the sky when they found you."

"I guess."

"You *know*. Oh, not Two Eagles, of course, not Bone. But the others . . ." Margaret nodded. Eight Minks smiled cryptically. "And are you Ataentsic?"

"You don't believe I am?"

"I am *shogasis*, it is my nature. *Shogasis,* I do not know your word for it."

"Skeptical? You doubt?"

"I do. Does that surprise you? Do not some of your people doubt that the one on the cross will return?"

"Some doubt He ever existed. Or had the powers Christians credit him with."

"Doubt is like fear of snakes. Everyone has some. Listen to me, I would not go around telling people you are Ataentsic, not if your heart is set on leaving."

"It is."

"And stay away from Graywind. You are safe in here, and at this end of the longhouse. But do not go near the other end or outside. If you must leave, use the rear door at this end."

"Maybe I'll get lucky. Maybe I'll leave tomorrow. Wouldn't that be marvelous?"

"*Nyoh,* marvelous."

Her expression said miraculous. Margaret sighed inwardly.

23

A warm moon invaded the swarming stars. The soft night air was cool and sweet to the nostrils in the chamber of Two Eagles and Graywind, and added to the scent of fresh pine boughs hanging among the dried fruits above them. Graywind lay beside her husband. He draped his arm across her, pressing his lips against her throat. She sighed lightly and brought her arms up over his back as he snuggled closer. A whole moon had passed without his warmth by her side, and the sweet song of his measured breathing as he slept, while she lay disdaining sleep, scouring her mind for visions.

His cool hands framed her face and slipped to her shoulders, down her slender body. She lay serene under his gentle touch; he was back to her arms, her body. Presently she would feel him, capture and delight in him.

On his knees, he moved his hands up and down her thighs. She began quivering and felt a dryness in her throat. Other than their breathing, there was no sound, not even wind outside. His hand asked her to turn over; she complied, lying on her breasts, her hands supporting her face. Lightly he rubbed her back, bringing erect the tiny hairs at her nape. A feeling of delicious languor came, from her calves, up her thighs, over her back, reaching her shoulders and spreading down her arms. For a long time, he stroked her, and within she tingled gloriously. She turned over on her back. With the flat of his hand he touched her yearning place. She held his head, drawing his mouth to hers.

Time moved the moon and the tireless stars stared fixedly as he mounted her and entered her place. She trembled, her eyelids sealed, her hips rose.

Time gave them each other, they went wild, they climaxed, they separated, lying shoulder to shoulder on their dampened backs, hands clasped, panting in unison. She kissed his cheek and ran a finger down his mouth.

"Do not leave me again."

"I do not want to."

"Will One-eye make you?"

"I have been thinking about that. I think he will do nothing, the doing has to be all mine. I must redeem myself in the eyes of our chiefs."

"You did no wrong; his cousin invited your vengeance."

"It is not that simple."

She sat up and ran her hand down his chest.

"I thank you for my gift, my husband. The slave."

He rolled over, talking to the bed under him. His tone had an edge. "I have already told you she is not a captive. Not your slave or anyone else's. Do not make me keep repeating myself."

"She thinks she can travel into New France. She is like a fish in a meadow that can never get to the water. She is here to stay. Why may I not have her? I can use her, even with her sharp tongue."

"That is spirit."

"I can break it. I have not had a slave since the Huron back in the early days of the war. Before we became man and wife."

"You killed him."

"I had no choice. He refused to obey me. He was useless. Why did you bring her back, if not for me?"

"I have already explained. You make me tired. Sleep."

Again she kissed his cheek. There was a long silence.

"Where is she?" she asked. "What did you do with her?"

"Sleep!"

24

Word got out that some of Two Eagles' friends who had accompanied him on the ill-fated search for his brother assumed Margaret to be the reincarnation of Ataentsic. She decided to neither confirm nor deny it. Obviously somebody had ignored Two Eagles' request to keep secret the arrival of the woman who fell from the sky; within hours, to many faces came the identical expression she'd seen on the faces of Fox, Red Paint and others back at the hollow tree.

She did not raise the subject again to Eight Minks, with whom she was speedily becoming friends. Her new guardian brought it up. Eight Minks sat cross-legged weaving a basket, skillfully interlocking splints. Out walking that morning, she had spied a black ash log. Splitting Moon had reduced it to length for her and skinned the bark. She had pounded it with a flat stone to loosen the lamina that joined bark to trunk, then carefully split and smoothed the peeled-off bark, which was cut into long flexible strips.

"When will you speak to the chiefs about my escort?" Margaret asked. "You did promise to."

"I already have. He Swallows says it is not their decision. The sachems must decide. Be patient, you will likely get your escort. Or help of some sort in getting there. If the sachems agree."

"You said they won't be back for weeks!"

"Shhh, you get very loud when you are upset. Someone could go to the treaty meeting that is about to begin and put the matter to them there. It is not as if we do not want to help you, but it is not an easy decision to make. Then too there is this business of Ataentsic. Someone has tipped over the kettle, and now half the people think you are Ataentsic. Do you want 'Ataentsic' in our midst? Would you want her in your castle back home? It is all getting as tangled as an old spider web. I have a thought."

She paused in her weaving. "Maybe Two Eagles . . ."

"What about him?"

"He knows you, so maybe he will volunteer to go to the sachems for you."

"It's true he'd like nothing better than to see me leave."

"You think he does not like you?"

"I know exactly how he feels."

"Then you are alone in this world. He never tells how he feels about others." She beamed. "Except, perhaps, the one-eyed Maquen."

She resumed weaving. Under her flying fingers the basket rapidly took shape.

"He won't go to the sachems for me."

"Make up your mind. I will talk to him. Who knows? Perhaps he has other things he will want to talk about to the sachems."

She worked on in silence, the basket nearly completed.

"How do you finish the rim?" Margaret asked.

"See those two splints?" She indicated the two that had been set aside. "Each one goes around half the rim and is fastened by a stitch. It is easy." Margaret had gotten up. "Where are you going?"

"I need some air."

"Go out the back door and not far. Keep out of Graywind's way."

"I'm not afraid of her."

"You should be. She has her heart set on making you her slave."

This Margaret dismissed with a shrug.

25

The issue of whether Margaret actually was "the woman who fell from the sky" sharply divided the Oneida. The decision rested with the tribal sachems and, as Eight Minks pointed out to Two Eagles, until they returned from the peace conference, which might not be until late fall, there was no hope of resolving the situation. Two Eagles wanted Margaret to be on her way as much as she herself did. He saw as inevitable a clash between her and Graywind. Now, with the war ended, no Oneida squaw had even a Huron prisoner-slave, let alone a whiteskin woman. In Graywind's eyes, a whiteskin slave would set her above every other squaw in the castle.

"She refuses to listen," said Two Eagles ruefully to Eight Minks.

They sat in Eight Minks' chamber. Margaret occupied

the chamber next door but was out at the moment. Graywind was at work in the fields.

"I have been thinking," said Eight Minks. "You and Kah-na-chi-wah-ne are very close. He has always been very fond of you . . ."

"He-big-kettle is at the peace conference," he reminded her impatiently.

"Will you let me finish? Why not go there yourself? Speak with him, tell him about Margaret. Get him to speak to Frontenac. When he hears what happened he will be pleased to take her back to Quebec and her husband. At the same time, you will have a chance to discuss with Kah-nah-chi-wah-ne your own problem. He has always given you sound advice. Perhaps he can help you with your problem with Ho-ka-ah-ta-ken."

Two Eagles pondered, biting a knuckle and narrowing an eye. "Graywind worries me."

"I will keep them apart. Margaret is not afraid of her."

"It is not a question of her fear. Graywind does not believe she is Ataentsic anymore than I. All she sees when she looks at her is a slave. If she should harm her . . ."

"She would not do anything behind your back to embarrass you."

He grunted. "I have heard that To-na-oh-ge-na does not believe Margaret is Ataentsic either. If, while I am gone, anything should happen to her, if trouble is stirred up, he would use it against me. I brought her here." He scowled. "I could strangle Sku-nak-su."

"Fox is your friend."

"He discovered her sitting in the tree. We could have passed her by."

"And left her to die? That is not you, Tékni-ska-je-a-nah." She lay her hand on his arm. "Go to the conference. Leave as quickly as possible. Speak to Kah-nah-chi-wah-ne and Frontenac before the talks begin. Once they start, they will have no ears for any words of yours."

"You will keep Graywind and Margaret apart?"

"Have I not already said I would?" Eight Minks smiled. "You worry about Margaret."

"We should have walked right by her." He sighed, then raised his eyebrows. "Why not take her with me?"

Eight Minks shook her head. "What if the French do not come, or come and go before you arrive? It is something that has to be planned carefully, for it has nothing to do with the peace. You must first ask Kah-nah-chi-wah-ne, not thrust her before his face."

"You are right. Graywind will burn the holes of my ears, but I will go."

26

Accompanied by Splitting Moon, Two Eagles left for the peace conference in Onondaga Territory. Once again, Graywind was alone. Now she sat in her dark chamber seeking a vision to guide her. Two Eagles' last words to her upon departing were to warn her to stay away from the whiteskin woman who was a guest, not a prisoner. And when he returned she would be escorted to the peace conference to be given over to Frontenac's protection.

And the Oneida would be rid of her forever.

Her husband's words were as bell tones in the channels of her ears, quickly forgotten. The counterfeit Ataentsic was her slave and it was now time to begin teaching her her place and putting her to use.

Graywind had already set by the chamber door offerings of green corn and porcelain beads for Agreskoue, whom the Iroquois worshiped both as the sun and their god of war. Into her mind Agreskoue would come as she lay sleeping. Into her "*ganno-gonr-ha*," her spirit, as well. Into her "*erienta*," the function of her heart and will.

Like all Iroquois, she believed that the soul acts independently of the body and makes long journeys at will, through the air, to the most hidden places. And as the soul itself is a spirit, nothing can obstruct or arrest its progress. Like all Iroquois, she believed that her dreams and the visions that occasionally appeared in them were actually occurrences, the doings of the soul while the body sleeps.

Confident that Agreskoue would not fail her, she disrobed, lay down and soon fell asleep. She was flying, arms outstretched before her, hair flaring wildly. Out of the swirling impenetrable darkness of her mind came a cloud of golden foxglove, saxifrage stars, twinkling foam flowers, dancing red gerardias, whirling around her as she tunneled through them. They clung to her, accumulating, covering her nakedness, and on she flew clad in color.

The blackness dissolved and Agreskoue appeared blazing, drenching with gold the meadows slipping by below. Agreskoue drew closer, his brightness stabbing her eyes, setting them throbbing with pain. Into his burning heart she flew, into a chamber, a haven of cool whiteness. She stood motionless. The pain fled her eyes. The flowers fell from her, heaping in a circle around her ankles.

Thunder startled her, and out of its rumbling echo came a voice questioning her presence. She dared not respond, dared not utter a sound. There was no need, for out of her mind came her request. Once more the thunder rolled and pounded. The white wall in front of her opened and in the white distance a figure appeared walking slowly toward her. She recognized "her." She, too, was naked. Around her neck hung a noose, the free end of the rope trailing after her. In one hand she held a stake, in the other a stone.

Graywind's heart leaped. Agreskoue approved; her purpose was right and must be achieved!

She awoke, looking around in the darkness, accustoming her eyes. She glanced toward the door, her heart sang.

The offerings had vanished.

She dressed in darkness and went outside. Down the length of the longhouse she walked. No one else was stirring. The silence was a robe wrapped around the castle. Moon and stars had disappeared. Then thunder spoke and lightning's jagged knife ripped the night, plunging into the earth to the east. The air was hung with rain that would fall before morning. Agreskoue would rest this coming day; in his absence the sky would wear gray.

Behind the longhouse were four cages made of osier branches. Three were occcupied by bear cubs. The smallest cage was empty. She untied the sinews holding its door closed. Then, opening the largest cage, she picked up the sleeping cub by the scruff of its neck, carried it struggling to the little cage and put it inside. She stood watching it fall back to sleep.

Thought of Two Eagles on his way to Onondaga Territory came to mind. And thoughts of their life together, their marriage.

Shortly after she had gone through the ceremony of maidenhood, she consulted Agreskoue. To her delight, he approved of Two Eagles for her husband. She told her mother of her decision to marry him. Her mother was already a good friend of Eight Minks. The alliance was agreed upon. Only would Two Eagles be attracted to her?

She waited one whole moon, as Agreskoue instructed. Then, gathering fresh corn, cooking and shredding it, she baked twenty-four double loaves of "ball biscuit." These she carried in a basket and hung at Two Eagles' door. If he ate just one he would be compelled by custom to propose marriage. Eight Minks reminded him of this, of the importance of such a step, the obligations and pressures that came with binding one's self to another for life. His eye having settled on Graywind, his ear became deaf to such reminders. He ate a biscuit and they were married the following week, only hours before he was to return to the war.

It had not been an easy marriage. Neither compliant nor cooperative by nature, Graywind did not look upon Two Eagles as her lord and master. Unlike some of his friends in their marriages, he did not require her to. They allied as two fiercely independent minds; agreement on anything, even something as trivial as what to eat for a meal, was rare. Other snags and tears appeared in the fabric of their relationship. Like many wives, she did not approve of some of her husband's friends. She disliked Anger Maker intensely, for his manner, his ways, the stench his foul-smelling pipe left in the chamber after his visits.

Over many things husband and wife bickered, but they seldom fought, for each respected the other and their hearts held a mutual loyalty, if not love. Iroquois husbands and wives did not seek love in marriage. The word was not in their vocabulary; its meaning was considered a wasteful emotion, non-contributive toward the relationship. Respect was all. Two Eagles and Graywind respected each other but hesitated to show it; their ingrained independence forbade it.

Graywind told herself that she was not jealous of Margaret. Two Eagles had never given her cause to be jealous of any woman. But all the talk about Margaret's husband waiting in Quebec and Two Eagles' responsibility for her until she rejoined him struck Graywind as pointless.

Agreskoue agreed.

The confirmation she had sought was hers. The way was clear!

27

Graywind searched the area around the longhouse for a stone, discarding a number before finding one that duplicated the size and shape of the one in Margaret's hand in her vision.

Back inside she pulled down two deer leg sinews from the storage shelf and, carrying the stone and a knife, started down the passageway to the rear. She found Margaret asleep. Graywind raised the stone and slammed it down on her temple. She flung the stone into a corner and proceeded to tie Margaret's wrists behind her with one sinew, her ankles with the other. She then cut away her clothing. Dragging her naked and unconscious to the rear door, Graywind placed her in the largest of the four cages.

Back in her chamber, she watched lightning brighten the interior and heard again the thunder speak. Using the long pole, she closed all the smoke-holes in the passageway. The rain came in a deluge. She fell asleep listening to it drum the roof.

Outside, the downpour woke Margaret. Her head ached furiously and she was stunned at how and where she found herself. She screamed for Eight Minks but could not make herself heard over the storm. Dizzy and exhausted, she stopped calling and lay motionless, the rain spattering her, mud splashing in her face and eyes so she sat up leaning against the side of the cage, head bowed against the low top. For hours, the rain swept unabated over the castle, reducing the grounds to a quagmire, assaulting the helpless captive.

Dawn was breaking when Graywind awoke. The storm was over but there was no sign of the sun. She appeared to be the earliest riser in the longhouse, for when she washed and dressed and went out into the passageway to open the smoke-hole covers no one else was about, not even Swift Doe's sons who were usually awake before anyone else.

After she had opened the last cover and left by the rear door, Eight Minks awoke. She washed, dressed and went at once to Margaret's chamber. Finding it empty, she ran out the rear door. There stood Graywind, watching her naked captive stirring and testing her wrist bindings.

Margaret sat shivering. Her hair hung pitifully. Her eyes were red from fear and pain, cold and anger. "You did this, you witch!"

"Shhh, you will wake the whole castle. You forced me. The first thing a slave must learn is obedience. You refused to obey me. You gave me no choice."

"You're mad!"

"You have spirit but I will break it. By the time my husband returns, you will be as docile as a baby."

"You *are* mad," said Eight Minks behind her.

Graywind whirled, eyes blazing. "Stay out of this, old aunt. It is no business of yours."

"Out of my way!"

"I warn you . . ."

Their shouting brought curious early risers. They stood gaping at the naked captive. Graywind continued loudly upbraiding her while Eight Minks went back inside. She reappeared with a moose-hide robe, striding past Graywind, swinging the cage door wide and arranging the robe over the captive.

"How dare you!" shrilled Graywind.

Eight Minks shook her head. "Mad, a hornet trapped in your head." She produced a knife, holding it out hilt first. "Cut her loose."

"Neh!"

Eight Minks shoved Graywind aside, reached inside the cage and cut Margaret's bindings. Quickly, she covered her nakedness.

"Come out," ordered Eight Minks, steel-eyeing Graywind.

"Stay where you are!"

Margaret crawled out, holding the sopping robe tight around her. Her cheeks glowed in humiliation.

Graywind started for her. Margaret swung her arm, fending her off. Two men held Graywind off as Eight Minks helped the captive into the longhouse. Graywind screamed protest. They went into Margaret's chamber.

Eight Minks got out a bearskin. "Keep covered," she cautioned. "You are catching cold."

"I'll kill her for this!"

"Shhh, we have had enough threats around here already." She clucked. "I blame myself for this. I never should have given in and let you live here by yourself. Two Eagles will be furious!"

Margaret sneezed. She felt half-drowned and could not control her shivering. Her teeth chattered. Her skin felt like ice.

Eight Minks shook her head worriedly. "Into bed, cover yourself. I will mix you *nosgah*." She disappeared into her own chamber, fumbled in a basket on the storage shelf and returned holding up a root the size of her little finger. "Bloodroot. It is fresh. I dug it up just the other day. I will grate it and boil it in water. You will drink a little many times today and by tomorrow your cold will leave you."

Graywind stormed in wielding a long stick, shoved Eight Minks out of the way, and began flogging Margaret. Eight Minks lunged to knock her away. She whirled, dropped the stick and seized Eight Minks by the throat. Margaret scrambled to her feet and grabbed Graywind from behind. Pain and rage infused her with astonishing strength.

Into the corner she hurled Graywind. As she fell, Graywind's forehead struck the discarded stone. She lay still. Eight Minks and Margaret stood staring at her. Eight Minks went to Graywind and turned her face up. Margaret gasped at the sight: Graywind's eyes gaped dully. Blood trickled from the corner of her mouth. Eight Minks knelt and listened at her heart.

"Is she . . ." began Margaret.

Eight Minks closed Graywind's eyes, straightened, looked toward Margaret and slowly shook her head.

— IV —

THE ASHES OF PEACE

28

The French delegation to the peace conference, escorted by B Company of the Second Battalion of the elite Carignon Regiment, had long since departed Quebec. The group numbered one hundred forty men, including four Huron scouts. A fleet of thirty-eight canoes had been assembled, the only craft light enough to be carried over the shoals and around the rapids that would impede the travelers along the one hundred and fifteen leagues of the St. Lawrence River from Quebec to Cataraqui, at the headwaters of the river in the northeast corner of Lake Ontario. Here General Frontenac himself had established a combined fur-trading and military post twenty-four years earlier, naming it for himself.

Now from Fort Frontenac the column headed south, crossed the river's rich alluvial meadows and entered the woodlands, the gateway to Onondaga Territory, a rectangular expanse wedged between the Cayuga territories on the west and the Oneida on the east.

In single file along the main trail, the French made their way through towering maple forests so dense the sunlight could barely be seen. Pierre walked behind his commander thinking about his already blistering feet and marveling at the redoubtable Frontenac's seemingly limitless energy and superb fitness (for one who had lived behind his escritoire for the past several months). Robins and black-capped chickadees trilled in the semi-darkness. The wind caressed the thick canopy of leaves. A strange low humming sound came from directly ahead. The birds stilled.

"Listen to the insects," said Frontenac, smiling. "We're invading their domain, and they resent it. Thank Him above us they don't carry tomahawks and bows and arrows, eh?"

Ironically prophetic words, for coming at them was an enemy bearing a weapon of another type. The humming grew louder. Into sight came a slender black cloud like an airborne serpent undulating through the trees, smudging the view, approaching at about fifteen feet above the ground.

From a muskeg about a hundred yards ahead where millions of eggs had hatched a few days before, the cloud of mosquitoes whirred toward human body heat. The peace delegation broke and fled, stumbling through the brush, flailing the humming air in futile defense against the onslaught. For nearly fifteen minutes the one-sided battle raged. Then, as speedily as they appeared, the attackers withdrew, their bellies bloated, returning to the muskeg.

Leaving the flower of the military in New France and the delegation scattered over a mile-square area cursing their painful bites and swellings. The governor general scratched both cheeks furiously and vented his annoyance on his equally uncomfortable aide. "You were in charge of supplies, why didn't you pack netting?"

"There was none to be had, Excellency."

Corpulent General Desmaines, puffing and sweating, his face and hands swollen in a dozen places, came up to them.

"Assemble the men, Leon," rasped Frontenac.

As he spoke, the bugler sounded assembly. From all directions the men came straggling back. Frontenac watched two Huron scouts standing together surrounded by scratching, suffering white men. Both were clad in leggings and deerskin shirts, but their arms, necks and faces were unprotected. Yet not a single red swelling could be seen on either man.

"What do you make of that?" Frontenac asked his general and his aide. "You two ..." He beckoned. "Come here."

The scouts approached, glancing curiously at each other.

"You weren't bitten?"

"No," said the older one.

"No, *sir*," interposed Pierre.

Frontenac grasped the scout's hand. On close examination he could see what appeared to be a salve of some kind; also evident on his arms, neck and face. Both men reeked of the stuff.

"Dog's tongue," explained the other scout.

"Dog's ..." Frontenac looked puzzled.

"Tongue."

The other scout pulled a cluster of limp, tongue-shaped leaves from his belt and rubbed them on his hand. "Keep away bugs."

"Where did you find that?" Frontenac asked.

"All over," said the first scout. "It keeps away mosquito."

"Yes, yes, so you said. We'll stop here for the night. You two men and your friends, go out and bring back all the dog's tongue you can. Bring it to the captain here. Go."

They trotted off.

"Filthy beggars," muttered Desmaines. "You'd think they would have warned us."

Frontenac grunted, shook his head and walked off to sit on a fallen log and resume scratching.

29

The scouts walking both forward points reported that the column's destination now lay less than ten leagues ahead. Here the trail widened and the forest thinned, more sunlight reached the floor. Game, mainly deer, was shot daily to augment the food supply.

It was midmorning. The column had stopped for fifteen minutes to rest. Pierre had shot a fully grown buck and two men were gutting it. The captain had just finished reaming and reloading his musket and stood talking to Frontenac, when movement in a tree directly behind the general caught his eye. Without hesitation, Pierre raised his weapon and fired.

Out of the tree fell a brave and his bow and arrow. The men quickly gathered around him. From his upper body tattoos—horizontal lines across the top of his chest and vertical lines descending either side of his breastbone, lines also decorating his neck and the lower half of his face—and his garb and five-feather headdress attached to a scalp knot, he was identified as a Cayuga sub-chief.

He was alone. The scouts speculated that he had been out hunting, had heard the column approaching, taken refuge in the tree, when the vanguard passed under him, he had recognized the general and resolved to assassinate him. Pierre's ball found his heart before he could let fly his arrow.

Frontenac exploded in gratitude. "You saved my life!"

In an instant the captain found himself surrounded by smiling admirers. Officers patted him on the back and pumped his hand as his commander grabbed his shoulders, beaming at him.

"Damned if you didn't!"

"You did indeed, Captain," said General LaFleur. "And I for one shudder to think what would have happened had you not." He addressed himself to Frontenac. "Imagine our showing up without you to do the talking—we'd be lost."

"Hardly," mumbled Frontenac.

"I beg to differ, *mon General*," said Desmaines. "You command the chiefs' savages' respect, admiration. We wouldn't get within a Provence mile of a treaty without you. Captain, you deserve a medal."

"It was just luck, sir," said Pierre. "I saw the leaves move. I couldn't take a chance. Anyone would have done the same."

Frontenac shook his head. "Not the point, Peter. The

hero's boots are yours. You spied him, fired, I'm alive. How can I ever repay you?"

"Excellency . . ."

"Look at him, my friends, he's blushing."

General LaFleur frowned. "Do you suppose more of them might be lurking in the trees up ahead?"

"No," said Frontenac. "To-do-da-ho and the other sachems would never permit it. They look upon the peace conference as seriously as we. This *renégat* was acting on his own. Peter, I am in your debt forever."

"Three cheers for Captain Lacroix," shouted a sergeant.

The cheering rose; Pierre lowered his face modestly and stuck his boot under the corpse, turning it over.

30

As dog's tongue eliminated the threat of mosquito bites, a decoction made from the inner bark of the tamarack tree eased the swelling and discomfort. Having trudged nearly one hundred miles overland from Fort Frontenac, General Frontenac's enviable endurance finally deserted him about three leagues from their destination.

A sedan chair was quickly fashioned and eight sturdy shoulders assigned to carry him the remainder of the way. It pricked the old man's pride as painfully as the mosquitoes pricked his face, to be transported like some flabby, self-indulgent Asian potentate, but he speedily became accustomed to it.

He spotted an open space early in the afternoon of the last day of their journey, called Pierre's attention to it, and ordered the column halted. The bugler blew assembly, everyone gathered.

"Men," said the general, "for any of you who might be curious, let me assure you I have no intention of entering Massowaganine in this ridiculous contraption. I propose to march in at the head of the column."

The men cheered.

He silenced them. "Before we arrive, I will remind you

again, as I did before we left Quebec, before we left Fort
Frontenac: there will be no 'incidents' in the days to come.
No man will raise his weapon against any Indian, even if
provoked. I repeat, *even if provoked*. To-do-da-ho has assured me that any of his people who misbehave toward us
will be severely dealt with. This is our chance to strike a
treaty with the Five Nations. I'll not have that chance
jeopardized by some trivial, uncalled for incident. You will
keep your swords sheathed, your muskets unloaded, your
tempers reined."

A groan went up.

"I mean it. Your personal enmity, all the black memo-
ries, you will leave in these woods. Our intention is to impress our hosts with our words, not weapons. We have not
come all this way to intimidate them but to gain their respect. And, whatever the outcome of our discussions,
when we leave we will leave no trace of resentment behind us."

Laughter.

Frontenac bristled. "Enough, the next man who laughs
will be flogged!"

He lowered his voice. "The British have deserted them.
They are at a low point. We are riding high. That should
be enough to assuage your bitterness. There is no love lost
between us *but there will be mutual respect*! Respect in
our discussions, in individual contact. No bullying, no
tempers, no weapons. I give you fair warning. That's all."

The march resumed with the scouts who had been walking the forward points being recalled. The last thing
Frontenac wanted just before arriving was a clash between
a Huron and an Onondaga out hunting for his dinner or
with another Cayuga wandering out of his tribal territory.

31

Two Eagles and Splitting Moon arrived at Massowaganine, the principal castle of the Onondaga Nation
and capital of the Iroquois Confederacy. Massowaganine

was situated on an eminence in a fertile valley, which produced an abundance of corn. The crop and the many fishing stations by the territorial rivers and lakes furnished ample food for the Onondaga. The castle itself was three times the size of Onneyuttahage and in the center, surrounded by conventional longhouses, stood the Council House of the Confederacy, two hundred feet long and twenty-five feet wide. The interior was not divided into chambers as in ordinary longhouses and therefore there were no interior walls to support the arched roof; instead, it was held up by a number of timber columns. Light and ventilation were provided by smoke-holes in the roof.

The floor was bare ground and the interior was filled with benches, leaving an aisle between the two sides. At the front was a raised platform for those who addressed the audience. The fifty sachem delegates to the conference would occupy the first two rows.

The two Oneidas had arrived early that morning. Already, the castle and surrounding area were crowded with visitors. All forty-one visiting sachems had brought large entourages. The newcomers more than doubled the population of the host Onondaga and lent a carnival atmosphere to the scene. Senecas, Cayugas, Oneidas and Mohawks were bartering goods with each other and with the host Onondagas. Food was shared, weapons and trinkets exchanged. Musicians and dancers entertained the gathering; from early morning until dark, the strains of the flute, the beat of the tom-tom, the water drum and various rattles were almost continuous.

A *baggataway* match was in progress, a game that the French called lacrosse, each side boasting at least a hundred players, the tribes mixing, providing participants to both teams. They flailed away with their webbed sticks, one in each hand, trying to snare the elusive deerskin ball, pass it to a teammate and move it toward the opponents' goal. The goal, defended by a player, was two slender twenty-foot poles joined at the top by a stick. The teams played barefoot and continuously until a goal was scored.

As was the custom, a solemn dance preceded the match, after which the ball was tossed in the air and the players rushed to catch it on their webbed sticks.

Splitting Moon loved playing and watching *baggataway*. The sport held little fascination for Two Eagles, however, particularly the match in progress. Upon arriving, they had gone immediately in search of Kah-nah-chi-wah-ne— He-big-kettle—only to be told that he and the other Oneida sachems were in a preliminary meeting that was expected to last until nightfall.

Two Eagles could not conceal his disappointment. Splitting Moon tried to cheer him up. "So you will see him tonight. He will speak to the others. You will have your answer before we go to sleep. Probably."

"Probably. Have you ever seen such a crowd? Why do they bring their squaws and children? Why the music and dancing, the *baggataway* . . . ? They are supposed to be negotiating a treaty."

"They will start as soon as the lace cuffs show up. How many tally sticks were attached to the wampum belts the sachems brought, do you think?"

Tally sticks indicated that a conference was about to begin. In this instance, each tally stick held twenty-five notches; one was removed each day until the French delegation arrived, whereupon the peace conference would begin. Three notches remained.

Two Eagles was not interest in discussing the tally sticks. "It is all a waste of everybody's time," he groused.

A player propelled the ball over the goalkeeper's shoulder between the poles, a loud cheer went up and, on the far side of the field, an unconscious player was carried off bleeding badly at his chest.

Two Eagles turned his back on the match. "There will be no peace treaty, you watch."

"They have to try," said Splitting Moon.

"They will offer us crumbs. One thing, they had better do away with the money."

Throughout the hostilities, the French King Louis had

offered standing rewards of ten silver *e'cus* for every Iroquois killed and twenty for every male prisoner.

"And they had better get off our lands and stay off, even their drunken trappers, who want our women as much as they want our beaver pelts."

Splitting Moon grinned. "It is a good thing you will not be in on the negotiations. There would not be any. Why so upset? You will talk to He-big-kettle. He will settle the business with the Englishwoman."

"He already knows about Ho-ka-ah-ta-ken and his cousin. All the sachems know. I will get a lecture from him like I got from To-na-oh-ge-na. This is stupid, we never should have come."

"He will not 'lecture' you. He has been fond of you since you were a *cian*. Was he not your father's best friend?"

"That was long ago, in another life. What do you suppose has happened to Frontenac? Where is he!"

The day wore on, the *baggataway* match continued, injuries thinned both teams, and Two Eagles' disposition deteriorated by the hour. When the match finally ended, the sun was well down beyond the Allegheny plateau. As the players were leaving the field, a tremor of excitement passed through the crowd; the French had been sighted. Two Eagles and Splitting Moon could see red, blue, white and gilt emerging from the woods. Marching at the head of the elite Cartignan company, his commander two steps behind him, his personal entourage and chief officers surrounding him, was Frontenac. He was resplendent: polished high dress boots, gilt-embroidered frock coat with lace cuffs that despite the heat reached almost to his elbows, a twelve-foot sash of white silk angling down from his right shoulder, circling his waist and draping down his left thigh almost to his boot top, full ruff, long white wig, white ermine-trimmed cocked hat.

The drums rattled, the fifes shrilled. The Indians stood gawking at Frontenac.

Two Eagles turned his back. "I cannot look at him. I hate him so," he growled.

"Did you see the Huron scouts?" asked Splitting Moon.
"He brings them to rub our noses in the dirt."

"Tonight I talk to Kah-nah-chi-wah-ne. Tomorrow we
leave."

"My friend . . ."

"Do not argue. I say again, we never should have come.
I should have stayed with Graywind. We have been apart
so long, and I come home from the years of red days and
go out looking for my brother, and now away again. I am
no husband. I am a flitting shadow in her life. Come."

32

In the pale light of the quarter moon filtering through the
trees, an Indian maiden sat by a quiet stream tossing
daisy heads into the water, watching the current set them
spinning. The water dipped and rose and curled sinuously
around shining stones, barely audible under the chirring of
the cricket thousands filling the night.

A twig snapped behind the girl but she failed to hear it.
It was not until a shadow fell over her and darkened the
water at her feet that she realized someone had approached
her from behind. The man bent smiling, taking firm hold
of her shoulders. She wrenched free.

"Now, now, pretty one, is that any way to welcome an
honored guest? Your conqueror?"

Fear twisted her pretty face, she began whimpering, her
eyes darting left and right. Up she sprang. He was too
quick for her. Seizing her braid in one hand, he gripped
her throat with the other, holding her rigid, fighting to
breathe.

"Relax, I won't hurt you. I'm very gentle, you'll see.
Such a pretty neck. It would be a pity to break it."

She didn't understand, but the threat he posed was clear.
Her eyes glazed with terror, she trembled in his grasp.

His eyes traveled down her face to her breasts, firm and
high under her tight dress. "Exquisite. Even lovelier than

little Two Buttons. You're fully a woman. Relax, I say, I won't hurt you."

Still smiling, he slowly released her throat, pulled her head forward and kissed her. She bit him. He howled and slapped her, sending her sprawling. His lip was bleeding. He reached down, grasped the front of her dress and ripped it open to her waist.

And clapped his other hand over her mouth to cut off her screams.

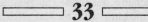 33

To-do-da-ho, He-great-wizard, was sixty but looked twenty years older. His eyes were a light brown with flecks of orange. His leathered face was usually in a radiant smile. Soft-spoken, intelligent, a gifted orator and debater, he was the leader of the Onondaga sachems, the host delegation.

In his chamber sat his lifelong friend Ta-ha-nah-gai-eh-ne, chief of the bear clan and acknowledged leader of the Onondaga. Two-horns-lying-down rarely surrendered his face to his emotions, rarely smiled. He was a man of action and hated idleness. Just sitting for a time finding nothing to do with his hands made him edgy. He was, at the moment, out of the arena of his expertise, and he showed it. He wore a British officer's red and white field jacket. He had introduced the sachem to their guest. Two Horns and the governor general had known each other for nearly seven years, in the way that opposing commanders in the field become acquainted, by reputation, each man sparking the other's respect by his exploits. Frontenac viewed his former enemy as a first-rate, albeit primitive strategist, on par with Genghis Khan. In Two-horns-lying-down's eyes, for a lace-cuff who would have been more at home directing his troops from behind a desk, Frontenac was remarkably adaptable and resourceful in a battle theater wholly unlike any in his previous experience.

A sharp distinction could be drawn between sachem and

chief in their views of the upcoming negotiations. He-great-wizard was determined to see that they be conducted in absolute good faith. But Two-horns-lying-down, having fought the French in the field, and having seen his people suffer at their hands for so long, could not turn off his bitterness simply because both sides had laid down their arms. In which respect he was not unlike the great majority of combatants on both sides.

Now the three had come together to set out the agenda for the opening day of the conference. Two-horns-lying-down asked Frontenac a question. The general, listening to He-great-wizard finishing what he was saying, did not respond.

Two-horns-lying-down repeated his question. "Why bring so many uniforms to a peace conference?"

"They are not that many. We came many miles through woodlands where there are many dangers. A Cayuga sub-chief lurking in a tree tried to kill me."

"Cayuga, not Onondaga," said Two-horns-lying-down. "You brought men of the vaunted Carignon Regiment. To impress us?"

Frontenac smiled.

"The general wished to show our people the Carignon Regiment, Ta-ha-nah-gai-eh-ne," said He-great-wizard, matching Frontenac's smile. "I *am* very impressed."

He stood up and began pacing. "Tomorrow we begin. If you agree, General, you will speak first and outline what you believe the treaty should embrace."

"There are seventeen major points," said Frontenac.

"Tomorrow, please, so that all the sachems may hear them directly from you. When you are done, the sachems heading each of the five delegations will speak in turn. The bones of disagreement will be laid out for all to see and understand. And we will begin picking them over one by one."

"Many trees must be burnt down, many stumps removed before the field of lasting peace can be sown," said Two-horns-lying-down.

"It can be done," said Frontenac. "It is in our hands. If

we fail, we can only blame ourselves." He unfolded a
sheet of parchment, squinting to read it in the flickering
light of the single torch. "I suggested twelve points, the
minister of war added five more. I tell you this so that you
will know we are in agreement among ourselves."

A brave burst in, nearly tearing loose the deerskin door
in his haste.

"I left word that we are not to be interrupted," snapped
He-great-wizard.

The brave went to the chief and whispered. Two-horns-
lying-down reacted with shock. He spoke rapidly in Onondaga to He-great-wizard, who gasped.

"What is it?" asked Frontenac.

"Something has occurred," said the chief. "It concerns
you, General." He nodded toward He-great-wizard. "You
tell him." The chief left with the messenger.

He-great-wizard sat back down, overcome with weari-
ness. "One of your officers is outside. A prisoner. He was
caught raping one of our women. My granddaughter, Willow Song."

Frontenac sucked a breath in sharply.

"Her two uncles were walking nearby, heard her
screams, rescued her. And captured the man."

Frontenac was ashen. He could not believe it had happened after all his warnings, on the very eve of negotiations!

"General?"

He snapped out of his thoughts. "Get him in here."

34

Captain Lacroix was pushed inside. His left cheek was
badly bruised. One sleeve hung by a thread from his
shoulder. A stout stick was thrust inside his elbows behind
his back, and his wrists tied so tightly in front of him that
the blood was cut off to his hands. Two angry-looking
warriors stood either side of him.

At the entrance, He-great-wizard turned back to
Frontenac. "You will want to talk in privacy."

"No, stay."

He-great-wizard shook his head and gestured to the warrior. "*Neh*, you two come . . ."

The three went out.

Pierre hung his head like a schoolboy called to account. Rage built in the old man. He still could not wholly believe this deliberate disobedience of an order after clear warning. His eyes burned into his aide.

"Please . . . loosen . . . my wrists."

Frontenac made no move. "I am listening."

"I did nothing, Excellency, I swear by Almighty God. They attacked me . . ."

"Enough! You don't start out by lying. Have you no shame? *Bastard! Canaille!* We have not even begun and you pull this!

"You . . . do . . . this . . . to . . . *me!*"

"Excell—"

"Silence!" Frontenac stared, his scowl softened, his narrow shoulders sagged. He threw up his hands. "Why am I angry? Why even surprised? I blame myself. I should have nipped this in the bud ages ago. You think your whoremongering goes unnoticed? That I don't know about the poor creatures you fetch to your bed? Your burning, uncontrollable urge to seduce and ravage every woman within reach? You and your perpetual erection?"

"Sir . . ."

"Don't speak, listen, damn you! I should break you to private and send you back in chains to Fort Frontenac to wait for us. You won't have to wait long, not now. Tomorrow in the negotiations we'll be shouting at each other, everything falling apart before we even start. No, not send you back, better I hand you over to her family. Her father will bury you up to your worthless neck, tie a rope around your neck with a bear at the other end, and dump honey on your head. It'll rip off your jaw to get at your tongue! Your screams will be heard all the way back to Quebec. And I will stand on the sidelines, cheering!"

"I implore you, let me speak!"

"You deny you raped her?"

"I did not rape her, I swear!"

"Of course. Her uncles hearing her screams saved her. Saved you. They could have slit your throat on the spot!"

"I did not lay a finger on her."

Frontenac leaned his face close and lowered his voice to a menacing whisper. "I could kill you myself for this. Skewer you where you stand. All this work, ruined before we start. You should be drawn and quartered, you miserable puppy!"

Pierre suddenly glared. "Enough! I have my rights. I am a French officer, entitled to speak. How dare you revile me? My father . . ."

"Don't. Don't throw that fat, greedy merchant-thief at me, puppy! Him, with a reputation as black as the pit. You come honestly by your lying tongue, your spoiled, self-indulgent ways, utter disregard of others' rights. Listen to me. If—I say if—He-great-wizard allows it—it is up to him. He and his family are the offended parties here—if he allows it, you will leave here before dawn with Colonel Depauw and a six-man escort. To return to Fort Frontenac where you'll be confined to quarters till we get back!"

He shoved Pierre roughly to one side and lifted the flap, calling to He-great-wizard. "Please send a man to bring Colonel Depauw and two of his men here to take this filth away and hold him under guard."

He-great-wizard hesitated, eyeing the captain.

"I know," said Frontenac, "you want him. You deserve him. I don't deny it. But he is under my command. Let me deal with him. I give you my word he will be severely punished."

He-great-wizard ruminated on this, bunching his lips, frowning into space. Then he slowly nodded.

"Thank you," muttered Frontenac.

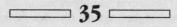

35

Two Eagles was relieved as he entered Kah-nah-chi-wah-ne's chamber and their eyes met. All the years of their friendship and mutual admiration rolled through his mind. He-big-kettle grinned, clasping his shoulders fondly, and warmth enveloped them both.

Then he frowned. "I have heard of your brother's death."

"Murder." Why did he have to correct everyone?

"The war is over, so you and Ho-ka-ah-ta-ken are now free to go at each other's throats, is that it? Tell me your version of what I have heard."

"What do you know?"

"I think all of it. Bad news has wings as powerful as the swift hawk."

Two Eagles recounted the incident, making no excuses for his impetuosity. "I need your advice. You are the wisest of our sachems . . ."

Up came the old man's hand. "Please, do not start by dripping honey into my ears. I cannot taste it there and it will not sweeten my opinion."

"Of course. I am sorry."

He-big-kettle sat cross-legged, fingering the silver disk hanging from a thong around his neck against his quill bib. At one time he had been one of the Oneida's fiercest warriors, but age and infirmity had kept him out of the recent war. While the younger men fought, he remained at Onneyuttahage to become the most highly respected sachem of the tribe.

"What will you do?" he asked.

"I have given much thought to that on my way here."

"And discussed it with Tyagohuens?"

"Neh."

"Good, good. Too much advice from one's friends can be harmful. We sometimes reach a point where we act on others' opinions instead of our own judgment."

A hint that whatever He-big-kettle might advise him should best be weighed against his own thinking. This he could not accept. He had thought so long and so hard about what he should do, it was all beginning to blur in his mind. And even before entering the chamber he decided that whatever He-big-kettle suggested, this he would accept and act on.

"What will you do?" repeated the sachem.

"I think go back to Onekahoncka and have it out with him. Get it over with. Better that than let it drag on for months."

"What does 'have it out with him' mean? A duel with knives? Giving your blood to the ground?" He shook his head. "You are wiser than that. Consider, you inflicted injury, why should he help to heal it? Why risk his skin to regain his face? It is for you to give it back, without his lifting a finger."

"We are talking about Ho-ka-ah-ta-ken. He will not rest until his knife turns in my heart. He wants to fight. On his terms, of course: where, when, how . . ."

"For you to return there would be like jumping into the sand that sinks and swallows. You would never leave there alive. It is not just his face you have taken, it is the face of his people."

"What do I do?"

"You must wait and let him come to you."

"He will not!"

"Shhh. It frustrates you, I understand. And I agree, he may delay approaching you with his demands for many moons."

It was the same view the chiefs had given him; and he had come all this way for an echo?

"Would it have been wiser for me first to avenge my brother's murder then give myself over to Ho-ka-ah-ta-ken? Surrender then and there?"

"You should not have retaliated."

"I should have let his cousin live? Pretend I did not know he was guilty? That is easy to say now, but if you had been there . . ."

"I would have controlled myself. I would have returned home and put the matter before the chiefs."

"And what would they have done for Swift Doe and her sons? Talked the thing to death and forgotten about it."

"That you will never know, not now. You ask my advice. I say stay clear of him." He stifled a yawn. "It has been a long day. I need to sleep."

"One other thing before I go." He told him about finding Margaret.

He-big-kettle grinned. "With her dog? Like Ataentsic?"

"Some of my friends *thought* she was Ataentsic. Still do. They have infected the whole castle. Half believe she is, the others . . ."

"Not you . . ."

"Whether she is or not is not important. What I was getting to is, she is married to a French long knife in Quebec and Eight Minks asked me to ask you to tell Frontenac, so that when they leave they can take her back with them. If he agrees to take her, I will fetch her here. Can you tell him?"

"Of course, but not right away. Not until we begin making headway in the negotiations. I cannot distract him with trifling matters that have no bearing on the treaty. But I promise I will tell him. You say she is English and married to a French? Such strange people to marry their blood enemies." Again he stifled a yawn.

"Good night, Kah-nah-chi-wah-ne," said Two Eagles. "And I thank you."

"For what? My bones tell me I have not helped you with your problem. Perhaps it is beyond anyone's power to help you."

"I think that is so."

"One other thing, my boy, stay away from the Maquen sachems here. Do not speak to any of them."

"I have no reason to. Good night."

"Wait, will you be staying until I can speak to Frontenac? Or shall I send his answer back to Onneyuttahage? Stay. You and I have not talked in so long. We used to talk often. Stay until I can ask him. Graywind will not mind. She must be used to your being away."

Two Eagles grunted.

"Stay and see some of your old friends from the war and we will talk again, I promise. Good night."

Two Eagles came away annoyed with himself. At foolishly expecting a great flash of wisdom that would solve his dilemma in the flap of a wing. What right had he to think such was possible? Foolish, stupid . . .

36

Early the next morning, Two Eagles was standing outside the longhouse where he and Splitting Moon had slept when his friend came pushing through the surging crowd pulling a man by one arm. He could not help but recognize him. The man stood six-foot-five, with shoulders even broader than his own, a mass of fiery red hair, a full beard concealing his huge neck, and mischievous eyes as blue as the sky.

"Duncan!"

Sergeant Gordon Duncan, formerly of the Second Scottish Highlanders, pushed past the beaming Splitting Moon to seize and embrace Two Eagles.

"What—?" began the Oneida.

"Am I doing here? I live here, auld skate. After the bloody war I married the bonniest wee lass in the whole spanking tribe. We're hoppy as twa frogs in a pond and our first wee bairn is on the way."

He pantomined rocking a baby in his arms.

"Lord love a duck, talk about a sight for sore eyes."

Two Eagles had never been able to completely understand Gordon but he delivered his words with such heartfelt warmth and friendliness he could not help liking him immensely, more than he liked any other English—which Duncan bridled at, explaining that he had "nae drop of Ainglish blood in any vein."

Into the waters of nostalgia they plunged: the attack on Ford Vercheres, the Battle of Schenectady, the defense at Toniata, the raids on the St. Lawrence.

They left the castle, strolling toward the stream, by coincidence toward the very spot where Willow Song had encountered Lacroix the night before. Two Eagles knew nothing of the incident, nor had Splitting Moon heard about it; Duncan knew everything.

"Some bloody frog officer tried to rape a lass and was caught in the act by her uncle, Shining Otter, who happens to be a good friend. He and an old friend of his. They fetched the culprit to Frontenac himself and early this morning the rotten bastard had to make his apologies to her and her family and the chiefs in front of everybody. Gifts were gi'en in reparation and noo he's on his way back to Canada in disgrace."

"He is lucky they did not cut off his thing and feed it to him," said Splitting Moon.

Duncan nodded. "They say the peacock general is still beside himself; when he gets bock he's liable to do worse wi' the bloody scoundrel. Serves him recht."

They spent all day with Duncan, meeting his wife, who appeared very pregnant, about to give birth during the conversation. They ate together, continued talking over old times and wondered along with everyone else unable to get into the Council House what, if any, progress was being made toward a treaty.

37

Graywind was buried. Her death had been accidental, so Eight Minks insisted, explaining to all who would listen and showing them the marks on her throat where Graywind had tried to strangle her. Had Margaret not intervened, she declared, "I would be the dead one."

Unfortunately, to many the truth is not as valid as the conclusions they so eagerly leapt to. Graywind's friends had earlier looked upon Margaret with curiosity; now in their eyes were suspicion and loathing. Others simply stared and talked about her behind their hands.

Whether or not she was the "woman who fell from the sky" no longer seemed to matter. She was the stranger in their midst and she had taken a life.

Now she sat in Eight Minks' chamber listening to Chief

His Longhouse and Eight Minks discuss her. They conversed in Oneida; she understood not a syllable.

To His Longhouse, Eight Minks recounted the incident in detail. He asked no questions. He understood that Margaret was a victim of circumstances. However, other aspects of the situation troubled him. Eight Minks had told him that Two Eagles had gone with Splitting Moon to Massowaganine to ask Frontenac to take Margaret back with him to Quebec after the peace conference.

"A bad idea now," observed His Longhouse, "to ask the husband of the woman she has killed to help her."

"Graywind was alive when he left," Eight Minks reminded him.

"She is dead now and he knows nothing about it."

"When he comes back, I will tell him exactly what happened."

"Your words will not interest him. His shock and anger will close his ears. His woman is dead and this woman is responsible. She should leave before he returns."

"For Quebec? By herself?"

"Get someone to go with her. Ask Do-wa-sku-ta, he knows her. Ask Sa-ga-na-qua-de."

"Ask Oneida warriors to venture into New France?"

His Longhouse felt Margaret's eyes on him, looked her way, did not smile or frown, showed nothing on his face.

Eight Minks brightened. "There are French at Da-yä́-hoo-wä́-quat."

"*Nyoh, coureurs de bois.*"

Eight Minks' smile fled. "*Neh,* they are dangerous."

"They would not harm her. If word got up to Quebec they would be dead men. They know that. The important thing is they are French and you say she is married to a French. And she can pay them to take her."

"You think they would not harm her? They are animals. They would ruin her. And murder her and bury the evidence."

"Does she know about Da-yä́-hoo-wä́-quat?"

"I doubt it."

"Tell her about the trappers. Let her be the one to decide."

"She will need protection getting there."

"Get it for her. Get her that far, then she will be on her own." He rose.

"Where are you going?"

"I have told you what I think you should do with her. Do what you like. I have to piss." He went out.

"Do you still want to leave here?" Eight Minks asked Margaret.

"Now, with this business, more than ever. Right away. When Two Eagles comes back and finds his wife dead . . ."

"You think he will take revenge on you? *Neh.* He has the worst temper I have ever seen, but he will not blame you, not after I tell him."

"I still don't want to be here when he gets back." Margaret avoided Eight Minks' eyes. "He's been good to me, helpful. He's trying to help now, out there. But I can't wait. Besides, he has enough problems of his own without my hanging around his neck."

"You are not hanging." Eight Minks moved closer and took hold of her hands. "There is a place on the river where the waters are shallow and canoes must be portaged. It is called the Carrying Place. Many French trappers come there."

"I can pay them to take me to Quebec!"

"*Nyoh,* but I must warn you, they are not men like your husband. They live in the woods. They do not bathe. They have lice. They trap beaver for months on end. They see no women. You understand?"

"They won't harm me. They wouldn't dare! I must go to them. Right away! Today!"

38

The first day of negotiations went poorly for the sachems. The British having deserted them, the Iroquois had little heart for the discussion, but had to take part; they would have to take the crumbs. Frontenac did not strut and threaten but he knew the power of his position; any prior limitations he might have put on his demands were jettisoned. He would expect the moon.

His seventeen points, if agreed upon *in toto*, would relegate the tribes to the status of indentured workers on their own lands. New France was in a heated competition with the British-controlled Hudson's Bay Company for domination of the fur trade in the New World. The trade in beaver pelfry had been the backbone of the Iroquoian economy. Now, insisted Frontenac, the tribes would collect the fur for the French government.

This the sachems unanimously rejected, which threatened to wreck negotiations almost before they began. Two-horns-lying-down blamed the tribes' former allies. Into the Council House he strode the second morning without his prized British officer's jacket. It was rumored that he had burned it shortly after the previous day's negotiations.

In his heart, Frontenac knew that even if the Iroquois gave their fur trade over to the victors, it would be impossible to enforce such a dictate. But the order came from his minister of war and it was his job to enter the demand.

Two Eagles, Splitting Moon and Gordon Duncan managed to get into the Council House for the second day's negotiations, standing just inside the entrance. He-big-kettle was speaking, striding back and forth in the manner of all Iroquois orators. Frontenac had announced his seventeen points. Before decision was reached on any single one of them the sachems had points of their own to put forth.

"The black robes must leave our lands," said He-big-kettle. "The missionary settlement near the salt springs, the one they call Jesuits' Well, the one at the branches of Kicking Creek and the other must be closed, the buildings taken down, the black robes leave. We are not Christians. We will not give up our beliefs to accept your beliefs in place of them. This is a thorn in our dignity that has pained us for many years. You have the power to remove it."

The sachems nodded vigorous agreement.

Frontenac looked perfectly solemn. "I understand your objection and it is valid. But the problem spawns another problem. I have not the power to withdraw the settlements. From your lands, from anywhere."

He-big-kettle frowned. "You are the governor general, in command."

"Of the government and the military. Not the religious community. The Jesuits are not a part of our government. They function independently; church and state are separate. The Jesuits do not answer to our gracious king but to the pope in Rome."

He-big-kettle was confused. "The black robes come here with you, you help them build their missions. You protect them and you say they do not answer to you? Obey you?"

"Their obedience is to the Mother Church. Let me ask you this: does their presence disturb you? Do they take from you? They bear no arms. They harm no one. They only seek converts. And they do not force the Catholic religion on your people. They ask for its acceptance. What is the harm in that? The Hurons have accepted them, the Miamis . . ."

"We are not Hurons. We do not want them around."

"They have made some converts among your people. The point is I cannot remove them. I cannot even ask them to leave. If their presence displeases you, I suggest you contact their general. Plead your case to him directly."

He-big-kettle smiled and shook his head.

"They agree on nothing," murmured Two Eagles. "Nothing!"

"They are like the banks of a river," said Splitting Moon. "Impossible to bring together."

"You two sound surprised," said Duncan. "Our people are in nae position to bargain and he kens it. The important thing is to keep talking."

"All our talking does not even get to their ears," Two Eagles scoffed. "They are closed to our words."

So it seemed. As the morning wore on and one sachem

after another raised an issue that favored the tribes,
Frontenac rejected it. But never, noted Two Eagles, directly. Each particular matter was out of his hands; it was
the opinion and the will of the minister of war or the king
himself.

"All firearms and ammunition, all swords must be
turned over to our representatives in the field, by order of
the Marquis de Barbezieux. Not my order."

Outside the skies had become overcast. Thunder spoke
angrily in the east. Lightning flashes carved the darkening
sky and attacked the earth.

He-great-wizard was speaking. "We are not blind, General. We see clearly that things will never be the same for
us. You invade our lands, steal our beaver and when we
protest you make war on us. Kill our people, burn our castles, reduce us to want and misery. Now you expect us to
beg for bones like dogs at a cookfire."

"But what you demand is impossible to give. You are a
proud people, so are we. Like you, we have been a victorious people. We have conquered the Huron, the Petun, the
Neutral. The Miami, the Ottawa and the Abnaki have fled
before our warriors. The fur trade was ours, our life's
blood was trading with the Dutch before you came here
with your war.

"You desire to enter the longhouse of the League of the
Iroquois by the smoke-hole, but that you cannot do. And
if you force us, we will resume the fighting.

"Your war with the English across the Wide Water is
over. You were defeated. This we know from the English.
Your chief with the hat of gold has no more stomach for
the blood of his enemies. The taste of war is like bitter
clover in the mouths of your people. If no treaty is to
come out of this conference, what then? We will both
sides bide our time. *We* will, so that you have no choice
but to do the same.

"The fabric of peace cannot be woven from scraps,
from your demands or ours; it must be whole cloth, woven
of concessions to and from both sides. Not iron clamps
made to control one side or the other . . ."

Thunder shook the Council Lodge, lightning crackled, hurling its eerie light through the opened air vents. A cry went up from the audience. A man was standing, pointing ...

"Oetseire!"

 **39**

Fire!
    Flame chewed at the roof above the speaker. Smoke poured down. A tongue of fire crackled up the far corner of the platform. The crowd panicked, screaming, surging toward the main entrance. Flaming pieces of the roof fell, creating human torches, the terror-stricken people nearest them fighting to get clear, finding no room to maneuver. Within seconds, all four walls were in flames, set by sparks and the blazing debris descending from above. Two Eagles, Splitting Moon and Duncan were forced to one side along the wall. As they began pushing toward the door, one then another roof column loosened and toppled into the crowd. Down came a large section of the roof, burying dozens of people in flames.

The screams were in all sides as fire and debris continued raining down. Many would never make it to the door and escape. Burned to death, suffocated or crushed, some could not fall, so tightly packed was the throng.

Two Eagles and Duncan carried a choking Splitting Moon outside to the shocking sight of fire all around them. The collapsing Council House, the flaming debris flying about, had ignited other longhouses. The fleeing crowd, swollen by people outside and French soldiers, surged toward the castle entrance, horror on every face.

Two Eagles and Splitting Moon, coughing, turned to help women and children get out while Duncan ran off to find his wife. Two Eagles spied him minutes later towering over those around him, roaring his frustration, his beard singed and smoking, eyes wild, battling his way through the crowd, carrying his wife over his head toward the castle entrance.

Around Two Eagles it appeared as if an evil giant had come striding through, setting his torch to one longhouse after another. Up they went crackling, hissing in the rain, billowing smoke, collapsing, reduced to blackened heaps. Now even the palisade had caught fire.

It was impossible for Two Eagles even to guess how many people had been trapped inside the Council House when the last sections of the roof fell in. Or how many had met their deaths outside. Most had escaped to stand shaken and silent a safe distance from the conflagration and watch helplessly as it consumed all that remained of their homes, their possessions and the bones of their dead.

Less than an hour later, with the rain coming down in torrents, Massowaganine, from entrance to rear wall, was completely razed. The survivors were in shock, everyone staring blankly, unable to believe what had befallen them. To Two Eagles the tragedy had happened too fast for recognition of its scope and pain; reality had yet to dislodge disbelief.

He and Splitting Moon found each other, Splitting Moon still coughing, his face reddened from the effort.

"Lightning," he murmured, shaking his head.

Two Eagles sneered: "Oh *nyoh, nyoh* . . ."

 **40**

Night. Massowaganine destroyed, not a single structure left standing. Frontenac sat with Two-horns-lying-down and He-great-wizard by the stream. A bow moon found them, the night sounds sang to them, the water idled by them. They sat as they had sat earlier in He-great-wizard's chamber the night before the peace conference began. Then the atmosphere had been cordial. Until interrupted by Lacroix and his captors. Frontenac had been in a good, expansive mood. Chief and sachem treated him with courtesy and respect; he reciprocated in kind.

No longer. Now tension braided the air like a taut rope of imminent violence. Suspicion nested in all eyes, mistrust guided every syllable. One thing only they agreed on: lightning as the cause was summarily dismissed; witnesses had seen flames spring up in two widely separated places at once—arson was the culprit.

"None of us can deny that negotiations were not going well," murmured the general, avoiding their eyes, pretending to focus his attention on one lace cuff.

Two-horns-lying-down grunted. "To negotiate is to give and to take, is that not so? I saw none of that."

He-great-wizard nodded.

"The fire had to be deliberately set," said Frontenac. "By more than one person. Not any of my people."

"Then by ours?" Two-horns-lying-down asked, his eyes narrowing, a tightness creeping into his tone. "That is what you are saying."

"Why would we burn down our own castle?" He-great-wizard asked.

"A good question. And I have a good answer. Let us be honest, here in this privacy where no one else can hear us. You don't want a treaty. You don't want peace."

Anger came slowly into He-great-wizard's face. "You know what is in our minds? Our hearts? You do not. You profess to want a treaty, so you keep insisting. But every word out of your mouth up on the platform was a threat. Your points were impossible demands on us." He leaned forward, slowing his words. "Intentionally impossible. You knew before you spoke what our answers would be, the only answers we could make. If you wanted peace out of your heart you would meet us in the middle of the bridge over the river that separates us."

"Why should I burn down your castle to terminate negotiations? When I can walk out at any time? Leave, return to Quebec. Resume the fighting, if it suits my purposes."

"You cannot," said Two-horns-lying-down. "Your superiors on the other side of the Wide Water would be angry. You would be removed."

He-great-wizard nodded. "All of this has been pretense. To satisfy your chiefs you must make it appear that you are sincere in negotiating."

"You think I came all this way under false colors? No!" Frontenac shot to his feet. "Enough talk. The fire was not our doing and was not caused by lightning. Someone among you, some faction that secretly desires war, not peace, is responsible."

"You think there are those of us who want war so badly they would sacrifice our people? Kill women and children to wreck the negotiations?" Two-horns-lying-down glared. "That is stupid and beneath you."

"Enough! We are wasting our breath. The conference is over. We leave at dawn."

41

Eight Minks was reluctant to help Margaret enlist men to escort her to the Carrying Place, but, under Margaret's persistence, capitulated. Aware that Red Paint and Fox were convinced that Margaret was indeed "the woman who fell from the sky," and still in awe of her, Eight Minks persuaded them to accompany her. Having grown fond of Thrown Bear, Margaret privately wished he'd volunteer to go along, but he did not and she demurred at asking him, or even broaching the suggestion to Eight Minks.

The sooner Margaret left Onneyuttahage, the sooner the tension caused by her presence would be relieved. She could see hatred on some women's faces, and prejudice. Even, she presumed, envy. She wondered why so many so stubbornly refused to believe Eight Minks' account of how Graywind had met her death. She thought of Two Eagles and pictured his arrival home. And Eight Minks telling him, if she were able to get to him before anyone else. Would he take it stoically, without any display of emotion? Would he rage? Would he shoulder the blame for bringing "an English" here and setting the stage, however unintentionally, for what happened?

He knew how Graywind felt about her, from the moment they first saw each other. When he left, Graywind saw her chance.

Now it almost seemed better if Margaret were to have submitted to her. She said as much.

Eight Minks disagreed. "You know you do not mean that. You could not. You have *eschucne otschtiénta*, a bone in your back. Not just like most people, but a warrior's *orochquine*: spine. Like ironwood. If Graywind so much as struck you, you would have . . ."

"Killed her."

The route to the Carrying Place did not parallel the return route from Onekahoncka. Leaving Onneyuttahage, they would head north before turning eastward, to where Otsquago Creek came down from the north. Two hours farther travel would bring them to a point where the Mohawk River—Eight Minks called it the Te-ugé-ga—descended from the northwest and turned east. The river had to be forded to reach the Carrying Place on the north bank. According to Eight Minks, *coureurs de bois* were to be found there in varying numbers year-round, so there was little chance the party would arrive to find the area deserted. . . .

"Have you ever been there?" Margaret asked.

"*Neh,* but I have heard so much about it I can see it clearly in my head. There are a few shacks in poor condition, holes in the roofs, broken doors or no doors; filthy, smelly." She smiled. "Like the trappers who come there. There are lean-tos and drying racks for beaver pelts. They come from all over to dry their pelfry and sell it to the traders who come down from Quebec and Montreal. It is the traders who carry the pelts north. The *coureurs de bois* sit around all day drinking, repairing and making traps, although mostly they steal them from us. They are like no men you have ever seen. You must be very careful."

"I can protect myself. If anyone tries to take liberties, I'll scratch his eyes out and yell until he sneaks away like a dog with his tail between his legs."

Eight Minks smiled. "You could, yes."

"You say that fur traders come down from Quebec."

"Sometimes. If you are lucky and meet a party of traders, they will take you back with them. They are all French, all snakes in one's blanket, but the traders are not like the *coureurs de bois*. I wish that Red Paint and Fox could stay with you, until you leave there, with the traders, but . . ."

"It would be dangerous for them."

"More dangerous even than for you." Eight Minks shook her head discouragedly. "I do not know about this, we may be making a terrible mistake. Fatal . . ."

Margaret embraced her, then held her away at arm's length to look at her. "You're so caring. Please don't worry. I have to go. I have no choice. And the longer I delay, the more worried poor Pierre will become. He'll be frantic, the poor dear. I can't let my misfortune upset him."

"I know. We have been through all that." Eight Minks sighed. "Is there anything else to pack in your basket?"

"No. I have so little." She chuckled, "When I think of all the beautiful clothes I left behind, my whole trousseau, every stitch I own. My jewelry, my gift for Pierre—I was bringing him a scandalously expensive, absolutely exquisite set of gold buckles. My world, my life, all up in smoke with the *Aventurier*. And the quicker I get to your Carrying Place, the quicker I'll get to him and I can breathe again!"

Eight Minks squeezed her hands fondly. "Let us go find your escort."

42

Two Eagles and Splitting Moon were saying their farewells the next morning. The rubble that had been Massowaganine no longer sent up smoke, but the stench still lingered in the air. Duncan seemed to take the tragedy philosophically. Two Eagles was impressed, his old friend was becoming an Onondaga in his thinking.

"Where will you rebuild Massowaganine?" Splitting Moon asked.

"Two-horns-lying-down and the other chiefs are already talking about a spot nae far from here to the west. There is plenty of good timber aboot and fresh water."

"Do they know yet how many died?" Two Eagles asked.

"Aboot seventy, nae any frogs, of course . . . and . . ." He lowered his eyes.

"He-big-kettle," said Splitting Moon. "We heard. We looked for his body to take back with us to Onneyuttahage but could not find it."

They discussed the sachem's death. He had evidently failed to get out of the Council House before the roof fell in. To the rear of the speakers' platform there was a small exit, just wide enough for one person to pass through at a time. During He-great-wizard's speech, He-big-kettle had been sitting with the Seneca, Cayuga and Mohawk delegation leaders, all of whom managed to get out unscathed, as did the other sachems occupying the first two rows in the audience.

"I should have thought of him when the fire first broke out," said Two Eagles.

"We could not have helped him," said Splitting Moon to Two Eagles. "Do not start blaming yourself. His heart was no longer strong. Everyone knew that."

Two Eagles shrugged. "Perhaps in all the excitement the drumming stopped, he fell, others around him were looking out for themselves . . ."

"I'm nae surprised you dinna find him," said Duncan. "They found charred pieces of many bodies but nae one could tell one corpse from anoother."

They wished him well and his people a swift recovery. As they started away Two Eagles turned and waved one last time. It might be many whole moons till they saw each other again, or it might be never. He had always liked the big red loud one, with his laugh like thunder, liked him better than any other whiteskin he had ever met. He fought like a wild man, drank like a trapper and carried a heart big enough for three men. Now he was one with the guardians of the council-fire of the Iroquois. Now he *was* an Iroquois.

Shoulder to shoulder they loped, following the well-traveled trail eastward to the border separating the Onondaga and Oneida nations. The sun blazed in their eyes directly ahead, burning free of the horizon. It was mid-August, when the moon is at its fullest, when the cooler nights begin.

Splitting Moon spoke as they trotted along. "The fire could have started as I said. When the young of the thunderbird are restless in their nest, the lightning is always sharp and strikes often. They could have been restless . . ."

"*They* did it," Two Eagles scoffed. "Or those Huron dogs they brought with them did it for them. Frontenac became bored with the game. He saw he could not win. The sachems rejected his every point. Neither side would give the width of a bowstring."

"He could have simply given up and left. He had no reason to burn the place down."

"He did!" Two Eagles stopped, glaring in exasperation. "Think! Put yourself in his head. To just give up and leave would make him look bad in the eyes of his chief with the gold hat. *He had to have an excuse.* What better excuse than to accuse the sachems of deliberately destroying the talking?"

"Not the sachems . . ."

"Then some wild heads acting for them."

"Burn down the whole castle?"

"The Council House. The fire got out of hand."

It made no sense to Splitting Moon, but so intense was Two Eagles' hatred of the lace-cuffs, for Frontenac especially, he found it easy to twist the facts to suit his prejudices.

Two Eagles went on. "Now Frontenac can claim the fire as proof of our bad faith."

They resumed running.

"I do not know . . ." mused Splitting Moon.

"I do not care!"

They followed the trail in silence for some time, both

sweating furiously in the broiling sun. In time they stopped to rest by a nearly dried-up pond. Green scum skinned the little water remaining. Splitting Moon knelt, made a hole in the scum, scooped up a handful of water, drank and spit it out. Two Eagles laughed. In the woods beside the trail they found a decaying beech, with water in the hollow places. It tasted bitter, medicinal; the tribes used it to cure scurf, scap, running teeter and other skin diseases, but it was potable and slaked their thirst. They sat refreshed and relaxed with their knees drawn up in the cool darkness of the trees.

"I feel bad about Graywind," said Two Eagles. "It is like some evil spirit always finding some reason to keep us apart."

"Star Daughter and me, too. Seven years is a long time. In all that time we saw each other only this often." He held up his splayed fingers. "Something else the lace-cuffs did for us, made us and our women strangers."

"Before we left this time, I felt I was lying with a stranger. When we get back it will be like we are starting our life together all over again."

Splitting Moon grinned. "That is good, you will avoid all the mistakes you made the first time."

"My biggest mistake was ever leaving."

They resumed running.

"Now this has happened," said Splitting Moon, "do you think the red days will start again?"

"*Neh,* they do not want blood anymore than we. Things will just go back to like they were before. No better, no worse, no good."

"Seven summers cut out of our lives for nothing."

"Nothing. Run faster, our women are waiting."

V

DESPERATE JOURNEY

43

It was with mixed feelings that Margaret left Onneyutta-hage with Red Paint and Fox. *Was* leaving for the Carrying Place the wisest decision? To place herself in the custody of strangers who, according to Eight Minks, were more like animals than men? Two Eagles would be speaking with Frontenac, asking him to take her back to Quebec. Would he agree? Was she being hasty?

And something else, something she should have remembered ages ago: Wouldn't Pierre, the governor-general's chief aide, be with him at the conference? Why hadn't she thought of that before Two Eagles and Splitting Moon left. What better reason for them to take her along? She could have talked them into it.

Such a stupid "oversight"!

All in all she had caused the Oneida, especially him, nothing but trouble since the hollow tree. So this had to be for the best: get away from these people, unburden them of their unwanted guest.

According to Red Paint, it was not far to the Carrying Place, a fraction of the distance from near the Shaw-na-taw-ty to Onekahoncka, and then on to Onneyuttahage. The trail, once they reached it, ran to the north of the main trail along the Wood Kill, north of Tenotoge, the western-most of the three Mohawk castles, located just over the border separating the Oneida and Mohawk Territories. Their first destination would be the Beaver Kill. They would ford it and continue on to where the Mohawk River descended from the northwest.

Carrying in her Mohawk basket her tattered wedding gown, extra moccasins and other belongings, Margaret walked behind Red Paint and in front of Fox. Again, she found herself wishing Thrown Bear had come along. He wanted to, but it turned out he was henpecked and his squaw refused to let him set foot out of the castle.

She should be grateful she'd gotten these two. They'd been unenthusiastic about escorting her, not because of awe of her, nor fear of confronting the *coureurs de bois* but, as Eight Minks privately disclosed as they said their goodbyes, because of Two Eagles. They would have preferred to get his approval of the assignment, but he wasn't around and she had no intention of waiting till he got back, so they had to leave without his knowing. Such was his friends' attitude toward him. He didn't bully people. He simply had the power to make everyone think twice about stepping on his toes. Perhaps, she thought, it was his size, maybe his reputation, like the way he'd dealt with Burnt Eye. Not that he'd conducted himself brilliantly in that unhappy episode, but he certainly knew how to take control of a situation and, unlike many who retreated from it, he eagerly embraced controversy.

He was at times annoyingly egotistical, but self-confidence was one of his main strengths. His blind spots, prejudices, other failings served only to prove he was human. He dealt fairly with others. He could be cold and distant, as he was with her. But he had helped her when he didn't have to, other than to satisfy a streak of kindliness in his makeup. And as time went on and they got to know each other better, mutual respect and even something resembling friendship came into play.

They could have raped her and left her where they found her. But did not. Because he was in command. Also because the others assumed she was "the woman who fell from the sky." She laughed. Red Paint looked at her.

"Nothing."

She thought about him, his small feet, his moccasins

she'd worn on the long walk. And Fox three paces behind her, the hideous French major's scalp dangling from his belt. What would the *coureurs de bois* say when they saw it? Would they recognize it as a white man's?

During the day they rested only twice, at noon when they ate their only meal and late in the afternoon. Shortly before noon, Red Paint found a large turtle trundling toward a nearby pond. She watched in horror as he straddled it and deftly lopped off its head. Taking care to avoid its jaws and claws even after it was dead, he built a fire, quartered the turtle's undershell, removed the entrails and roasted the meat in its upper shell.

She found it delicious. The oil extracted from its fat in the heat of the sun was, according to Fox, very savory.

"If there is no water to be had," said Red Paint, "the blood and juices are good."

She was not *that* thirsty. They also shared *sagamité* and bread, and Red Paint captured two fat grasshoppers, removed their wings and legs and ate the bodies raw.

They walked until the sun behind them slid down the sky and settled into the trees. That night they made camp not far from their destination. Fox sighted a lone black bear making its way through the woods to the north. He called their attention to it and she stood rigid holding her breath as the Oneidas nocked arrows to their bows. But it lumbered from sight before they could take aim.

She was too tired to sleep. She lay studying the stars through the trees, listening to Red Paint and Fox snoring on either side of her. By now they had acquired the status of old acquaintants. Having accepted responsibility for her they would hardly ill-treat her. Not without answering to Two Eagles.

Her only fear at the moment was of tomorrow and the meeting with the *coureurs de bois*. Asking their help. Demanding it, if they hesitated to escort her.

44

Two Eagles and Splitting Moon returned and went straight to their respective homes. So preoccupied was he with thoughts of Graywind, Two Eagles did not notice the staring directed at him, the heads being shaken, the looks of sympathy on the way to his longhouse. He was too busy thinking, resolving never to leave her again for any reason.

He found their chamber empty. Down the passageway he wandered toward Eight Minks' chamber, calling for Graywind.

Eight Minks was playing bowl dice with Swift Doe, with the two boys looking on; six smoothed hickory nuts painted black on one side were the dice, shaken in a flat-bottomed bowl and dumped on the ground. Red beans were used as counters. The player who accumulated all the beans was the winner. Sometimes the game went on for days.

They stopped playing to greet him.

"Where is Graywind?"

"Sit," said Eight Minks, putting aside the bowl and dice. "There is something you must know."

Swift Doe, who had taken to wearing Long Feather's English medal around her waist, got up, taking her boys by the hands. "I will leave you to talk."

"Answer me. Is she outside somewhere?"

"Neh."

"Something is wrong in your face. Is she sick, hurt?"

"She is dead."

He jerked as if an arrow had struck between his shoulderblades.

"She was killed, an accident."

"How? Who did it? Who?" He grabbed her by the shoulders, pulling her to her feet, shaking her. "Who?"

She pulled free and held him away with her outstretched

arms. "If you do not calm down, I will tell you nothing. Sit down, be quiet and listen."

"Where is Margaret?"

"Gone."

"Run away . . . ? She did it!"

"Will you listen?" She quietly told him what had happened, without criticizing Graywind for causing her own death, and taking pains to remind him of her feelings toward Margaret.

"Never mind that, where did you bury her?"

"In the grove that she loved, where she always went to be by herself and speak with her visions. When we buried her everyone came. Come let me show you."

He made no move to get up. He sat shaking his head slowly in his hands as her words sank in. "I never should have gone to Massowaganine." He touched his chest. "In here I had a feeling something bad would happen while I was away, something I could have stopped if I had been here."

"You would not have stopped it. Graywind was a wild woman."

"She would not have behaved so if I were here."

"If . . . if . . ." Her eyes softened. She laid a hand on his shoulder. "I know that this gives you much pain but you must not blame Margaret."

"I blame myself for bringing her here in the first place."

"You could not leave her where Sku-nak-su found her."

"When did she go?"

"Before the sun broke fully from the horizon."

"Alone?"

"With O-kwen-cha and Sku-nak-su."

He exploded. "To Quebec? They are crazy!"

"*Neh, neh, neh,* to Da-yä´-hoo-wä´-quat."

He grew angrier. "She thinks she can get trappers to take her all the way up there? Crazy. Whose idea was that? Not hers . . ."

"My idea."

He flung his hands. "Stupid, stupid!"

"I told her all about them. I warned her it might be dangerous . . . "

"*Might* be?"

"Can we talk without shouting? My ears are ringing. It was her decision. I did not urge her. I tried to discourage her."

"Why even tell her about that place?"

"She had a right to know!" Eight Minks lowered her voice. "She wanted to leave. She did not need your approval. After what happened, she did not feel safe here. Can you blame her? And she is willing to take the risks. She loves her husband very much. I could not have kept her from going if I had tied her down."

"That French filth will take one look at her. . . . And forget O-kwen-cha and Sku-nak-su, they are dead! What were they thinking? They will walk into trappers' knives as thick as corn!"

"Why should the trappers harm them?"

"They will destroy her! You know nothing about them. How could you do such a thing? Send her to certain death. Crazy! Stupid! I must go and catch up with them. I must find Tyagohuens, Do-wa-sku-ta . . ."

"*Neh!*"

"First, I will go to Graywind's grave. I must bring gifts for Agreskoue."

"You do not believe in Agreskoue."

"She did. And I must paint the pickets around her grave."

"*Nyoh,* that was left for you to do. What of the peace conference?"

"There is no more 'peace conference.' " He told her what had happened.

"Have our sachems returned?"

"They are coming. Kah-nah-chi-wah-ne is dead, killed in the fire. The French left. It is all finished, up in smoke. 'Peace.' " He sneered. "What does it always turn out to be but a time for lying and cheating between the months of red days."

He started for the door. "I want to be alone with Graywind. Go, find my friends for me."

45

Margaret gasped. The Carrying Place had been destroyed. The bodies of scalped trappers lay about, horribly disemboweled, heads and limbs cut off, faces stabbed and sliced, rendering their features unrecognizable. The stink of death hung over the area.

Margaret turned her back, holding one hand over her mouth, the other on her stomach. Red Paint came up carrying a scalp, the blood dry on it.

"They were attacked just before we came. If we did not stop to eat we would have walked into it."

"God in heaven," she murmured, "what am I to do now?"

Fox joined them. "All dead."

"We rest, then start back," said Red Paint.

She looked from one to the other. Having come this far, she had no intention of returning. But to go on alone would be insane. They were talking in Oneida, paying no attention to her. Did they still think her to be Ataentsic? She might not persuade them to go on to Quebec as "the whiteskin woman," but would they dare refuse Ataentsic?

"This is good for you," said Red Paint. "You would not have been safe with them."

Fox was scanning the sky. "Rain coming, we had better start back."

"No," she said firmly, "we're going on." She pointed to four canoes lying bottoms up on the river bank. "We'll take the one in the best condition, follow the river to the Hudson, then start north. We can make it. With just the three of us we'll travel fast."

"We do not go to Quebec," said Red Paint.

"We do not know the way," said Fox.

They knew the route all right. She pretended she hadn't

heard. "Let's go look at the canoes. From here they look
to be usable. Come."

Neither moved.

"We will go back to Onneyuttahage," said Red Paint.

"Fiddlesticks and rot! Look at me, you know who I am.
We have come this far, we will go on."

They looked at each other, then back at her. Fox swallowed grimly.

"I will protect you, take care of you. You know that I
have the power. For good or for evil. It's your choice. If
you disobey me, I will turn my power against you."

Her conversation with Eight Minks came swiftly back to
her, all that Eight Minks had told her of the woman who
fell from the sky, the other tales, the names of spirits.

"Don't think Jouskeha will help you. My grandson and
I have talked. He has no part in this. He knows why I must
get to Quebec and he won't side with you."

She narrowed her eyes at one, then the other. "This is
you two and me."

Again they exchanged glances. Red Paint frowned worriedly and cleared his throat. "Two Eagles says . . ."

"What?"

"You are not the woman who fell from the sky."

"Do you believe him or me? Decide!"

They gawked.

She had them! They would not dare refuse her. "I will
tell you this and no more. You go with me and your lives
will be safe and peaceful and without sickness or pain
from now on. You abandon me and not even Jouskeha can
save you from my wrath. Now, which is it to be?"

Red Paint lowered his head. "Let us go look at the canoes."

46

Eight Minks assembled Anger Maker, Splitting Moon,
Bone and Thrown Bear, coming upon the one-handed
one in the midst of a loud domestic dispute. Of the four,

he was the most eager to join the party and gain a respite from the nagging of his squaw, Moon Dancer. Also, he had come to know Margaret better than had the others, and he liked her. Moon Dancer threatened to bar him from the longhouse if he was not back by sundown.

Arming themselves, they set out under a sun so bright it bleached out the blue. Only Splitting Moon had no enthusiasm for the chase.

"I do not understand why you want to do this," he complained, minutes after they set out. "All along you have wanted her to leave and now that she has . . ."

"To leave, *nyoh*, not to be raped and murdered."

"What do you care if she is? She killed Graywind."

"It was an accident, Eight Minks saw it all."

"Whatever happened, your wife is dead. Because of her."

"My friend, if I can accept what happened, why should you worry about it?"

"All she has ever talked about is getting to Quebec. Now you want to bring her back? Against her will."

"There are ways of getting up to Quebec without dealing with the trapper scum," growled Two Eagles. "If Frontenac had not left Massowaganine this would not have happened."

Splitting Moon shook his head. "She still would not have waited till we got back. Not after she murdered Graywind."

"It was not murder!"

"Anybody would think she is your woman, stolen by somebody."

"Will you stop picking, picking? You are like an old squaw!"

Splitting Moon stopped short. "And what do you need with an 'old squaw' to help catch up with them? I am going back."

"Go!"

"Wait . . ." Thrown Bear intervened, pushing Splitting Moon back gently, his tone conciliatory. "Do not leave,

Tyagohuens. He does not want you to. He is not himself. He has just lost his woman."

"Oh, you want to catch her and punish her. That is it!"

"That is not it!" snapped Two Eagles. He looked appealingly at Thrown Bear. "He twists everything into knots!"

Thrown Bear addressed Splitting Moon. "He does not want revenge. He . . . feels responsible for Mar-gar-et."

"Why? She is not his blood, not even one of us. She is one of those who deserted our people with Phips. All English are dogs. You go after her. I have better things to do. I am going back." He started off.

"Tyagohuens," called Thrown Bear.

"Let him go," growled Two Eagles.

All four watched him head back along the trail toward Onneyuttahage. He ran about fifty feet, stopped, stood for a time, his back to them, then turned and came back.

"Do not say anything," Thrown Bear cautioned Two Eagles. "Do not tease him."

Splitting Moon looked sheepish as he came up. "Why are we standing around? They are getting farther and farther away."

Two Eagles clapped him around his shoulders. They went on.

=== 47 ===

Fat black rain clouds were gathering in the east as Red Paint and Fox went to work. All four canoes proved to be damaged; the attackers had driven their tomahawks through the bottoms. One canoe showed only two fist-size holes on either side of the keel strip. Red Paint and Fox cut eight-inch-square sections of bark out of the canoe beside it, squared off the holes and fit the pieces in place.

Then Red Paint sent Fox off into the woods. Red Paint began examining one corpse after another. Finding the biggest trapper lying on his chest, his head and both arms hacked off, he turned him over. Margaret watched in horror and fascination as he knelt, cut away the man's shirt, sliced through his belt and cut away his trousers across his massive belly. Then he set the point of the knife on the exposed flesh about six inches from the navel, pierced the flesh and cut a neat circle.

Margaret turned away when he lifted the circle of dripping flesh and held it up to inspect the underside. The cavity gleamed crimson and almost at once two bluejays winging in and, perching on the edge of the cavity across from each other, began pecking at the exposed flesh.

Red Paint, meanwhile, took his trophy down to the river and washed the blood from it. He brought it back draped over one wrist. He ripped a piece of bark from one of the damaged canoes, and on it placed the stomach flesh, skin side down. Fox returned with a quantity of pine resin in the front of his breechclout. Red Paint went to the nearest hut and came back with a shallow pan. Into it, Fox spilled the resin. They gathered sticks and started a fire, using Fox's corncob punk cylinder. Red Paint scraped the fat from the inside of the stomach skin, added it to the resin in the pan and mixed it into a paste that was heated. The result was a tallow-like substance. They brought it to the canoe and carefully gummed the edges of the two squares.

They waited a time to let the seaming harden, then turned the canoe over and slid it into the water. Not a single leak showed, but Margaret could not take her eyes off the two new squares of bark and the stomach fat mixed with the resin. They selected four paddles, two for spares, and set out, paddling on their knees, Margaret sitting in the middle. In the middle of the river, they caught the current and glided eastward toward the Hudson.

Fox, sitting forward, sniffed the wind coming toward them. "Rain coming this way," he called back.

The clouds, now blended into a single, pillow-shaped mass, appeared twelve or fifteen leagues away but the wind from the east behind it was pushing it their way. Fox estimated that this, combined with the swift easterly progress of the canoe, would bring the cloud overhead in about four hours. He assured Margaret that should the water become dangerously turbulent they would put to shore, find shelter and wait out the storm.

His estimate of four hours was far too generous. In a short time the cloud spread to the four corners of the sky, turning the day as dark as evening.

It did not *start* to rain; one moment the air was dry, the next the rain came down like a cataract, setting the river boiling, inundating them before Red Paint and Fox could paddle toward the safety of the bank.

48

In seconds, the canoe was waist-deep in water. Seized by the suddenly raging river, it tipped over. Margaret sank deep and came up gasping. Water swept over her, and again down she went. Surfacing, she managed this time to stay afloat long enough to refill her lungs.

She could not see the canoe, could not see Red Paint or Fox, but ahead was the bank. She made for it flailing, kicking, struggling to cut through the powerful pull of the current and the turbulent water. If she did not make it to land, she would be swept downstream and drown as had, apparently, her two companions. The storm muddied the water so when it surged into her mouth, up her nostrils, she choked on the grit. The current tossed her like a stick, the rain blinded her. The bank appeared, vanished. On she struggled. A boulder appeared. Would the current smash her against it? She battled toward the bank, losing and regaining sight of it, drawing on her rapidly waning strength, and cleared the boulder by inches, sweeping on, downstream.

She swam until her arms felt like granite, until her heart threatened to burst, until one foot touched bottom! She surged ahead and stood briefly in water up to her waist grasping for breath, only to be knocked over. Regaining her feet, grabbing the limb of a tree extending over the river, she pulled herself to the bank and up it to safety.

Face-down she lay in the driving rain, heart thundering, her throat and lungs on fire. And passed out.

49

She was awakened by a repeated sharp pain in her side. Her eyes opened on four Indians looking down at her. One toed her in the ribs.

"Don't! Please!"

Mist hung all around her. She pulled herself up on all fours, then painfully stood up and smoothed her wet skirt. They were Mohawks. She could tell by their shaven heads, gleaming pates around the distinctive center strip of hair with no feathers, not even the single one Two Eagles wore. And their chests and stomachs were painted with blue stripes. Three carried rabbits slung over their shoulders.

"Go away, leave me alone!"

One was jabbering to the others, looking her way again and again. She began shivering. They made no move to touch her. She would treat them as haughtily as she had the Oneidas when they found her, intimidation her only possible protection. She scanned the river. The rain had stopped, the water was still muddy and turbulent, the sun still hidden. Upstream and down she glanced. No sign of Red Paint or Fox. Why bother to look? A hand gripped her arm.

"You come ..."

She looked from one stone face to the next, and started up the bank.

50

Two Eagles and the others reached the Carrying Place to find the carnage Margaret, Red Paint and Fox had found the day before. They examined the rotting corpses, whisking away black flies. Anger Maker found the shallow pan in which Red Paint had mixed and heated the tallow to repair the canoe. On the bottom of the pan were traces of the hardened substance. They found the corpse from which Red Paint had taken the stomach skin.

"They were here," said Two Eagles. "They repaired one of the canoes and left in it."

"How did she talk Red Paint and Fox into going on with her?" Anger Maker asked.

No one bothered to answer him.

"They left here and were caught by the storm out in the middle of the river," said Splitting Moon. "And drowned."

"Not Fox," protested Anger Maker. "He is too good a swimmer."

"*She* drowned," said Splitting Moon. "She must have."

"You do not know that!" snapped Two Eagles. "They could have made it to shore and taken cover before the storm hit."

Splitting Moon shook his head. "It hit like a whiteskin's cannon. Like the river turned upside down. No thunder, no lightning . . ."

"Enough!" snapped Two Eagles. "You see black in everything. In the sun. Talk is only guessing. Who can say for certain what happened to them? Not you."

"If they survived, we can still catch up with them," said Thrown Bear. "We should go on."

Splitting Moon groaned. Two Eagles ignored it. He threw down the tallow pan and looked toward the three damaged canoes.

Bone read his thinking. "If we repair one like they did and go on by the river, we will not see them."

"He is right," said Anger Maker.

Two Eagles nodded. The trail followed the river within sight of it. They walked through twilight and into night. Around the moon a halo had formed, inside it four stars gleamed, a sure sign that rain would come again four days hence. At Splitting Moon's urging, Two Eagles put a four-day limit on the search.

They sat around at the campfire. Splitting Moon nodded approvingly at Two Eagles' decision.

"Now you are making sense," he said.

The flames fired sparks at the haloed moon. The night sounds, now and then dominated by the distant deep booming whoos of a great gray owl, relaxed them and brought weight to their eyelids. They slept, excepting Two Eagles; he lay staring heavenward, speculating on what had happened to Margaret and his friends. He worried in his heart about her, wondering at the same time why he should. Splitting Moon was right: She was not his blood, not even an Oneida. He had not invited her into his life, she had blundered in, with her carping tongue, her demands. A distraction that, like an annoying insect, would not go away. Home to Onneyuttahage they had brought her and now Graywind was dead, all because of her. And Red Paint and Fox, as well.

Had they never found her, his friends would be alive now and he would be home with Graywind, sleeping beside her, feeling her warmth, his heart stirring for her as he held her. All these problems, this disruption to his life over a whiteskin woman. Why did any of them leave England? English, French, Dutch, all crossing the O-jik-ha-dä-gé-ga, bringing their disputes with each other, their red days to his people.

He tensed; twigs snapped underfoot, the sound coming from behind him, upriver. His hand slid to his knife. He arose without a sound and looked around. The others lay snoring. The fire had lowered to embers. He listened; again he heard the snapping. Then low voices speaking Oneida.

Out of the trees came a bedraggled Red Paint and Fox. Spotting Two Eagles, they ran forward.

"We thought you drowned!" he cried, rousing the others.

"We almost drowned," said Red Paint, dropping to his knees, heaving an exhausted sigh.

Fox nodded. "The storm struck, our canoe was swamped, we turned over."

Two Eagles looked past them. "Where is . . . ?"

Their faces darkened. "Drowned," said Red Paint.

"You saw her?"

"I saw her go under," said Fox. "When I came up and looked around for her . . ."

"Drowned," repeated Red Paint.

Splitting Moon rubbed his eyes, yawned. "I told you. We can talk about it tomorrow. Go back to sleep. It is a long way home."

"Wait," said Two Eagles, "where did your canoe turn over?"

"Just upstream from where the big boulder lives in the river," said Fox. "I think the current carried her into the boulder, broke her back."

"Neh," said Red Paint, "she drowned before that."

"How do you know?" Two Eagles asked. "You did not see."

"I did," said Fox.

Two Eagles knit his brow. "There is no way she could have made it to the bank before the boulder?"

Red Paint shook his head. "The current was too strong."

"But it was raining so hard you could not see clearly."

Red Paint grunted. "She went down, she did not come up. How many times must we tell you? She is dead. By now her body is almost to the Shaw-na-taw-ty, if it did not catch on a branch."

"How close to the bank was she when you lost sight of her?" Two Eagles persisted.

"Not far," Fox said.

"She is dead!" exploded Red Paint.

"Maybe not," murmured Two Eagles.

Splitting Moon snorted in exasperation. "You are not going on looking for her?"

"She may have made it to the bank and climbed up into the trees," said Thrown Bear. "That is why you did not see her again after she went down."

"Neh," said Fox, "she was fighting the water, swallowing it, the current was too strong. If I thought she had a chance I would say so. But . . ."

"Accept it," snapped Splitting Moon, "be satisfied and relieved. She will never trouble any of us again."

Two Eagles considered this. He nodded. *"Nyoh."*

On his way back to Fort Frontenac from Massowaga-nine, Captain Pierre Lacroix had a great deal of time to search his soul and question the direction of his life. And more time upon arriving, as he had been ordered to sit and wait for the return of his commander. He had no idea how long it would be before Frontenac returned but he resolved to put the time to purposeful use.

He resolved to change.

It was out of conscience as well as concern, even fear, for his future, that he decided to confront and dismiss his dissolute way of life. He knew he had been given every opportunity in the service of his country. His road to his captaincy had been so easy as to be all but strewn with flowers. Born with a silver spoon on his tongue, in his entire life he had never known want or suffering, never experienced disappointment in anything of consequence. The world and the military, in particular the governor general, treated him like the only child of the wealthy man that he was. His most offensive trait was his shameless profligacy, closely followed by his conceit, his imperious behavior toward underlings, especially Nez, and his deceit and his toadyism toward his superior. He was also a consummate liar.

All these flaws he accused himself of having. Then congratulated himself for such a "candid self-appraisal."

Upon arriving at Fort Frontenac and being assigned quarters much too comfortable for one guilty of such heinous behavior, behavior that jeopardized the very peace conference itself, he took to spending hours in front of his mirror agreeing with his image's criticisms of himself, even to volunteering additional ones. What pained him more than anything else was his belief that underneath lurked the makings of a good soldier and good man. His many admirable traits had turned Margaret's head. In her company—and only in her company—he was a perfect gentleman: witty, urbane, considerate, altogether a paragon of manhood.

Chevalier sans peur, sans reproche.

Her love for him was boundless. And he loved her. He did.

But he was as deserving of her as is a fox of the helpless chicken it steals. He deceived her, deceived Frontenac, deceived himself, deceived the world.

"No more!" he announced to the mirror. "Louis ... the governor general will arrive to find me a changed man. Completely. A credit to myself, to him, to her, to the army."

When the old man showed up and confronted him, he must acknowledge his transgressions, strip away his conceits and vow to change with heart-wringing sincerity. Frontenac must be made to believe him. All he wanted, all he felt entitled to, was another chance. And deep down he knew he wasn't "entitled" even to that. He would not play on the governor's heartstrings; not now, not ever again; he would not appeal to his innate fondness for him. He would present himself in sackcloth and ashes and, if luck was with him, would convince Frontenac that he deserved the opportunity to prove he had come to his senses at last.

And when he was done baring his soul and wallowing in contrition, he would offer to give up his captaincy in exchange for the rank of private. He frowned and eyed his image.

"Would that be going too far?"

He would have to think about it.

VI
NIGHTMARE

52

The four hunters brought Margaret straight to Oneka-honcka, as she feared, straight to Ho-ka-ah-ta-ken. He was alone, sitting cross-legged, sharpening his knife on a stone. When they walked in, he looked up and leered at her, his eye rounding with lust.

"English!"

He dismissed the hunters and got to his feet. "So, you come back."

"Listen to me ... Chief." She explained how his men had come to find her on the riverbank. "We were on our way to Quebec."

"Quebec."

"The ten men in my escort all drowned. I will need a whole new escort. Ten, twelve men. Well-armed and who know the best route to Quebec. They will be paid well. And you too for helping me."

"Quebec."

He circled her slowly, his eye undressing her. He laid his hand on her breast.

She shrank away from him. "Don't do that!"

He yawned. *"Tekátyahks."*

"I don't know what that means," she said icily. She began to tremble. Her heart thundered.

"I am tired. You are tired." he reached under his breech-clout to unfasten his belt. "We will sleep."

"No! Don't you dare. Do you know who I am?"

"English."

"I am Ataentsic. Yes, the woman who fell from the sky. Returned to earth. The Oneida know, Two Eagles knows, everyone. I demanded to go to Quebec and they gave me warriors to escort me, their best men."

She had his attention. She had to convince him. She drew herself up straight and moved toward him, bringing her face close to his.

"You do not sleep with Ataentsic. No man but my husband sleeps with me. You will do as I say, summon warriors to escort me, Ataentsic. Now! At once!"

"You are not Ataentsic. Ataentsic is no whiteskin, no English. Ataentsic is Maquen."

He reached out and ripped her dress, exposing her breasts. Then, seizing her by the hair, he pulled her close and muttered, his free hand creeping to her breast, "We will sleep."

 **53**

Night. Margaret came to. Pain radiated through her. She cried out softly. Every bone in her body felt broken. She was certain her ribs on her right side were fractured. She hesitated to breathe, and when at last she had to she cried out again.

She was covered with dirt and sweat and felt ugly, contaminated. Her jumbled thoughts went back to the start of the nightmare. Once more he tore off her clothing and threw her down. She fought him, kicking, driving her fists into his chest, his face, his leering eye. Pinning her to the ground, he attacked her like a wild beast. Twice she blacked out, coming to while he was still ravishing her.

It was then, in the midst of her agony, that it dawned on her. In his twisted mind, her suffering was transferred to Two Eagles. The more he hurt her, the more he hurt Two Eagles. She was the instrument of his vengeance.

Did he plan to kill her in the end? Cripple her so she'd be worthless and would have to die? Would he prolong the nightmare only until he felt avenged? She must get away! Get away? She couldn't move.

A voice spoke. She turned her head and recognized Dreamer. In her hand was apiece of chamois. Dipping it in a bowl of water, she wrung it out and patted Margaret's forehead and cheeks.

"Is he . . . ?" she began. Speaking triggered a searing pain in her windpipe. Had he broken the cartilage? She hesitated even to touch her throat.

Between her thighs a fire raged. With a groan, she guided Dreamer's hand holding the chamois down to her thighs. It momentarily cooled the pain. Dreamer drew a bearskin robe over her, raised her head and gave her water. She managed, through knifing pain, to down half a cup.

"You . . . ?" began Dreamer.

She knew some English, asking her how she felt, where it hurt. And knew as well what her husband was capable of. The look of sympathy in her luminous eyes testified to that.

Burnt Eye didn't believe she was Ataentsic. Could Margaret persuade Dreamer, instill in her the same awe that Fox, Red Paint and others of the Oneidas had shown back at the hollow tree? She spoke. "Ataentsic."

Dreamer stared, puzzled.

"Ataentsic! I fell from the sky near the Shaw-na-taw-ty. Ask Jouskeha, my grandson. The sun. I, Ataentsic, am the moon." She pointed at a slit in the bark wall, through it at the unseen moon. "Ataentsic, me!" she tapped her sore chest.

"Ataentsic, Jouskeha *ohserú ni ni teru*," murmured Dreamer.

Margaret repeated it.

Dreamer's large eyes were suddenly wide. She signed. "You . . . come from . . . sky?"

"To wreak my vengeance on Ho-ka-ah-ta-ken!"

"Ahhh . . ."

"My grandson Jouskeha and I, Ataentsic. I come, Ho-ka-ah-ta-ken does this to me, violates me. He must die!" She mimed stabbing her heart.

"Die . . ." repeated Dreamer, her eyes huge.

Margaret gestured animatedly as she continued. "He does not believe I am Ataentsic. He will find out. I will bring the lightning to flay him, the thunder to crush his heart. I will kill him. Kill Ho-ka-ah-ta-ken!"

Dreamer understood.

She had her!

"Kill Ho-ka-ah-ta-ken!" Margaret repeated.

"Neh!" Dreamer shook her head vigorously.

"Nyoh!"

Dreamer patted her forehead with the chamois.

Margaret grabbed her wrist. "Kill! Kill!"

For a moment Dreamer stared horrified. She said nothing. Margaret asked for a salve like the one Eight Minks had given her for her feet. Dreamer brought the same salve, rubbing her entire body with it. It helped. In time she fell asleep.

54

Eight Minks had carefully removed the hair from the green deer hide and soaked it in water for several days. Now she draped it over the graining log, from which the bark had been removed. She began scraping off the particles of flesh, fat and sinew, using an instrument resembling a small hoe, with a heavy handle of moose horn.

Two Eagles, feeling dismal, sat watching her work. Eight Minks strove to immerse herself in her task in the hope of diminishing her anger at Red Paint and Fox.

"Those two fumblers could not even get her as far as the Shaw-na-taw-ty," she groused.

"The river was a boiling kettle. The rain came down like falling stones. They could not control their canoe. They were lucky to save themselves."

"Maybe she reached the bank, climbed up. Maybe Ho-ka-ah-ta-ken's men found her."

"Neh."

"How can you be so sure? You just finished saying

O-kwen-cha and Sku-nak-su admitted they did not see her. If Maquen hunters did find her, you know where she is now."

"I tell you, she drowned. She is dead. Why keep pounding at it?"

"Perhaps because of your face. You say it but you do not believe it." On she scraped. "How easy it is to see when your face and heart disagree."

She was right. All the way back from the Carrying Place doubt had nagged at him like a wasp that will not go away. For a woman, Margaret had remarkable stamina. She could be as strong a swimmer as Fox. If the current didn't smash her against the boulder, she could have made it to shore. And there were many trees with branches overhanging the river on both sides. It was possible she'd pulled herself ashore right behind Onekahoncka. And been found.

He jumped up and began pacing.

"What is it now?" snapped Eight Minks. She turned the hide over on the graining log and began removing the last few bits of hair with a beaming tool fashioned from the cannon bone of a deer, sharpened on both sides.

"Nothing," he growled.

"You think she did save herself?"

"Neh."

"Onewachten!"

"I am not lying. I . . . you!" he burst. "You never should have let her go with them! There is no way they could have made it . . ."

"To Da-yä´-hoo-wä´-quat?"

"To Quebec!"

"Calm down and think. How was I to know they would find what they found at Da-yä´-hoo-wä´-quat? And that she would talk them into going on?" Her scowl softened, tenderness came into her tone. "Do not blame me. Do not blame yourself. You are probably right, O-kwen-cha and Sku-nak-su are right: She did drown." She lowered her head, gazing at him from under her lashes. "Too bad, you were becoming fond of her . . ."

"*Neh,* I only felt responsible for her."

"At first, when you found her, but time stirred your heart for her. And hers for you."

"That is stupid talk."

"Is it? While you were away we talked many times. It was easy to see how she felt about you."

She began washing the scraped deer hide in a large bowl of water, to be wrung out, then stretched on a wooden frame, laced to it by leather thongs. Before framing, the skin would be worked and twisted to render it pliable.

"You are seeing things," he said, with a dismissing wave. "I feel nothing in here for her." He tapped his chest.

"Nothing, *nyoh.*" She laughed, then sobered. "Tell the truth, do you think it possible that she survived? You do. Your face answers. You know what that means."

"You will tell me."

"Anyone can. Ho-ka-ah-ta-ken has her, his prisoner, his slave, his *cannawarori.*"

"He would not dare touch her!"

"Not so loud, he will hear you."

"I would sheathe my knife with his heart!"

"Shhh. My point is, you must somehow find out if she is with him. I do not mean *you*; someone must find out for you. You dare not go near Onekahoncka—you walk in, they would carry your body out."

Now Eight Minks prepared to brain the hide, mixing a batter of the deer's brain, dissolving it in warm water and crushing it with her fingers, working it into a paste while Two Eagles worked at rendering the hide pliable for her.

"I cannot send someone to find out for me," he said. "If he does have her, he would not admit it."

"I disagree. He would be eager to admit it, knowing it will distress you. He would like nothing better than to see you turning on a spit over the fire of his hatred for you. He might even challenge you to come and bargain for her freedom. He would love to see you grovel in front of his people."

"I hate him so my blood stings in me."

"So much that when you see him your brain goes to sleep and your hand goes to your knife. Do not remind me. I have a thought. Perhaps Do-wa-sku-ta, Sa-ga-na-qua-de, or one of your other friends could venture into the Maquen's hunting grounds and intentionally injure himself so that he cannot walk. And be found by hunters and taken to Onekahoncka. He would have to stay until he recovers ..."

"*Neh!* That is stupid, *I* have to do it. Me! No one else."

"Of course, what must I be thinking? Only you can tear down the moon and conquer the sun. Before you start hand me that small knife there beside the drying rack."

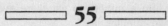

55

Captain Pierre Lacroix awoke to the rattle of drums and sharp, clear sound of fifes. He hurriedly dressed. In the mirror, he noted that he could use a shave, but there was no time. Governor General Frontenac and his entourage came marching spritedly into the fort, giving no outward sign that the peace conference had turned out anything but a rousing success.

Why had they come back so soon? Had the savages seen the futility of their position and knuckled under to the old man's every demand? Frontenac's expression as he marched by said otherwise. Pierre watched the group disperse. Frontenac, accompanied by Generals Desmaines and LeFleur, ambled over. Clicking his heels smartly, Pierre snapped off a salute. Frontenac returned it in his customary half-hearted fashion.

"Welcome back, Excellency."

"In my office in ten minutes," said Frontenac, as if merely speaking to his subordinate was distasteful.

Pierre's mood sagged. "Yes, sir."

He returned to his quarters and shaved. He was preparing to dab on essence of lavender but thought better of it. Why add fop to the old man's list of criticisms of his character? He sighed.

"This is it, Captain, and this may be the last time I address you so ... sir."

It was as unfair as it was depressing, that his whole future should hang on the next half-hour. Of course, he could resign his commission, quit the army. But what then? Go home with his tail between his legs and hear the titters the rest of his days? And what of Margaret? The poor darling must be sitting in Château St-Louis in Quebec at that very moment, wondering when he'll be back, so eagerly anticipating reunion at last with her "hero" husband.

"*Mon Dieu*, what a frightful mess you've made of things, you *idiot!*"

He snatched up his watch. Already eleven minutes gone. It would take him a minute to get there even if he ran. Making him two minutes late!

"Late for your own execution, *idiot!*"

56

Captain Lacroix stood before his commanding officer and quietly and determinedly stripped his soul naked, waving the banner of contrition with all the humility and sincerity he could muster. The governor general listened with eyes downcast, his hands folded across his midriff. Anyone entering the room might have assumed he'd nodded off. The captain had rehearsed his speech no fewer than thirty-one times, and his delivery was flawless. He was almost done when Frontenac held up his hand, stopping him in mid-sentence.

"Enough. Meritorious words. Let us both hope your actions will live up to them."

"They will, they will!"

"We shall see."

Frontenac stretched and yawned. "It's good to be back, even halfway back. You will see to assembling our fleet for the return to Quebec."

Pierre blinked. "Then I am ..."

"Still a captain, still my aide. And beginning now, on probation."

"Yes sir, yes sir, I understand."

Frontenac eyed him jaundicedly. "I sincerely hope you do. Now let's put it behind us."

"Yes, Excellency, oh yes," he beamed.

"I . . . have not forgotten that you saved my life."

"Yes, Excellency. Ahem, may I inquire, how did the negotiations go?"

"They didn't. In all fairness, your conduct—as despicable as it was—in no way affected the discussions. The sachems had their wall of resistance up even before we got there."

He told him about the fire. Pierre registered appropriate shock.

"Oh, it wasn't the sachems' doing, I'm sure," Frontenac went on, "more likely a handful of hotheads dead against any accord. Rash fools killed seventy of their own people. There's just no understanding the savage mentality. I've been here since seventy-two. I can't tell you any more about their thinking processes now than I could the day I stepped off the ship."

"What happens now, sir?"

"Isn't it obvious? They'll sit on their hands, we'll sit on ours."

"Perhaps it's not as bad as it seems."

"Isn't it? I can't imagine how it could be any worse."

"You did your best, sir."

"Please . . . my boots are much too muddy to kiss."

"Yes sir, yes sir."

Frontenac smiled. "That's one thing I can always count on with you, my boy."

"Sir?"

"Your consistency. You never miss an opportunity to make me think that you and I think alike."

"No. Sir!"

"You know what that's called?"

"*Ahem* . . . toadyism, sir."

"Correct. Dismissed."

Pierre stood outside taking huge breaths. He had survived unscathed. He had his precious chance and he would make good on it. It had gone far better than he'd expected; or had a right to.

But for one thing. The way the old man had looked at him, mistrust if he ever saw it on a face. Would their relationship heal in time? Would the old devil ever feel the affection he felt before?

Like the treaty, that remained to be seen.

57

Three days had passed. For Margaret, three days as if suspended from tenterhooks over a fire. The rapist had come nowhere near her. She stayed in the bed provided her by Dreamer and healed. And plotted escape, though realistically she had no idea how she might get away. One thing was certain: She could not expect to be rescued. If either Red Pain or Fox survived, which was doubtful, and got back to Onneyuttahage, they would be sure to tell Two Eagles and Eight Minks that she'd drowned in the storm.

Her pain had reduced to a dull aching. Nothing was fractured. Her windpipe healed overnight. By this, her third day, she felt able to get up, but hesitated to. Perhaps Burnt Eye was staying away because he assumed she was too battered to "perform," to satisfy his lust. She was on her own—except for Dreamer. But how induce Dreamer to help her get away, to defy and deceive her own husband? Using Ataentsic?

She sat up to press her eye to a slit in the wall between the bark sections. Men were working up high on the palisades, replacing rotted timbers to the overhead wall. The wall walk was shaking. A water jug teetered and fell.

Straight down it plunged, smashing the right shoulder of Burnt Eye who was talking to Hole Face and two warriors. He howled in pain, grabbing for his shoulder. Hole Face went to him, a crowd gathered quickly. People were shouting. Burnt Eye was helped toward the longhouse. Margaret lay down smiling through her discomfort.

Outside her door she could hear voices and Burnt Eye, groaning in pain, being helped inside and down the passageway.

She dozed and was awakened by Dreamer with the salve.

"Ho-ka-ah-ta-ken . . ." Dreamer began.

"I broke his shoulder," said Margaret.

Dreamer gasped.

"Next time it will be his neck."

Dreamer left the salve and withdrew, gaping fearfully, her eyes huge.

"Pity," murmured Margaret, stifling the urge to cheer. He would be in no condition to brutalize anybody for at least a week!

At dawn on the fourth day of her captivity, she was awakened by loud arguing. She recognized Burnt Eye's voice, and the indistinct woman's voice had to be that of Dreamer. They were outside in the passageway, moving closer. Again and again she recognized one word: Ataentsic. From the tone of their voices she deduced that Dreamer was appealing to him, and he was rejecting whatever it was she wanted.

Was she warning him that Ataentsic was to blame for his broken shoulder? That this was just the beginning of her threatened reprisal for his brutality toward her? Strange. Dreamer impressed her as being passive, living in all but abject fear of him, for which she could hardly be blamed. Now she was berating him like a stern mother scolding a thoughtless child. The argument ended abruptly when Burnt Eye came stomping up the passageway. She tensed as he stopped by her door. Lifting the flap, he peered in. His right arm was bound to his side with rawhide. His injured shoulder, uncovered, looked badly swollen. Pain contorted his features, his malevolent eye stared. He grunted and dropped the flap. She heard him go out.

Disappointment struck.

Had he been standing a few inches to his right under the

overhead walkway, the jug would have solved her problem.

She did not stir from bed all morning. Dreamer came in around noon bringing a bowl of *onädoonondä*, a delicious dried corn soup. They communicated quite well but it was the surprising change in Dreamer that interested Margaret. She seemed in awe of her. Burnt Eye's accident had evidently convinced her that her patient had been telling the truth, she actually was Ataentsic. Entitled to her respect, even the fear now filling Dreamer's eyes. She seemed reluctant to touch Margaret to apply the salve, keeping her distance and preferring to stand in her presence.

She did not come back again that day. Margaret concentrated on escape plans all afternoon. The list of essentials was growing. She would need a disguise. Her hair had to be concealed. She would need food for the long trek back to Onneyuttahage. Going back was disheartening but continuing on to Quebec alone was out of the question. She would have to escape under cover of darkness; a drenching rainstorm like the one that had gotten her into this mess would be a godsend. She would need a good head start.

Would it be wise to head back to the Oneidas? When Burnt Eye discovered she was gone he'd assume right off that that was where she would go. It might be better to cross the river and make for the Carrying Place or somewhere near it; his pursuing path might be parallel but he wouldn't see her. The problem was getting across the Mohawk; it was so wide and the current, even in good weather, so strong.

More than anything else, she would need luck. Dreamer would help her. It was plain that Dreamer wanted her out of there, out of both their lives as soon as possible. She would willingly risk helping her.

And risk it was. . . .

58

The black bird of night spread its great wings over the castle, stilling the sounds of activity, and the star-millions appeared, brightening as the sky darkened. Moonlight poured through the slit in the wall, laying a band of light across Margaret's legs.

Still plotting escape, she fell asleep. Pain struck the right side of her neck, waking her. She could smell him even before her eyes focused and she recognized him. He stood over her staring down. She cried out. He had hold of her hair, and pulled her head sharply right causing the pain. His right arm was still strapped to his side. With his left hand, he lifted her up by the hair to a sitting position. The bearskin fell away revealing her naked breasts. His eye narrowed. A growl of lust rumbled in his throat.

59

Never good at bridling his temper, Two Eagles now became all but uncontrollable. Most of his friends kept their distance from him, all but Thrown Bear who, as always, gave as good as he was given. Eight Minks, too, yielded no quarter in arguing with her nephew. His problem was obvious to all. She became bored with the way it gripped his conscience and set his tongue rattling.

Aunt and nephew sat in her chamber, Two Eagles steeped in sullenness, as he had been for the past few days. It was now well into the second week since the night Red Paint and Fox had joined him and the others at the Carrying Place. To Two Eagles it seemed like months ago. Eight Minks had given up trying to persuade him that Burnt Eye was not holding Margaret prisoner. She did not even believe that herself.

Eight Minks worked on her deer hide. Having rubbed it thoroughly with the brain paste, she had removed the hide from the drying frame to soak again, and was now wringing it out, twisting it lengthwise around the graining log and twisting it again by means of a stick thrust through a loop. This process repeated over and over removed the cellular filling, producing a clean sheet of pelt fiber. When the skin was soft, pliable and white, it would be sewn up in the form of an irregular bag with crossed sticks thrust in the mouth to keep it open. The bag was then filled with smoke to set the color and finish the hide.

"Are you going to sulk around here until Gâ´-oh blows winter into our houses and our bones?" she asked.

"Leave me alone."

"Leave *me*. This is my chamber. Who asked you to barge in here and make me a party to your misery and frustration? I do not remember inviting you."

"Thank you," he rasped, "for your understanding."

"Understanding for twisted thinking I do not have. Or sympathy."

"I did not ask for your sympathy!"

"Please, do not start shouting again. And for the last time, *do not even think about going near Onekahoncka*."

"You know she is there."

"I know nothing of the sort!"

"He is using her to get back at me. He will end up killing her. Part payment for what he thinks I did to him."

"What you *did*, you mean."

"He wants me to come, wants me to humiliate myself by asking, begging him to release her. Wants *me*, not Saga-na-qua-de, not O-kwen-cha, or someone else to act for me."

"You have done many stupid things in your life out of your famous temper. But stupidest of all would be to go there."

"You do not understand, none of you."

"Control yourself. Shouting does not help anything. Your temper is what got you into this." She softened her tone and laid a hand on his forearm. "I know you have grown fond of her."

"*Neh,* that is foolish talk. You of all people should understand. I brought her here. I am responsible for her. That is all."

"She left of her own free will. If she is in trouble, it is of her own making, not yours."

"It is mine!" He sighed heavily. "Let us stop, it is circle talk. We repeat and repeat ourselves and solve nothing."

"All I am doing is working."

The flap was lifted revealing Splitting Moon. He looked as angry as Two Eagles; they had argued heatedly about the situation earlier. Anger Maker had to separate them. He nodded greeting to Eight Minks and frowned at Two Eagles.

"A Maquen has come for you."

Two Eagles jumped to his feet. "Where?"

"Outside by the entrance gate."

People on all sides stopped their work and their conversations to stare at the messenger. Splitting Moon stood with Two Eagles as the Mohawk and he exchanged greetings. The man glistened with sweat; dust covered his calves. He appeared exhausted, as if he'd run all the way from Onekahoncka. He proffered a small deerskin pouch. Two Eagles noticed a second pouch in his breech-clout belt.

"What is it?" Splitting Moon asked, while others crowded around. Eight Minks stood in the doorway behind Two Eagles. he thrust his hand into the pouch and brought out a medal that looked identical to Long Feather's, even to the nick on the top.

"Your brother's medal," murmured Splitting Moon.

Two Eagles grunted. "*Neh*, Swift Doe wears his around her waist."

Thrown Bear nodded. "One-eye wants you to think this one is his, wants you to think his cousin did not kill your brother. He is a clever one."

"He is *oeuda*."

"Shit, that too."

"Clever shit," muttered Splitting Moon.

Two Eagles frowned. The messenger offered the second

pouch. Two Eagles ignored his grin and stuck his hand inside. And brought out a handful of blond hairs.

 **60**

The second nightmare was more hideous than the first. Ignoring the pain of his broken shoulder, Burnt Eye raped her mercilessly, leaving her battered and unconscious shortly before dawn. The sun was breaking the shoulder of the distant Taconic Mountains when Dreamer came into Margaret's chamber with water and her chamois and awoke her.

Only vaguely aware of Dreamer sitting beside her bed applying the salve, Margaret's mind wandered in and out of delirium. Just breathing sent pain piercing up her spine. Dreamer stanched the bleeding between her thighs with cobwebs and fed her a tea that combined the bulb and leaves of adder's-tongue with horsetail grass to hasten healing.

All that day and the following night she lay in unremitting agony, not caring whether she lived or died. He did not come near her. It wasn't until midmorning the next day—while Dreamer was patiently trying to feed her dried-corn soup—that she heard him. He thundered into the longhouse in the company of Hole Face and some of his warriors carrying on angrily. Dreamer went out and came back moments later. She stood in the doorway holding the flap up. Combining words and gestures, she told Margaret what had happened. A copperhead had bitten Burnt Eye in the lower leg. He was now in bed, his friends attending him, rubbing the puncture with bruised blacksnake root and dosing him with a small quantity of juice extracted from the root.

Margaret managed a feeble smile. So Ataentsic had struck again! By simply being told of his accident, she could feel her strength returning, the incessant throbbing pain easing; as long as she lay perfectly still. When she could move, she would leave. With or without Dreamer's help, she would get away. Somehow.

The next assault she would not survive.

61

Dreamer returned that evening to tell Margaret that the copperhead bite Burnt Eye had suffered was not serious, that he was very strong and would recover in a few days.

"I sent the snake," Margaret said coldly. "I caused both." She indicated her shoulder and lower right leg. "*Neh*, he will not recover, his heart will stop, he'll die."

Dreamer shrank from her, swallowing, her beautiful eyes rounding with fear. "*Neh, neh . . .*"

"*Nyoh.* I can't even move. He has to pay, he must die."

Dreamer panicked. She offered to give Margaret clothing, food and a knife and help her get away. Margaret pretended she had no desire to leave. "Not while he still lives."

To her surprise, Dreamer had already worked out a plan of escape for her. Wearing a shawl over her head, Dreamer would leave the castle by the rear entrance carrying a deerskin sling full of trash of one sort or another. Three times she would leave and come back with her sling empty. Then give Margaret her shawl and the sling. *She* would leave the same way, except that the sling would be filled with food, extra moccasins and other essentials for the long journey back to Onneyuttahage.

By the time Burnt Eye awoke she would be precious hours away. He would guess she'd be headed for Onneyuttahage but reject the too obvious route following the river. And with his injured leg, he'd be slow coming after. Dreamer emphasized repeatedly that she must follow the Mohawk west. In time she would reach a spot across from the Carrying Place. From there on, she could make her way south to the main trail that ran from Onekahoncka

past the other two Mohawk castles all the way to
Onneyuttahage.

When Margaret finally gave in and agreed to leave,
Dreamer's relief was remarkable; she all but embraced her
in gratitude. There was, of course, one immediate problem.
Margaret was in no condition to get out of bed and walk
to the chamber entrance, much less journey on foot for the
better part of a week. She resolved to give herself two
more days to recover her strength and let her spine heal so
that the pain became at least bearable.

Hosting pain of his own, Burnt Eye did not come near
her the next two nights. According to Dreamer, he did not
leave their chamber. Margaret stayed an additional night,
which proved wise. By the time darkness settled over
Onekahoncka, she felt nearly as restored physically as she
was emotionally. Dreamer dressed for her role in the plan,
donning her shawl and shouldering the sling carrying
trash. She left by the rear gate, returned with her sling
empty, repeated the performance a second and third time—
Margaret left in her place the fourth time. Easing the gate
closed behind her, she made her way swiftly through the
trees down to the river's edge and headed upstream. She
would travel all night the first night, she was up to it after
so long flat on her back. If not, she'd force herself to go
on. Come daylight, she'd find a hiding place, sleep for as
long as her body demanded, eat some of her cold rations
and be on her way again.

As Dreamer had warned, between her and her destination lay dangers of a dozen different kinds: animals, hunters, possible *coureurs de bois*, uncertain weather, even her
own questionable, untested stamina.

She would make it. But what then? She was no more
than returning to her starting point, where so many people
resented her. Clearly, the Oneidas felt no obligation to help
her get to Quebec. Eight Minks and Swift Doe were on her
side, as was Thrown Bear, for that matter. But none of
them could escort her. Two Eagles could, if he were so inclined.

But he wasn't. That he'd already made abundantly clear.

62

Hurrying along, already beginning to feel weary, stumbling, pushing obstructing branches aside, lashing her face with one then another, her mind flew back to that terrible night of her flight from the *Aventurier*. The same panic as then did not seize her, but fear of her surroundings was just as intense, the blackness, the unseen eyes watching her pass, the wilderness in its vastness, its primeval menace.

Time and again she glanced behind her expecting to see pursuers. But no sight, no sound of anyone. Back in the blackness Ho-ta-ah-ta-ken slept and the distance from him, his sadism, his viciousness slowly lengthened. Thinking of Burnt Eye prodded her to move faster for perhaps twenty paces before she realized she was only squandering the little stamina she had left. Again she thought back to her escape from the ship, running until she couldn't manage another step, finding the hollow tree, plumping down inside it, telling herself it was protection. Niche in her lap. In the darkness, so absorbed in the need to escape, failing to notice that he had died, poor creature.

Two Eagles and the others finding her and all that had happened since, pictures flipping before her mind's eye. None of what she'd been through moved her any closer to Quebec and Pierre. Would she *ever* reach there? Was it written on some slate in heaven that they'd never see each other again? Someone, something would take her life before she got any nearer to him than these woods, this river? Fear forced a shiver. And like a cloak tightening, the night closed on her as once more she picked up the pace.

63

Burnt Eye lay awake beside Dreamer. Minutes before he had finished enjoying her. Although he did not cause

Dreamer to scream in pain as he did Margaret, he took a woman only to please himself, on his terms only.

Dreamer had taken very good care of him during his recovery from his broken shoulder and from the snakebite. The poison was out of his system, his vigor had returned, and there was no pain in his shoulder—unless he accidentally bumped it, as he had on their chamber door, setting him bellowing. Dreamer was a good woman. He did not tell her so, only because she *was* a woman and would surely take advantage of any compliment. Any sentiment shown her was a sign of weakness, so he did not compliment her on anything, unlike Joshu´we-agoochsa and some of his other friends who even went so far as to display their admiration for their women in public.

He pushed her shoulder, waking her.

She sat up rubbing her eyes. "What is it, my husband? Is something wrong? Can I get you anything?"

"Shhh, stop rattling your tongue. I just wanted to say . . . ah . . ."

"Nyoh?"

"You are a good woman."

"Thank you."

"Go back to sleep."

They both fell asleep, but he awoke an hour later when he turned on his side, onto his ailing shoulder. She was deep in sleep and from her expression enjoying a pleasant dream. She invariably looked so when sleeping. He was envious of her gift and the name it inspired. He sat up watching her sleep and thought about Margaret in her chamber down at the front of the longhouse. Two-thirds of the twenty-four chambers were vacant. He wanted it that way, liked the privacy. It never occurred to him that most of their relatives had no desire to share their longhouse.

He got up and went out. It had been too many days since he last enjoyed his whiteskin slave. His lust suddenly became overwhelming. He hurried to her chamber, jerked aside the door flap. Moonlight slipping through the slit between the bark panels revealed her empty bed.

He growled, spun about, raced back to his chamber and

shook Dreamer awake. "Sit up. Clear your head of your foolish dream. Answer me, where is she?"

"Who?"

He slapped her so hard she fell. She crawled clear and sat looking up at him fearfully.

"Where ... is ... she?"

"Gone."

"Where?"

"She left hours ago."

He bent over, his eyes burning into hers. "You helped her escape?"

"Listen to me, my husband, please. She was the woman who fell from the sky."

"Was she?"

"*Nyoh, nyoh.* It was she who caused your shoulder to break and the copperhead to bite you. She wanted to stop your heart, kill you, she told me! She would have! She was very angry for the way you treated her. I was terribly afraid for you. So I helped her get away. Now there is no more danger for you. I did it to save you from her!"

"Save me from her ..." He straightened. He spoke quietly. "Get up, go get my knife."

She shrank back, frightened. *"Neh ..."*

He smiled. "Do not look so. I am not going to hurt you. I merely want to cut this loose string from my legging. Get it."

She brought the knife to him.

"I saved you," she said timidly.

"*Nyoh.* And I am grateful."

She offered the knife hilt first, smiling tentatively. He accepted it, turned it, and swept it before him, slitting her throat.

"Too bad you cannot save yourself. That was very stupid of you, the worst mistake you have ever made. But now you have paid for it, so I can forgive you. I do, I forgive you."

64

Margaret made her way along the south bank of the Mohawk River, passing the boulder that she had nearly crashed against. Moonlight bathed the slowly moving water but broke through the leafy canopy overhead only rarely. The path appeared and vanished, evidence that it was little used. It was studded with roots and jagged stones and again and again she tripped and nearly fell.

Night sounds were all around her. It was darker than the night she stood at the stern of the *Aventurier* before the savages came pouring out of the woods. Here alone, struggling to put distance between her and her tormentor, with so far yet to go to safety, the dangers and uncertainties ahead, the test of endurance confronting her, all were so daunting she was fleetingly tempted to give up then and there.

But Burnt Eye, bad leg and all, would come after her. That spurred her on. Would he pursue her even into Oneida territory that, according to Red Paint, began the other side of the Beaver Kill, well beyond the Carrying Place?

What about the other Mohawk castles? Could she stop off at one to rest, perhaps engage men to escort her to Onneyuttahage? Would they protect her from him? Would a Mohawk protect a whiteskin woman against another Mohawk?

Her thoughts tumbled about in her head, winging her back to the canoe and the storm striking, to her wedding gown lost when the canoe turned over. She had brought it all this way. Was losing it in such a manner symbolic? Had fate deliberately caused it?

Was losing it a sign, a warning not to bother to travel to Quebec, for she and Pierre would never be married?

Poor Pierre. He had to be worried to distraction over her. Had news of the massacre reached Quebec by now? If he'd heard about it, he'd have to assume she'd been killed along with the others. It would shatter him, poor darling . . .

Damn that storm! Had it missed them, they'd be half-way to Quebec by now. How could Dreamer or anyone believe she actually was Ataentsic? But they did, and it had gotten her away from Onekahoncka. Hopefully, Dreamer was all right. Burnt Eye would know she helped in the escape, Dreamer wouldn't try to deceive him. But she'd done it only for him, out of fear that Ataentsic would made good on her threat to stop his heart.

On she trudged, ignoring the disabling aches in her legs and the cuts on her face from lashing branches. Along with a knife and food, Dreamer had given her a quantity of some kind of berries, instructing her to crush them and darken her complexion.

She had no idea how far she'd come from the boulder in the river. She was stumbling more often now, approaching total exhaustion. The birds awoke, filling the woodland with song. Dawn erased the moon, and the sun rose behind her as white as a lingah pearl. She looked for a hiding place but it was some time before she found one: a small cave. Actually, it was only a space between two large outcroppings with a massive hop hornbeam growing atop them, holding soil with its roots to form a roof. The "cave" was only eight or ten feet deep. There was no animal odor, no evidence that anything or anyone had stayed there recently. She examined her rations. *Onye' sta* and *djistaga'on*: chestnuts and hickory nuts; *ganeo-^{n}-te'do^n*, "early bread," unhulled corn mixed with a little water in a mortar and beaten into a paste, formed into loaves and boiled. There were *ganya'oya* and *oya'gane gowa*, apples and wild cherries, *ogon'sä'gan'on'da*, succotash, and salted dried venison.

She knelt by the river to slake her overpowering thirst and studied her reflection: She must be careful about her hair, so blond it would be a beacon to any hunters or trappers roaming about. Every strand must be concealed under the shawl when she resumed walking.

She ate a little of everything Dreamer had given her,

keeping in mind the Iroquois' sensible habit of eating but one full meal a day.

She found two large stones and managed to roll both up close to the mouth of her "cave." They blocked the entrance fairly well. She massaged her feet with a small quantity of the same salve Dreamer had applied to her bruises. She fell asleep in seconds. The last sound she heard was the soft burbling of the river by the near bank.

 **65**

A soft sound like a child's toy rattle woke her. Into focus came eyes the yellow of marigolds.

The snake stood rigid, its head elevated perhaps eight inches, its fat pink, gray and brown body coiling back to its tail beating the ground. Its forked tongue flicked, testing the air, "smelling" her. It hissed. Her heart froze, she dared not breathe. Again it hissed and held its eyes on hers.

Now, it slithered slowly forward, bringing its flat coppery head to within inches of her face. Little more than a yard separated her from the rear wall. Was a stone or stick within reach? She was afraid to turn her head. The knife was in her shoulder sack with her food, back by the wall. The snake continued to stare, slapping its tail against the ground. Lowering its head slightly, it hissed again. Its jaws slowly parted, its fangs slid from their sheaths. Then, amazingly, it lowered its head to the ground, turned and slithered away.

She fainted.

 **66**

Margaret endured a dismal fourth night, utterly discouraged, her nerves taut as bowstrings, too tired to sleep. Each of the first three nights had been harder than the one preceding it. Since the copperhead, every root she stepped on, every stick, every loose vine hanging in front of her was a snake. Unable to find a safe hiding place, she tried a sprawling tree limb, spreading it with pine boughs. It proved impossible to sleep there. The sun was well up into the sky when she finally dozed off on a large, flat boulder.

The little sleep she managed only partially restored her energy. She no longer noticed the persistent aching in her bones and joints. She continued rationing her food carefully, knowing that even when she deserted the riverbank for the main trail it would still be the better part of three days before she came within sight of the castle. She hurried by the rear palisades of one of the Mohawk castles, the third and final one before Mohawk Territory changed to Oneida Territory.

The sun was burning away the horizon directly ahead. Once on the main trail, she need only follow it in the same direction. She ventured down to the water's edge, kneeling and moistening her face and neck. She was filthy, her hair a mass of tangles. Never in her life had she gone more than a day without bathing.

She removed her clothing, scrubbed it with sand and laid it on the rocks to dry while she washed her hair and body, trying to scrub away the last two weeks. It took nearly an hour out of her precious time but was worth it. She dressed in her still damp top and skirt and regained the trail. She had not gone more than two hundred yards before she stopped, her heart rising.

Directly across the river was the Carrying Place. Just as they'd left it, the rotting corpses still lying about, the canoes upside down, side by side, bows nudging the water. But only two? There had been four. She, Red Paint and Fox had taken one. Since then, someone had evidently taken a second one.

Voices. She retreated into the trees, squinting through the leaves. Men were approaching from the north. She could hear brush crackling underfoot, the voices louder now, speaking French. Three *coureurs de bois* came into view: bearded, filthy, carrying muskets and beaver traps with pelts slung over their shoulders. She watched them wander among the corpses, joking, it appeared. The stink didn't seem to bother them. What was there to laugh about? She backed father into the trees. She glanced about for her bearings. To the south, less than thirty minutes away, lay the main trail.

She started for it, creeping softly through the woods. About thirty yards from the river she broke into a run. There was no trail, not even a path. She pushed through the brush and tangling vines, then stopped short.

Directly in front of her, not twenty feet away in a small clearing, several wolves were feasting on the carcass of a bull moose, ripping the flesh greedily, their jaws dripping blood. As she watched, two more wolves came loping into the clearing to join the feast.

She slipped behind a big maple out of their sight; would the breeze from the river carry her scent to them? She retreated the way she had come to within sight of the river. One of the trappers was examining the canoes. She turned west and walked in a wide circle around the clearing and the bloody wolf banquet.

Twilight was ambering the woods, bringing the peacefulness of the day's end by the time she sighted the main trail. The longer part of her journey still lay ahead but it would be easier, she'd cover more than twice the distance she'd managed each night up to now. And no more whipping branches and rustling, menacing snakes.

The woodland now behind her, her spirits lifted, and she suddenly felt strong enough to walk all night up to noon tomorrow. Not that the main trail would be without danger; there was still the risk of meeting savages. She reached the trail and stood a moment looking down it back toward Onekahoncka, Burnt Eye's castle. Thought of him revived the aching.

She started west up the trail, proud of her endurance. Who among her friends back home would have survived what she'd survived and come all this way under their own power? She would make it to safety, to Quebec, with or without Two Eagles' help.

No, she'd talk him into helping her, as she'd done with his friends.

Heart high, confidence restored and brimming, she did not look back. Had she, she would have seen the wolves appearing one by one at the edge of the woods; stomachs full, eyes glinting, moving in single file through the trees, following her.

67

She came onto the trail well past the mound where Two Eagles had found the mutilated bodies of Long Feather and his friends, and went on until the afterglow surrendered to darkness pinned to the vault of heaven by the stars.

Not until then did she realize she was being followed. The eyes of her pursuers trapped moonlight, gleaming like diamonds. She nearly panicked at the sight of them. Several started out of the trees toward her slowly as a pack behind their leader, heads down, tongues lolling.

Trembling, she fumbled the knife out of her shoulder sack, dropped the sack, held the blade angled upward, and stood perfectly still. Could they smell her fear? She held her breath. They had approached to within twenty feet of her and split up, encircling her.

They couldn't be hungry. Did they kill humans for the pleasure of it? Were human beings natural prey to them? She knew little about them, which only magnified her fear.

They circled her slowly, not growling, not baring their fangs, not slavering. They seemed intent on inspecting her, as they would any prospective meal. Would that she had a torch, that would send them scooting!

Should she go on? Show them they didn't scare her? Walk boldly through the circle? They had stopped moving. A few sat on their haunches, one lay prone. The leader approached her slowly, to within three feet, then dropped on its haunches, bared its teeth, growled. Not daring to breathe, she pushed the knife up to its muzzle, almost

touching it. Did it recognize it as a threat? She strove to
steady her hand.

It stopped growling, settling on its belly, lowering its
head, between its paws. She filled her lungs and resumed
walking. She walked between two wolves and out of the
circle. And continued on. Still holding the knife upright,
she gave in to the trembling that seized her shoulders and
upper body. She counted a hundred paces before looking
back.

Their curiosity apparently satisfied, they had vanished.

68

Two Eagles plunged his paddle into the placid water,
driving the canoe forward toward the right bank. Driving hard, he pushed the bow up onto the mud and got out.
He pulled the canoe three-quarters of the way up the bank
and turned it over to dry. The paddle he hid in the bushes
nearby. He could see the rear of Onekahoncka rising into
the cloud-strewn sky.

Providing she was still alive, Margaret would be in
Burnt Eye's longhouse, of that he was certain. He would
enter by the gate and likely be recognized and intercepted,
be stripped of his weapons and taken to Burnt Eye. At
worst, the one-eyed one's knife would find his heart before
he could get a word out.

Hopefully, they would at least get to talk. Two Eagles
would try to persuade him that Margaret was only the unfortunate victim of their feud. "How can a chief of Ho-ka-
ah-ta-ken's stature lower himself to punish a stranger, an
innocent to relieve his antagonism toward his enemy?"

They could have it out then and there.

The gate was open. People recognized him. A familiar
voice called to him. It was Joshu'we-agoochsa: Hole Face.

"Tékni-ska-je-a-nah . . ."

"Joshu'we-agoochsa."

The sachem looked astonished. His jaw hung exposing
his uneven teeth. "What are you doing here?"

He held out his hands. Two Eagles gave him his toma-hawk and knife.

"I asked you . . ." began Hole Face.

"I have come for the white woman, the English."

"Ho-ka-ah-ta-ken's *cannawarori*."

"His captive."

"She had gone."

"What?"

"Dreamer helped her escape, for which Ho-ka-ah-ta-ken gave her a red bib."

"He killed his woman?"

Hole Face grinned, slitting his throat with his finger. Then his pitted face darkened. "Not wise for a wise man. She sleeps now with dirt in her mouth and he sleeps alone."

"I do not believe this. Margaret left by herself?"

"Who would go with her?"

"Without help, she knows she cannot get to Quebec," said Two Eagles, thinking aloud. "She must be heading for Onneyuttahage."

"What difference where?" He looked puzzled. "Is she important to you, is she your *cannawarori*?"

"Did he hurt her?"

"How should I know? All I do know is that he is sorry now he gave his knife to Dreamer's throat. The clan mothers are outraged. No Maquen kills his woman over another woman, over anything. We respect our women as you respect yours. It was stupid of him. His fire burns much too hot for his own good."

"Where is he?"

"He stays in his chamber."

"A prisoner?"

"Not a prisoner. He stays there until the mothers decide his punishment. With our people no one gives the knife to another without paying some price."

"What will they do to him?"

Hole Face smiled icily. "Is that your concern?"

While they talked others crowded around them. The warriors had their hands on their knife hilts.

"Now you know all that I know about it," said Hole
Face to Two Eagles. "You had better leave while you can."
He handed back his weapons and spoke to the crowd. "He
is leaving. Make way for him to the gate."

The crowd split in two, giving him a narrow path to the
gate. Eyes drilled his bones as he walked the gauntlet.
Outside, the gate closed behind him, he drew a cavernous
breath of relief and started on Margaret's trail.

69

He paddled against the current until his arms felt
leaden, and his muscles became taut to snapping and
viciously cramped. Putting ashore, he abandoned the canoe
and continued on foot. He would keep going day and night
until he caught up with her. Or her corpse. How far had
she gotten? Was she now on the main trail?

Ho-ka-ah-ta-ken would have caught up with her by now
if the clan mothers hadn't detained him. Which, as far as
he could see, was the first luck to come Margaret's way.
But she had no way of knowing of their actions regarding
his crime or even of the crime itself.

If she made it over the border into Oneida territory she
might make it to Onneyuttahage. But only if luck walked
with her.

Why did Dreamer help her? Risk her life for her.
Strange creatures, women. He did not understand any of
them, not even Graywind.

Graywind. His conscience whispered, causing him to
wince. What must her friends think of him, his own
friends, risking his life to save the woman who had killed
his woman? And an English whiteskin, at that. Who cares.
This was no one's concern but his own. No one else had
the right to make it their concern. Only why was her sur-
vival so important to him? Something beyond the sense of
responsibility he carried. In the beginning he couldn't
stand her. Her mouth and her ways. She did not act like a
woman. She refused to defer to his or any of the others'

judgment or wisdom. And the more Do-wa-sku-ta and the others treated her as if she really were Ataentsic, the more vexed he became. But time had changed his thinking, she had changed it. Now he marveled at her; *nyoh*, she did have *eshucne otschtiénta*. No Oneida woman he knew carried a stronger bone in her back.

Although why should he feel even more warmly toward her now that she was missing?

And why, when she filled his mind, did this strange, uncomfortable feeling arise in his heart?

Did she get the same feeling?

"This is not right. When a man starts worrying about what a woman thinks of him it is wrong, wrong!"

70

During her second night on the main trail to Onne-yuttahage, Margaret heard the chilling sound of wolves howling and for a moment thought that the pack was returning: now hungry, seeking a fresh kill. She stopped to listen. The howling became louder, braided together in one long, piercing ululation. Then it broke off sharply. She resumed walking.

The wind rose. The sun had vanished from an indigo sky; the sky was as black overhead as were the woods on either side. Fat raindrops fell, splashing on her head and shoulders and pocking the dusty ground.

She doubled her pace, almost running. Realizing it, she slowed, listening intently for the pack.

The downpour increased, a cold, steady rain that gradually skinned the trail with mud that caked her moccasins and spattered her bare legs. The temperature seemed to have dropped twenty degrees; she shivered. What she wouldn't give for a comfortable haystack to dive into, burrow into its warmth and concealment and sleep like a child for the next ten hours! The Indians did not collect hay and stack it; corn provided no hay. She closed her eyes and could see the green hills rolling all the way to Birmingham, the herds of cattle, the pastures and haystacks dotting the landscape. Hundreds of them, thousands. From overhead it must look like they were buttoning the grass to the earth.

The rain dimmed her sight of the way ahead, and she was seized by a gnawing homesickness. And she'd never see Pierre again; fate heartlessly forbade their reunion.

"What is not meant to be can never come to pass."

Would she ever see Quebec?

"Not in this life, milady."

The rain fell harder. She deserted the trail for the trees. She hoped to find enough dry leaves to wriggle beneath and at least keep her warm.

Sore and depressed, she was also harrowingly lonely. She made her bed and lay down, stuffing dry leaves under and atop her. Her shoulder sack served as her pillow as usual. It was getting lighter, not much food left. She got out her knife to hold under her leaf blanket while she slept. If anything or anyone woke her, at least she'd have a fighting chance.

Dawn would not come for at least two or three hours, she guessed. She could not fall asleep with the rain pelting her cheeks. She lay on her side, staring into the darkness.

She gasped; a man was standing at the edge of the woods, his outline barely visible. He stood perfectly still less than thirty feet from her. He started forward, heading straight for her. He had seen her! Gripping her knife, she rolled over out of his path, and crawled behind a tree.

Standing, she chanced another look. He continued toward the spot she had just vacated. He looked around, no more than six feet from her, with only the tree—too thin to conceal her—between them. His silhouette showed the handle of his tomahawk on one hip, his knife on the other. Any moment now he would draw one of them. Her scalp tingled. She could feel the warm blood running down her face, the excruciating pain, hear her shriek . . .

Raising the knife, she lunged at him.

71

Two Eagles roared in pain, staggering backwards. The point of Margaret's knife had sliced his upper arm. He grabbed her wrist and shook the knife loose. Their faces were inches apart. She gasped. "You . . . !"

He grunted, seething. His hand went to the wound on his upper arm. Blood seeped between his fingers. She tried to rip a strip from the hem of her skirt to bandage his wound but she could not tear the deerskin.

"Never mind," he growled.

He had turned and walked back toward the trail. She stepped over her knife on the ground and followed him. "That has to be bandaged."

He stood at the edge of the woods. The rain was letting up. "You are quick with your knife."

"Why didn't you call out, identify yourself?"

"I did not think you would try to kill me."

"I thought you would kill *me*!"

"Stop shouting!"

She retrieved her knife and cut a strip from her shawl but when she tried to bind his wound, Two Eagles pushed her away.

"You'd rather bleed to death?"

"It is nothing. I am lucky you do not know how to use a knife."

"It doesn't take any particular talent. I could have stabbed you in the heart."

He shook his head disdainfully. "*Neh*, you do not have the belly for killing."

A thought struck her. "My God, you weren't on your way to Onekahoncka!"

"I came from there."

"You could have been killed!"

"Not by Burnt Eye, I could not even get to see him. He killed Dreamer."

"No!"

"For helping you get away."

Shame overwhelmed her. "What have I done? I might as well have held the knife myself . . ."

She explained how she had used Ataentsic to scare Dreamer into helping, after failing to convince Burnt Eye. "But *she* believed me, I made her. Oh God, oh God, this is horrible!"

"Why blame yourself? She knew the risk if she helped you."

"The sad, sick part of it is she did it for him." She told him how she had threatened to stop Burnt Eye's heart for his brutality toward her. "What am I thinking? How could things have turned out otherwise? Poor, good-hearted, naive creature. My God . . . What will his people do to him? Kill him?"

"*Neh*. He is too clever to let that happen. Any other man murdering his woman would be burned to death, or at least exiled. But he will probably claim she was a witch."

"Fiddlesticks and rot, who would believe that?"

"Among our people witchcraft is punishable by death."

"What rubbish. Damn his black soul. How can he get away with it?"

"He is their chief. They will accept his word for it. There is anger toward him, but that will pass."

She was staring so at him that he averted his eyes. "How did you know I didn't drown in the storm?"

"Red Paint and Fox were sure that you did."

"Because I'm a woman and not strong enough to make it. It's a relief to know *they* didn't drown. They're . . . good souls."

"They were taking you to Quebec when the storm struck. How did you talk them into doing that? Like you did Dreamer? Putting the Ataentsic fear into their hearts?"

"They've believed all along I'm Ataentsic."

He grunted.

"One other thing," she said, "I'm . . . sorry."

"Sorry?"

"About Graywind . . ."

Again he grunted. "Do not speak of that."

"I expect I should have waited for you to come back from the conference, to tell you myself, explain. Actually, I should have gone with you. Did you get to speak with Frontenac about taking me back with him?"

"Neh."

"Did you see my husband?"

"Neh. They left too soon." He told her about the collapse of the negotiations.

"Pierre *was* there, he had to be."

He shrugged and glanced skyward. "No more rain tonight. Let us sleep. Find dry leaves, make our beds."

"Make your own." She hesitated. "Oh very well."

It seemed the very least she could do. But why had he risked his life to come after her? After what she'd done to Graywind it astounded her. Perhaps Indians didn't mourn their lost loved ones the way civilized people did. Perhaps mourning was a sign of weakness. Was it possible he was becoming fond of her?

For his sake, she hoped not.

72

Even with sufficient sleep, Margaret found that approaching the final leg of the journey she could no longer manage more than a few hundred yards. She was simply too depleted to go on. Two Eagles had to carry her.

This indignity took its toll on her disposition. For the next two days they squabbled like sparrows over a nest. Long intervals of icy silence separated their quarrels. Once he set her down and walked on. She hobbled after him and he picked her up.

"You cannot even hobble anymore," he growled. "You should see your face. It is only a few more hours to Onneyuttahage. You are as light as a bow."

"It's . . . embarrassing. Put me down!" She struggled in his arms.

"Ogechta. Your mouth is too close to my ear for shout-

ing. Be embarrassed, be angry, just do not shout. Although that is like asking Gâ´-oh to hold his breath."

"You really despise me, don't you?"

"Why should I?"

"Graywind was an accident."

"I know that."

"I've caused you nothing but trouble since you found me."

"Believe me, Margaret, you have no part in my troubles. What happened with Burnt Eye would have happened if we never found you."

"Put me down!" she burst.

"My ear!" He set her down. She sat on the ground. He squatted close to her, picking aimlessly at an imbedded stone, avoiding her eyes.

"You called me Margaret."

"That is your name."

"It's the first time."

He grunted.

"Every time I bring up something you don't want to talk about, you grunt like a pig."

He shrugged and looked off under his hand in the direction they were heading. It was midafternoon. The sky was the identical color of her eyes. Fair weather would continue. But last night had been cool and now, with the sun still four hands from its bed, the air was again becoming chilly. It was September. Maple and ash were already dressing in their colors.

"What are you thinking?" she asked.

"Nothing."

"You're obviously thinking about something."

"It is not worth giving words to," he said coldly.

"You think I talk too much."

"I did not say that."

"It's written all over your face."

He stood up gesturing for her to rise.

She did so painfully, wincing as she shifted her feet. "I can walk."

He picked her up. She decided against protesting; she

couldn't walk ten paces without falling. He was so strong, she must indeed be "light as a bow" to him. She felt like an infant comforted in its father's arms. She was tempted to lay her head against his shoulder, but he might see it as brazen. Besides, why give him ideas? On he walked in silence.

She broke it. "I ... haven't thanked you for rescuing me. I'm truly grateful." He grunted. "I'm sorry I've been such a dreadful burden to you, disrupting your life in so many ways. It's all been just bad luck, actually. Neither of us has had much luck these past few weeks." She sighed heavily. "It's beginning to look like I'll never get to Quebec."

She snuffled, closing her eyes.

"It is getting late in the year to travel north," he said.

"It's barely into September."

"The leaves change. *Ochquari* looks for his cave to sleep. The *kahanckt* and the small birds fly over the Ganawageha Mountains to where the sun keeps its warmth away from here. *Augustuske* starts early and lasts long in our lands. It gets very cold. The earth wears white for many moons."

"So, the sooner I leave the better, is that what you're saying?"

"I said the leaves change, *ochquari* ..."

"Yes, yes. Listen to me, if you help me get to Quebec you'll be handsomely rewarded. I told you that before. You'll be rid of me. You'd like that, admit it. It would be worthwhile to you in so many ways to help me."

"What ways? What do I need with French money? For you to leave ..." He shrugged.

"What does that mean? You don't care one way or the other? I find that hard to believe."

"I find it easy. I do not want to talk."

"Then I won't. See? I can cooperate. I'll sing you a song: 'There she stands, a love-ly creature, who she is, I do not know; I have caught her for her beau-ty, let her answer, yes or no ...' "

"I do not understand your song."

"It was my favorite when I was a little girl. Scarcely a day went by when I didn't sing it. We lived out in the country. I had no one to play with. I had to amuse myself. I made up games and imaginary friends and sang songs. What did you like to play when you were little?"

"I cannot remember."

"You can, tell me."

"We played *gä-na'-gä-o.*"

"What is that?"

"You throw a spear at a hoop rolling on the ground. The spear is as tall as a man and as thick as your thumb. Sharpened at one end and striped. The hoop is as wide as your two hands flat, side by side. You throw your spear so." Holding her with one arm he gestured throwing the spear. "The winner gets all the spears."

"I bet you were good at it."

He grunted.

"What other games?"

"*Ga-wá-sa.* Snow snake. You throw the spear like in spear-and-hoop. Only the head is round, not sharp, and turned up slightly and pointed with a stone to make the snake go farther. It goes very fast across the snow crust, like an arrow, and far."

He described *gus-kä-eh*, a game played with a bowl and peachstones. Young and old competed in foot races. There was also *baggataway*, lacrosse, and other games played with a ball.

"What was your favorite game?"

"The foot race. Thrown Bear, Splitting Moon, Anger Maker, all of us would race for hours."

"And you always won."

"Sometimes." He suddenly looked saddened. "What does it matter? It was so many summers ago, as many whole moons as there are leaves on that tree. And we were children. And now we are grown and Thrown Bear has lost a hand, Long Feather his life, Anger Maker his woman."

And you, too, she almost said.

"It was better back then, before the whiteskins came

and the long years of red days and the dying. Much better."

He was done talking. He walked faster.

73

Late summer gave way to autumn's motley as the trees abandoned their growing leaves in the woodlands. The oaks surrendered their acorns. The purple loosestrife hordes in the meadows turned crimson. Swift Doe gave to the world of the Oneida a son, naming him Ochobi-coza— Dawn Maker. With her nephew, Eight Minks sat in her chamber sipping a refreshing drink made from the tips of hemlock boughs boiled in water, flavored with maple syrup and cooled. Coolness was not her mood of the moment; fury rose in her, ripening her cheeks. Two Eagles had given up trying to calm her, choosing to submit to listening until she tired of listening to herself.

"You could have been killed! You are stupid!"

"You repeat yourself like a *tiswate* rattling his tree."

"And what of the discord between you and Ho-ka-ah-taken? Our sachems have returned from Massowaganine. They will consult with the Maquen sachems."

"Good," he snapped, "let them talk it to death. Does what they decide mean anything to anyone but themselves? Ho-ka-ah-ta-ken is not holding his breath waiting for their wisdom. He has bigger problems."

When she spoke again her voice was controlled and sympathetic, despite admonishing him. "You could have told me you were going, instead of sneaking off like a *seronquatse* in the night."

"If I had told you we would have had all this shouting talk back then. And I still would have gone. There was no danger, not with Ho-ka-ah-ta-ken confined to his chamber."

"You did not know he would be. That monster . . ." She clucked. "Their clan mothers should make him run a gauntlet and flay him to death. His miserable life should be forfeit for the way he treats women. Margaret . . . did he . . . ?"

"Whatever horrible and shocking you see in your mind he did to her."

"She told you?"

"She did not have to. I know him. But she will recover." He sighed. "And with all she has been through she still wants to go to Quebec."

"It is all she thinks about."

"She wishes to be with her husband. Is that unnatural?"

"Impossible, is what it is, and the sooner she accepts it the better for all." Eight Minks shook her head.

"Not impossible . . ." He began to bite his knuckle, shutting one eye, plunging into thought.

"*Neh!* You do not take her there! It would be like an *aque* wandering into an *ochquoha's* den. Worse for you even than Onekahoncka. If the Ottawa do not kill you, the Huron or the French will. It is being said the French hate our people more than ever because of the treaty that was burnt before it could be signed."

"They were to blame. They want peace like you want poison."

"Who cares?" She refilled their cups with the cool liquid. "I have thought much about her and Quebec. The dead trappers at Da-yä'-hoo-wä'-quat are not the only ones around. They wander about our lands like the *sinte* they are so eager to trap. You must find others, not to escort her—that is still too dangerous."

"What then?"

"To give a message to take to Frontenac. Sooner or later they all get up to Quebec."

"They cannot be trusted with a message any more than they can with her, all are dogs and liars. Besides, even if they did contact Frontenac, he might refuse to send down an escort."

"Why would he? She is married to one of his officers. When she wakes, when she recovers from her injuries, I will suggest it to her. As for you, if you want to help her so much, go find her some trappers. You will not even have to go as far as Da-yä´-hoo-wä´-quat."

He grunted and drained his cup. "I will think about it."

74

In glorious bloom around Lake Oneida was the vanguard of the arriving aster legions. The breeze off the water was cool but the sun on Two Eagles' scalp lock provided a comfortably warm cap. He sat on a rock that projected over the water, his deer sinew line descending to the wing bone hook baited with deer suet. Fishing with him were Thrown Bear, Splitting Moon, and Anger Maker. Bone watched them. As always, the fishing was excellent. Fat speckled trout, fatter walleye and grass pickerel were being taken in abundance. The catch, laid out in an orderly row on the ground and covered with wet grass, already stretched nearly three paces.

At the moment Bone was the object of everyone's taunts. Even before the birth of her third son the Mohican was looking with favor upon Swift Doe. The recent loss of her husband precluded any friendly overtures on his part. Still, Swift Doe in her loneliness was not averse to him. Two Eagles thought they should marry. Eight Minks counseled patience, reminding him that his brother's bones were still warm in the earth and it could even be that his spirit had not yet settled in the Village of the Dead. Any proposal would come from Swift Doe, for it always came from the woman. They were not of the same clan: He was of the turtle clan, she of the bear clan, so that was no bar to their marrying. Her mother was dead, and her father, like all Iroquoian fathers, would not be expected to interest himself in her plans. To interfere would be an invasion of female jurisdiction, an area of privacy as sacredly regarded by him as he regarded his own. All of Onneyuttahage knew that the two were "looking at each other," as the clan mothers were so fond of phrasing it. Therefore, Bone could expect to be teased by his friends.

"You had better be good to her," advised Thrown Bear, "or her sons will punish you."

"Will you carry the cradle board?" Anger Maker asked, puffing vigorously on his pipe and waving a great cloud of smoke toward Splitting Moon beside him, who reacted with a scowl, waving the smoke on past. To Bone's relief, Thrown Bear, whose own marriage was not something to be bragged about, got the company off the subject.

"Mar-gar-et is well now," he said to Two Eagles.

Two Eagles grunted.

"Aunt Téklq´-eyo says that all she talks about is leaving. She cannot go alone and the trapper scum cannot help her."

"Do you want to fish or talk?"

Thrown Bear rested his chin on his upraised stump. "We can do both. Aunt Téklq´-eyo is telling everyone that you plan to escort Mar-gar-et to Quebec. It is also being said such talk is upsetting to To-na-oh-ge-na."

"It is no business of To-na-oh-ge-na's what I do. He is not my chief."

"Then it is true, you do plan to escort her?"

"I did not say that."

"Then you do not plan to escort her."

"Fish."

Anger Maker's line jerked, he pulled it up. A speckled trout a foot long danced from the hook. He unhooked it and threw it back as too small. "He is going. I am going with him," he said.

"I will discuss it with Moon Dancer," said Thrown Bear.

Two Eagles shook his head resignedly. "If you ask her, she will not let you go."

Thrown Bear bristled. "My woman does not tell me what I can do! I will go if I want to."

Anger Maker and Splitting Moon chuckled.

"None of us can go," ventured Splitting Moon, eyeing Two Eagles. "Did you not hear? The chiefs and sachems have decided to hold an *Ononharoia*."

Two Eagles asked when the White Dog Sacrifice was

scheduled to begin. No one knew exactly, but Anger Maker and Splitting Moon were certain it would be soon.

"By the time it is over, it will be too late in the year to go to Quebec," said Splitting Moon. "To go anywhere north."

"Not so," said Two Eagles. "We are barely begun the season of colored leaves. We could do it. By way of Te-uge´-ga, the river of the Maquen, to the Shaw-na-taw-ty and north would not be wise ..."

Thrown Bear laughed. "You will never go near Onekahoncka again, we know."

Two Eagles ignored him. "We paddle up the big lake, Ne-ah´-ga-te-car-ne-o-di, to the Kanawage, that runs all the way to the Wide Water."

As Two Eagles saw it, they would make their way through friendly Onondaga Territory to Osh-we-geh, "the pouring out place."

"Then up the lake to ..."

"Fort Frontenac," rasped Splitting Moon, "where the lace-cuffs will shoot us like *schawariwane*."

"Not if we paddle by with the darkness in their eyes," said Two Eagles.

Splitting Moon shook his head. "Then what? Up the Kanawage to the arrows of the shiteaters and more French guns? If I want to die I will pick up a big stone, let out my breath and jump into the lake. It will be easier, less pain-ful."

"Did I ask you to come with us?" Two Eagles asked.

"Do not bother, I will not go."

"Let us not argue about it," said Thrown Bear. "Our words can wait until after the *Ononharoia*."

It was agreed. The fishing resumed. Splitting Moon did not speak further to Two Eagles but Two Eagles knew his friend well and sensed that for all his objections, all the boulders he rolled in the path of the idea, in the end he would join the escort.

If there were no problems, by water all the way—save for occasional portaging—they would reach Quebec in less than a whole moon.

To be sure, fair weather could not be taken for granted this time of year and it was unlikely the Ottawa and Huron and French would let them pass without notice. But in most places the St. Lawrence was very wide; distance would protect them from their enemies. And Margaret was key. With her, a French officer's wife, along, they could actually depend upon the French if they needed help.

Not the lace-cuffs, but their moccasin allies, were the only problem Two Eagles could foresee.

 **75**

Two Eagles' prediction was on target: Burnt Eye's crime was all that the Maquen sachems wanted to deal with for the time being. The feud and its bloody consequences were set aside. Much to Two-branches-of-water's disgust. Predictably, he had taken an intense dislike to "the false Ataentsic." Hearing that Two Eagles and his friends were planning to escort her to Quebec aggravated his displeasure. Were it up to him, said he, he would have turned her out of Onneyuttahage barefoot.

Fortunately for Margaret, it was not up to him. The turtle clan chief's views on the subject found Eight Minks' ears; she, in turn, imparted them to her nephew, who said he wasn't interested in Two-branches-of-water's opinions or suggestions as to what should be done with Margaret. Eight Minks, nevertheless, persisted in issuing daily reports to Two Eagles on the subject.

Six regular thanksgivings were annually observed by the Iroquois. The first was the Maple Festival, in appreciation of the tree, for yielding its sweet water. Next was the Planting Festival, when the seed was blessed before it was covered with soil. Third came the Strawberry Festival, in gratitude for all the fruits of the earth. Fourth was the Green Corn Festival, when thanks was given for the ripening of the corn, beans and squashes. Then came the Harvest Festival, after the gathering of the harvest. Last came the great jubilee of the Five Nations, the Festival of the New Year.

The White Dog Sacrifice was not a festival, not an annual affair. The last such sacrifice had been held two years before the war with the French. Before that, according to the elders, more than thirty years had elapsed between ceremonies. In the Oneida rite three white dogs would be strangled. One was hung on a twelve-foot pole to be left until it decayed. The two remaining dogs were cast into the ceremonial fire, then a basket of tobacco was thrown in. The speaker delivered his speech. The two dogs were removed from the fire, cut into pieces and served to those taking part in the ceremony.

"That is followed by a war dance and a dance for everyone that will last all night," Two Eagles explained to Margaret.

They were walking outside the castle for privacy. He did not want to risk meeting Two-branches-of-water while in Margaret's company. An argument, like a trap, is best avoided, his friend He-big-kettle had advised him as a boy. Not advice he had taken seriously, save in Two Branches' case. No one was better at heating up words than Two Branches, except perhaps Anger Maker. Two Eagles was inclined to believe that eventually he would finish what he had started years before: kill the turtle clan chieftain, if sufficiently provoked. Two Branches' repeatedly voiced dislike of Margaret was only the latest pricker in the sensitive flesh around Two Eagles' protective instinct.

It had been freezing cold the night before, laying a skin of ice on Lake Oneida and ruining large quantities of corn on the stalk. Freezing temperatures this early in the year surprised and worried Margaret. She had asked him when the days would normally begin turning cold in this part of the world. He admitted that signs did indicate the weather for two or three days hence but not weeks ahead. The "short summer" was due later in the year."

"After the trees give their leaves to the earth."

"That's some time from now. It could become deathly cold before that. With snow, freezing . . ."

"The White Dog Sacrifice begins tomorrow. For four days. As soon as it is over we will leave."

She stopped him, touching his arm. "I cannot find the words to thank you, all of you." She hesitated. "The others have agreed to go?"

"Bone has and Splitting Moon will. He carries on so in refusing, I know he will end up going. And the others, too. For a good reason, we want to visit Quebec."

He'd made a joke! Weak, but a joke. It was a first. Impulsively, she kissed his cheek. He recoiled, rubbing the spot with the back of his hand and frowning.

"That's just like you," she said. "It didn't hurt, did it?"

He grunted.

"You despise showing affection, don't you? None of you do, except Eight Minks. Why? Is it a sign of weakness?" She bent and plucked a wild daisy, twirling it in her fingers, pretending it held her attention.

"It is not a sign of anything," he said. "It is just not done. Like a woman does not show her breasts to others."

"But affection is felt. Everyone feels it. Why not show it? Affection, love . . ."

"Because . . ."

"Yes?" She suddenly had him on the defensive.

"Because affection, love, is not a part of you. It is put on, like moccasins."

"Fiddlesticks and rot. It's as much part of you as your heart or your soul. Love comes from the heart, it rises in you."

"We have no use for such a feeling."

"It's not a question of usefulness. It's something you have no control over." She was confusing him. "Love . . . just happens between a man and woman. Like between Bone and Swift Doe."

"What is happening between them is not love. Love is for your people. Our people have no use for it."

"You're wrong but I shan't argue with you." Such a strange people, she thought. Bone and Swift Doe loved one another fully as much as she and Pierre, anyone could see. Their hearts knew they were in love even if their minds ignored or denied it.

Such a strange people, he thought. Love. Rising from the heart, she said? As if one's heart guided one. What was the mind doing, then, resting? Where was the spirit, sleeping?

Strange, strange people.

The Feather Dance and War Dance, both costumed, were the two greatest of the thirty-two Iroquoian dances. The Feather Dance was a dance of thanksgiving, the War Dance patriotic. The War Dance, Thrown Bear explained to Margaret, was performed as often as possible in peace time, to keep warriors aware that war, like rain, could return at any time. It was to be the climax of the White Dog Sacrifice.

Twenty-five select warriors, Two Eagles and Anger Maker among them, were chosen to perform the War Dance. The participants were chiefly distinguished for their endurance, for the dance could last from evening to dawn. Margaret had never seen Two Eagles in costume. He looked impressive: a beaded deerskin kilt with two tassels that hung below his knees, the kilt fringed and embroidered with beads and porcupine quill work; his tall headdress, supported by a frame, from the crown of which hung a cluster of white feathers and a single large eagle plume set in the center in a manner that allowed the plume to revolve. His upper body was naked; his leggings, ornamented with quill work, were fastened above the knee and descended to his moccasins, also decorated with porcupine quills and beadwork. His prized belt was interwoven with white beads. He wore deerskin and dogskin arm bands, and knee rattles fashioned of deer hooves. His ornate, engraved ceremonial war club was decorated with feathers at both ends.

With other participants, he danced to the beat of many

drums and turtle shell rattles, in a circular area. The dancers stood close together, four chanters recited the war song, the drums beat, the rattles shook and the dancers made the ground quiver. One followed another, each more spirited than the one before. The dancers were more violent than graceful, each warrior dancing individually: one attacking, another defending, one drawing a bow, another striking with a war club, others in the act of hurling tomahawks. The music and dancing became wild.

Standing beside Thrown Bear at the front of the watching crowd, Margaret was fascinated. She could not take her eyes off Two Eagles, who danced like a man possessed. A voice heavy with bitterness spoke in Oneida behind her.

Thrown Bear glanced back. "To-na-oh-ge-na, Two-branches-of-water, the turtle clan chief," he whispered.

Two Branches ranted on, haranguing anyone who would listen.

"What is he saying? I heard Tékni-ska-je-a-nah . . ."

"He and Two Eagles are not friendly."

"He hates Two Eagles," she said.

And before Thrown Bear could stop her, she turned on Two Branches.

Two Branches sneered and addressed her in Oneida. The men closest to him laughed.

"What did he say?" she hissed. "It was something about me!"

Thrown Bear hung his head and lowered his voice. "Shhh. He says Two Eagles has taken his woman's whiteskin killer for his . . . prostitute."

She whirled. "How dare you!"

Thrown Bear grabbed her arm and pulled her away, hurrying along down the front of the crowd until he found a safer place. "Please do not say anything to Two Eagles," said Thrown Bear. "Please, Mar-gar-et."

"The old pig, what right has he . . . ?"

"Shhh, pay no attention. He *is* old; and bitter, filled with hate for everything. But do not say a word to Two Eagles."

"All right, all right."

Now, between the dances, a man addressed the gathering. Margaret recognized His Longhouse, chief of the bear clan, the clan of Two Eagles, Swift Doe and Eight Minks.

"Friends, I am much pleased with the dance. My thanks to the dancers for their spirit."

The dancers and crowd reacted with approval. Except for Two-branches-of-water, who was still talking to those around him. Margaret continued watching him, he lifted his bony finger to point at Two Eagles.

She bristled. "He's still chopping him up!"

"Shhh . . . chop-ping?" Thrown Bear looked confused.

"Picking on him, saying terrible things about him."

"What of it? Words are like drops of rain. They fall on your shoulders and roll off."

The dancing resumed. During the intervals more speeches were given in the hope that the White Dog Sacrifice would cure the ill. An elder whom Margaret did not recognize now spoke.

Thrown Bear translated for her:

"Friends and relatives, we glory and rightfully in the victories of our brave warriors and ancestors of our warriors. Once the war cry and the painted band were the terror of our enemies. Then our fathers were strong and their power was felt throughout the land of many tribes. Now we are reduced to begging, that we be allowed to live on our own lands, cultivate our own fields, hunt in our own woodlands, drink from our own springs, and mingle our bones with those of our fathers.

"Many snows ago our ancestors were told that a great monster, with white skin and white eyes, would come and invade us and consume our land. And this has come to pass and we are doomed, we are doomed. Our only hope of rescue is the grave."

His unexpected words shocked his listeners by their frankness and their clear vision of the people's plight. All joy and enthusiasm seemed suddenly to drain from audience and performers alike, like rainfall from high ground.

The dance was over. The crowd broke up slowly. Mar-

garet stared at Thrown Bear. She had never seen him looking so melancholy. Everyone seemed to be looking at the
ground.

Two Eagles approached. "Not a very long dance," he
murmured to Thrown Bear.

"Hi-sen should not have spoken so, not here, in front of
so many."

"What did he say? Only what is in all our minds and is
the truth."

Thrown Bear shook his head. "It was not suitable for tonight. It was a very good dance up to then."

"The White Dog Sacrifice is over," said Two Eagles to
Margaret. "Tomorrow or the next day we will leave."

"Tomorrow?"

"Perhaps. I will speak to the others in the morning."

Eight Minks joined them. She, too, looked uncharacteristically sober. For another reason entirely.

"Pay no attention to Two-branches-of-water," she said.
"Yes, I heard. He cannot open his mouth without mud falling out."

Thrown Bear sighed agreement.

"What are you talking about?" Two Eagles asked.

Eight Minks perceived her error too late. She said nothing further.

He turned to Thrown Bear. "What is she talking about?"

Thrown Bear shook his head.

Margaret glanced at Eight Minks and Thrown Bear, then
told him, avoiding his eyes as she did so.

"His heart is a dung heap," said Eight Minks. "Insults
grow in it like the white worms in rotten meat and his
mouth spills them out. Ignore him, everyone does."

Two Eagles said nothing but turned angrily away. Margaret sighed to herself; she had given him yet another
problem.

77

Thrown Bear and Splitting Moon barged into Two Eagles' chamber the next morning shouting and shaking him awake.

"Get up!" boomed Splitting Moon.

Two Eagles blinked. "What . . . ?"

"Why did you do it? How could you be so stupid!"

"What are you talking about?"

Splitting Moon shook his head. "Why did you kill him?"

"To-na-oh-ge-na is dead," said Thrown Bear.

"As if he did not know," exclaimed Splitting Moon.

"They found him behind his longhouse just a few minutes ago," Thrown Bear went on.

Two Eagles yawned. "Good, it pleases me to hear it. What . . ." His glance shifted from one to the other. "You think *I* killed him?" He scoffed and rolled over to resume sleeping.

"After what happened last night, *everybody* knows you did," snapped Splitting Moon.

"Everybody is stupid. I never went near him. I came home with the women last night and went right to bed. The war dance is always tiring, even one as short as that one. Go away, let me sleep."

"You are taking this much too lightly, my friend," said Thrown Bear.

"I do not kill people over insults. Go, let me sleep."

Thrown Bear laid a hand on Two Eagles' shoulder. "Get up, dress and go straight to Sho-non-ses."

"Before he comes to you," growled Splitting Moon.

Two Eagles moaned his displeasure as he dressed. The three of them met His Longhouse moments after stepping out the door. The old chief silently motioned them to follow him to Two-branches-of-water's longhouse on the other side of the castle. The body lay on the ground near the rear door. A crowd was gathering. A squaw moved to cover the body with a bear robe. His Longhouse stopped her.

Two Eagles knelt and carefully examined the body front and back, then got to his feet.

"There is not mark on him," he said to His Longhouse. "Only the blue color of death on his lips. Or maybe it comes from so many insults out of his mouth."

"It is not funny," rasped His Longhouse.

"The drum of his heart stopped," said Two Eagles. "The pain that turns his hands into *schawariwane* claws stopped it. I did not kill him. No one did. Death took him. Look and see for yourself."

His Longhouse looked doubtful. "To-na-oh-ge-na and you hated each other. He has stood against you in all things since what happened at the stirring of the ashes at the New Year's Festival, when you attacked him, would have strangled him had not others intervened. Last night he threw dirt on you and your whiteskin woman."

"She is not *my* whiteskin woman!"

"She heard his insult as did you, Do-wa-sku-ta, and others. You were told . . ."

"So? We avoid each other. Last night was no different. If he died by my knife or an arrow from my bow or my hands around his throat his body would tell you. You can see nothing." He addressed the crowd. "Nothing. I did not kill him. That is all I have to say." Again he fixed his eyes on His Longhouse. "I refuse to waste more of my breath. With you or anyone."

With this, he waved him from his sight and stalked off.

VII

INTO THE WEB

78

The sun had not yet escaped the ridge of the Taconic Mountains when Two Eagles, Splitting Moon, Anger Maker and Bone assembled at the door to Thrown Bear's longhouse. Attired in vests and leggings in place of their breechclouts, carrying their personal effects and weapons, they stood listening as Thrown Bear and Moon Dancer argued heatedly. Margaret stood at a discreet distance, able to overhear husband and wife. Everyone in that part of the castle could hear Moon Dancer.

To Margaret, she did not look like a dancer of any type. She was short and fat and she waddled. Whatever beauty there was in her face was hidden beneath fat; fat closed her eyes to slits and weighted her cheeks so they hung like pouches, and concealed her neck. Her hands waving angrily resembled tight bunches of fat mushrooms.

Her voice cut like an angry crow's. "You will not go!" she shrilled.

Two Eagles rolled his eyes.

"Calm down," Thrown Bear repeated.

"*Neh!* If you go you will die. I have seen it! I danced into a frenzy and fell down and saw you dead. As clearly as I see you now."

"Moon Dancer . . ."

"Dead! And you killed him!" she screamed at Two Eagles, jabbing his chest with her pudgy fingers.

"That is enough!" spat Thrown Bear.

"Not enough! When I am done you will know. Listen to
me. When I dance and fall down I see things with these
eyes no one else can. Did I not see the logs that belched
fire and smoke? The black sun that covered the golden sun
and brought darkness at noon? The fish that leaped from
the lake by the hundreds to die in the grass? Everything I
see after I fall down comes to pass. As will this. You leave
here, you will die, I will never see you again!"

She grabbed his vest and shook him. He broke loose.
"Stop this, you are embarrassing me." He took off the lanyard holding his withered hand and placed it around her
neck. "Wear this till we return."

"You will never! It will be all I will have of you. You
are a dead man. And you will kill him!" Again she jabbed
Two Eagles' chest.

He backed away. Thrown Bear threw up hand and
stump in exasperation. Margaret hated the feeling rising in
her that the squabble was her fault.

"I am leaving," boomed Thrown Bear.

Moon Dancer's tears all but jumped from her eyes.
"You are dead, you are dead, dead, dead . . . !"

The others were walking away; Thrown Bear joined
them.

"I'm sorry," Margaret said quietly to Thrown Bear.

He waved his stump, dismissing her concern.

"You do not have to come," said Two Eagles.

"What should I do? Stay behind while all of you go and
have everyone point and whisper that Moon Dancer would
not let me go? I come and go as I please. . . . My woman
does not order me."

"She said you would be killed," said Splitting Moon.

"She thinks she can predict everything," said Thrown
Bear. "She can predict the day the corn is to be picked, but
that is all."

Splitting Moon wasn't so certain. "What about the logs
that belched fire?"

"The French cannons," said Two Eagles. "Everyone
knew they were coming."

"The black sun that covered the golden sun. Other

things. She said you, Do-wa-sku-ta, will die and you, Tékni-ska-je-a-nah, will kill him."

"And you believe that?" Two Eagles asked.

Splitting Moon shrugged.

"Never mind, let us get out of here."

They headed toward the main gate.

Splitting Moon spoke again. "I hear that the chiefs and the sachems will assemble with the elders to discuss To-na-oh-ge-na's death."

"Good," said Two Eagles, "it will give them something to do."

"But will they not want to speak with you?"

"If they do they can come to Quebec."

Margaret stopped. "I can't leave without saying good-bye to Eight Minks."

"She is asleep."

"Wait, I'll just be a minute."

She ran back toward the longhouse. Eight Minks was up, stumbling sleepily down the passageway. Margaret ran up and embraced her.

"You are going now? Be careful. If the Ottawas see you they will draw lots to see who gets the golden scalp."

"We'll never see each other again," said Margaret.

"We have met, that was a good thing. They are waiting, your husband up there is, go."

Again Margaret embraced her.

"Goodbye, Margaret, and do not let Tékni-ska-je-a-nah bully you."

"When have I ever?"

Eight Minks grinned like a glorious sunrise.

Margaret rejoined them, hurrying to catch up. "How far will we walk today?" she asked.

"Just to the lake," said Two Eagles.

"I do wish Red Paint and Fox could come," she said wistfully. "It would be a reunion for all of us."

"They are coming," said Anger Maker, lighting his pipe.

Two Eagles nodded. "They wait for us by the lake.

They have been there for some time making our canoes. We will be traveling by water all the way."

He explained that they would cross Oneida Lake to the Oneida River and follow it upstream to where it joined the Seneca River at Three Rivers Point. From there they would head north on the Oswego River. "It flows into the big lake."

"Lake Ontario . . ."

"We will cross the lake to Cataraqui."

"Fort Frontenac. Will getting past there be a problem?"

"We will slip under their guns by night," said Thrown Bear. "A canoe is as quiet as an egg."

He somehow looked undressed to her, without his relic hand bobbing at his chest. Used to seeing it, she no longer found it repulsive. But her conscience still troubled her over the unpleasant farewell. Thank the Lord she was leaving for good and would no longer have to contend with the glares and gossip directed at her by Graywind's friends. And she would be leaving Ataentsic behind as well.

She was told that they would be about three hours crossing Lake Oneida, another four hours reaching Three Rivers Point. Crossing Lake Oneida they would leave Oneida Territory for friendly Onondaga. The Oswego River ran through Onondaga Territory and the entire eastern shore of Lake Ontario up to Fort Frontenac was Onondaga land as well.

Their difficulties, if they were to meet any, would come getting past the fort and up the St. Lawrence to Quebec.

If they were to meet any?

"Is this route safer than eastward to the Hudson then north?" she asked Two Eagles.

He shrugged. "It is easier, faster."

"Is it dangerous?"

"Everywhere is dangerous when you leave your own territory," commented Splitting Moon.

Thrown Bear's grunt said he agreed.

"I have an idea," she said. "Just listen, don't throw cold water on it right away. It's this: When we get to Fort Frontenac, I think instead of sneaking by we should stop.

I'll speak with the commandant, explain the situation and get him to supply me with an escort the rest of the way. Then all of you can return. That way you'll not even have to enter enemy territory. The last thing I want is for anyone to be hurt on my account."

No one spoke.

"Well, what do you think? Doesn't it make sense?"

Two Eagles grunted, which she took as signaling an end to discussion. Nevertheless, it was a sound idea, she thought, inspired actually. But he obviously was in no mood for suggestions from her. When was he ever?

 79

Surrounded by fleecy clouds, like a court surrounding its monarch, the sun blazed from the tranquil surface of Lake Oneida. Shading her eyes, Margaret followed it for more than two leagues to the horizon.

Red Paint and Fox had worked on the canoes nearly three full days, selecting the elms, girdling them with clay and then with fire at their bases, the burnt wood chiseled away, the cut burned again, cleaned again and so on until the tree toppled. Then carefully removing the bark and cutting it into panels, before felling the single white ash that supplied the framework.

Each finished canoe comfortably carried three, and together had ample room for the baggage, including bearskin robes for all eight members of the party.

Two Eagles assigned paddlers and passengers: He and Splitting Moon would paddle one canoe, with Margaret as their passenger; Fox and Red Paint the second, with Thrown Bear, who was able to paddle only with difficulty; Anger Maker and Bone would paddle the third, which carried the party's bearskins piled in the center, spare paddles, and other supplies.

They pushed off. The embarkation was a solemn moment, the launching of a bold journey that no one in the party had ever before undertaken. While she sat comfort-

ably, clutching the gunwales, Margaret's canoe glided with
the ease of a feather blown across glass. Two-thirds of the
way across Lake Oneida a sunshower struck, ruffling the
water and drenching them. But by the time they gained
the opposite shore and found the Oneida River everyone
had dried out.

She marveled at the ease with which they paddled, down
on their knees driving the sleek vessels forward at a steady
rate, the only sound the plunging of the paddles into the
dark water. Two Eagles cautioned her that the river would
be a different matter. They must be on the alert for rocks
and bottom sand that created shallows.

Midafternoon, the sun halfway down its path over the
lush, flat terrain to the west. They came to the confluence
of the three rivers and turned northward into the Oswego.
Along the banks gravelly hills rose, separating rock-strewn
lowlands dotted with shallow swamps. Forests of one-
hundred-foot white pines, and shorter, lacy crowned hem-
locks and spruce crowded the sandy soils and bogs.

They would enter Lake Ontario before dark and keep
the eastern shore within view, and when night lit the stars
they would put ashore to camp. They were in no rush to
reach Fort Frontenac, which they planned to sight during
daylight. And wait until nightfall to sneak under the
French guns.

"Why sneak by?" Margaret asked Two Eagles. "Why
not put ashore as soon as we see it and you and I go on
ahead? I'll speak to the commandant. They won't even
have to know others are with us." She turned, calling back
past him. "Thrown Bear, doesn't it make sense?"

"It does to me," growled Splitting Moon, manning the
bow paddle in front of her. "Any idea that keeps bullets
out of my body and my hair on my head is a good idea.
Tékni-ska-je-a-nah?"

Two Eagles grunted.

"It is a good idea," called Thrown Bear from behind
them.

Red Paint, in the bow of the second canoe, agreed. Mar-

garet watched Two Eagles in thought. Everyone rested
their paddles and watched him.

"All right, all right," he snapped at length, "if it is so
important to you."

"It's important to you," she said. "And, on second
thought, why don't I speak to the commandant by myself?"

"*Neh*, I will come."

"Oh, very well, but please, I beg you, don't start anything."

The others laughed.

"Just do not think the moon will fall in your lap," he
warned soberly. "Getting their help may not be as easy as
you think."

"He is right," said Splitting Moon. "They may not have
the men to spare for an escort. They may be all drunk, they
may be too busy counting beaver pelts to help you,
they . . ."

"Tyagohuens," said Two Eagles. "Can we wait and see
what can be done? Can you save some of your dark shadows?"

The Oswego River dropped one hundred feet over its
eight-league course; they came within sight of Lake Ontario, which cheered Margaret's heart. Two Eagles dragged
his paddle, steering for the right bank, ordering Splitting
Moon to do the same and calling for the other two canoes
to follow.

"What are you doing?" she asked. "Keep on, keep
on . . ."

"Listen," said Splitting Moon, "and you will understand."

From directly ahead came a sound like a steady wind.

Splitting Moon turned to her. "There are falls ahead
higher than the palisades at Onneyuttahage, as high as six
men."

"We will portage around them to the lake," said Two
Eagles to her. "You will carry as much as you can."

Carrying their canoes, they walked by the falls studded
with gleaming outcroppings, the water crashing down so

loudly they had to shout to make themselves heard. By the
time they reached the shore of the lake the sun was melting into the horizon, spilling copper across the water.

"We will camp here," said Two Eagles.

"It's still early," she said. "Can't we at least start
across?"

"Tomorrow."

She was in no position to question any of his decisions.
He'd conceded her Fort Frontenac. *Would* she be able to
change escorts there? Thank the Oneidas and send them
home before they entered hostile territory?

Whoever was in command at the fort wouldn't dare refuse her!

<hr>

========= **80** =========

A bloodred sun wounded the sky in the west, just above
the horizon, oddly casting no image on the surface of
the lake. To the east, so densely massed were the trees that
the darkness was like a wall of coal. Not a whisper of
wind, the water dead calm, to Margaret, as if it had gelled.
The eerie silence was broken only by the soft dipping of
the paddles.

She glanced skyward. A sheet of cirrus clouds resembling a row of scimitars bent by high winds stretched
above the lake. Hazy layers gradually blended into a single
sheet as white as a shroud. The wind came up, blowing
from the southwest.

Bone, manning the steering paddle of the third canoe in
the line, called out, pointing: *"Gionto!"*

A chilling sight followed the wind: a great black curtain
bore down on them. Margaret gasped; it looked like every
thundercloud she had ever seen combined in one, devour-
ing the sky.

The wind now ridged the surface of the lake with a
chop. Then waves rose, roiling the water white, rocking
the canoes. Two Eagles shouted the order to make for
shore but it was at least half a league distant and the black

curtain was coming faster. She gasped and trembled as one, another, a third funnel appeared, twisting down from the curtain, writhing obscenely, like enormous arteries drilling into the water. Pulling the black monster forward.

Lightning snapped and flogged the curtain. The furious wind nearly upset her canoe. The steerers had turned all three vessels toward shore, digging deep with their paddles, driving the bows of the canoes into the heaving waves. They rose precariously and dropped like stones; water spilled in, flooding around her ankles.

Her eyes were riveted to the lightning and the black funnels, as the curtain picked up speed. Rain, whipped by the wind, struck from all directions.

The lake boiled like a gigantic cauldron, tossing the canoes. She hung on. . . .

"Gionto! Gionto!" screamed Bone, above the roaring wind.

The curtain had closed on them. The canoes sank and rose, slewing and spinning out of control. The paddlers ducked against the mounting fury, hanging on.

Margaret prayed for deliverance, begging to reach the distant shore. The wind bent the trees, snapping off crowns, toppling one, then another, but the sounds of destruction were inaudible above the screaming tempest.

They were within a hundred yards of land when Anger Maker's and Bone's canoe turned over. They fought to stay afloat. Then the other canoes capsized.

Down she plunged, to find the water deeper than the Mohawk River and surging and swirling more violently; and when she came up the wild rain made it difficult to catch her breath. She struck out frantically for the shore she could not see.

Two Eagles surfaced nearby and grabbed her waist, swimming with her.

"I can make it . . ." she cried.

He pulled them forward with his free arm to shallow water. They stumbled through the bottom muck, onto shore, waves breaking over them and collapsed face-down

on the sand. The others joined them. In front of her, the
trees bent like giant dancers.

Above the shrieking wind, she heard crackling sounds.
They got to their feet and started forward, all but Splitting
Moon.

"We will be killed in there," he shouted. "Stay here,
stay here!" One by one the others stopped and dropped
down on the narrow strip of sand, the water from the
breaking waves swirling around them. With a loud crack,
the crown of a huge maple near the water broke cleanly
off, dropping straight down toward Anger Maker and
Bone, burying them in its branches. But miraculously, the
trunk missed them. They emerged in a daze, checking
themselves for injuries.

"Get back underneath it!" yelled Two Eagles.

They hesitated, then got back inside the branches. The
others ran to the crown, throwing themselves inside, like
boys diving into a haystack. Two Eagles gripped her hand
and they, too, got inside, just as a second crown came
crashing down a few yards beyond.

The blackness boiled overhead for what seemed hours
as they lay shivering in their meager protection. The wind
increased in fury, so powerful she feared it would pluck
them from their cover and hurl them one by one into the
woods.

Then, abruptly, the wind and the rain stopped and the
sky turned blue. Slowly, they emerged from the branches
and stood looking about them. There was no sign of the
canoes, or any of their supplies. All the weapons had been
lost save their knives.

"*Gionto!*" shouted Bone, again pointing southwest.

"Oh dear God . . ." she murmured.

A second cloud was approaching. A decision had to be
made before the new fury hit: Should they move into the
trees and take their chances?

"We stay here," declared Two Eagles.

Splitting Moon protested loudly, as did Fox.

"There may be a cave in there we can hide in," Fox
suggested.

"There may not be," countered Two Eagles. "And while we search for it, the water-lizard that makes the wind is crawling out of his pool again." He gestured toward the approaching storm. "I do not want Margaret's head or mine cracked by a falling tree. Do you?"

He scowled witheringly at Splitting Moon, at Fox.

"We stay here."

81

The second phase of the storm was even more terrifying, more destructive than the first. Thrown Bear was struck in the knee by flying debris and Anger Maker hit his forehead on a rock. When at last the skies cleared, the first stars welcomed the oncoming darkness and a smudged, yellow moon supplanted the bloody sun, they held council to discuss their next move.

They decided to wait until daylight to retrieve whatever belongings and supplies that might have washed ashore. Splitting Moon had lost his tooth-ball tomahawk, Anger Maker his cherished pipe, Bone his fire cob. But for the clothes on their backs and their knives, everyone had lost everything. Losing all their weapons troubled Two Eagles, for eventually they would be entering hostile territory. There was no hope that any of the canoes had escaped damage, so they would either have to build new ones, delaying the journey for the better part of two days, or continue on foot through the woodlands.

In this choice the party was split. Those who wanted to continue on foot optimistically believed that Margaret would find a fresh escort at Fort Frontenac. Two Eagles, Thrown Bear, Bone and Red Paint were certain they would have to journey all the way to Quebec and would therefore need canoes.

Margaret adamantly favored walking on. She repeatedly reminded Two Eagles of his estimate that it would probably take less than six hours on foot to the fort. Thrown Bear pointed out that they were still in Onondaga Territory, minimizing any threat from hostile tribes. If any Ottawas or Hurons had invaded the area to hunt or poach beaver, their numbers would be insignificant and the Oneidas would have little difficulty dealing with them.

"We have only our knives," Two Eagles reminded him and, with a sweeping glance, the whole company.

"We can make bows and arrows," insisted Red Paint. "Then we can take the trail that runs from the fort to Massowaganine. There are no dogshit eaters here, no Huron snakes."

"And if you're right," said Margaret to Two Eagles, "and it turns out I can't get men at the fort, we can always build canoes there, can't we?"

"We can build them anywhere," said Thrown Bear, rubbing his injured knee. "She is right."

"She is right, she is right," rasped Two Eagles, "always right. I am too tired to talk about it now. Tomorrow is time enough."

Confident that no hostile hunters would happen on them while they slept, he saw no need to post a guard.

Splitting Moon disagreed. "You sleep if you want, everybody. I will stay awake."

"And fall asleep before the sun rises tomorrow," said Thrown Bear.

The others laughed.

Two Eagles was the first to awaken, yawning and grinding his eyes with his fists shortly before sunrise. He found Splitting Moon, knife in hand, sitting against a tree fast asleep.

Before he woke him he resolved to say nothing about it to the others, in particular to Thrown Bear.

82

Because of the swelling in his knee, Thrown Bear was excused from the early morning search of the beach. Margaret kept him company while the others wandered in pairs up and down the sand looking for salvage from the storm. Thrown Bear sat on a bounder.

Margaret eyed him sympathetically. "I'm sorry about Moon Dancer."

"Because we heated our words? It is how we keep our fire warm. Sometimes I think if we did not argue we would not talk at all."

"I'm sure that's not true. She *was* firm against your coming."

"Not so much against it, more that she wanted it her own way. She is a good woman, but she worries too much about me. I am not her child."

Margaret stared at him. "All of you are good ..." she murmured.

"Good?"

"You've helped me, fed and clothed me, protected me, even risked your lives for me, a stranger, intruder. Why?"

"Why do you think?"

"Is it because you think I'm Ataentsic?"

"Two Eagles does not think so."

"Then why?"

"It is no great mystery. We found you lost, a helpless woman."

"When I think what all of you ..."

"All us savages, what we could have done to you?" He snorted.

"You do believe women are inferior to men. I've seen that."

"Inferior?"

"Beneath men, lower in importance."

"*Neh*. Only separate from men."

He glanced out from under his hand over the lake, then back toward the woods and the wide swath of broken and fallen timber made by the storm. He flexed his knee, wincing.

"Whatever you have seen, we respect our women. They have a high place in the clans. The clan mothers appoint chiefs and can depose them. The women keep the wampum belts with the hereditary names of the chiefs. And

women have much say in our affairs, even in our wars.
Their wishes are always listened to in council. Among our
people, women have more say and more control than they
do among your people, I would guess."

"Well . . ."

"At the same time, they need our protection. They, like
the children, are . . . what is your word?"

"Vulnerable? Like a deer in a circle of hunters."

"*Nyoh, nyoh.* As you were. No Iroquois warrior would
have harmed you back at the hollow tree or left you there.
Not even your friend Burnt Eye. The last we heard he is
still a prisoner of the clan mothers. You need our help to
get to your husband. That is our way. We help anyone.
Would not whiteskin soldiers do the same for an Iroquois
woman?"

"I . . . suppose."

He grinned. "You do not know."

The others straggled back empty-handed. Only one canoe was found, shattered, useless. Everyone stood watching Two Eagles as he pondered the situation, his knuckle
between his teeth.

Finally he spoke. "We will find the main trail to the
fort."

Thrown Bear grunted painfully. Two Eagles looked this
way. "It is all right," said Thrown Bear. "I can walk. I will
not hold you back."

Red Paint and Fox had already fashioned spears out of
straight hickory branches and announced their intention of
bringing down the first deer they sighted.

They started into the woods, Two Eagles and Margaret
in the lead, the others following in single file, Thrown
Bear in the middle. But as they went on, stepping over
fallen trees and around tall, craggy stumps, he fell behind;
until Bone, next to last in line, called out.

"We have lost one."

Two Eagles dispatched Bone and Anger Marker to find
Thrown Bear. Thrown Bear reappeared, limping badly.

"You walk too fast," he protested.

"Tyagohuens and I can make a litter and carry him," declared Anger Maker.

"Carry yourself!" snapped Thrown Bear.

They went on, Thrown Bear hobbling behind. When they stopped to rest, Bone found a spindly-looking plant with small green flowers and a dull green stem covered with hairs. He handed it to Thrown Bear.

"What is that?" Margaret asked.

"Stinging nettle," said Two Eagles. "The hairs on the stem sting, but the roots and leaves are good for pain and swelling."

Thrown Bear selected the tenderest leaves, pounded them with a stone and gently rubbed his knee with them.

"You will notice," said Two Eagles smugly to Splitting Moon and Fox, "we have yet to see a single cave."

"We have not looked for any," said Splitting Moon.

He moved ahead until he led the company by about twenty paces. He found the main trail and called back just as Red Paint sighted a solitary doe, standing nibbling red maple leaves, its white rump to them. They chased it with their spears but it eluded them easily. They came back grumbling, ignoring the others' laughter. The party reached the main trail and started north. It was only a few minutes later that a throaty, insistent *ka'-ka'-ka' cow cow* call sounded directly in front of them and was immediately repeated behind.

"What is that bird?" Margaret asked.

Two Eagles was frowning. The call repeated ahead and left and right of them. "That is no bird," he said quietly. "It is a man imitating *tite-ti*."

"The cuckoo, yellow bill," said Anger Maker behind them. "He is right, it is a man."

83

Thirty braves surrounded them, a dozen or more holding arrows, ready to shoot, others menacing the Oneidas with muskets and tomahawks. They wore breechclouts and

deerskin leggings, wide white-and-purple beaded head-
bands and short feather headdresses. No paint on their
faces or chests but some displayed copper disks suspended
from woven belts around their necks. Two, standing five
paces in front of them—one aiming his bow—began jabbering loudly. The sound of crackling twigs was heard,
three white men appeared, bearded and slovenly.

Margaret's heart, already pounding, wrenched in her
chest at the sight of the *coureurs de bois*. The biggest of
the three, and presumably their leader, wore a patch over
his right eye and a dirty battered tricorn hat. Had he a
sword, he would have looked like a pirate. His belt hung
over his potbelly as he swaggered up to her and Two Eagles. He pretended surprise at sight of her. His eye settled
on her breasts, reminding her of Burnt Eye.

"*Sacre bleu*, what have we here?"

"Who are you?" she snapped in French. "How dare you
accost us like this? Tell them to lower their weapons and
get out of our way. At once!"

"At once!" he repeated. And shoving his thumbs in his
belt, threw back his head laughing uproariously. "Listen to
this, *comrades*, a blond squaw with blue eyes speaking
French. And beautiful. Look at that hair, spun gold, no?"

He seized her hair. Two Eagles growled, started to move
between them. And was pushed back so hard he nearly
fell.

"Stay where you are, *sauvage*. Look, *mon ami*, he is a
tall one. Watch me cut him down . . ."

Wincing in pain, Margaret yanked her hair free from his
fist. "Animal!"

"Look at this lot, Jean-Paul," he said, ignoring the insult. "Oneidas. What are Oneidas doing on Onondaga
lands?"

"We're on our way to Fort Frontenac," she rasped. "On
. . . official business."

"Official business, Jean-Paul, ooooo."

"Get out of our way, let us pass. At once!"

"Ho, ho, ho, orders, orders. And a temper, too, Jean-

Paul." He pushed too close. His breath was vile. "And such a pretty mouth."

Again he grabbed her hair. Again, Two Eagles took a step forward. The two men behind her tormentor brought up their muskets and two braves with bows pushed flint-locks to within inches of Two Eagles' chest.

"Tell your tall friend, pretty mouth, that if he wants to die where he stands, just take one more step."

She struggled to free herself.

"Hold still. Don't make me pull your lovely hair out by the roots."

He pulled her downward. Her knees buckled. Down he pulled her until her face was against his manhood. She jerked to one side, flattening her cheek against him. He laughed. Two Eagles looked on seething.

The Frenchmen sneered at him. "You have seen nothing yet. You want to watch? Look at his eyes, Jean-Paul, he wants to watch."

"You're hurting me," she whispered.

One of his companions spoke.

He snapped a response. "*Me* first, then you and Marcel can chose or draw a card to see who's next." He released her.

She rose slowly, glowering.

"Keep your filthy hands to yourself. Will you let me pass or do I report you to the governor general himself for detaining us, molesting me, threatening us all?"

He roared with laughter so loud it echoed. And barked an order. The Oneidas' wrists were tied behind them. A long rope was produced, a noose fashioned, placed around Two Eagles' neck and tightened. Then the rope looped around the neck of each prisoner in line, joining all six.

Six?

She whispered to Two Eagles: "Where is Thrown Bear?"

He started to reply. A musket butt hammered his stom-ach viciously, doubling him over, gasping. Escorted by the Ottawas, the *coureurs de bois* led them off the trail along a narrow path to a clearing stacked with hundreds of plews and a pile of dead beaver. Three squaws were so busy scraping hides free of tissue and sinew they did not even look up. Other women were stretching finished hides on willow frames. The area reeked of beaver musk. A fire with a number of wide-mouthed earthen pots beside it occupied the center of the clearing, sending up wisps of smoke.

The leader was talking to his two companions and two Ottawas. Again and again, he looked back at Margaret. His men smirked. He came over to her, taking her by the hand. She pulled away.

"Now, now, be nice to me, I will be nice to you. Come along, we must have privacy."

"Leave me alone. I'm not going anywhere with you!"

"Will you be nice or must I drag you by your beautiful hair? Which?"

"Get away from me, you pig!"

He struck her with his fist. She cried out and fell. The tethered Oneidas started forward. The brave holding the end of their rope jerked them to a standstill.

"Get up," growled the trapper, "or the next one I'll break your . . ."

A shot as loud as a cannon cut him off. The ball obliterated his face.

84

The attack came from all sides. Within seconds, half the Ottawas lay dead, struck by bullets and arrows. A Frenchman fell to a screaming warrior's tomahawk that halved his skull, spilling his brains. The third *coureur de bois* ran for his life, but two arrows struck him in the back. His right hand feebly reaching for them, he fell.

The squaws scattered. The attackers paid no attention to them. The few fleeing Ottawas were cut down. Within two minutes, the clearing came to resemble the Carrying Place, but with many more corpses. The attackers now set about methodically scalping the dead while two men released the captives. Fallen from the punch of her antagonist, Margaret had remained on the ground, not daring to budge, throughout the attack. Two Eagles rubbed the rope burns at his throat and helped her to her feet.

"Well, auld skate, that was a lark, wouldn'nae you say?"

"Gordon! Gordon! Gordon!" boomed Two Eagles.

He embraced Sergeant Gordon Duncan, attired in deerskins and feathers and to Margaret, every inch an Onondaga warrior but for his flaming red hair and beard and baby-pink complexion.

"Angels from heaven," she murmured, testing her jaw to make sure it wasn't broken.

"Ond who might this pretty loss be, Tékni-ska-je-a-nah? Dinna joost stand there, mon, introduce us."

She extended her hand. "Margaret Addison Lacroix."

"Sergeant Gordon Andrew Dooncan, formerly of the Second Scottish Highlanders, noo ond forever moore an Oonondaga. Returned to the wars, it would appear."

"What in the world are you doing here?" she asked.

"Honest labor, trocking beaver poachers for Chief Hegreat-wizard. Orders are to clear our lands of every lost thieving rascal. We've been trocking this bunch for a week."

The Onondagas had outnumbered the Ottawas better than two to one. She averted her eyes at the sight of a final scalping, in front of her.

"Not a one got away," she murmured.

"We let their squaws go, Missus. They'll report the disoster and the chiefs and their frog mosters will think twice befoor sending oot anoother bunch. But what are you doing here so far from Onneyuttahage?"

Two Eagles explained.

"Ah, the storm, the storm. We took cover in a bluddy cave. You were actually on the lake when it struck? A miracle you survived!"

"We lost Thrown Bear," said Two Eagles.

"One hand? Nae . . ."

Margaret told him what had happened.

Splitting Moon shook his head. "He is dead."

"Dinna' go jumping to concloosions."

Gordon and the Oneidas began searching for Thrown Bear. Margaret sat waiting in the clearing with Bone and two of the Onondagas. Did the Ottawas find him, kill him, as Splitting Moon thought? Clearly, Two Eagles didn't think so.

The sun was dissolving along the horizon when the first few searchers came straggling back.

"Didn't anybody see anything?" she asked Duncan.

He shook his head. Still, he did not appear as pessimistic as the others. "It dinna necessorily mean the dogshi ... the Ottawas found him. He could have circled aroond and be halfway to the fort by noo."

"Not on that knee," said Two Eagles.

"He is dead," said Splitting Moon. "I know in here." He tapped his chest.

Two Eagles frowned. "You think in there instead of in your head? Maybe that is why you can never see the sun in anything."

"Say what you like, he is dead. Just as Moon Dancer predicted. She is never wrong."

"Fiddlesticks and rot!" burst Margaret. "Talk all you want. The only thing we know for certain is that none of us knows a blessed thing."

"The lady's recht, auld skate," said Gordon.

"She is always right," said Two Eagles. "We will camp here and go on in the morning."

"We may find him waiting for us when we get to the fort," said Red Paint.

Two Eagles scowled. "That is crazy talk. A lone Oneida, walking into that place?"

"He is dead," repeated Splitting Moon.

85

Gordon Duncan had acquired the Onondagan name Gäde-a-yo, which translated into "Lobster"—not inappropriate, considering his overall appearance. With the

Oneidas he walked about the carnage. It had been a massacre, not a battle, all happening so fast. They found all sorts of weapons. Splitting Moon was disappointed in not being able to find a tooth-ball tomahawk to replace his, lost in the storm. Nor did Anger Maker find a pipe not combined with a tomahawk. The party rearmed with bows and arrows, tomahawks and four muskets, along with small quantities of powder and ball.

Gordon's men packed the stolen beaver pelts to carry back to Massowaganine—now, he disclosed, rebuilt, nearby the original site. The Scotsman shared the Onondagas' food supply with the Oneidas, including hard corn bread, apples and salted venison.

Margaret eyed the meat suspiciously. "It's not *sateeni*," she muttered.

Gordon laughed. "The bluddy Mohawks eat dog, not the Oonondagas. We've a much moore selective palate, partial to *gohanha-yä* ond *ati:ru owanisse*."

Two Eagles flashed a rare smile. "Raw eel and raccoon tongues."

"The raccoon pickled in brine," added Gordon.

"Delightful." She excused herself and walked off.

"Beautiful loss," murmured Gordon.

Two Eagles grunted.

"She likes you, auld skate."

"She is grateful to me, that is all."

"She's married, she said. Pity. Of course, what am I saying, you are yourself. Did she ond your missus get on?"

Again Two Eagles grunted.

Duncan laughed. "I'll take thot for yes. That one is fond of you, though. Ond why not? Turn you loose in Edinburgh and all the lossies on the street would look your way."

"We have to go on."

"We do, too."

They shook hands.

Gordon's men picked up stacks of forty and fifty pelts, each stack weighing upwards of a hundred pounds, and started toward the cave they had used earlier as a refuge from the storm. Ten paces away, Gordon paused and waved. Two Eagles returned it.

"I like him," she said. "You two fought together."

"Many times, so many places most of them have washed out of my memory. A brave man, for a whiteskin, good soldier."

"What did he say about me?"

"Nothing important. Your jaw, where the stinking one hit you, looks worse than Thrown Bear's knee. Ask Splitting Moon or one of the others to find you some stinging nettle."

"I'm not helpless. I'll find my own." She frowned. "Poor Thrown Bear . . . you can blame me for just about everything bad that's happened."

"Please, do not start that again."

She bristled and walked off, nearly tripping over the body of a *coureur de bois*.

He felt a twinge of pity for her. Nothing that had happened to them from the hollow tree on, least of all Thrown Bear's disappearance, was her fault.

And Gordon was wrong. How could she be fond of him? Like Eight Minks and like so many others, he confused gratitude with something else. She had her man in her heart. And whenever his name came up, up came that foolish word.

Love.

He missed Thrown Bear, despising the nagging thought that he was dead, his scalp hanging dripping from some Ottawa's belt.

And when they got back to Onneyuttahage he would have to be the one to tell Moon Dancer.

 **86**

Thrown Bear's loss gnawed at Two Eagles. Still, they'd found no trace of his body and his murderers would have had no reason to carry it away. Had he somehow survived?

Before decamping she wandered over to where lay the *coureur de bois* who had been about to take her away to rape her. The single shot to the face had rendered him unrecognizable. She had been looking at him when the bullet fired by Gordon Duncan struck; in her mind his leer remained frozen as before he fell. She looked at the other corpses, the flies sucking their sweat—wood rats, weasels and other vermin would arrive, then the wolves, and by noon tomorrow a good part of every corpse would be eaten away.

By now those at the Carrying Place must be reduced to skeletons. Life, so easily disposed of.

She noticed Two Eagles staring at Eye Patch expressionlessly. A dead whiteskin, so dirty was this one it wasn't easy to confirm the color of his skin.

The Oneidas, delivered from certain death by their fellow Iroquoians by timing and luck, took no more notice of the carnage than they would have of dead branches and stones.

"What are you thinking?" she asked.

"Thinking?"

"The way you're staring at him."

He nudged the corpse with his toe. "Only that killing this one and the other two is nothing. Or the ones at the Carrying Place. They are so many, like the black flies in mid-summer; whiteskins: trappers, traders, farmers, soldiers, black robes, whiteskins, whiteskins. The brook becomes a stream, the stream a river, the river a flood. They are so many, we are so few. Hi-sen was right."

"Who?"

"Hi-sen, Red Squirrel, the elder who spoke at the White Dog Sacrifice war dance."

She recalled the wrinkled old doomsayer whose speech had so depressed the gathering that it ended the dance.

Two Eagles smiled grimly. "He spoke for everyone there, even the smallest child."

"Are you a doomsayer, too? Will the Iroquois just give up and move on to other lands?"

"What good would that do? The river is becoming a

flood that will spread all over. I am glad that I have no son
to pass on this empty gourd that was our world and our
life. When I think of the many who died in the red days,
what they died for: only to hasten the flood. A long time
ago Kah-nah-chi-wah-ne, He-big-kettle, my father's old
friend and my counselor who died in the fire at Massowaganine, said a curious thing that I will always remember. He asked me: What if our people built our canoes as
big as the wooden islands of the whiteskins and we paddled across the O-jik´-ha-dä-ge´-ga to their lands? The
British, the French, the Dutch. Would we be able to chase
them out, steal their land and settled and grow in numbers? And bring our friends and relatives over? What
would the whiteskins do?"

He snickered.

"He knew the answer to that. Even I, only a boy, knew.
This place is beginning to smell. We will leave."

87

The destruction in the woodland lessened as they moved
north. The stinging nettle leaves Margaret applied to
her swollen jaw helped greatly. Two Eagles wasn't interested. His rankling regret over Thrown Bear permitted his
mind no room for anything else. He brooded. He sulked.
The others in the party stayed clear of him.

At noon the following day, Splitting Moon, the self-
appointed scout for the party, came running back out of
breath.

"We are there!"

"We will stop here," declared Two Eagles. "All of you
stay and wait for us. Margaret?"

"I'm coming."

They started off.

"Now, remember," she said. "You promised to let me do
all the talking."

He sniffed disdainfully. "I have nothing to say to any
French long-knife."

"No matter what the commandant says, even if he refuses me, *don't get mad*."

He stopped, staring indignantly. "Do not talk to me like I am your child."

She sighed. A yellow warbler flew across their path, looking like a feathered lemon. "I apologize," she said, avoiding his eyes. "I did. It's just that this is so important to me. Please God, they dare not refuse me an escort. They must be in contact with Quebec, sending supplies back and forth or whatever, don't you think?"

He shrugged. "What would I know about that?"

"If they happen to be sending a boat to Quebec, I certainly wouldn't be any burden to take along."

"Can we go on?"

"Yes, yes, I'm sorry."

The trees finally broke to reveal the shoreline at the foot of a long, sparsely wooded rise, the lake to their left, the headwaters to the river on their right.

Panic seized her. "Good God! Where's the fort? There is none!"

He pointed to an island directly ahead, so heavily wooded it looked at first glance like a gigantic green-feathered headdress.

"The fort is on the other side of that island."

"Fiddlesticks and rot, if this doesn't beat all! What do we do now, swim?"

"Swim."

"Oh no . . ."

"It is not that far."

"I could never make it."

"The current does not run fast like the Mohawk. You are a good swimmer."

She had plumped down, discouraged. He knelt beside her, looking out over the island, which blocked completely the view of the fort on the opposite side.

"We can swim it," he said. "When we reach the island, we cross it and on the other side is a smaller island. From there it is a short way to the mainland, to Canada. Take off your clothes."

"I will not!"

"You cannot swim so far in deerskins. It will not be like when you swam ashore in the storm." He fingered the fringe of her jacket. She pulled away. "They will become heavy, weigh you down. I will carry them for you, keep them dry."

"I am not swimming over there in the ... without clothes, and that's final."

"Go behind that tree. I will not look at you."

"Can't we find a log and float over on it?"

"The current would carry us too far downriver. Go."

"It's indecent, cavorting about with nothing on."

"The fish do not think so."

"Don't you dare look ..." She hid behind a tree and began removing her clothing. "Everything?"

"Everything," he said, his back still to her. "Throw them out."

He collected her clothes and wrapped hers along with his own jacket, leggings and moccasins, in his trousers, securing them with his belt around his neck, so that in the water the bundle would ride on his upper back.

Standing naked, his back to her, he spoke. "I will go first. Stay upriver of me." He indicated with his left hand. "'I will catch you if the current carries you past me."

"Don't you dare touch me!"

He waved, ran to the river, dove in, surfaced, whipped his head, adjusting the bundle on his back and looking straight ahead. "Come!"

She dove in behind him. He pointed upriver and down; two spits projected up and downriver. He pointed midway between them, directly ahead.

"There is where we want to beach." His hand swung upriver, to the spit nearest the lake. "Aim for that and the current will carry us to the center. Come."

"It's freezing."

"You will get used to it."

She swam behind him, marveling at how swiftly and smoothly he knifed through the water. She was a strong swimmer but in less than a minute he was thirty yards ahead.

"Slow down ..."

He braked and turned around, treading water. "Are you all right?"

"Stop showing off. It's not a race, you know."

"I will go slower for you. Swim."

It was nearly an hour before she could feel the river bottom underfoot. Already dressed, he tossed her clothes out to her. To her surprise, they were but slightly damp.

VIII
QUEBEC

88

The three strands of braid on the Austrian knot denoting his rank were almost as precious to Pierre as his appearance. Gazing into his mirror, he shuddered at how close he had come to being stripped of his captaincy. Since that black hour, when he'd been hauled before the old man and dressed down, he could proudly say he had executed a complete about-face in his conduct, in his philosophy toward life.

The new Captain Pierre Lacroix was conscientiously keeping his handsome profile low, carrying out his duties with dispatch, conducting himself as a consummate professional under the critical eye of his commander. In addition to what he liked to call his "reincarnation" on the job, he had cut down on his drinking and reined in his fondness for bedding Huron and Ottawa maidens—although managing to avoid total chastity, confining his lust to Two Buttons. Word of his near-miraculous transformation quickly got about the fort. His fellow officers and the enlisted men came to be almost equally divided between believing that he actually had changed his ways or that he was merely putting on an elaborate show of doing so strictly for the governor general. He cared not a whit what others might think. He knew he had turned himself around. And would be a better soldier and better husband for it, when Margaret arrived. Which he was beginning to wonder about, since she should have shown up two weeks ago.

Nez had finished shaving him. He was dressed and prepared to seize the morning, eager as a child confronted with sweets to please his commander anew, when a knock rattled the door. Nez opened it to the man-sized tin soldier, Corporal Claude Lemieux, who promptly clicked his heels and saluted his musket.

"Message for the captain."

"Good morning to you, Claude," muttered Nez.

"What is it, Corporal?" Pierre asked, powdering his cheeks and neck before coming over. Again the corporal clicked and saluted. "Must you carry that musket about? Nobody else does."

"Sir, good morning, sir."

"Good morning, Claude. Spit it out."

"Sir, the general is ill and confined to his bed. General Desmaines has taken over as interim commander. Lieutenant Salgues, his aide, has asked me to inform you that your services will not be required. That is, sir, until the general resumes his duties, sir."

Pierre stifled a cheer. "Thank you, Corporal, thank you, thank you. That'll be all. Don't salute." Lacroix withdrew. Nez kicked the door shut with his back turned to it.

"*Mon Capitaine,* what does this mean?"

"Are you deaf? I am unemployed, dutiless. I can go back to bed. I can spend the day at dice and cards. I can start drinking at noon. Of course, I won't. I have better things to do." He winked.

"At six o'clock in the morning, sir?"

"Of course not, lad. The new Captain Lacroix has a firm hand on the rein of his lust." He strolled back to his mirror. "How do I look?"

"*Magnifique.*"

"My first duty of my first day of no duty will be to call on the general. To extend him my deepest sympathies and heartfelt wishes for a speedy recovery. I'm expected, Nez, I must be off. Where's my sword?"

Nez buckled it on for him. "I wonder how bad the general is?"

"He's been complaining about pain in his legs ever

since we got back from that fiasco with the savages. He's an old man, Nez, illness and infirmity come with years. Aren't you glad you're still a boy? Oh, happy day!"

He all but danced out the door.

89

The city of Quebec, which included the fort, nestled high in a corner formed by the entry of the St. Charles River into the St. Lawrence. The Château St-Louis was by far the most imposing structure in the area. In erecting and recently renovating it, Governor-general Frontenac had endeavored to duplicate his own family's estate on the Indre River in central France, but the wherewithal was unavailable. So he settled for plank instead of parquet or marble floors, oak walls in place of plaster, and other substitutions of inferior quality, although many of the furnishings were on a par with those in his office. The jewel of his furniture was a sumptuous sixteenth-century Venetian bed, a four-poster draped with Milanese silk hangings; a bed to rival the king's at Versailles, with a goose-down mattress.

At the moment, though, the general was not enjoying his cherished bed. His unnaturally pale face was carved with pain, above and below his mustaches; his bald head gleamed with sweat so it nearly reflected the two Jesuits hovering like birds of prey over him. General Desmaines, in his pink, perspiring corpulence, stood at the foot of the bed. Major Boulanger stood behind the priests, more concerned with the balance of his mustachios, tweaking the end of the left one, then the right. Dr. Blaise, runty, acidulous and reputedly a butcher in the practice of surgery, sat at the bed opposite the priests, frowning over his ignorance of what to do further for his patient, beyond elevating both his legs on a pile of pillows. According to Boulanger, who whispered the information to Pierre, Frontenac was suffering from inflammation of the veins of both legs. What the doctor had prescribed so far appeared to make sense: complete rest in the recumbent position, splints applied to both legs to reduce the possibility of injury from accidental movement, and elevating the legs.

"We will hold off on applying fomentations until tomorrow, Excellency," declared Dr. Blaise. "In the hopes that a good night's sleep will ease the pain."

"How can I sleep with the pain?" Frontenac asked.

"Tonight I shall give you laudanum."

As the doctor carried on, one of the front-door guards appeared and went to Major Boulanger, whispering to him at length. The guard withdrew. Boulanger glanced Pierre's way and cleared his throat.

"General, *ahem* . . . I'm afraid bad news has just arrived."

Frontenac shut the doctor up with a wave of his hand. "Yes, Hertel?"

"It . . . concerns Captain Lacroix, mainly."

"Well, what is it? Speak up, man."

"Word has just arrived that the *Aventurier* was attacked by savages on its way up the Hudson. All on board were massacred."

The group gasped as one, the priests crossed themselves, everyone looked at Pierre.

He swallowed. "My wife . . ."

"All massacred?" Frontenac asked. "Are you sure?"

"That's what they say. *Coureurs de bois* found the burnt skeleton of the ship, corpses strewn about."

"My God," whispered Pierre.

"The ship got stuck," Boulanger went on, "and evidently, while the crew was attempting to dislodge it, the savages attacked."

"May I be excused, General?" Pierre asked.

"Yes, yes, go."

He hurried out, Boulanger following. The major set a hand on his shoulder and moved them out of earshot of the front entrance guards.

"I'm so sorry, Pierre." Boulanger shook his head. "A woman's body was found still clutching her rosary beads."

"Rosary beads? Margaret was not Catholic."

Boulanger shrugged. "Perhaps she converted."

"She said nothing about it in her letters." He covered his face with his hands.

"Let's go back to my office. I've a new bottle of Calvados."

"I was beginning to worry," said Pierre, following him. "They should have been here two weeks ago."

"This place is a bitch, plague take it," burst Boulanger. "No place for humans. I can't wait to get relieved and Jeanette and me on a ship bound for home."

"Incroyable," mused Pierre, not hearing him. They'd held their breaths waiting for the war to end so Frontenac could no longer deny them his permission to marry. Now this. Hertel was the smart one, marrying a local beauty, an option the general had no control over. Poor, poor Margaret. It was no easy trek from New York City but she'd have had a twelve-man escort. They'd sailed upriver through hostile territory, granted, but by the time they reached the first falls, at whatever the savages called it, and portaged, they'd be only two lakes and the Richelieu River away from the St. Lawrence.

A massacre . . .

When the two of them got to Boulanger's office and sat down and the major got out tumblers and the bottle, Pierre's heart was thrashing wildly, and he could feel heat in his face. Again and again he shook his head.

"Are you all right?" Boulanger asked.

Boulanger poured the cider, tasted it and made a face. "Tastes like a toad drowned in it. Sorry, old man, it's all I've got."

"It's all right. I'm not in the mood anyway." Pierre rose to his feet.

"You're not going . . . ?"

"I appreciate your concern, Hertel. I don't want to seem ungrateful but, if you don't mind, I'd like to be my myself."

"Of course."

Pierre left the fort, taking the path west toward the Lorette Huron castle. Feeling a need for consolation other than that the major and his inferior Calvados could provide.

90

To Margaret, standing a stone's throw from it, Fort Frontenac looked distressingly ramshackle and neglected. Duty in such a rundown place, so far from civilization, had to be as bad as solitary confinement. Although Two Eagles had crossed the St. Lawrence many times in raids on settlements, he had never had occasion to travel the river and this was his first glimpse of the fort, as well.

The fort was constructed of logs and rambled in all directions in haphazard additions. The muzzles of four cannons pointed at the lake. No flag fluttered from the pole, no sounds of activity came from within.

He had started for the main gate. She hurried to catch up. "It looks deserted."

"They may all be behind doors."

"But shouldn't there be sentries?"

"I do not think they expect an attack."

"Don't walk so fast. You'll be rid of me soon enough. Remember, I'll do the talking."

He walked boldly in the open gate without a glance left or right. She followed hesitantly. Inside, they wandered from dusty room to room, at length coming to the mess hall, seeing no sign of recent occupancy, no clothing, no food or drink about. The only sound was the wind blowing over the palisade into the little parade ground.

"I knew it," she murmured. "They've abandoned it. Isn't this just my luck!"

Would the Oneidas have to escort her all the way? The possibility suddenly threatened in earnest.

"Let us go look at the barracks," he said.

"Do you think there'll be bodies?"

Not a sign of conflict anywhere, no discarded weapons, no bloodstains. It looked like the personnel had simply picked up and left. Why? No treaty had been reached.

Thrown Bear and others had said that the fighting could resume at any time. Why would the French desert such a strategically situated post that commanded view of the entire northeast corner of the lake and both banks of the river? And when not in military use, the fort was purportedly the fur-trading center of the area. Had it become too expensive and distant for the government of New France to man?

"I just don't understand," she said over and over.

They walked down a hallway toward a door marked COMMANDANTE. Two Eagles opened it and went in. Sunlight flooded in through the window onto a dusty desktop. All the drawers had been pulled open, all were empty. He looked out at the lake. "Look," he said pointing. On the beach a single canoe was pulled halfway out of the water.

No sooner was the word out of his mouth than a side door burst wide and two braves brandishing knives came running in screaming.

"Get out!" he shouted to her.

She backed toward the door, her teeth chattering absurdly. She watched in horror as, unable to get out his knife, he ducked under the first attacker and shoved his ribs against the brave's midsection, knocking him into the other one, who went down, his elbow hitting the floor, knocking his knife from his grasp.

She moved to retrieve it; he yelled.

"Back! Back!"

The first brave whirled about, slashing the air. His knife barely missed Two Eagles' shoulder. Up came the Oneida's knee, hammering the other's groin. The brave screamed, doubling over in agony. Two Eagles jerked out his knife and plunged it into his attacker's belly. Pulling it out, releasing a freshet of blood, gloving his hand crimson. As the brave dropped, Two Eagles pivoted, lifted his knife high with both hands and, falling downward, drove it hilt-deep into the second brave's heart.

He lay atop him for fully ten seconds while Margaret stood staring transfixed. Then he got to his feet, wiped the blade between thumb and forefinger and sheathed it.

Margaret gagged, vomited and stumbled off down the hallway.

91

H uron snakes," Two Eagles murmured. They walked toward the beached canoe. "You feel better?"

Embarrassed, she held reply. The dead men had worn breechclouts and their hair was shaved on both sides of their heads to a center strip like that worn by Mohawk braves. But these two wore two feathers: white with wide painted red tips.

The canoe appeared to be in good condition. It was made of white birch bark, lighter and sleeker looking than Iroquoian canoes. In it they found a tooth-ball tomahawk, an almost exact duplicate of Splitting Moon's that was lost in the storm. They also found bows and arrows and a number of small paddle-like objects on the floor at one end.

"Beaver tails," he explained. "They are burned in a fire till they are black, the skin peeled off, then the tail is boiled. It tastes good." He smiled. "As good as *sateeni*."

"Disgusting, the poor little creatures. They're so clever and work so hard and they slaughter them and you do and the French."

"The English. Get in carefully. You will help paddle."

"I don't know how."

"You have seen us. Does it look so hard? You kneel in the front and paddle on the shore side. I will steer."

"First, would you mind . . . ?"

"What?"

She grimaced. "Get rid of those . . . things."

"You."

She picked them up by her fingertips, dropping them one by one into the water. When the bottom was empty she got in, taking up a paddle.

"Wait," he said. "Stay here, I am going back. They may

have left behind some musket powder and balls. We will need them going on." He trotted away toward the fort.

Her heart quickened: He'd already made up his mind to go on to Quebec. Would the others after what had happened to Thrown Bear?

He must expect to encounter trouble, else why go back to look for more ammunition? How many settlements would they have to pass, under how many guns? Montreal, she knew, lay between here and Quebec. And at least a dozen other settlements, all heavily armed against attack from the south.

If only she could get word to Pierre, have him send an escort down for her. She could send the Oneidas home with heartfelt thanks. And never see them again. She'd grown fond of them, enjoying their protection like that of big brothers.

She would miss them. She saw Two Eagles coming back and thought how dreadfully she would miss him; his caring and strength.

He held up a metal box. "Powder and balls!"

They set out to round the big island for the spot where they had landed swimming over. About two hundred yards from shore her upper arms began aching. She gritted her teeth, she could stand it. She got up from her knees to paddle sitting.

He was silent behind her.

The soft sounds of their paddles dipping in unison clashed with the swallows bickering high up in a tree.

"You do not have to paddle," he said at last.

"I want to help."

"Your arms are already hurting. I can see it in your back. You will suffer much pain tonight. And you will grow *wakó-kas*." He rubbed his thumb against his finger.

"Blisters."

"*Nyoh*. We still have far to go, stop paddling."

"I must . . ."

"All right, all right."

The day lengthened, the birds flocked and rested, the shadows grew longer. It did seem a long way back, paddling southwest against the current between the small island and the big one, clear round the latter.

At length, when the darkness had settled over the land and the moon silvered the lake, they finished rounding the big island and started up the south fork, now aided by the current. The others had come down to the shore. As they drew closer and exchanged handwaves, she saw Splitting Moon. She could see him clearly in the moonlight, and he looked a portrait of disappointment.

"Do not tell Tyagohuens about the *ga-ja´-wa* we found for him."

"The tooth-ball tomahawk. Yes, we'll surprise him."

Perhaps pick up his spirits? She noticed Two Eagles was more and more lately calling his friends by their Indian names, using Oneida words for obvious things. What made him decide to teach her his language at this late date?

"Margaret, Tyagohuens will want to go back. He will make a big speech. Be prepared for him to fill all our ears with his protests. But they are only noise. In the end, he always goes along with the rest of us."

"I wouldn't feel right about forcing any of them."

"He will force himself. He likes to carry on. You should know that by now. And listen, when we land, *I* will do the talking. You will say nothing. Just walk away so that you cannot hear us. Go pick flowers."

"Yes."

92

Margaret did as he asked. She walked off feeling worse than ever about the situation, distressingly selfish. He was asking them to go back to war for her, practically. There was sure to be more fighting, more casualties. But she couldn't go on alone. Even if they gave her the canoe, she couldn't paddle hour after hour like they did. The woodlands must be full of hunting parties, especially this time of year, with winter just ahead. She picked wildflowers aimlessly, yellow daisies and blazing stars, which reminded her of home—filling her fist with them. There was one possibility: If she made it to the first settlement, whatever it was, she could get her escort there. She dropped the flowers and stood straight up. That was the answer!

Anger Maker was shouting, Splitting Moon shouted back; she could see Two Eagles trying to act as peacemaker between them. They quieted down. He had given Splitting Moon the tomahawk, but it didn't appear to improve his mood. Now everyone was talking at once in low tones. Two Eagles was nodding his head vigorously.

Anger Maker called out. "Margaret!"

She ran to them.

"We are all going on," said Two Eagles.

"I did not say I was!" burst Splitting Moon.

"You know you are," said Anger Maker, "it is settled."

"No," she said quietly. "Give me a chance, please. What is the first settlement we would pass on the way?"

Anger Maker who evidently was familiar with the river said, "Gananoque. Where the islands are like corn in a basket."

"Gananoque. The people are French?"

"In every settlement up here," said Two Eagles. "We are in Canada, in New France."

"Good. How far is Gananoque?"

"Less than half a morning," said Anger Maker.

"All of you listen, please. If you can get me as far as Gananoque, I'll get my escort there for the rest of the way." She turned to Two Eagles. "Remember, I speak French. If I just mention the governor's name . . ."

"*Neh.*"

"May I finish?"

"You have said enough, it is a bad idea."

"It's the perfect solution. It means you won't have to risk your lives on my account after all."

"It is *your* life you would be risking. And you think speaking their language would help you? Not with their kind. They are not peaceful farmers who will welcome you. They are like the trappers: thieves, liars, murderers.

Worse, for you. You would be as safe with them as with the Ottawa dogshit eaters."

"He is right," said Anger Maker. "Anyone of them would slit your throat to sell your hair for money."

The others nodded, except for Splitting Moon, who seemed dedicated to holding out to the last.

"I don't believe any of you," she snapped. "You're just saying that to frighten me."

"Why would we do that?" Two Eagles asked.

She could not think of an answer.

"You think that from here to Quebec is like running a gauntlet," he went on. "That we will be like war captives who must run between women beating us with sticks and switches. It will not be like that. The river is so wide we can avoid every settlement."

"Most are on the north bank," said Red Paint. "Except the Sokoki Abnakis to the south."

"The downriver current is strong here," said Two Eagles. "We can make as far in one sleep as it took us five to get home from Onekahoncka after we found you."

"But that's only half of it," she protested. "Even if we make it to Quebec you'll all have to return. Against the current."

Two Eagles shrugged. "It can be done. Your friend Frontenac did it. How do you think he came to Massowaganine to the peace conference? Are his men better paddlers than we are? Why are you now against the idea?"

"I . . . didn't think about what we might be coming up against. Hasn't it been terrifically hard getting this far, through friendly territory? If it hadn't been for Sergeant Duncan the Ottawas would have massacred us. Now we have to invade their territory."

"No more talk. It is late. Tomorrow we must build two canoes. We can build them in one day."

"Two Eagles . . ."

"I said no more talk. Are you hungry?"

"Famished."

"If that is hungry, then eat." He smiled. "You should not

have thrown away those beaver tails. They really are very good."

Should she steal a Huron canoe and flee in the night? She would probably drown before she got ten miles downriver. Besides, they'd be certain to come after her.

He simply couldn't resist the challenge. To desert her at this point and return home would be cowardly. He would lose precious face. Men. Wherever they came from in the world, whatever their tribe, their standing, their intelligence, their influence, they were all the same.

"All idiots!"

 **93**

Governor-general Frontenac's condition was not improving; his legs kept their owner on his back and in pain. His lungs conspired to send up a wracking cough. Dr. Blaise hovered over his patient for hours shaking his head, putting on an expression that he hoped others would interpret as combining compassion with wisdom, and poking both legs with a tongue depressor repeatedly asking, "Does this hurt?" It did, the patient told him.

Pierre watched the playlet all week and decided that the old man was on his way out. He would not see October at the rate he was slipping. Blaise could do little to ease the inflammation in his throat. Frontenac did not complain; whining over his discomfort was beneath him, but he was not about to grope for optimism. This Pierre could see in his rheumy eyes.

The two Jesuits had brought the Bishop to see the patient. To Pierre, although their intentions were good, their black presence and the heavy crosses around their necks and their rosaries mutely spoke of the hereafter, which did little to cheer the old man.

"Peter," he said, "I'm sure you've better things to do than stand and watch me shrivel on the vine day in, day out. Go. Take a walk, get some fresh air." He winked and attempted a smile. "Stick your nose into the office and see if General Desmaines is doing his job. My job."

Pierre chuckled. "Espionage, sir?"

"Tomorrow I'll either be dead or up and dancing the gavotte."

He began coughing. Dr. Blaise filled a spoon with reddish medicine and got most of it down the patient's throat. It tasted vile, but it stopped his hacking. He lifted a hand feebly, dismissing his aide. Pierre saluted and withdrew.

 **94**

Major Boulanger eyed the center of his personal universe in his mirror, clicked the little pair of scissors resembling a peacock and carefully snipped.

"Parfait!"

"Are we going to play backgammon or must I sit here all day watching you fiddle with your face?" Pierre rasped.

"Sorry, old man. All done."

"Your throw." Pierre disliked his friend's office: too small, cramped.

The dice came up a doublet. With a flourish, the major moved two stones. "This is turning out to be the Massacre of the Huguenots," he murmured, smirking.

"It's not over yet. You're on a blot. Watch me knock you out on this throw."

The game didn't interest Pierre enough to take seriously. It passed the time, as did napping and cards and drinking. For he had resumed drinking "in earnest," as Boulanger put it, three days after the general took to his bed.

"It's none of my business, old man," said the major, "but we *are* friends and friends don't shy away from frankness and . . ."

"And what? Damn, these dice are jinxed!"

"I can't help noticing that a certain three-stripe friend and colleague is rapidly slipping back into his old ways."

"I'm in mourning."

"Really? I would have thought you were celebrating something."

"That's not nice, Hertel. Am I not allowed to mourn in my own way? Would you rather I bury myself in church?"

"I'm sorry."

"Deciding to accept my loss and go on with my life is no sin. I loved poor Margaret, couldn't wait for her to get here, but it wasn't to be. There's nothing I can do to change things."

"Agreed, agreed. I just don't see what this has to do with Margaret or mourning."

"This?"

"You slipping back into your old ways. I hear you brought your fair Indian maid to your quarters last night. Half the guard saw her slipping out just before reveille."

"So?"

"So that way lies disaster. Need I remind you you came within a butcher's inch of getting booted out? You did a complete aboutface. . . ."

Up came Pierre's hand stopping him. "Please, no lecture." He drained his tumbler. Boulanger refilled it with Calvados, a brand that was a distinct improvement over the last bottle. "Consider my situation, Hertel. The old war horse is as good as dead. I'm out of a job. I've just lost the only woman in the world who means a thing to me. What would you have me do, crawl under a rock? No thank you. I'm going back to enjoying life. What can Louis do, break me and cashier me from the grave? Somehow I don't think that's a danger."

"He could recover."

"Could he? You haven't seen him since last Monday. I visit every day. He's going downhill like an avalanche. By this time next week, they'll be draping him with the flag and blowing the bugle over him with not a dry eye in the cemetery. Your toss."

95

The Huron birchbark canoe was set on the ground and eighteen two-foot stakes driven around it, framing it. Two red elm trees were burnt down with fire rings. Two sections of bark of a size necessary to build a fourteen-foot canoe were carefully peeled away. The rough outside bark was scraped off, and torches made of waste bark were then applied to both inner surfaces to toast and flatten them. Meanwhile, a single white ash was felled to supply rim pieces about the width of a hand to run around the edge, outside and in and, using bark twine from the same tree, stitched through and through to secure them to the body of the canoe.

Margaret was fascinated with the process of the work. Two Eagles had divided the men into two three-man crews, with Red Paint in charge of his crew and of the other, Fox, whom she could see had the most experience for the job. Red Paint enjoyed being in charge, barking orders to Splitting Moon and Bone. Pitched into a position of authority, he behaved like a young boy. Bone took Red Paint's instructions and comments good-naturedly. He seemed a changed man since becoming friendly with Swift Doe, not so private and lonely. Swift Doe was bringing him out of himself.

Two Eagles had told her that he considered him one of the brightest people he'd ever met. It was a pity he didn't understand English, nor she Oneida or Mohican, precluding any chance at real conversation between them.

The canoe ribs consisted of narrow strips of ash, set a foot apart along the bottom of the canoe and secured under the side rim. Once the bark was set in the framing stakes, the work of fastening the gunwales began. Temporary spreaders were set in the required places, which would give way later to the well-formed thwarts, pierced at the ends and sewn through the bark, the cords passing over the gunwales.

Fox she found intriguing, mainly because of all the stories that went around about his conquests of women much older than he.

As the day wore on, the work advanced with dispatch, though more complicated than she had imagined: lining the bark with long strips of basket splints; laying the lining under the ribs to protect the vessel from abrasion; laying the sheathing, difficult to fasten at bow and stern without splitting the ends.

Anger Maker approached her, his hands moving aimlessly with nothing to occupy them, without his pipe to puff on—which made conversation with him welcome for a change. Notwithstanding his reputation, she found him a gentle giant. He picked up a discarded strip of wood and knelt, motioning her to do likewise. He drew a long line in the dirt with an egg-shaped outline at one end.

"The Kanawage."

"Saint Lawrence."

"Saint Law-rence." He indicated the first few inches up from the lake. "Here are all islands, as many as the flies on Eye-patch's corpse."

"Are there rapids?"

He frowned, puzzled. She mimed falling water.

"No ra-pids. For three sleeps we will travel without stopping, except to eat and sleep. But there are many rocks and the paddler at the front must keep his eyes wide. Whoever is in the Huron canoe must, it is not made for ra-pids. Too light. From here there are no more islands but the rapids begin. Going downriver, as we will go, they are easy to get over. Coming back, we will have to portage around them." He marked an X. "Here is Hochelaga, where the mountain is that the lace-cuffs call royal."

"Montreal."

"Passing there, we will stay close to the bank on this side. Farther on, here, is where three rivers come together. There are villages on both sides. We stay in the middle of the river. We go on. Here is Stadacona."

"Quebec?"

He nodded. "On the far bank. But between . . ."

"Montreal . . ."

"And Stadocona are places with big ra-pids. We will have to portage around them."

"How many leagues from here to Quebec, do you make it?"

He furrowed his brow, shrugged, held up six fingers, changed his mind, held up seven. "So many sleeps."

"That's not long at all. For some reason, I thought it would take at least twice that." She lowered her voice. "Sa-ga-na-qua-de . . ." He seemed pleased at hearing his name from her in his language. "Tell me the truth, is Tékni-ska-je-a-nah right? Will there be no danger?"

He looked uncomfortable. "The ra-pids between Hochelaga and Stadocona . . ."

"I don't mean the river, you know what I mean."

He shrugged. "Ask Tékni-ska-je-a-nah."

"I'm asking you."

"I do not know."

"Will we see many Ottawas?"

Aiming an anxious look at Two Eagles, he too lowered his voice.

"The tribes here . . ." He indicated the stretch from before Montreal to Quebec. "They are mostly Ottawa, some Huron snakes, like the two you and Tékni-ska-je-a-nah found at the fort."

"Are they more dangerous than the Ottawas?"

Two Eagles had come over. "Are we building canoes?" he asked Anger Maker.

Anger Maker smiled sheepishly and went back to work.

"He says we'll see Ottawas and Hurons," said Margaret.

"*Nyoh*, they will see *us*, we will pass them by."

"How does he know so much about the river?"

"He is the only one of us who has been down it almost to Quebec. He was captured with others by the French in a raid near here. They took them almost all the way down-river to work building a fort at Quebec. There was a storm near some rapids. Their canoes tipped over. Many escaped. That was the closest he ever got to Quebec."

"Until now."

"Until now." He jabbed his thumb against his chest. "*I* look forward to seeing it. All these years I have heard so much about it."

96

The moon painted the lake. The second canoe was finished, removed from the frame and turned over. Red Paint and Fox began gumming the stitched seams, rendering them waterproof. Bone and Splitting Moon carved the four paddles out of ash. The tedious job would not be completed until morning, with a few hours off for sleep.

While the others slept, Two Eagles and Margaret sat looking out over the lake. Two Eagles never seemed to tire. He was in a somber mood. With the day's activities behind them, was he back to thinking about Thrown Bear? A mosquito lit on her upper arm. She slapped and scratched. It drew his attention.

"*Wa'tkata'tenake,*" she murmured.

" 'I scratched myself.' Where did you learn that?"

"Do-wa-sku-ta."

Immediately, she regretted mentioning Thrown Bear. "He survived," she said quietly. "I feel it in my bones. You know how resourceful he is, how tough."

"In your bones." He tapped his heart. "I wish I could feel it in here. And not what is in there now. A stone I should cut out with my knife."

Impulsively, she set her hand on his arm. "He's alive."

He grunted. "We must sleep. The paddles will be finished early. We will travel through the islands all day. More than half as far as from Onekahoncka to Onneyutta-hage."

He lay down and was asleep. Supporting herself on one arm, she studied him. There were things about him, qualities, abilities no man she'd ever known had. He was the strongest man she'd ever seen; lifting one end of the canoe log, carrying it into the open while it took three, including the powerful Splitting Moon, to carry the other end. If tragedy touched him he failed to show it like others. To the death of his wife he reacted with the stoicism of a martyr of old. Eight Minks said fittingly: "He is even stronger inside than out."

He stood taller than other men, in the way of rulers and generals and great intellects.

He had qualities she didn't like, his temper and stubbornness, but vanity was not among them. Dear, darling Pierre was vain, of course anyone as handsome and dashing as he had justification. Two Eagles was handsome, becoming more so in her eyes as time went on, though she couldn't explain that. Apart from all else, he seemed to personify his people: *the* Oneida warrior-chief. Surely, John Riley back home, who captured so capably kings and statesmen on canvas, could do honor to his portrait, depict the real Two Eagles.

Watching him sleep, she felt a twinge of regret for Thrown Bear and one of conscience for contending that he was still alive; when in her heart she thought otherwise. But he was so sad about him, she had to say something hopeful.

"You . . ." she murmured. "You fine and gentle and brazen and courageous and considerate and obstinate and intelligent and single-minded creation of God's hand. What a man you are." She owed him what she could never possibly repay, her life.

She bent and kissed him lightly on the forehead.

"Sir Galahad."

He did not stir.

97

Thick and motionless was the fog snugging the river when Margaret and the Oneidas awoke. The fog was still as dense as wood smoke when, an hour later, Splitting Moon and Bone pronounced the last two paddles finished. The weapons and supplies were loaded aboard the three canoes and, with Margaret sitting in the middle and Splitting Moon paddling the bow, Two Eagles pushed them off.

She let her hand slip through the water as they glided out into mid-stream. Forward to Quebec, the final leg, journey's end, and at long last, Pierre.

"Slowly," Two Eagles called to the others in the canoes following, "until we can see better ahead."

Like a woman of rare beauty slowly raising her veil, the fog lifted, revealing the first cluster of islands through which they would weave all day. Autumn's early colors showed on tufts of land crowded with oak, elm and large white ash, every island so thickly wooded there appeared scarcely room for another sapling.

Stately blue herons perched on slender legs and plucked breakfast from the river. Beautiful crested, iridescent green, purple and blue wood ducks abounded. Birds filled the morning with their music. And everywhere wildflowers; nature in all her splendor. Margaret reveled in it, pointing out one sight after another, eliciting only passive grunts from her two companions. Behind them, the two new canoes were holding up as well as their birchbark one. About an hour after departing, well after the fog had lifted, rounding a bend they came upon a grassy area along the right bank, richly green and strewn with mica-studded boulders.

Splitting Moon called out, pointing toward the bank. Two Eagles steered for the bank. Splitting Moon was carrying on loudly, gesticulating, jabbing his index finger toward something. Shading her eyes, she saw what was exciting his attention.

Sitting on a boulder was a man, an Indian, his back against a flat rock that rose like a throne to a height of about six feet behind him. He sat with his legs tucked under him, his arms at his sides, eyes straight ahead, as if in a trance. They rapidly drew closer. Splitting Moon's shouting turned his face toward them.

Thrown Bear.

98

Recognizing his friends, he called weakly, "Tékni-ska-je-a-nahhhhhh, Tyagohuensssss ..."

"Do-wa-sku-ta!" burst Splitting Moon, dropping his paddle and shooting to his feet, shaking the canoe.

Now they were directly in front of him. She watched transfixed as Thrown Bear slowly raised his stump. Then raised his hand. No hand; it too was a stump, blackened at the end, caked with what looked to be pitch or black mud. With agony etching his face, leaning for support against the stone at his back, he lifted both legs. Just enough to reveal that both feet had been severed, the stumps blackened like his wrist stump.

"Tékni-ska-je-a-nahhhhhh," he called again, his voice piercing her heart. And he added something in Oneida she could not understand.

Sickened by the sight, she turned to Two Eagles. In horror, unable to speak, to intervene, she watched as Two Eagles picked up his bow, nocked an arrow, drew, let fly.

"Nooooooo!" she screamed.

The shaft sank into Thrown Bear's chest, stiffening him. The suffering on his face eased, the start of a smile softening his features. Over he fell, rolling off the rock to the ground.

Lowering his bow, Two Eagles flung it overboard.

99

Murderer!" she screamed, the echo shouting it from all sides. She jumped up, rocking the canoe. Splitting Moon grabbed her shoulders, drawing her down. Two Eagles stared at Thrown Bear's mutilated body.

"Why? Why?" she shouted.

"He begged Two Eagles to kill him," murmured Anger

Maker, as his canoe came up on theirs, the paddlers holding their place against the current.

"But . . ."

"Who would want to live like that?" Red Paint asked her. The others grunted, nodded.

She turned again to Two Eagles. Slowly, he got back down on his knees. They headed for the bank.

"His woman was right," said Splitting Moon. "She said he would die and you . . ."

"Ogechta!" the others snapped in chorus.

Splitting Moon sealed his lips. They landed and pulled up the canoes. The stood in a semicircle looking down at the body. Two Eagles still had not uttered a sound.

"The dogshit eaters did this," growled Splitting Moon. "Back before they ambushed us. He was lagging behind, they cut him off."

"Nyoh, nyoh," rasped Anger Maker. "Why tell us what we already know?"

Thrown Bear's captors had pitched all three stumps, obviously to keep him alive until the Oneidas passed this spot.

"How did they know we planned to come down the St. Lawrence?" she asked Two Eagles.

Without responding, he knelt beside the body, setting his hand on the dead man's cheek. Fox called from close by. He held up Thrown Bear's severed feet.

"His hand is here, too."

"We will bury them with him," said Red Paint.

They loosened the earth with their knives and, using the paddles for shovels, dug a grave about five feet deep and in it placed Thrown Bear seated, with his knees drawn up, his severed hand in his lap. Unable to watch, she walked off, occupying herself with picking wildflowers.

Unlike Splitting Moon, Two Eagles had never conceded that Thrown Bear was dead. As depressed as he became, he had maintained a spark of hope. Hadn't she herself fanned that spark, her heart holding the same optimism? Now he was dead; his wish. To go on living without hands or feet would have been intolerable for anybody. He preferred death. Two Eagles accommodated him. An heroic act. But one it would be painful to live with.

Could she kill a friend to save him?

A yellow summer warbler perched on the back of the throne, flicking its tail, raising its *sweet-sweet-sweet* song to the sun. Then it cocked its head and eyed her inquisitively.

A nightmare in this idyllic setting. The grave filled in, they started for the canoes, leaving Two Eagles looking down at the mounded earth. So still he looked as if he was not even breathing. No sound came from him.

The birds sang, the breeze played among the trees, the river slipped by on its way to the distant ocean. For hours he stood looking down while the others waited patiently. The sun climbed its path and was poised directly overhead when at last he looked up.

He turned from the grave, lifting his head in a terrifying primal scream. Then he walked off away from the river. Locating the tallest tree, he climbed it almost to the top, jammed his knife into the trunk, descended and headed down the bank toward the canoes.

"Tékni-sha-je-a-nah," murmured Fox, "it is time to eat."

He stopped, nodded. They got the Ottawas' pot out of one of the canoes, started a fire, cooked venison, warmed succotash and ate. He said nothing.

She watched him. Would he never speak again?

══ 100 ══

Two Eagles and Splitting Moon rested their paddles, letting the current carry them. Late-afternoon shadows banded the river. Still he had not uttered a sound. Had he taken a vow of silence? They were still traveling through the islands and, with the delay, would not see the end of them today, so Anger Maker assured her.

They camped that night on an island, selecting the smallest they could find. No fire was lit. There was no conversation. The moon wore a ragged cloud mask, the breeze rested, they slept.

Not until early afternoon of the next day did they put the last of the islands behind them, passing a tiny settlement on the distant north bank, little more than a collection of shacks; no protective palisade, no sign of life. It slipped behind them out of sight. The river narrowed. The rapids ahead would slow them, in particular the three between Montreal and Quebec, but here no rocks disturbed the quiet water sliding between crags and shadowed by woodlands.

The canoes now traveled side by side, Margaret's in the middle. Anger Maker, on their right, called over to her.

"No ra-pids, I told you. Water like this the rest of today and all day tomorrow. Then we will come to small rapids."

"No big ones till Montreal," she said.

He grinned. "Hochelaga." She repeated it to please him. "And some before Hochelaga," he added.

"Will we have to portage?"

"At Lachine, maybe. That is where we raided in the war. There the ra-pids are strong and very long. You will see. When the land becomes flat again listen for the sound."

Vines festooned the trees on both banks. Splitting Moon had told her earlier that wild grapes grew everywhere, even near Onneyuttahage, and were in season now. The paddlers let the current carry the canoes around a long bend in the river.

To come upon a sight that caused her to swallow painfully hard.

Six canoes.

"Dogshit eaters," growled Splitting Moon.

For the first time since Thrown Bear was discovered sitting against the rock, Two Eagles spoke. "Lie down," he ordered her. "Face down! Do not talk or move until I tell you." He knelt with his paddle across the gunwales looking out from under his hand. The Ottawas' canoes were moving closer. Red Paint called out. Two Eagles looked behind him. Eight more canoes carrying four men each, two standing, bows drawn, arrows aimed. Within seconds they were surrounded.

"What is happening?" she asked, raising her head slightly, and saw the Ottawas paddling closer, tightening the ring. Her heart was suddenly thumping so she thought the others must hear it. Was this to be as far as she would get? "No!"

"Shhhh . . . !" He pushed her down. "Stay down, if you do not want an arrow through you."

"*Sa-dogga-cho-sa!* came a voice as brittle as a dry twig snapping.

Again, she raised her head. He growled but this time didn't push her back down. Slipping through the circle came a canoe fully thirty feet long, gliding swiftly, powered by two muscular giants. Seated in the middle was a wizened little man, a chief, from his headdress and ornate attire, although sitting hunched forward as he was, he looked more like a wolf spider squatting at the hub of its web. Small brown feathers descending from his temples framed his face and gleaming coal-black eyes. He was ancient, his face so dark and deeply wrinkled it was almost impossible to make out his features.

"*Sa-dogga-cho-sa!*" Up came one withered talon commandingly.

She sat up.

As bizarre as he appeared, he could not hold her attention, for standing behind him was a towering priest in his robes resembling a giant black stork, his emaciated face paper white, his eyes jet, pink-rimmed, huge, hypnotic.

The sight of him and the threat of death encircling her set her trembling. Struggling for control, she cleared her throat and in a tremulous voice addressed the priest in French. He was staring at her piercingly, his long arms folded across his chest. For a long moment, like a sword suspended from a thread, silence hung in the air. And the warriors held their aim.

The priest coughed and then replied.

"What did he say?" Two Eagles asked.

"Be quiet," she rasped. "I'll handle this."

Again she addressed him. Now he spoke in turn to the chief, then to the warriors, gesturing for them to lower their bows. Not one moved. She could feel drops of sweat falling from her chin onto her chest, while ice ascended her spine. At last the chief shouted an order. The bows and arrows angled toward them dropped. A second order, and the arrows were restored to their quivers. She sighed in relief, and again spoke to the priest, explaining their presence, the purpose of their journey.

At the word *Quebec* the old man broke into a grin so broad it threatened to crack his furrowed face.

"Stadacona, Stadacona."

"Quebec."

"Stadacona," repeated the chief. "Fron-ten-ac. *Mon ami* Fron-ten-ac."

The priest eyed her appraisingly. "You speak French but you are not French."

"I am English."

"Ahhh. Are you a Catholic?"

"Catholique!" burst the chief. And waggled a large wooden crucifix. *"Chrétien!"*

"My husband is."

"You're not."

"No."

"Are you planning to join the Holy Mother Church?"

"No."

"A pity." He smiled toothily. "Ah, but your husband will not convert to Protestantism. You will not ask him to."

"No."

"Catholique!" sang the chief. *"Chrétien. Jésus Christ!"*

"Perhaps the day will come when you will convert to our religion, the 'true' religion. The former Mother Superior at the Ursuline Convent in Quebec was an English convert. May I ask your name?"

"Addison-Lacroix. Margaret."

"La-qua, a most distinguished name. 'The cross.' Interesting, an omen for your future conversion? Forgive me, I am detaining you. I bid you *adieu*, Madame Lacroix, and safe journey. And do not worry about Indians. My children along these banks will not harm you. But downriver live the Tete de Boule Cree, the Huron and the Sokoki Abnaki across from them. I'm afraid I cannot guarantee your safety traveling through their lands. Catholics or not, all are enemies of the Iroquois."

"Catholique! Jésus Christ! Dieu!"

"And watch for the rapids ahead. And beyond, just this side of Montreal, are the Lachine Rapids. They go on for five leagues."

"That far?"

"And strong. You will want to portage."

"Chrétien!"

"Definitely, around the rapids between Montreal and Quebec. Three spots."

"I'll remember. You've been very helpful, Father . . ."

"Gilbert. Of the Order of Sulpicians. The seigneury of Montreal is our order's. The Sulpicians were founded by the blessed Abbé Olier. Do forgive my chattering. God go with you to your destination and your husband, Madame. God bless your reunion. Tonight I shall pray to St. Denis for your safe arrival in Quebec. *Adieu*, Madame Lacroix."

"Adieu, Father Gilbert."

Off went the chief's canoe followed by his fleet of warriors.

Two Eagles grunted. "Dogshit eaters . . . black robe . . ."

"That 'black robe' just saved our skins. Ah." She dismissed him with both hands. "Let's get out of here."

"I give the orders, not you." All eyes fixed on him expectantly. "Go on, *Ísene!*"

She resumed sitting and had to stifle a laugh with her fist. Paddling at the bow, Splitting Moon said something in Oneida.

"I know, I know!" burst Two Eagles.

Curious, she leaned forward to tap Splitting Moon on the shoulder.

"I just told him he should be grateful to you. You saved all our lives."

101

Here, in a glade of young elms, was privacy incomparable, a quite accidental discovery of which Captain Pierre Lacroix was once more taking full advantage. Looking through the trees to the brook he could see the pool where he had first come upon Two Buttons bathing. Little Cloud, her grandfather had called her, and there *was* something ephemeral about her, as pure as a white cloud or had been before he conquered her. He smiled to himself. Now, not so pure, and Two Buttons suited her better.

She was indeed a conquest, not like the others he bedded, Indians and town women, who smelled and scratched and pretended interest, whores, one and all. Not Two Buttons, she was his . . .

"Concubine. *Precisement*."

Her lovely eyes questioned as she looked up. He patted her cheek, ran his hand down from her shoulder, over her small breast, her velvety stomach, down her vee, feeling its moistness. She shivered deliciously. Worship was in her eyes, in her eagerness to please, her pliancy; whatever he wished, she gave. She made him feel her lord and master as Margaret never had. And it had taken some mighty and inspired persuading to get *her* into bed. Now dear Margaret was dead, poor soul, her bones rotting in some corner of the forest.

"Poor darling."

"Dar-ling?"

"Are you my darling, you delicious little creature? Lie back."

He was preparing to mount her when a voice called.

"*Capitaine . . . Capitaine* Lacroix . . ."

Twigs snapped underfoot, branches swished. It was Nez, embarrassed and nervous. Pierre sat up. Two Buttons snatched her clothes, covering herself. Nez turned his head to avoid looking at her and addressed the tree beside him.

"You must come back at once, sir."

"Goddamn you, you beak-nosed imbecile, how dare you come barging . . ."

"His Excellency wants you."

"How did you find me?"

"I . . . followed the children, sir." Nez pointed through the trees at the large bush. Four little faces poked through the trees, giggling, then vanished.

"Goddamn my soul!"

Major Boulanger came up behind Nez, ignoring Two Buttons completely. "Get your clothes on, Pierre."

He was already fumbling into his things. Two Buttons sprinted away.

"Damn! Now see what you've done!"

"On your feet!" bawled Boulanger. He softened his tone. "Listen to me, the general's been yelling for you for an hour."

Pierre closed his fly and buckled his belt. "If this is a joke, Hertel, it's in the poorest possible taste."

"It's no joke. He's recovered. He's back at his desk and he wants you."

"He can't be. He's on his death bed. I saw him."

"He's completely recovered. The way he's carrying on, you'd think he was never sick.

"Impossible! If this is a joke . . ."

"I'm trying to save what's left of your ass, *idiot!* Shut up and come along."

====== **102** ======

Where the devil have you been, Peter? Hiding? I've had men out looking since I came in."

"My most abject apologies, Excellency. I went for a walk in the woods."

"Alone?"

"Of course."

"Collecting birds' eggs or just communing with nature?"

"Just walking, Excellency, thinking about Margaret and the unfairness of life."

Clad in the uniform of a French marshal, laces of gold and silver with ribbons; perfumed, powdered, bewigged; Frontenac sat behind his escritoire like a great white bear. It was amazing. Pierre had seen him not four hours earlier lying in his bed, a pale and wraith-like replica of his former self, his limbs elevated, his cough climbing his throat with savage regularity, a man most definitely bound for the grave.

"What, may I ask, are you staring at?"

"You're completely recovered, sir. It's a miracle!"

"I can thank some old squaw. The mother superior of the Ursuline Convent came to see me the other day. Blaise was fussing over me as usual, so frustrated with his failure to cure me he seemed on the verge of rattling a gourd over me and chanting incantations. The mother superior stopped in, saw what ailed me and mentioned that one of the sisters came down with the same thing and a squaw suggested rubbing her legs with the bark and leaves of witch hazel steeped in boiling water. It cured her in two days. Cured me. And some kind of ivy leaves dissolved in plain water cured my throat in two hours. These heathens with their barks and leaves and such can cure anything. I should force Blaise to live with them for six months, learn all their secrets, learn his trade properly, the useless fake, quake! Will you please stop staring?"

Frontenac leaned back and stroked his mustache, grinning impishly. "Tell me the truth, Peter, have you been behaving yourself?"

"Of course, Excellency."

"No drunken rampages, no whoring amongst the Huron maidens? No deflowering twelve-year-olds?"

"You misjudge me, sir." Pierre tried to look indignant.

"I think not. You've done a good job of establishing your reputation."

"May I remind you, sir, my wife . . ."

"You're in mourning, I know. A first-rate excuse for any kind of behavior. We've heard from Paris. They're furious at the failure to negotiate a peace treaty. Hardly surprising."

"Not our failure, Excellency."

"Who's to blame isn't important."

"What can we do?"

"I don't know." The general suddenly looked far away, wearied of it all. "I'm well again but the miracle of the leaves and bark can't cure my biggest affliction: old age. More and more, since the collapse of negotiations, I've been getting the feeling it's too late for me to make a peace."

"Nonsense, Excellency, look at you. Would that I were as fit, as energetic . . ."

"Please, don't start that." He shifted papers in front of him. "Our esteemed chief minister, the Marquis de Barbezieux, is faulting me for closing up Fort Frontenac. I explained why it makes sense to consolidate our manpower here in Quebec. If, God forbid, the fighting resumes, Fort Frontenac would be destroyed, the personnel massacred. It happened once—before your time. It eats at me to be given the job, one I never asked for, and feel twine around my wrists behind my back. How can anyone a thousand leagues away make judgements and decisions on these things? In my reports, I give them the facts, and they sit down with His Majesty and twist them like pretzels and second-guess me . . ."

On and on he rambled, boring his listener. He stopped listening, sending his mind back to the blade, to Two Buttons. She did make him feel absolutely regal. Whey didn't Margaret? She didn't make him feel anything like Two Buttons did. Why didn't she at least try?

Dear God, what was he thinking? Poor Margaret was dead. Never again would he hold her, enjoy her. Thank God a hundred times over for Two Buttons! His isle in the sea of his sorrow.

"Are you listening to me, Peter?"

"Of course, sir."

"What did I just say?"

"You were talking about consolidating our forces."

"What I was talking about when you drifted off was the English. Sir William Phips may get it into his head to take advantage of the impasse and visit us again."

"Is that possible?"

"We should be on guard. We've received some new artillery. It only took two years. I want new batteries deployed at salient points. At the Dufferin Terrace, we'll increase the four guns to eight. I want the high cliff of the Sault-au-Matelot and the barricade at Palace Hill, at present defended by four guns each, increased to six. I want the windmill on Mount Carmel converted into a small battery, and whatever's left in the way of light pieces collected in the square opposite the Jesuits' College to serve as a reserve battery for any weak spots in our defenses."

"And the Lower Town?"

"We've already six eighteen- and twenty-four-pounders mounted on the wharves, I see no need for augmenting our defenses there. You'll see to the disposition of the other guns. It's all written down; here you are. Go find General LaFleur, he'll assign men to help you."

Pierre saluted. "Excellency, again it's a relief, an absolute joy, to see you on your feet again."

"Mmmmm. Thank you, you can go."

Pierre clicked his heels, spun and left.

"Peter, Peter, I do love you like a son. I only wish you had as much stomach for the job as you've almighty gall."

103

Down, down, down, the water plunged them. Up from the bottom it boiled, whipping furiously, rushing into a deafening roar, as if all the waters of the earth were gushing from all directions into a maelstrom; and shooting them out of it into a pool as tranquil as tea cooling in its cup: the end of the rapids of the Long Sault.

Into a pool and out of it, and the churning water resumed, writhing, roping around a curve, walls of water rising on both sides. Out of the cauldron they hurtled into calm water. The banks receded, the river spread into a lake; serene, enclosed by the woodlands showing their vivid colors, the sight so glorious that, with the relief, it brought a lump to her throat.

And the lake they were gliding across became a mammoth diamond, shining blue in the setting of the wilderness.

The night before, Two Eagles had consulted his óyaron. He had told only Splitting Moon of the result, much less cryptic than the response to his question concerning his brother's whereabouts. This time he had asked if they would reach their destination without further loss of life. It was all he wanted to know. Holding himself responsible for everyone's welfare, he could not abide the thought of losing another friend. The answer he got was "not one of you will die but a woman."

Splitting Moon told Margaret. He felt she was entitled to know; he believed the prediction and was concerned for her. She thanked him, not at all tempted to disclose that she put no stock whatsoever in Two Eagles' medicine. Any power credited to it was in the mind of the user. All the same, she harbored as much superstition as the average intelligent, educated person. A bit. Enough. She thought about the prediction.

"Not one of you will die but a woman." Common sense insisted that his óyaron had no more validity in her own scheme of things than Moon Dancer's wild prophecies. Of course, the one about Thrown Bear came true. In every respect. She vowed not to let multiple coincidence prey on her mind, which only proved it was doing exactly that.

Margaret thought about Two Eagles paddling behind her, thought back to the tree he'd climbed to plunge his knife into the trunk—the one he'd carried since the Ottawa campsite, replacing his own, lost in the ambush earlier. What was the significance of the gesture? He hadn't "stabbed a tree" when he discovered Long Feather's body.

Curious how his mind worked, how all their minds

worked. She was tempted to ask Splitting Moon or Anger Maker about the knife in the tree trunk but she didn't want to pry into what seemed such a personal and private act. Thrown Bear's death consumed him, putting a dreary, absolutely wretched expression on his face that rarely left these days.

In plunging through the rapids they'd taken on at least four inches of water. It lapped cold against her. They headed for the nearer south bank. Pulling the canoes up, they emptied them of their supplies and turned them over, dumping the water. Red Paint and Fox examined them for any damage. Splitting Moon, Anger Maker and Bone went off to pick grapes.

She and Two Eagles walked together. He seemed oddly thoughtful. Purple twilight was beginning to softly drape the woodlands.

"I know you do not believe in my óyaron," he said.

"That you believe in it is all that matters."

"Last night it said that for you danger lies ahead. Waiting like the snake waits for the mouse to cross its path. Danger that perhaps ... cannot be avoided. I worry."

"You mustn't."

"You take it lightly."

"It's not my óyaron."

"You think what it tells is false?"

"I ... don't have an opinion."

"We have come a long way together. We have only three, maybe four more sleeps before it ends. I would hate to see anything happen. You must be careful."

"I try to be. I don't go wandering off. I don't take chances, certainly not now when we're getting so close. If you think about it, I'm completely in your hands."

They faced each other in the fading light. He looked down at her; she read his eyes. In them she could see his mind move ahead to their parting and sensed that this upset him. She would stand on the wharf with Pierre and watch them board their canoes. They would look at each other for the last time, murmur their farewells quite form-

ally and off they'd go. He realized this and it sobered him.
Even saddened him? It did appear so.

Spurred by impulse, she seized his hands and squeezed
them. "Don't look such a sobersides, so glum."

And yet the prospect of their separation growing closer
saddened her as well. It suddenly seemed eons since the
hollow tree.

"Margaret . . ."

"Yes?" she asked.

He wanted very much to relieve his mind of something,
she could see. But then the rigorous code that governed his
words, his actions, his very life reasserted itself.

"Nothing."

The others had come back loaded with grapes. *Sku-nak-
sus*, Anger Maker called them, fox grapes. They were delicious. She ate too many and fell asleep that night with a
stomachache.

IX

THE BEST LAID PLANS

104

Major Hertel Boulanger was in a foul mood and there-fore less than good company, beginning with his barging into Captain Pierre Lacroix's quarters unannounced.

"I can't really talk now, Hertel, dear boy, I must go call on General LaFleur. The old man's got it into his head to turn the entire town into a fortress."

Boulanger put a hand on Pierre's chest. "Shut up and listen, *Capitaine Incorrigible*. I'm telling you this as a friend. Get rid of your little Huron flower, before our revered leader catches you. Once and for all, button your fly, straighten your hat and behave yourself!"

"Don't shout. I still have a headache from last night."

"And stay out of the bottle."

Pierre smiled sheepishly and gripped his friend's shoulders. "Hertel, Hertel, be reasonable. What would you have me do, take vows, become a monk? I'm not slipping back down into the hole, trust me, everything in moderation. He can't fault me for that."

"He can, *idiot!* I swear sometimes you've the brains of a fish. You practically took a vow of chastity and sobriety when he let you off the hook the first time. He won't stand for another slip."

"All right, all right, I'll be a good boy. You're obviously right, my friend. It's just that the news of my poor darling was such a shock it . . . it drove me off the deep end."

"Oh, drop it."

"Hertel, I love you. You've more common sense in your little finger than I'll ever have in my whole self. I straightened out before, I can do it again. I swear to you as an officer and a gentleman, no more carousing and whoring, no more *bouse*, not a drop."

"You'll stay away from your Huron?"

"For good. Introducing the new Captain Lacroix, the celibate captain, sole proprietor of the straight and narrow."

"It's not funny!"

"It's so deadly serious I'm trying to lighten it, dear boy. Now, if that's all, I mean my word is my bond, I have to get to work. On your way out, would you send in Nez?"

Boulanger eyed him for a long moment, nodded, left. In came Private Campeau. Pierre repaired to his mirror to brush his hair.

"Sir?"

"Listen to me, Nez, and this is strictly *entre nous*. From now on, no more trysts in the woods, okay? Things will have to be arranged differently. More . . . prudently. I want you to go into town and rent a room, something with a bed that's not filled with rocks, understand? That'll be where you'll bring my dessert from now on." He counted money into his hand. "Bring back the address and the key. Look around, be choosy: no lice, no rats."

"Yes, sir."

"Good boy."

"Will that be all, *Capitaine*?"

"Oh, while you're engaging the room, pick up a couple of bottles. A decent brandy, if you can find one. And tonight you'll fetch her. If you tell a single soul I'll strangle you. Go!"

Off went Nez, muttering, wondering out loud who he'd be assigned to next.

105

The Lachine Ra-pids are coming," called Anger Maker in the canoe beside theirs. "They are very many and long."

"Father Gilbert said five leagues long," remarked Margaret.

"When the French were taking you and the other prisoners to Quebec, did they portage these rapids?" Two Eagles asked.

"*Neh.*"

"If they can make them, so can we."

"*Nyoh,*" asserted Anger Maker with exaggerated resolve.

They easily negotiated the first churnings and thrashings but as time went on, exhaustion set in. Margaret gripped the gunwales, tense as a spring. Bone and Red Paint fought the water.

The canoe of Anger Maker and Bone shot ahead and in seconds was lost from sight. Anger Maker shouted over the relentless roaring that they were coming to the end. A small lake showed through the spume raised by the dashing waters. Like boulders in a road, islands cropped up on both sides. On they rushed between scrub woods and irregular shores, and the Ottawa River appeared, entering from the north, bringing down its mud to tint the lake ahead. And the rapids shot out into the lake and were swallowed.

"Look!" Fox hollered.

Anger Maker's and Bone's canoe was floating capsized, bubbles issuing from the under one gunwale. The final thrust of the rapids had driven the two surviving canoes to within thirty yards of the empty one. They slowly approached it. Water was spilling into a bow hole, pulling the canoe slowly down.

Drowned. Vanished when their canoe shot ahead. And now there were three. Dead, sacrificed to this reckless trek of hers. The storm, the Ottawas, now this and what next? Thinking of Swift Doe waiting for Bone's return and Moon Dancer, she could feel tears welling. For the first time, Two eagles looked utterly crushed. This was a journey doomed. Forget Two Eagles' óyaron's prediction that she would be the one to die; none would survive.

She wanted to hold and comfort him. She studied her hands in her lap and guilt surged, threatening to choke her.

"Aiiiiiii!"

She could hear splashing.

"Bone!" bellowed Red Paint. "Bone! Bone!"

Red Paint and Fox pulled him aboard, sputtering and gasping.

"Sa-ga-na-qua-de?" asked Two Eagles, hopefully.

Bone shook his head and pointed back up the rapids. To his right, with a soft, burbling sound, his canoe sank.

"We turned over," he gasped. "I was thrown clear. I saw him go down but I was swept away . . ." He touched the side of his head. "My head, my shoulder, my legs . . ."

"Sa-ga-na-qua-de is dead," declared Splitting Moon. "Drowned."

There was no need to put it into words. Two Eagles' scowl told him so.

"Drowned," he repeated, thrusting out his bottom lip defiantly.

"Dear God . . ." she murmured and buried her face in her hands.

"Look!" bawled Fox again.

He pointed toward the rapids roaring down. A dark shape appeared, vanished, reappeared, arms flailing. Toward them the surging waters carried him, heaving him into the lake. Down he went like a stone, leaving circles of water rippling outward. They held their breaths, up came bubbles. Up he came, flinging water from his head, grinning out of his battered face.

They cheered. On Two Eagles' face relief spread like the sun rising.

106

After tumbling through the rapids for a quarter mile, Anger Maker returned to life battered and bleeding in a dozen places. He groaned when Fox, Red Paint and Bone pulled him into their canoe.

"I am dead," he declared dramatically.

"I told you we should have portaged," grumbled Splitting Moon.

Through his pain, Anger Maker managed a frown. "Shut his mouth, somebody, before I tear his head off and throw it where he cannot find it."

It was decided that Red Paint and Fox would accommodate the survivors and the journey would be completed with but two canoes.

"We should not try to pass Montreal till after dark," said Two Eagles, shading his eyes, looking back into the sun as it inched down toward the turbulent waters.

Anger Maker nodded between groans. "Hochelaga, yes, and where the three rivers meet beyond there."

"How many more rapids?" Splitting Moon asked.

"Three bad," sand Anger Maker. "We will have to portage."

"Have you anything broken?" Two Eagles asked Anger Maker.

"Everything."

"Nothing," said Splitting Moon. "If he did he would be howling, not groaning."

"We will put to shore and wait for dark," said Two Eagles. "And find yellow thistle for him."

Margaret shook her head. "Would that we had a bottle of arnica."

"Yellow thistle *is* arnica," said Two Eagles.

The thistle blossomed in July and August, so the yellow petals had faded and dropped now, but the plant itself was easily identified by Red Paint and Fox. The patient was laid on a heap of leaves. Red Paint and Fox boiled the

slender, black rhizome of the plant in water. Compresses
soaked in the solution were applied all over Anger Maker's body. Two Eagles and Margaret sat watching the treatment.

"By the time we see the sun again he will feel much
better," he said.

She smiled. "It's so much less trouble back home. One
walks into the apothecary's and for six-pence you get a
bottleful all prepared."

"A . . . poth . . . ?"

"A store where one buys drugs and medicines, everything for what ails one."

He swept an arm, taking in every direction. "This is our
store."

"All free and you never run out of anything. Good
point."

"How far from Montreal to Quebec?" he asked Anger
Maker in Oneida.

"Three more sleeps, so long only because of portaging.
The end of the trail."

"Yes," she said. "When we arrive, please let me do the
talking. You'll be under my protection. Of course, Pierre
will smooth things for us. He'll get right to Governor
Frontenac and explain everything."

Two Eagles grunted. "Every feather there will be our
enemy. There is much hatred, many wounds that did not
heal, will never heal."

"I know."

"Do you? I do not think you have ever seen hatred so
deep. Like an arrowhead plunged into your side that you
cannot pull out because the blood will spill and take your
life out of you. So you keep the arrowhead in you and live
with the pain. Seven years and the blood on both sides
running like the winter snows into the rivers. They do not
forget. We do not."

"No harm will come to you. I swear it. Still, getting
past Montreal after dark gives me an idea. What if we approach Quebec the same way? Put ashore well before and
let me go on alone in one of the canoes."

"You cannot paddle a canoe."

"I did all the way from Fort Frontenac to the mainland."

"You did well, but you could not have by yourself."

"But it'll only be a few hundred yards. If we're lucky, there's no moon. Why are you smiling?"

Two Eagles shrugged. "Strange. For them to see you paddling up as if you had paddled all the way from Lake Oneida."

"I'm being serious. It's a capital idea. They can't possibly harm you if they don't see you. You can be off and away before I even get there."

"In one canoe?" Splitting Moon asked. "Six of us?"

"Oh. Well then . . ."

Two Eagles, still smiling, leaned forward. *"Nyoh?"*

"Maybe . . . maybe one of you can bring me up and drop me off." He had begun shaking his head at her first word. "Why not, for pity's sake?"

"You would ask us, who have come all this way for you, to drop you and sneak away like Huron snakes? Like men without spines with fear fat in their throats? We do not fear the snakes, the dogshit eaters."

"Or the lace cuffs with their hairy faces and long knives," added Splitting Moon. He fisted his chest. "We are the warriors of the People of the Longhouse, the Onayotekaono."

"Never since the birth of our day have we shrunk from our enemies or hidden from them," said Two Eagles. "The warrior who does has milk for blood. All of us here, even Bone, who comes late to our people, would dress in oil and run the fire gauntlet before we turned from facing the murderers of our children!"

She sighed to herself. At stake suddenly was their manhood, never to be doubted. Not to carry their mission to completion would be dishonorable. And they would return home without face. "You mustn't look at it that way. You're letting pride cloud your perception. Would you risk your lives for no reason?"

Every face held the same stubborn frown. She had unwittingly touched a nerve, and nothing she could say would change their thinking. It was something lodged in their temperaments at birth, tempered through conflict and hardship.

"We will take you to Quebec," said Two Eagles, "and see you step onto the land and be welcomed by your husband."

The others, apart from Bone, who understood not a word of English, nodded with finality.

She sighed inside. "Men."

107

Two priests, in black *soutanes* and floppy, broad-brimmed hats, hurried by as Pierre inserted the key into the door to the three-story house on the narrow, cobbled street in the Lower Town. The Recollet church bell tolled the second hour, hastening the holy fathers' steps, leaving the captain alone. Nez had brought back two keys for his money; one for the front door, the other for the attic room for which three months' rent was paid in advance. The house was dark, the *propriétaire* and his wife deep in their dreams, along with their other tenants, so advised Nez when he returned at midnight with both keys and assurance that Two Buttons was eagerly awaiting her lord and master in the little room. Nez had not put it in those words. He simply said, "All set, *mon Capitaine*." Said with a glum face, Pierre recalled; did he think of himself as a pimp? Stupid fellow, all he'd done was make lodging arrangements.

Gingerly testing the stairs, Pierre went up. The room was tiny, the ceiling slanting down to a single dormer overlooking a dark cul-de-sac below. She lay awake, naked, her small, firm breasts washed in the white light of the moon. He flung off his clothes, crouched naked like a panther and prowled to the bed, leaping on her growling. She giggled, flinging her arms around him. It was like entering heaven must be, delicious, and no one but his faithful lackey knew of this secret place. He might even have a second set of keys made for her, eliminate Nez from the process altogether.

No, she'd lose the keys, for she had no brain. She seemed incapable of learning even two words of French. She had to be led in everything, including their lovemaking. But she was the absolute soul of cooperation. One day when she became a woman, she'd make some Huron warrior a good squaw. He'd be done with her by then.

But right now she was all his and she worshiped him, which guaranteed her faithfulness. Frenchwomen did not worship their men slavishly as she did. Margaret didn't worship him. Her eyes sparkled with love when he looked into them, and she was obliging. But she had a mind of her own, not like this one, whose mind was the mind he gave her and controlled.

He climaxed, wondered if she had, and rolled off her.

"Amour, amour . . ."

The only French she grasped enough to remember and use. Why even bother trying to teach her? They communicated without any difficulty simply by gestures.

"Don't be in such a rush," he said, "we've hours."

"Ow-ers."

"You haven't the vaguest idea what I say. *Mon Dieu,* but you're *merveilleuse,* you delicious little pagan, *sauvage*! What have I done to deserve such a rare creature?" He ran his hand down her slender body. "Aphrodite in the wilds!"

He supported himself above her, staring down admiringly, his crucifix swinging lightly from its chain, catching the moonlight. She giggled and snatched it, pulling hard, the chain cutting into his neck.

"Owwwww! Bitch!"

He slapped her. She cried out. Up shot her hand, slashing his cheek with her fingernails. He bellowed, struck her viciously, clapped a hand around her throat and squeezed hard. There came a soft snapping sound. He stiffened and slowly released her. Her eyes were shut, her head lolling awkwardly to one side.

"Mon Dieu . . ." He gasped. "No . . ." He leaped up.

He panicked, pacing the floor, smashing his fist against his palm again and again, babbling like one unhinged.

"*Mon Dieu, mon Dieu,* what have I done? It's murder, the poor creature. These hands, I don't know my own strength!"

His cheek stung. He slid his hand down it and studied the four fingertips of blood.

"How could she do such a thing? Like an animal, a cat. Whatever possessed her? *Damnation,* what to do, what to do . . . ?"

He spied two bottles in a corner, snatched up the brands and downed a generous swig. He sat catching his breath on the edge of the bed staring down at her. Beautiful, dead.

"*Mon Dieu.* What now? What now?"

The brandy settled his nerves enough to enable him to dress and dress her. No one had seen him enter the house. The two priests walking by hadn't even looked at him; and his back had been to them. All they could have seen would have been a man in the uniform of an officer of the dragoons. Leaving without being seen shouldn't be too hard.

Nez, and the landlord would know, of course, although he now recalled Nez telling him he hadn't bumped into a soul inside the house or out when he brought her upstairs. So no one could know she was even there!

Opening the dormer, he looked down into the cul-de-sac. He could not even make out the pavement. Leaning out as far as he could, he held his breath and listened. A dog barked in the distance. The river lapped at the wharf. Rain was falling softly.

Moving to the bed, he checked her clothing, then carried her to the window. She was surprisingly light. He eased her out onto the slate roof and pushed hard. She landed with a thump. He tensed. No lights went on, no windows opened downstairs or across the way or at the closed end of the street. No one heard anything. He remade the bed, taking pains to remove every wrinkle. Nothing whatsoever betrayed occupancy. He retrieved both bottles—the other was a red wine, an outstanding vintage, he should congratulate Nez on his taste—and went out, locking the door.

Down the stairs he stole, like a housebreaker, "Better a thief than a murderer ..." He caught himself. Why hang that sign around his neck? Self-defense was what it was. "Hardly, old boy ..."

Still, she *had* brought it on herself. How would he explain the scabs on his cheek? Nez would have to get hold of some makeup, perhaps flesh-colored powder, if such a thing could be found here at the end of the world. He could say he'd scratched himself in his sleep.

Scratches on the cheek were like lovebites on the neck. Everyone knew they came from the same inflictor. Oh well, at the moment, his scratches were the least of his worries.

He got safely out of the house and hurried around the corner into the cul-de-sac without being seen, he was sure. At least, he saw no lights. She lay in a heap, one arm flung over her head, blood curling out of the corner of her mouth. The rain fell harder, washing the blood away as he inspected her.

"Poor little *sauvage*. I'm so sorry. Forgive me, forgive me."

Away he ran.

▭ 108 ▭

Demons ran after him, sticking to his heels all the way back to the garrison and into his quarters. He flung himself onto the bed.

"Murderer!"

It wasn't intentional, but murder it was. How could anyone be so fragile? His demons worked on him; one by one the factors he banked on to shield him from discovery were stripped from his optimism. No one had seen him near the place? The two priests had. His uniform was like a red flag. Also someone must have seen Nez bring her in. Hurons wandered into town at all hours, but a white man accompanying an Indian girl would be certain to draw attention. So he could not say for sure that no one had seen her enter the house. And she was there by herself for upwards of an hour. Maybe somebody had knocked on her door, and she'd opened it thinking it was he. Maybe she'd gone back downstairs for something, and been seen coming or going. He could hardly assume that *no one* knew she was there.

When her body was discovered, the first thing the police would do would be to determine where it had come from. They'd see that it had been thrown down. They'd question everyone in the area and sooner or later pinpoint the room. Once they did, they'd connect it with Nez and then him.

Dear God, it *was* an accident. Should he go straight to the police and make a clean breast of it? Of course, the old man would get wind of it and pull the rug out from under his career so fast he wouldn't get two minutes to defend himself. He'd given him his solemn word to give up whoring. He must keep it quiet and pray that no one would connect her to him. How many rooms surrounded the spot where she landed? At least twenty windows out of which she could have fallen.

"Fallen?"

The police would think about the windows right off. They'd question the tenants behind every window, reduce the pool of suspects to six, five, down to one: the captain of the dragoons who'd taken the room for three months, for obvious purposes.

He had executed a complete about face. Within hours the hand of the law would come down on his shoulder. He wrestled with his guilt, a beast out of a nightmare, already begun to wear him down.

Confession! In church!

"That's it!"

He would go first thing in the morning. He hadn't made a confession in months, years. Actually, he couldn't recall the last time. He had never intentionally harmed anyone, not counting the Cayuga in the tree on the way to the peace conference, and a handful of other Iroquois, which was an altogether different sack of beans.

Was this a mortal sin? A mortal sin involved spiritual death and loss of divine grace. If not mortal then venial.

"Yes, venial." An offense committed without reflection or full consent. *Should* he make his confession? A priest hearing his story was forbidden to divulge it to anyone. His secret would be safe forever. And this terrible creature eating at his conscience like a rat gnawing a corpse would let go.

He reached under the bed for the brandy and drank two long swigs. His head ached enough to echo.

No more than a couple of hours till reveille. He groaned. What a picture he'd present to the general reporting for work tomorrow. He must at least try to cover the scratches. Scabs were even harder to conceal. He yawned. Tonight there'd be no sleep. If he could somehow drag through tomorrow, hopefully tomorrow night he'd be able to get some.

He emptied the bottle. The brandy settled in his stomach and ballooned in nausea worse than before. All drinking ever did was make a bad situation worse. His confession would have to be rehearsed, phrased perfectly. The fact that he was willing to confess a sin of such magnitude had to put him in a good light.

If he got through the next two days without a knock at the door, he'd be in the clear!

Then make his confession?

He should. He'd think about it.

=== **109** ===

Pierre got through the next day better than anticipated. The ever-reliable Nez skillfully mixed talcum powder with rouge, creating a flesh-colored powder that effectively concealed the scratches.

He worked with General LaFleur all day at the Château St-Louis, in what the governor designated as his "war room." In it was a crude but useful scale model of Quebec, both Upper and Lower Towns, the garrison, Palace Hill, across a slender mirror that represented the St. Charles River, the Jesuit monastery, general hospital where Dr. Blaise reigned, the Ursuline convent, the Recollet church, residences from the mansions of wealthy merchants to the hovels of the poorest citizens. Even, Pierre noticed, the house overlooking the cul-de-sac.

General LaFleur was intelligent and attentive to detail. They worked on plans for the deployment of the recently arrived artillery pieces. Pierre came away from the château that evening so exhausted he could scarcely see, but relieved that the interminable day was behind him. Not a whisper had come from the authorities regarding the incident (he no longer referred to it as a crime in discussing it with himself).

He passed up supper to catch a couple hours' sleep and arose feeling slightly refreshed. Returning to town, he wandered about aimlessly, passing one tavern after another, fighting back the temptation to slake his thirst. When he was sure that no one was following him, he set out for the cul-de-sac.

The body had been removed, as expected. Was it at the *commissariat* now? When would they return it to her people at the Lorette Huron castle? Was the death of an Indian important enough to investigate? Would anyone be questioned?

The first day had gone by without repercussion. Today was Saturday, tomorrow the day of rest. By midnight Monday, his worries would be over. He'd be in the clear.

Mere anticipation of this so lifted his spirits that he decided to repair to the nearest *taverne* and treat himself to a drink. He found a little place and a table no larger than his hat in a reasonably private corner.

Two slightly tipsy girls said hello. He graciously invited both to join him for a cognac. They began drinking in earnest. In about twenty minutes, the blowzy redhead with the ear-splitting laugh had to leave. With Pierre still was her friend, a small, buxom brunette, whose sensuous mouth became the focus of his attention. She moved her chair closer, slipping her arm through his, pressing one ample breast against it.

His thoughts flew back to the rented room. In the inside pocket of his tunic were the two keys. He whispered in her ear. She tittered. He put down money for their drinks, they left.

110

Anger Maker recovered speedily, as did Bone who wasn't in nearly such bad shape. Under cover of darkness, keeping as close to the south bank as they could, they departed Lac St. Louis, paddled between the islands and shortly put the royal mountain and the sleeping citizenry well behind them.

The three rapids between Montreal and Quebec were portaged. Finally, when Quebec was an hour distant and it was again growing dark, Two Eagles ordered them ashore.

Margaret protested. "We're almost there."

"We will get there early tomorrow and not be so tired."

"He means we will be able to defend ourselves better," said Splitting Moon.

"Fiddlesticks and rot! Nobody's going to attack us. Besides, if we reach there this evening, there'll be fewer people around the wharf, won't there? I can go ashore by myself, find an officer, and have him take me straight to the governor general. And see to your protection before anything else, even Pierre."

Two Eagles considered this, crinkling his brow.

"You can paddle back out to midchannel where you won't be seen," she added.

"Why would we not want to be seen?"

"Oh, don't start that again. Let's just go on and land me so you'll be rid of me."

"You cannot wait to see your husband."

"I can't."

"We will go on."

"Excellent! And don't forget, you promised to let me do all the talking."

"You always do."

The others laughed. They paddled in silence. Quebec rose on the top of a high peninsula extending out into the St. Lawrence from its northern shore. To the north and west it was guarded by the St. Charles River, while high bluffs guarded its eastern and southern flank. As they drew closer she gazed at the night-shrouded city, piled like an immense sand castle studded with toy cannon. In half an hour, even less, she would feel him holding her, reunited at last! How many times had her pessimism persuaded her that they would never see each other again? From the *Aventurier* to here it was their love that had sustained her.

Now the ordeal was over, they'd won out. She began trembling. The instant the canoe touched the wharf she'd climb up and run off to the garrison, to his quarters, to his arms. He would hold her, keep her. Forever. "Can't we go faster?"

Two Eagles dug in, calling to Splitting Moon to do the same. The wharf appeared deserted, the wall behind it rising to the Lower Town, the moon the sole source of light. So far was it back to Fort Frontenac and Lake Ontario, it almost seemed as if they'd come from another planet. Now the wharf was only thirty feet distant. She could hear the water lapping against. it. Two Eagles turned the canoe to approach sideways.

He ascended the wharf, bent down and offered his hand. Red Paint and Fox's canoe kept clear of the wharf, pointing upriver, as if they couldn't wait to get out of there. There came a shout and out of the shadows at the wall six soldiers sprang, aiming their muskets at them.

"Don't shoot!" she cried in French.

A lieutenant strode forward, his sword drawn and held upward. "Bring that canoe in," he snapped, pointing his sword at Red Paint.

She hurriedly identified herself and explained how they came to be there at such an odd hour. He didn't understand or didn't want to.

He glared at Two Eagles and the others, in arrogant hatred. "They're Iroquois. Tell them to climb up here, all of them! At once or we shoot!"

"These men are under my protection . . ."

"Fire!"

A musket boomed. Red Paint ducked. The shot whizzed over his head, plunking into the water.

"Damn you!"

Two people were approaching, an officer in dress uniform and a woman.

"What is going on here, Lieutenant Girard?"

"These savages were trying to sneak ashore, Major Boulanger, sir."

"Nobody's 'sneaking ashore,'" she burst, "this idiot . . ."

"Please, calm down," said the major.

Margaret again explained the situation.

"You're alive . . ." murmured Boulanger. "Amazing. We heard that everyone aboard your ship en route from New York was massacred. Oh, forgive me, may I present Madame Boulanger. Jeanette, this is Pierre's wife, whom we all thought was . . . Astonishing, a miracle. Wait till he sees you!"

"I can't wait myself, except that this has to be straightened out first. Lieutenant, these men must be allowed to leave without further delay."

"*Mais non, Madame, impossible!*" burst Girard. "They are Iroquois. They must come ashore. They will be incarcerated."

"Major . . . !"

Boulanger gestured helplessness. "I am sorry, Madame. He is in charge."

"You outrank him."

"I could be a full general, still I could not countermand his order. Regulations, Madame. This is 'his' wharf."

"Ridiculous!"

"Please, I'm sure it can all be straightened out in the morning. I'll inform the governor immediately."

"*I* will, and my escort comes with me. He'll be the one to decide."

"No one moves!" barked the lieutenant.

"Lieutenant Girard," said Boulanger, "I want your word that these men will not be harmed, not a hair. Lock them up if you must, but leave them alone. And see that their canoes are properly taken care of. Understand?"

"Yes, sir."

"Be assured, Madame Lacroix, they will be safer behind bars than out on the river at night." He lowered his voice. "In the morning, when he hears your story, I'm sure the governor will see to their immediate release. Please, this is the only way."

Margaret hesitated, glancing toward Madame Boulanger. But Madame Boulanger, who looked like a beautiful, life-size china doll, appeared mystified by the whole situation. And afraid of Two Eagles, standing close to her. She had slipped behind her husband and was gripping his arm.

"Two Eagles . . ." began Margaret.

"It is up to you," he said quietly. "We are not afraid of their guns. If you say to go with them, we will go."

Would getting them out of jail be harder than keeping them out? "I hate this," she muttered.

"Madame . . ." began the major.

"I know, I know. Two Eagles, Splitting Moon, all of you, please, let's not have anyone get hurt. Go with them. I shall be there myself as soon as I can." She turned to Boulanger. "Take me to the governor."

"He is at the château."

"At once. Then, would you please collect Pierre and bring him there?"

"With pleasure, Madame." He struck her as immensely relieved. "My dear Jeanette, will you forgive me for aban-doning you?"

She smiled, the first expression other than fear on her lovely, polished face. "It's all right, I know my way home. You go."

Margaret turned back to Two Eagles. "I'll be there in a

few minutes, I promise. No harm will come to you. You heard the major."

He grunted. Red Paint, Fox, Anger Maker and Bone put ashore, and the muskets aimed at them were lowered. She watched gloomily as one by one they handed their weapons to the lieutentant and his men.

They were marched away, the lieutenant barking orders, high-stepping and swinging his sword.

She went off in the other direction with the major.

Governor Frontenac and General LaFleur were in the war room on the second floor of Château St-Louis, hovering over the scale model of the city. His Excellency held a tin cannon above the high cliff of the Sault-au-Matelot. Where to place each individual toy gun had become a battle of opinions.

"The cliff commands the whole river, my dear Eugene," asserted Frontenac.

"Governor . . ."

Margaret, Major Boulanger and a private entered. Both Frontenac and LaFleur gasped at the sight of a white woman in the deerskins of a squaw, with a beaded band around her blond hair. Margaret introduced herself.

The governor's eyes bulged. "*Incroyable!* You, alive? How can this be? We received word . . ."

She explained her escape from the *Aventurier*, her rescue by the Oneidas. "They escorted me all the way from their castle. One was brutally murdered by Ottawas. No sooner did the others set foot on the wharf than your men marched them off to jail. Your Excellency, they must be released at once, their weapons returned and given permission to leave. I gave my word."

Boulanger interrupted, telling what had happened.

"The wharf lieutenant is in charge," LaFleur reminded Frontenac.

"Amazing," said the old man, lifting his arms to clasp hers. "Pierre will be overjoyed. Private . . ." The soldier who had brought them upstairs stepped forward, clicking his heels. "Go at once and fetch Captain Lacroix. Bring him here. Don't tell him why, just get him here fast as you can."

"Your Excellency," interrupted the major, "may I be permitted to get him?"

"If you like, but don't tell him the good news."

The major left.

Margaret's temper rose. "Governor, I want those men released. At once, please."

"Madame, forgive me, but the general is quite right, it's the lieutenant's authority. And believe me, they'll be much safer staying put. By now, word is all over the garrison that Iroquois are behind bars. They would not get halfway back to the wharf before trouble started. There are Hurons all about the area. Not to mention our men, many of whom are still understandably bitter. Tomorrow, we will escort them to the wharf under protective guard, return their weapons and see them off."

"If you can do it tomorrow, why not now?"

"The lieutenant's decision will be reviewed. I will secure his permission to release them."

"I've never heard such nonsense."

"Regulations."

"Regulations be damned!"

He placed a consoling arm around her. "Indeed, many's the time I wish certain rules could be dispensed with. They'll be inside only for a few more hours. Tomorrow's Sunday. Before I go to Mass, I'll summon the lieutenant. I'm sure we can work it all out to your satisfaction. Let me show you to your room. You and your husband will be my guests. You look exhausted."

"I must go to them."

"The prisoners?"

"They aren't prisoners! I can see now I never should have let it happen, that damned spit-and-polish lieutenant! Have your private take me to the jail."

"Madame . . ." began Frontenac.

"If you don't mind, Governor!"

Frontenac's affable smile concealed his annoyance. He nodded once.

* * *

Major Boulanger threw open the door to Pierre's quarters. The bed was empty.

"Damn! I might have known."

Private Campeau appeared in his nightshirt, bleary eyed and yawning.

"Where is he?"

"I don't know, sir."

"You do, too. Where, in town? At the Huron castle, romping with his Indian? Speak up, man!"

"I . . ."

"His wife has shown up. Alive!"

"Mon Dieu . . . !" Nez hurriedly crossed himself, and told the major about the rooming house.

Boulanger growled, "Go fetch him. Run, man!"

111

They had been crowded into two cells, Two Eagles, Splitting Moon and Fox in the smaller one. She strode past the corporal at the desk sitting under a rack displaying four pistols, dismissing his protest as he jumped to his feet. He hurried to catch up with her.

"Keep out!" she burst.

He backed off in confusion. She slammed the inner door in his face. The Oneidas were sitting on the stone floor. They got up and came to the bars.

"I'm so dreadfully sorry," she began. "I don't know what to say, except that if you did put up a fight when they were aiming their muskets . . ."

"When do we get out?" Two Eagles asked coldly.

"First thing in the morning, Frontenac has to discuss it with the lieutenant beforehand. It's their ridiculous regulations."

"What did they do with our knives and bows?" Splitting Moon asked. "And the muskets we took from the dogshit eaters?"

"You'll get everything back, Frontenac said so."

Two Eagles scowled. "You believe him?"

She returned his stare, the dread thought springing to mind that she'd been duped to quiet her. Frontenac had no intention of releasing them.

"I could kick myself," she murmured. "This is all my fault."

"*Neh,* we surrendered our weapons, gave ourselves up."

"We should have cut them down like corn," said Splitting Moon. "They could not see that we had loaded muskets. We could have been back out in the middle of the river and on our way home before other soldiers got there."

Red Paint nodded. "We should have caught them by surprise."

"Should have, should have," rasped Two Eagles. "Is it not late for crowing talk? We are in this cage like bear cubs. It is done and talk will not unlock the door."

"I'll get you out," she said. "I swear by Almighty God. Please be patient, don't cause any trouble."

Two Eagles grunted. "What trouble can a deer fallen into a pit trap cause?"

"If Frontenac goes back on his word, I'll, I'll . . ."

"Talk to him, we know."

He let go of the bars and turned from her. Not having the heart to continue the conversation, she left. Thinking as she made her way back to the château with her escort that yes, they could have fought back and probably gotten away.

But for her. Concern for her safety had to be Two Eagles' only reason for surrendering.

Pierre sat up awake. Pebbles rattled against the windowpane. He threw open the window.

"Who is down there? What in hell do you think you're doing!"

"It's me, *mon Capitaine,* Campeau."

"Nez! What are you, drunk?"

"No, sir. Major Boulanger sent me to tell you your wife has arrived and is waiting for you at the château."

"You *are* drunk, imbecile, my wife is dead!"

"What's all the racket?" his companion asked sleepily, propping on one elbow and frowning at him.

"Nothing, go back to sleep. Nez?"

"It is the truth, my right hand to God, sir. She has come with some Iroquois, from a long way away. She is well and safe and wants you to come."

"*Mon Dieu,* it can't be. Margaret, here?"

"Margaret who?" the woman asked.

"Meet me around front." Pierre began pulling on his trousers.

"What are you doing?" she asked, "deserting me? Come, get back into bed, make love to me."

"Are you deaf? I have to go."

He kissed her hurriedly, pulled on his boots and was out the door and starting down the stairs tucking his shirt in, fastening his buttons.

"Margaret. Alive." He burst out the front door, all but bowling Nez over.

"She is waiting, sir."

"You've seen her?"

"*Mais non,* Major Boulanger . . ."

"All right, all right, let's go."

112

The tester bed was so like her own back home. The same sensation of the feather mattress swallowing her, of floating in a canopied royal barge on a quiet stream.

Despite her exhaustion, she was so excited she couldn't sleep. At the same time, regret flooded her conscience over the Oneidas.

In he rushed, throwing his arms around her, covering her with kisses. "My darling . . ."

"Don't talk, just hold me, kiss me and everything else, the whole mad story can wait till morning."

He undressed and climbed in beside her. She trembled as his flesh came in contact with hers. And she surrendered, utterly transported. Journey's end, home to his arms at last!

A gentle knocking sound opened her eyes to the sunshine streaming through the window, bringing the warmth of a late September morning.

"Breakfast in fifteen minutes," sang the muffled voice.

Pierre awoke, kissed her neck, her face, clasping her hand. She started slightly.

"What is it?" he asked.

She moved her fingertip down his finger. "Where's your ring?"

"I . . . Sometimes, I don't wear it."

"*Some*times? Darling, we made a pact. February fifth, three P.M. sharp, rings on, exchange vows and 'I do.' Just as I promised I married you by proxy in that chapel in Knightsbridge. And you were to marry me by proxy, same day, same hour. Only you didn't. Why not?"

"Darling, we were fighting. Up to our necks. I was nowhere near here. It was impossible . . ."

"You could have postponed it. The war's been over for months."

"I did think about doing it when we got back here, but since I couldn't back in February, it didn't seem right."

"Right? Or necessary?"

"Margaret, darling, if you must know, I didn't do it because . . . I didn't think it had any meaning. It wouldn't have been the real thing without you beside me. It just seemed so make-believe, such a sham."

"You think *I* didn't feel the same way? But *we made a pact.*"

"All right, all right. I made a mistake. The blunder of the age. I'm an insensitive lout. But can't you find it in your heart to forgive me?" He embraced her. "I'll make it up to you. We'll be married today. The real thing: priest, witnesses, guests."

"What have you done with the ring I gave you?"

"It's back in my quarters, in my jewelry cask. I didn't

lose it, if that's what you're implying. Where's your wedding gown?"

She studied him archly. "I was bringing it. It was lost in a storm on the Te-ugé-ga."

"The what?"

"The Mohawk River. O-kwen-cha, Sku-nak-su and I were on our way to the Shaw-na-taw-ty . . ." He suddenly looked as blank as an unstamped coin. "Never mind."

Another knock. A servant called a reminder of breakfast.

"We'd better go down," said Pierre.

"I have to see the governor." She got up and started dressing.

"Can't we eat first? I'm starving. What's so important?"

She explained, adding: "He gave me his word they'd be released and permitted to leave. This morning."

"Iroquois warriors brought you here? I don't believe it!"

She summarized events up to her meeting with Frontenac. "He gave me his word, I gave them mine."

"This Two Eagles, is he some sort of chief?"

"A Pine Tree chief."

"Practically all of them are 'Pine Tree chiefs.' What you're really saying is he's just another upright animal like the rest, even our Hurons."

"He's not an animal! How dare you say such a thing? He's decent, honest, ethical. He's my friend, they all are. I've never known better, more trustworthy friends."

"He sounds a *parangon*, your feathered *gaillard* of the wilderness, your *sauvage*, I absolutely must meet him."

"He's . . . not your concern."

"He's obviously yours. Which makes him mine, since we're married. As good as."

"I've been under the impression *I* was. Or should I say delusion?"

"Darling, darling, we've been apart so long. I've been so excruciatingly lonely waiting, my heart keeping this . . . vigil. Must we start out sniping at each other over details? All that matters is that we love each other. The waiting's

over, life starts today." He held her and kissed her tenderly.

"You're right," she murmured. "I'm sorry."

"And I'm sorry I insulted your feathered knight in no
armor." He turned to the mirror to attend to his collar.
"But don't get your hopes up too high."

"About what?"

"Your Iroquois. Frontenac gave you his word, I know.
Unfortunately, circumstances may prevent him from keeping it. We've already consolidated our forces in anticipation of a possible attack by the English. And with them, of
course, their Iroquois allies. Which makes six Iroquois
warriors falling into our laps quite a windfall, wouldn't
you say?"

"He wouldn't . . ."

"Six fewer screaming *sauvages* attacking, raping and
scalping our women, butchering our children. Where are
you going?"

Out the door she swept without responding, without
even looking back at him.

════ 113 ════

On her way across the parade ground to the governor's
office everyone gaped at the blond woman in deerskins. Oblivious, she prayed that the meeting with
Frontenac wouldn't end up in confrontation.

He had no legal right to hold the Oneidas. The war was
over. There was as yet no peace treaty, but if hostilities
were about to break out again, Two Eagles would have
heard, and they wouldn't have ventured within fifty
leagues of here. What did Frontenac know that the Oneidas didn't? What did Pierre know?

If Frontenac intended to go back on his word, why give
it in the first place? After all, he could order all six Oneidas taken out and shot, term it "retribution against known
enemies of the king," or some such. And she could carry

on in protest like a madwoman at St. Nun's pool, for all the good it would do.

If it all came apart in the next few minutes, she'd simply have to enlist Pierre's help. Frontenac was fond of him, and he might listen. Of course, she'd first have to win Pierre over to her point of view. At the moment he seemed even further away from it than the governor.

He already disliked Two Eagles. And hadn't even met him. "He's jealous. How could he be?" She didn't want him visiting Two Eagles.

Frontenac looked up as she entered. "Madame Lacroix, welcome, welcome. Did you sleep well? Did you enjoy your breakfast?"

"It's still waiting for me, I'm afraid."

"We must get you some clothes, my dear. You've come about your escort. I've already discussed the situation with Lieutenant Girard, the Wharf Officer last night."

"Yes, and?"

"He's left it up to me." He winked. "I had a suspicion he would."

He came out from behind his escritoire, hands behind his back and began pacing. "I'd be delighted to see them off. There's only one hitch, I'm afraid."

" 'Hitch'?" She flinched.

"Yes, their canoes were destroyed last night. Kicked in, chopped to pieces."

She gasped. "Disgraceful! Major Boulanger specifically warned him . . ."

"Oh, don't blame Girard. After all, we could hardly ask him to stand watch over two canoes all night. It seems they were brought ashore and stored and someone found out, either Hurons or our men; chips on their shoulders, probably drunk. It *was* Saturday night."

"So replace the canoes."

"That wouldn't be easy, I'm afraid. We can hardly ask the Hurons to provide transportation for their blood enemies. And all we have on the river are *chaloupes*: sloops. Better than the longboats but no match for canoes. We don't even attempt the rapids in *chaloupes*."

"How many can one hold?"

"Seven or eight, ten in a pinch."

"Fine. Assign somebody to sail or row the Oneidas across. They'll build their own canoes on the other side."

"Mmmmmm."

"Will you please? Governor, I understand your reluctance. Six Iroquois warriors walk into your arms . . ."

"You think I worry about the Iroquois attacking? Who told you that, Pierre?" He chuckled. "He's exaggerating. I have no such concern."

"Someone must have."

He pursed his lips somberly. "General LaFleur, for one."

"To hell with him! And anybody else shaking in their boots. You gave me your word. Your reputation is one of a man of great courage."

"I have not said I refuse to release them."

"When?"

"I'll have to ask you for some time."

"How long?"

He shrugged. "Let me explain. Quebec, every town, every village along the St. Lawrence has suffered grievously for years from the depredations of the Iroquois. By now, everyone here knows that your six companions are behind bars. Perhaps locking them up was a mistake."

"No 'perhaps' about it."

"But now that they are, the garrison, the townspeople, the Hurons, all feel a sense of triumph. Public opinion is not something I can turn a blind eye to. If I were to unlock the door, supply them with transport and bid them farewell, it would go down a lot of throats very hard."

"You're saying your image is at stake. If you can't release them, why not take them out, line them up and shoot them? That should please everybody."

"My dear . . ."

"I've asked you to release them. You've just finished telling me you can. Only you won't."

"I didn't say that. I just asked for some time."

"If you'll excuse me, they're entitled to know what's going on. I doubt they'll be surprised."

=== **114** ===

The chapel bells of the Ursuline convent sang beautifully. Sunshine flooded the dusty parade ground. Pierre stood with Major Boulanger outside the major's cottage. In the front window, sitting embroidering—a framed portrait of an officer's wife on domestic duty—Jeanette waved to the captain. Told by Margaret that the Boulangers had been present at the landing the night before, Pierre was curious.

"The one she calls Two Eagles ...," he began. "How did she talk to him? Did they seem on unusually friendly terms?"

The major finished tweaking the ends of his mustachios and restored his hand mirror to his pocket. "Not 'unusually,' why?"

"When his name came up this morning, she was very defensive."

"You think she's fond of him?"

"Who knows? They've been together a long time. Sleeping in the woods night after night ... You should see the look in her eyes at mere mention of his name."

"Don't be an ass, my friend. Do you ever stop to think before you go spouting off? They saved her life, risked their lives escorting her here through hostile territory. Why shouldn't she be grateful? *Mon Dieu,* if it were me, I'd fall down on my knees and kiss their stinking moccasins."

"I'm not talking about the others. Just him. *You* think about it: How in the world did she ever induce them to help her?"

"You think she gave herself?"

"What do you think?"

"You're ridiculous."

"I'm realistic, Hertel. I see things as they are."

"You're jealous."

"That's ridiculous. Forget it, then. Forgive me for detaining you."

Off walked Pierre muttering to himself. Then he turned and came back.

"You don't understand, Hertel. I love her so much I ache all over. Last night, when Nez called up to the window . . ."

"By the way, how is your Indian playmate?"

"When he told me she'd shown up, I thought it was an awful joke. But when I walked into that bedroom and saw her lying there, the world fell out from under me. I was in paradise. I felt like I'd been pulled back from the grave, my life restored!"

Boulanger laid a hand on his arm. "She'd never have put herself through all the difficulty and danger to get here if she wasn't in love with you."

"You're right, as always. I'm sorry. I do spout off without thinking. Thank God I've you to straighten me out."

He patted Hertel on the back and walked off whistling. The Ursuline bells rang.

▭▭ 115 ▭▭

Pierre arrived at Frontenac's office just as Margaret came out, crestfallen.

"What did he say?" he asked.

"He's decided to hang on to them, and gave me all sorts of gibberish trying to justify it. Your brave general is as soft at the core as the basest coward, afraid to keep his word. Why did you tell me he wants to keep them locked up because as Iroquois they're a threat? He denied that."

"He's very good at that, bending the truth to spare people's feelings. He should have gone into politics."

They walked toward the château. Fort St-Louis was a quiet, lazy place on Sunday. Townspeople and Indians mingled with the off-duty soldiers.

"You'd like to see them leave, wouldn't you?" she asked, breaking a long, weighty silence.

"Locking them up was a mistake."

She brightened. "You do want to be rid of them. Darling, talk to him, please. He respects you."

"If you want, darling, but not today. Let him sleep on it, maybe he'll change his mind. I'll see him in the office tomorrow morning."

She kissed him loudly on the cheek. "That's all I ask."

"Tomorrow you should go into town and shop for clothes. You look ... peculiar, to say the least."

"I've gotten used to deerskins. They're cool, comfortable. I know it doesn't look proper for a captain's wife to be strolling about imitating a squaw, but speaking of the captain's 'wife,' I think we should get married this coming Saturday."

"Of course, darling, the sooner the better. Saturday, it is."

They had reached the front door of the château. She paused.

"I should go and see Two ..., see the Oneidas."

"Would that be wise? I wouldn't, darling, you can't do them any good just now, nor yourself. Cheer up. As I told you, I'll discuss it with him first thing in the morning."

"It's all so stupid!"

"Calm down. What say we go visit Hertel and Jeanette? Maybe the four of us can go for a boat ride on the river." She frowned. "Sorry, bad idea. Maybe just for a walk. Do cheer up, darling." He took her in his arms. "It'll all work out. At least they're safe. No hotheads can get at them, like the ones who wrecked their canoes. Lieutenant Porior is a fine guard officer, and the ramrod is on the desk."

"Ramrod?"

"Corporal Claude Lemieux, the walking encyclopedia of army regulations. Believe me, your *sauvages* can't possibly be better protected."

They spent the remainder of the day with the Boulangers. Margaret was getting to know Jeanette better, and she liked her. She was animated and charming, despite her narrow world and limited interests and outlook.

By seven o'clock, Margaret's conscience got the better
of her reasoning and, instead of going back to the château
with Pierre, over his objections, she detoured to the jail.
Corporal Lemieux sat at attention at his little desk when
she walked in. She eyed the four pistols on the rack on the
wall behind him. Why not snatch down a couple, force
him to open the cells, knock him cold and head for the
wharf? There must be a boat of some kind about. He escorted her back to the cells.

She told Two Eagles about her discussion with
Frontenac. Neither he nor any of the others seemed surprised or disappointed by the bad news. She promised
she'd get them out "one way or another" and came away
soberly realizing that every one of them seemed to know
the governor general as well as Pierre did.

What an unfair world it was!

116

They lay holding hands in the silence of the night. He
had wanted to make love. Preoccupied with pessimism
over the situation, she wasn't in the mood but could not
bring herself to tell him, and submitted. A mistake. She
was leagues distant and unable to conceal it.

Furious, he turned up the lamp and got out of bed. "If
this is the way things are going to be from now on maybe
we should think twice about marriage."

"I'm sorry, darling, I'm just . . ."

"Not in the mood, that's obvious. More specifically,
I've failed utterly to get you in the mood. You're not even
here. You're back in bloody England or across the way in
the cell with him. Which?"

She sat up covering her breasts. "I said I was sorry, darling. There's no need to get nasty."

"You can't get him out of your head, can you? Not that
you're trying."

"Pierre, listen to me. Stop carrying on like a little boy

whose favorite toy just got smashed. You should see your face. Grow up!"

He sat on the edge of the bed and stared at her. "Tell me the truth, my darling. I have to know. I won't be angry. I'll understand."

"What are you talking about?"

"How many times have you slept with him?"

It struck her like a hammer. For a moment, she couldn't speak. "How dare you!"

She got up and started dressing.

"What are you doing?"

"What does it look like?"

He grabbed her arm, turning her toward him.

She jerked free. "Don't do that. Ever! I'm not one of your Pigalle trollops you can manhandle. Or the one who scratched your cheek!"

"Your display of moral indignation is most convincing, but you still haven't answered the question. Just tell me you haven't slept with him. Is that so much to ask?"

"You disgusting bastard! You call yourself a man, but you're as jealous and insecure as a stripling."

"Darling, come tell me all about your upright animal. I can take it."

"That's the second time you've called him that. If he's an animal, you're a bloody insect he can step on without even knowing it."

"Crazy about him, aren't you? Totally infatuated. What it is, his nakedness? He must be six feet seven. I'll bet he's hung like a . . ."

"Shut your foul mouth and get out of here!"

"Gladly, my darling."

Clutching his clothes and boots, he left. She sat gazing at the closed door.

She whispered, "What have I done?"

She should have simply told the truth, that Two Eagles had never so much as looked at her suggestively. Instead, she lit into him, which only served to reinforce his suspicions. She should go find him. Sit and discuss it. Tell him the truth, that he's the only man on the face of the earth she loved. Hadn't she proved it, coming all this way?

She leaned against the door. She couldn't go after him. "Why?"

═══ 117 ═══

Histor his fury unabated, he could not sleep. He could kill her, the cheating bitch! With a filthy *sauvage*, a stinking feathered blunder of nature, no better than the dogs he ate. To be humiliated, cuckolded by such scum, the mud of mankind . . . !

He'd heard about such women: happily married, abducted by Indians, taking up with a warrior, eventually rescued and refusing to return to civilization. Becoming as low as the animals they lived with. And proud of it.

"Damnable bitch!"

The gray fringe of the night was painting the windows when he got up, dressed and left the château. Reveille was still twenty minutes away when he crossed the parade ground, knocked on the door to the jail office, and went in. Spelling Corporal Lemieux was a private he didn't recognize.

"I want to see the Indians."

"Yes, sir, right away, sir. I don't know if they're awake."

"Stay put. I know my way around back there."

They were awake, sitting on the floor staring into space. They looked up as he entered. He recognized Two Eagles. "You . . ." He gestured. "Get up. I want a word with you."

Two Eagles got to his feet, towering over the captain's six-feet-one.

"She wants to tell you the governor's refused her. He won't let you go. There's nothing more she can do."

"Margaret said this?"

"Margaret? Madame Lacroix. I am Captain Lacroix."

"I know who you are. I do not believe you. She would come herself, not send somebody. Not even you."

The bars between them, Pierre took one step backward, drawing his sword. Two Eagles showed no reaction.

"Are you calling me a liar?"

"You lie. Your face says it. So what should I call you, tell me."

The others relaxed and chuckled. Splitting Moon said something in Oneida, which brought a laugh. Pierre growled. All his hatred, frustration and humiliation collected in his throat. He lowered his sword and thrust it forward. Like a cat, Two Eagles shifted to one side, grabbing the top of the blade with both hands and swinging it sharply forward, wrenching it from the captain's grip. Against one bar, he snapped the sword cleanly in two and casually tossed the pieces to the floor.

Pierre threw himself against the bars, grabbing Two Eagles' throat with both hands. Up came the Oneida's forearms between Pierre's, breaking the hold easily. And reaching out with one hand, Two Eagles gripped *his* throat. The captain struggled, fighting for breath. He finally broke free and staggered back, gasping, his eyes bulging, sputum stringing from his mouth. He could not speak. The others looked on, fascinated. Turning, he jerked open the door, ran out and behind the desk, nearly bowling over the guard in his chair. He snatched down a pistol and, ignoring the guard's shouts, ran back inside, hastily aimed and fired.

The explosion was deafening. The ball tore through Two Eagles' upper arm and struck the wall. Men came running.

In seconds pandemonium reigned. Pierre stepped back and lowered his hand, letting the smoking gun fall to the floor.

========== **118** ==========

Captain Pierre Lacroix was brought to Frontenac's office by the Prévôt Maréchal, along with the jail guard on duty and others attracted to the scene by the sound of the discharged gun. Someone, Margaret wasn't sure who, alerted a guard at the château, who informed the servant, who woke her.

Ignoring the outside guard, she burst into the office. By then the only ones still present were the captain and the governor.

Frontenac paid no attention to her intrusion. He was firing questions. "What I'm still waiting to hear, is why you went there in the first place."

"I'm sorry, Excellency . . ."

"Intending to shoot him."

"Sir, forgive me but it's a personal matter involving . . ."

"What is all this!" she cried.

Frontenac placed a chair for her. She sat. He explained. She listened open-mouthed. Glaring at Pierre. "You killed him!"

"A flesh wound in the arm," said Frontenac, "nothing serious. The doctor's attending to him." He looked from one to the other. "I'm sure you two would like a little privacy. Perhaps together you can agree on an explanation. I myself need a little fresh air. Margaret, you'll be pleased to hear that your Iroquois friends are leaving. Their weapons will be returned, except their muskets. They'll be given a *chaloupe* to get them across the river and upstream to where the bluffs end and they can get ashore. After that they'll be on their own. They'll be released before dawn tomorrow when their departure will be less conspicuous and safer for them."

"Thank you, Governor."

"As for you, Captain, there'll be a hearing on this unfortunate affair in a day or two, when I can find the time. Until then you'll attend to your duties as usual. You're lucky you didn't kill him."

"Yes, sir."

He left.

She bristled. "What happened? The truth!"

He hung his head. "I have no intention of lying to you. It's all gone too far."

"Talk, damn you!"

"After we argued last night, I couldn't sleep. All I could

think about was you and him. I went there to pin him down."

"To kill him, you mean."

"No, I just had to know. Only it never got to that." He studied the wall to avoid looking at her. "He didn't provoke me, not really. Don't you understand! I love you so much I can't put it into words. I lived hour to hour thinking about nothing but you, waiting for you to get here, then word came of the massacre and it broke me into pieces, destroyed me. When you showed up it all turned around, suddenly I was in heaven. Yes, I was consumed with jealousy. To think any other should even come near you. I should have controlled myself, but from the first moment I saw you, we've had upheaval, misunderstandings. It wasn't supposed to be like this. What happened?"

She studied him in silence.

Now he turned to her. "I love you. God, but I love you!"

"Pierre, Pierre ..." she sighed. "And I love you. For better or for worse, eh?"

He ran to her, embraced her. "Can you forgive me?"

"Let's not talk about 'forgiving.' Let's just push all that's happened since I got here behind us, pretend it never did happen. Start fresh here, now."

"Yes, yes ..."

"What will happen at the hearing he spoke about? What will they do to you?"

"I don't know, nothing too severe. A slap on the wrist. I deserve it. I was an *idiot*."

"Perhaps if I spoke ..."

"No, no, no. I went berserk. I should be made to pay." He smiled thinly. "This has been like a bucket of ice water thrown at me. Bringing me to my senses. What time is it? We'd better give him back his office. I have to get to work. Will you go shopping after all?"

"I'll ask Jeanette. You'd better give me some money."

He handed her a generous amount. "Will you buy a wedding gown?"

"Just about everyone here assumes we're already mar-

ried. Saturday, why don't we just sneak into town and find
somebody to marry us?"

"Yes, yes. You'll still marry me?"

"Darling, I didn't come all this way to go back. Now, if
you don't mind, I want to go to him."

"Two Eagles. Yes, yes of course."

119

Margaret came away from a lengthy visit with Two Eagles relieved that his wound did not appear to
threaten his life. He wouldn't admit it was painful. News
that they would be leaving before dawn the next day tempered his anger. She did not mention the attack or Pierre,
nor did he.

Early that afternoon she went into town with Jeanette
Boulanger, straight to Madame Tourette's Fashions of
Paris, "the only decent dress shop in town." She didn't expect to see a stitch in the latest fashions and walking in
was pleasantly surprised. A black mantle trimmed with
embroidery, with an overdress looped up for walking,
showing an embroidered underskirt immediately caught
her eye. The sleeves were finished with plaited ruffles in
the same material as the gown. She bought it on the spot;
and a pair of long kid gloves, a muff decorated with a bow
and ends of brocaded ribbon.

They were the only patrons and could talk about anything they pleased in a normal tone.

Jeanette had heard about the incident and tried to ease
Margaret's embarrassment. "Jealousy is the fuel that fires
love."

Margaret laughed. "Where did you hear that?"

"I made it up." They were standing by the front window. Jeanette looked at her questioningly. "You do love
Pierre . . ."

"Of course. It's just that he's different."

"It's here: the fort, Quebec, the wilds of New France.

Everybody's different. It's a whole different world. People change."

"I guess. Oh, look . . ."

She ran to a gown of rich silk trimmed with pre-tintailles, patterns cut out and laid on in rows across the petticoat. The flounce and gown were edged with gold lace. A stiff, high stomacher; loose sleeves, ending below the elbow with full ruffles of lace to match a commode headdress, which had streamers down the back.

"It's adorable!"

"Buy it. Your rich husband expects you to take advantage of him. Don't disappoint him. You'll need it for balls, formal occasions, the few there are. Did I tell you that the governor's crazy about the theater and that they'll be building a playhouse come spring?"

"Wonderful."

"I've done a little acting, just little playlets at church, mostly comedies. Though we did attempt *Phèdra* last summer, by Racine. We did it in the open air, on the parade ground. No stage. I played the nurse."

"You surprise me, Jeanette."

"Did you think my whole life was needle and thread and keeping house? Sweet heaven, I'd go utterly mad. Let's get everything wrapped, then we'll go round the corner to Roget's for an absinthe. Shopping always makes me thirsty. And tomorrow, when Pierre gives you more money, we'll buy shoes."

Madame Tourette, a slim, pretty woman in her fifties, came out from behind the drape. Margaret paid for her purchases and, at Jeanette's suggestion, changed from her deerskins into a purple and gold atlas gown laced over tight stays, open at the front displaying a black velvet petticoat edged with two silver orrices. They were preparing to leave when Madame Tourette reappeared with the deerskins neatly folded.

"Shall I burn these, Madame?"

"No! Wrap them, I'll take them with me."

"As you wish."

The indulgent smile appeared genuine, if ever-so-slightly disapproving.

It was different making love that night, the peace that follows hostilities. Gone was the distraction: his fixation on Two Eagles. Gone, too, was her resentment over his baseless jealousy.

She came to him untouched by any other man. He knew that now and he'd changed back to what he'd been, the man she'd all but fallen in love with at first sight at the cotillion in Montmartre so long ago.

Now, for the first time since she arrived, they could relax. Listening to him breathing beside her as he slept, she could tell herself they were right for each other, they belonged together. And she would hate leaving his side when the scheduled knock came at the door an hour before dawn. But, as she explained earlier, she could not let them leave without saying goodbye, and he agreed.

— X —

DECISION AT DAWN

120

Only the murmur of the St. Charles River flowing south past Quebec and Fort St.-Louis trespassed the silence of the waning night as Margaret made her way down the stone steps to the wharf. With her was Jeanette, who refused to let her "prowl the area alone at such an ungodly hour." The night guards, as Jeanette had said, were off somewhere dozing. Lieutenant Girard was nowhere to be seen. Frontenac had kept his word: A *chaloupe* was secured to the pilings. It looked to be in fair condition, adequate to the job of ferrying them across. There were six paddles they could keep to use with the canoes they'd build on the other side. What was left of their weapons after the rapids—no muskets, their tomahawks, bows and the few arrows that hadn't gone overboard—had been placed in the *chaloupe*.

"Where are your Indians?" Jeanette asked. "You don't suppose the governor changed his mind?"

"If he did the boat wouldn't be here."

A sullen pre-dawn cloud left wisps of mist clinging to the dark river. From upstream came the clear, low-pitched croak of a great blue heron, a sound so forlorn that Margaret sighed, so appropriate was it to her mood.

They came down the steps and across the wharf in single file, raising their hands in greeting. Unsmiling, looking in a hurry to get away.

"How is your arm?" Margaret asked Two Eagles.

He grunted. They inspected the *chaloupe*.

She handed him her folded deerskins. "Please give these to Eight Minks. Somebody can use them."

He handed them to Fox who placed them on board.

She lowered her eyes self-consciously. "I'm sorry you had to be put through all this."

"It was not your fault," said Anger Maker. The others nodded.

She moved to the edge of the wharf and, leaning down, offered her hand to him. "Goodbye, Sa-ga-na-qua-de, and thank you for everything. I hope you find a new pipe to your liking. Goodbye, Bone, my friend, I know you'll be a good father to Swift Doe's boys."

She shook his hand in turn as Anger Maker translated for him. He nodded looking unaccountably grim. All of them seemed saddened by this. There wasn't the eagerness they should have shown, being freed to leave enemy territory. She turned to Red Paint and Fox.

"O-kwen-cha, Sku-nak-su, I'll never forget any of you. Tyagohuens, you never wanted to come, but you did and I thank you from my heart. I thank you all, my Oneidas, my friends."

All were in the boat except Two Eagles. By the time she turned to him the mist in her eyes was blurring her vision. She felt a tear slide down her cheek. Two Eagles gazed down at her. Crooking his finger, he caught the tear on the back of it, and showed it to her glistening, then lifted his finger, setting it against his own eye.

"The day comes," he murmured. "We must go."

She said nothing. She could only hold his eyes with her own. He clasped her hand, squeezing it fondly, then started to turn.

"Wait . . ." she burst.

She grabbed Jeanette's wrists. She spoke in French. "You won't believe this."

"What?"

"I'm insane, daft as a loon, you'll think I am. Last night I lay thinking and suddenly realized I didn't feel at all what I should be. Something was terribly missing. I couldn't understand. I told myself we belong together. Over and over, like I was trying to convince myself. Oh, Jeanette, I wanted so much to love him. But it's just not there. God knows if it ever really was.

"Brace yourself, I'm gong back with Two Eagles, back into the wilds, into a world I don't understand and probably never shall. Where I don't fit. How could I? How could any of us? Still, I have to go, it's pulling at me. Aren't you shocked? Am I stupid, feverish, crazy, what? I'm sputtering gibberish ..."

"You're not, my dear. Your heart is talking to you." She set a finger to Margaret's lips. "Don't you talk, don't even think, just listen."

"You do understand!"

"I'm standing here watching you two, I'd have to be blind and thick as a wall not to."

"I can't help myself."

"Don't try. Go with your heart. You should see your face. You're not standing in the dark on this god-forsaken wharf, you're in heaven!"

"Will you tell him for me?"

"As gently as I know how."

"He'll be angry for what he'll see in everybody's eyes, what I put there, Frontenac's, Hertel's ..."

"Not mine."

"Bless you. And yet, deep down, you know, I think he'll be relieved."

"He will. He's dashing, he's fun. Women adore him. But marriage is not for him."

"They're waiting." She held Jeanette and kissed her and turned back to Two Eagles. "Tékní-ska-je-a-nah ..."

"Margaret?"

"Take me home."

━━━ **121** ━━━

No sooner had the *chaloupe* reached the precipitous opposite bank and they turned upriver to where they could get ashore on level ground than Margaret snatched up the bundled deerskins and ran off into the woods. Minutes later she reappeared wearing them, the day dress wrapped in a ball and placed in the stern of the boat to be returned to the wharf.

"Some woman back there will have more use for it than I."

The *chaloupe* was tied at the water's edge where it would be picked up later on. The Oneidas worked all day building the two canoes. The sun was setting, searing the clouds a cornflower purple, when the second canoe was declared completed by Red Paint and Fox.

On the north side of the river, meanwhile, Governor Frontenac sat at his escritoire looking over a lengthy dispatch that had recently arrived from Paris, a litany of suggestions on how to expedite the peace treaty with the Iroquois. Repeatedly as he read he felt the urge to crumple the dispatch into a ball and fling it into his wastebasket. A knock interrupted his annoyance.

"Come."

With the guard was an angular individual in the black uniform of a *gendarme*. He introduced himself as Sergeant Bordagary. He displayed a well-timed tick under one eye and his voice squeaked absurdly.

"I hope this is important, Officer, I have work to do."

"Vitally important, Your Excellency. Last week the body of an Indian girl was found in a cul-de-sac in town. I determined that she was thrown from an upstairs window. Three buildings overlook the spot. Her skull was fractured, her neck and back, both legs and one arm broken."

"Thrown? Couldn't she have jumped?"

"No sir. She had been strangled. There were finger marks around her throat. The body was discovered early in the morning, brought to headquarters and kept there until early evening. It was then brought to the Lorette Huron castle."

"Sergeant, this is all very interesting, but how does it concern us?"

"Your Excellency, I have two people waiting outside. With your permission . . ."

"Bring them in, let's get it over with."

In strode the white-haired Winter Heart and a *coureur de bois*, a young and—for a man of the woods—surprisingly clean-looking fellow. Even his clothes were neat and he didn't smell like most of the *coureurs de bois* Frontenac had come in contact with.

The sergeant introduced both. "Jacques, here, has offered to interpret for Winter Heart," he said.

"Yes, yes, get on with it."

"Excellency," said the sergeant, "the girl was Winter Heart's granddaughter. Her people called her Little Cloud. We've determined that she was strangled and thrown out the window by one of your officers."

Up went Frontenac's right eyebrow. "Oh? Go on."

"Jacques . . . ?" said the sergeant.

The *coureur de bois* questioned the old man in Huron. He answered at some length.

"Sir, he says that the girl knew her murderer well. That he, himself, had met him."

"And what is this 'presumed' murderer's name?"

The question was put to the old man.

"He says he doesn't know his name."

"Does he know his rank?"

He could not differentiate one rank from another.

Frontenac suppressed a smile. "Can he describe him?"

Again, Winter Heart carried on for some time.

"Sir," said Jacques, "he says his eyesight's not what it used to be. He can't be sure what the murderer looks like."

"You're telling me that one of my officers killed this poor girl, you don't know his name, his rank, you can't even tell me the color of his hair. How can you accuse anybody?"

"We know who he is, Excellency," said the police sergeant, "but you will have to be the one to identify him."

"You're not making sense."

"Please bear with me, Excellency."

"I'm doing my best," said Frontenac crisply.

"He has proof," said the sergeant. "Winter Heart, show His Excellency."

Jacques communicated the request to the old man. Frontenac watched him dig his fingers inside his shirt and bring out a small square of deerskin. Laying it on the escritoire, he slowly unfolded it.

To reveal two regulation officer's tunic brass buttons.

 **122**

Late afternoon, the sun burnishing a fleet of clouds anchored above the horizon. Paddling against the current, the Oneidas' pace was considerably slower than traveling downriver when they covered the more than fifty leagues from Montreal to Quebec. They rested more often. They quit for the day when twilight was barely begun. When it was necessary to portage, she insisted on helping, for they were no longer just escorting her. Now she was one of them.

Second thoughts had assaulted her even before they reached the south bank, three days before. On the way to the wharf with Jeanette, she had thought only about Pierre, not Two Eagles, and definitely not about leaving. But walking along, coming to the stone steps and starting down them to the wharf, weighing her heart against her mind, she recognized for the first time: Pierre was not the man for her, she was not the woman for him.

When she and Two Eagles had looked in each other's eyes, when she saw the painful yearning mirroring her own, it was all it took.

He had yet to say the three words. He probably never would. Pierre did, over and over, twenty times or more every night in bed. But Two Eagles expressed his feelings in more subtle ways: with his eyes, his little attentions and big considerations. Gone was his reserve of the past. His attitude toward her now opened like a morning glory. Mostly he was as taciturn as a tree but now he talked more and more easily. Not once since they departed the wharf had she heard a grunt from him. He was content.

She must see it for what it was, a sea change in her life.

Daddy and mother would have to be told. She'd have to write and explain and somehow get a letter to the nearest Jesuit missionary, to someone who could get it aboard a ship to England. She'd spend hours framing it. How would she justify such a shocking decision?

She went over to join her husband, and ran off with an Indian. A red Indian, my dear, a savage who paints his cheeks and chest and wears feathers and shoots things with a bow and arrow. Insane? Of course. Totally demented. Snakebite or a fever caused by the wilds, something. And such a sweet young thing she was . . .

"What are you thinking?" Two Eagles asked.

They were walking upriver, watching the water swirl. Here, just beyond Lac St. Pierre, where the banks narrowed considerably, accelerating the current, they could look out on the beautiful foliage.

"Just about things in general," she answered. "At the fort one Sunday, we spent the afternoon with Jeanette and her husband. The major had a collection of maps and I looked over our route coming here, all the way from the lake. I know where we are now. We're getting close to Montreal."

"We will not pass it." He stopped, picking up a stick and clearing the leaves from the ground. "The mouth of the O-chog-wä River is just ahead."

"That would be the Richelieu River, named for a famous French cardinal."

He gave in to a rare grin. "The lace-cuffs here call it the Iroquois River."

He drew the St. Lawrence and Richelieu River entering it. At the other end of the Richelieu he drew an oval. At the far end of the oval, another lake, one more river, then a tributary running westward. He came back to the St. Lawrence, indicating it.

"The Kanawage, the Rapid River here . . ." He pointed. "Here the O-chog-wä spills its waters into it. We move up it and here portage, to get around the falls. Four leagues, and sneak under the guns of the lace-cuff forts on the opposite side. And two sleeps up the O-chog-wä brings us to lake O-ne-ä-da-lote."

"Lake Champlain."

"Him we know. He came many summers before any of us were born. He fought and killed three Maquen chiefs and many warriors. That is what started the bleeding between the lace-cuffs and our people." He indicated the south end of the lake. "Here we enter a smaller lake."

"Lake St. Sacrement."

"Andia-ta-roc-te. And down here at the bottom of it, portage to the Shaw-na-taw-ty."

"The Hudson!"

"You remember the Shaw-na-taw-ty. The current will be with us down to here."

"The Mohawk."

"Te-ugé-ga. From there we paddle into the sunset to Da-yä´-hoo-wä´-quat."

"The Carrying Place."

"You should remember 'the Carrying Place.' "

"This route is so easy. And shorter, why didn't we come up this way?"

"The way we came was safer for you." He indicated the Mohawk River. "Coming along here we would have passed Onekahoncka, and your old friend. Back then the fire in him was still burning. Now, it has had time to cool. We will not slip by without being seen by his warriors, but I do not think they will try to stop us. Also, this way, down the O-chog-wä, is dangerous. French forts and villages. We must sneak through the woods on the side of the sunrise."

Choosing the other route coming up to Quebec seemed to make sense. Besides, what would getting there a few days earlier have accomplished in light of what had happened since?

"It's getting colder," she said, rubbing her arms briskly. "The nights and mornings are a lot colder."

"Up here *augustuske* awakens early from his sleep." He

glanced skyward. "We may even see snow before we reach the Shaw-na-taw-ty."

"How is your wound?"

"All wounds heal."

"Let me see it."

"Neh."

"Let me!"

He shrugged. She undid the bandage carefully. The wound looked an unhealthy purplish red.

"Does it hurt?"

"Neh."

She touched it lightly. He didn't wince but she could tell it was tender. "It looks infected. What did the doctor put on it? Anything? Did he clean it first?"

Again he shrugged.

"What do the Oneidas put on gunshot wounds?"

"The green parts of cornsilk."

"Small chance of getting any around here. Is there anything else they use?"

Anger Maker had come up. "There is a flower, *o-käsa-äta*, the one with five yellow fingers that grows in the corn fields."

"Five petals."

"With yellow strings in the center. When the flower dies, small round heads with black seeds are left. They smell like the blood of the pine tree."

"Resin."

"There are no more *o-käsa-äta*," said Two Eagles. "They blossom only until the last whole moon."

"Eight Minks must have some dried petals. She should know how to treat your wound."

"She has all medicines," he said.

"We must get you home before it becomes mortified, before your arm has to be amputated."

His hand covered his wound. "No one takes my arm."

He glanced toward Anger Maker, who took the hint and left them.

"I . . . am glad you have come back with us," Two Eagles said.

"I had to. I couldn't stay there. I didn't belong. It was all wrong."

"Will you be happy, living with savages?"

"I'll learn your ways. I'll become one of you. You must be patient with me."

"You must be patient with us. Some will not like an Englishwoman living among us. Some old men will shake their heads. Some women, Graywind's friends, will say things to your back."

"I know. I've thought about that."

"But most will accept you. Most people know how to open their hearts. And in time, like us, they will come to admire you."

"What on earth for?"

"For being what you are. You have fought like a starving wolf fights to protect its young. You got away with your scalp when the Maquens took all the others' and burned your ship. You walked your feet raw, hurting every step, with tears in your eyes but no complaint from your lips. When the Te-ugé-ga went wild, you fought it and stole your life from it. With your wits and your iron heart you got away from Burnt Eye. When the storm tore the lake like the side off a beaver and broke the woods you showed it your back and your courage. You saved us all from the arrows of the dogshit eaters talking to the black robe. You made Frontenac open the bars that held us. Your *eshucne otschtiénta*, your spine, is stronger than a French captain's long knife. Even danger cannot bend it. Fear is afraid of you."

"Two Eagles . . ."

"You are not Ataentsic. You do not wear her flesh and bones, and your blood is your own. But in you is her spirit; in you, Margaret Englishwoman. Back there, when I thought we would never see each other again, I felt as sad as the bird sounds that stands on tall sticks and croaks out over the river."

"Me, too . . ."

"Then you said, 'Take me home.' And like a bird rising, the sadness lifted from my heart."

She threw her arms around him. He looked down at her. He spoke.

"I love you, love you."

123

The Richelieu was to provide an exhausting stretch, on stamina, on nerves; an ordeal. Margaret insisted vainly on helping with the paddling. The six Oneidas rotated at it. Along the river was danger on both sides, the French end of the war road. Forts St. Jean, Thérèse and Chambly rose behind stockaded walls. Between them on both banks were stockaded villages called *cotés*. Eyes watched the river day and night. The Oneidas would have to get through the gauntlet as swiftly as they could, paddling against the current. To where they would have to portage more than three leagues past the rapids.

Trees on the banks were heavily roped with vines, the grapes approaching the peak of their season. Grapes made her think of wine, wine of Pierre, Pierre of four days ago, Quebec and an interlude in her life that was better barred from memory. Would she ever forget him? One thing she wouldn't do, compare the two—as futile as comparing their two worlds. The news Jeanette delivered, however gently, must still have crushed him. But he'd have no trouble finding another woman. She watched a butterfly flitting among blue asters.

With luck and strong shoulders and arms they got through the gauntlet without mishap. Shortly before dawn chased the stars and gilded the ridge of the Green Mountains, they put the Richelieu behind them and swinging around the uninhabited Isle aux Noix entered Lake Champlain. Four huge islands dominated the northern end of the lake, which, according to Hertel Boulanger's map, stretched more than forty leagues southward. Throngs of chestnut trees and grapevines even thicker than those along the Richelieu reached down to the water, and the un-

spoiled landscape was the most gloriously beautiful she'd
seen since leaving Lake Oneida.

A fish jumped, a silver gray monster fully five feet in
length. Splitting Moon pointed. *"Causar!"*

She couldn't have guessed what it was, but it was as big
around as a man's thigh and had a double row of fright-
fully sharp teeth.

Down the lake they slipped hugging the west shore. To
the east they could see the lofty Green Mountains at first
appearing snowcapped but actually crowned with white
rock. To the west rose the familiar Adirondacks, the "Tree-
Eater Mountains."

This was Mohawk Territory, Two Eagles told her, but
their hunters rarely ventured this far from Onekahoncka
for there was sufficient game closer to the easternmost
castle of the tribe. To the east and below was Mohican
Territory, where Bone had come from. Lake St. Sacrement,
which they would reach eventually, was smaller than Lake
Champlain, only ten or eleven leagues long. Her attempts
to pronounce the Oneida name for it—Andia-ta-roc-te—
elicited laughter; still, her command of the language was
improving daily. They saw neither Mohawks nor Mohicans
and passed through Lake St. Sacrement and its hundreds
of small islands without incident.

From the lower end of the lake, a trail led to a short
river, evidently of minor importance along the war road
that comprised the two lakes above and the Richelieu
River and stretched from the St. Lawrence down to Albany. No one knew the name of the trail, if it had one.

But its significance became enormous to Margaret when
they reached the southeast end of it, where it emptied into
the Shaw-na-taw-ty.

124

A yellowthroat, black-masked like a raccoon, landed on
the prow of the canoe, flicked its olive tail, warbled
briefly and flew off. They had passed Onekahoncka and

the boulder that identified the spot where Margaret had swum ashore in the storm. Two Eagles' gunshot wound was infected and he was running a slight fever, which worried her. Bone found cinquefoil, boiled the root in deer's blood and applied it to the wound. It reduced his fever but not her anxiety.

Worry was not among Two Eagles' emotions. And for future problems, he held nothing but disdain. He was right, she conceded, in that most anticipated calamities fail to materialize, or can be dealt with. But she saw impending mortification as well worth worrying about.

They passed the Carrying Place and counted three skeletons picked bare and washed clean by the rain. They saw no canoes. The area looked as if no *coureurs de bois* had visited it since the three she'd seen on her way back to Onneyuttahage after fleeing Burnt Eye.

"What's happened to Burnt Eye, I wonder?" she asked Two Eagles.

"He is still chief. That cannot change. And like a snake, when you close its hole with your foot, he has found a way to wriggle out of his problem."

"He has not forgotten you," murmured Splitting Moon, paddling behind her.

"If I am still in his head he can chew on me till his teeth crack, I do not care."

"You took his face. He wants it back."

"He'll fight you, won't he?" she asked. "You can't fight anybody with that arm. You can barely lift it."

At which Two Eagles lifted his arm straight up. The others laughed as pain stretched his jaw cords.

"You're such a child," she rasped. "Men . . ."

"Do not give him room in your thoughts," he said. "Anymore than you would give the French bones back there."

They reached the bend where the Mohawk River turned northwest. Deserting the canoes, they set out on foot, gaining the southbound trail. She was coming to know it as well as the walkway down to the cider pippin orchard back home.

Home. Never again would she see it, nor England, her
family, friends ... Some choices in life were difficult.
Strangely, this one hadn't been at all. She hadn't wrestled
with her conscience, at least not in deciding. Staying in
Quebec and going through with the marriage would have
been completely wrong. Going back to England would be.
She'd let her heart do the deciding and was satisfied.
Pierre would be relieved, also disgusted with her. And embarrassed. How would he explain it?

*My fiancée became deranged, poor girl. It all started
when she escaped a massacre. From then on her travail
was such, she lived such a nightmare, in time she completely lost her mind.*

"No, found it."

Two Eagles looked her way. She moved closer to him,
slipping her arm through his uninjured left one. She
walked faster, forcing him along.

They must hurry. He would not lose his wounded arm.
Or his life!

=====   **125**   =====

Margaret arrived home acutely footsore but not weary.
The company was greeted on all sides but on some
faces smiles of welcome were quickly supplanted by
worry. At not seeing Thrown Bear with them? So murmured Two Eagles.

"I must go and speak with Moon Dancer."

Above the entrance to Eight Minks' longhouse hung a
grisly spectacle: two dead birds bound together, feathers
stained with dried blood.

Two Eagles saw that Margaret was upset. "Eagles," he
said quietly, "from your friend."

Eight Minks appeared in the doorway and ran to Margaret, embracing her. "I knew you would come back! I saw
it in your eyes, in his the morning you left. I knew, I
knew ..."

Moon Dancer came out and beckoned to Two Eagles. "*How* did you kill him?" she asked, as he approached.

"The dogshit eaters captured him," said Splitting Moon, stepping in front of Two Eagles. "And gave him a long death. Tékni-ska-je-a-nah spared him much agony, for which Do-wa-sku-ta was grateful."

"How?" repeated Moon Dancer, ignoring Splitting Moon.

Two Eagles endeavored to explain. Moon Dancer said nothing, showed nothing on her face. In mid-sentence, she turned from him and walked off.

"She knew it would happen," he said to Eight Minks. "I had to kill him."

Eight Minks shook her head. "But when you did you killed the hope in her that it would not happen, that she could be wrong."

"I will go to her."

She stopped him. "She is not angry with you but with him for going. Leave her with her sorrow for now." She glanced at the two dead eagles. "Two Maquens came four days ago and asked to hang them there. I let them, as was proper."

"It's disgusting," muttered Margaret, averting her eyes.

"They are his challenge," said Splitting Moon.

Two Eagles whirled on him. "Why do you always have to say what I already know, what everybody . . . ?"

"I was talking to Margaret," Splitting Moon sniffed indignantly.

Anger Maker thumbed his chest. "I am happy in here you came home with us."

"Thank you, Sa-ga-na-qua-de. Eight Minks," she said, turning to her, "this is a gunshot wound. It's badly infected. Do you have any of the yellow flowers?"

Eight Minks beckoned them inside, down the passageway to her chamber. From the overhead shelf, she got down two large baskets, picking through one, then the other, at length finding what she was looking for. The flowers were dried but the yellow petals were still intact.

"That's Johnswort, St. Johns grass!" exclaimed Margaret. "It grows in the meadows back home, common as clams."

"Here it grows in the cornfields," said Eight Minks.

She felt Two Eagles' forehead for fever and turned down the corners of her small mouth. She then set about boiling the entire plant and concocting a solution. She removed the doctor's bandage to expose the festering wound, which she bathed liberally.

"The air will help it," she explained. "It will have to be bathed often for three days. The scab should be scraped off."

"Do it."

"There is much sickness in the scab," she explained to Margaret. "The o-käsa-äta must get deep into the wound."

Two Eagles pulled his knife. "Scrape it."

Eight Minks held the knife over the fire till the blade turned red. She plunged it into the decoction water, setting it sizzling. Then prepared to remove the scab.

"You scrape it," said Two Eagles to Margaret.

Eight Minks handed her the knife. She did not demur. In her heart he was already her husband. It was her duty. One hand on the hilt and the other on the tip, she set the blade to his arm above the wound. Fighting for steadiness, she inhaled as inconspicuoulsy as possible, braced herself, closed her eyes and scraped off the two-inch scab in one piece. The pain had to be excruciating. Sweat gleamed on his forehead and cheeks but he did not move or utter a sound, did not take his eyes from the debridement. Blood streamed down his arm. Eight Minks applied the deerskin pad saturated with the solution.

"There is rawhide in that small basket on the shelf. Get some and tie this on. Not too tight."

It was done. Even covered as it was, Two Eagles continued staring at the wound.

"Can you move your arm freely?" Eight Minks asked.

"Of course."

"Do not. If I see you moving it we will strap it to your side. If you move it, the tunnels like threads will send out more blood. You need all you have to heal."

"She's right," said Margaret.

Outnumbered, he sagged in annoyance, but said nothing.

══ 126 ══

In the longhouses of the Oneidas the passageway fires burned all night. In the morning, water kettles were found frozen and ice the thinness of a dragonfly's wing glazed Lake Oneida. Margaret worked with Swift Doe and other women harvesting and burying the last of the corn. In the middle of the morning, the white sun still struggling to send warmth, she saw Bone approach Swift Doe, looking every inch the suitor. He was neither handsome nor impressively muscled, and that a woman of Swift Doe's rare beauty should favor him so cheered him that his happiness remained fixed to his face for as long as he was in her presence. With him were her sons and he had come to ask her permission to take them fishing. She asked if they wanted to go. They yelled happily and jumped up and down.

But it wasn't their eagerness to go fishing that held her attention, it was Bone and Swift Doe. He had come into her life at precisely the right time: Her mourning was ended, loneliness and the bleak prospect of raising her sons without a father shadowed her life. Among the Iroquois, nearly two thirds of the women were widows and the widow who found a new husband was looked upon as most fortunate. In the Mohican Swift Doe saw another chance for companionship and protection, all the things Long Feather had once given her.

While the boys tugged at Bone's arms, Margaret watched him and Swift Doe talk in low tones. Like a golden cloud, affection settled about them, holding them together, bound with private warmth as if no others existed around them. They seemed unaware that she was nearby, unaware of anyone, even the boys. Love as such, so it was claimed, did not exist between men and women among the tribes. But there was no other word to describe what they were sharing at the moment.

She and Two Eagles shared it. And he had broken the rule, had shed his reserve and said the words.

I love you, love you. Hearing it just once satisfied her. He'd said it solely because he knew she wanted to hear it, wanted him to step out of his ways into hers, just for a moment. And that she would treasure, forever.

They were to be married that evening. Since neither of their mothers was involved, the customary negotiations were overlooked. At twilight, with Eight Minks' help, she would bake a single cake of unleavened corn bread and present it to Two Eagles. He would eat it in her presence, signifying his acceptance of her. It was customary for the bridegroom through his mother to give the bride a gift in exchange, generally venison or some other meat, to ratify the contract. But, since this was not possible, the giving of the cake and Two Eagles' offer to share it would suffice.

When the shadows lengthened and the sun lowered to rest, the cake was shared and bride and groom were led to a place outside the castle. There the squaws sat in a circle, with Two Eagles and Margaret in the center kneeling facing each other.

Eight Minks produced a string of rawhide as long as Two Eagles was tall. It was passed among the onlookers, each adding a single knot to it. When it was returned to Eight Minks she tied the ends together and twisted a loop into a figure eight, placing one loop about Two Eagles' neck, the other about Margaret's.

So simply they were bound in marriage.

They lay in their wedding bed, the chamber made fragrant with hemlock boughs and the sweet-smelling white flowers of the basswood tree.

He leaned his face against her neck, breathing in her fragrance, and fondled her shining blond hair. Tenderly, he stroked her arms and hands and the smoothness of her belly and on down her legs to her feet. Her breasts he did not caress, for they were not for the husband but for the child. They were her as mother, not as wife. Softly she moaned. He pressed his lips to her cheek and her mouth. Her nakedness, her trembling, her hurried breathing, her scent in his nostrils aroused him and his hand sought her place, pushing his finger slowly, gently inside.

He lifted her buttocks, pulling her upward onto his manhood. Together they moved and reveled in each other quietly but with great passion. And she adored him: her husband.

Despite the heat thrown by the cookfires in the passageway, the cold found its way to them, prompting her to pull the bearskin robe up from their thighs to cover them. She felt pierced with joy, her body incandescent. And tasted the honey of contentment. Until into her mind slipped a buzz of worry.

"What will you do about Burnt Eye?"

"He has challenged me. We will fight."

"When?"

"The first day after the new moon."

She swallowed. "That's only five days from now. You can't . . ."

"That is the day all such disputes are settled."

"I don't care. It's too soon. Your arm has barely started healing."

"He knows that."

"It'll be at least three weeks before you can even move it without pain." She caught herself. "Did you say *he knows that*?"

"He knows of my wound, yes."

"How could he?"

"Do you remember the night before we left for Quebec? During the dancing, when Two-branches-of-water said black words about you and was found dead the next morning?"

"But you didn't kill him . . ."

"He has friends who tell themselves I did, believe it and hate me for it. And ache in their guts to see Burnt Eye take my life. You can be sure they have told him of my wound."

"I don't care. You can't fight him!"

"He has given me the challenge. I must accept it. And because he is the wronged one, I cannot ask favors. And all the choices are his: the time, the place, all."

"Tell him you want to put it off for one month."

"I cannot. A challenge, like a blow struck, must be returned right away. But do not worry. In the five sleeps to come, my arm will heal."

"It's suicide!"

"Shhh, there is no reason to shout on this, of all nights."

"How will you fight?"

"With knives, of course, the only way. To give my arm rest when it needs it I will defend with my left hand."

"How can you? You're right-handed. Look at me, listen, you've simply got to postpone it, absolutely must! He's taking unfair advantage. Everybody can see that, even his people. They'll understand." She searched his eyes. "But you won't ask him because he'll think you a coward. What does it matter what he thinks?"

"I care as much for my face as he does for his. Red Paint and Fox are already on their way to Onekahoncka to accept his challenge for me." He squeezed her hand. "It is our way, the only way to smother the fire that rages between us."

"He'll kill you."

He shrugged. "No one has yet and I have fought hand-to-hand many times."

"You told Bone on the way to Onekahoncka that Burnt Eye is fearless, the bravest warrior you've ever seen. Your very words!"

"Fearless, the bravest, but not the best. I will do better. No more talk. I am tired. We will sleep."

"Sleep? You must be joking!"

She would never sleep again, now that she knew the bride could be a widow before the week was out. All thanks to Pierre!

127

Thunder hurled its wrath, lightning speared the robe of night, rain fell heavily, pooling on the ground. The entrance to Onekahoncka opened to admit two visitors. Red Paint and Fox were greeted as if expected and led to Burnt Eye's longhouse. Long before departing for Quebec they had learned that the matrons of the clans were holding the one-eyed one a virtual prisoner in his own house while they and the tribal elders discussed what, if any, punishment should be his for murdering his wife. Since that time he had evidently been exonerated. Or perhaps he'd appealed for the chance to absolve himself by defeating Two Eagles in hand-to-hand combat, pointing to the Oneida as the original cause of all his problems and indirectly responsible for Dreamer's death. Whatever the justification for his release, Red Paint and Fox found him sitting unguarded in the chamber of his longhouse where they had earlier shared food. Hole Face stood by.

Burnt Eye nodded, recognizing them. "*Se-go-li*, O-kwen-cha, Sku-nak-su."

"*Se-go-li*, Ho-ka-ah-ta-ken and *se-go-li* from Tékni-ska-je-a-nah," said Red Paint.

Food was brought and all ate. When the meal was done, fingers licked clean and the kettle removed, Burnt Eye surveyed his visitors and belched.

"I trust that he is well?"

Fox nodded. "He is."

"You have come a long distance in angry weather. What is your mission?"

"We bring his answer to your challenge, Ho-ka-ah-ta-ken," said Red Paint.

Burnt Eye leaned forward. "Does he accept?"

"We ask you, great chief, to show us the circle of blood."

Burnt Eye grinned triumphantly. Hole Face clapped his hands and a warrior appeared carrying a struggling wood-

chuck. A knife was produced, the creature's throat slit. As
it slowly died, its blood was drained into a bowl. The carcass was taken away. Burnt Eye held the bowl at eye level,
rose to his feet and poured a circle the length of his arm
in diameter between himself and his visitors.

"You have brought Tékni-ska-je-a-nah's knife?" he
asked, resuming his seat.

From his belt, Fox drew Two Eagles' knife wrapped in
deerskin. Unwrapping it, he plunged it into the ground in
the center of the circle. Burnt Eye did the same thing with
his knife. Less than an inch separated the two blades.
Burnt Eye then picked up Two Eagles' knife and sheathed
it.

Red Paint picked up the Mohawk's knife, wrapped it in
the deerskin and stuck it behind his belt. "Tékni-ska-je-a-
nah accepts your challenge," he muttered.

Burnt Eye nodded. "Tell him we will fight when the sun
shines on our heads on the first day after the new moon.
At a place near Onneyuttahage where all our people may
watch. We will fight for our knives."

Red Paint nodded. "He who retrieves his own knife is
the winner."

"Agreed."

Red Paint and Fox rose to leave. Burnt Eye stayed them
with a gesture.

"One other thing. We will fight with our knife hands
only, with our free arms strapped to our sides."

Red Paint and Fox exchanged glances.

"Unless Tékni-ska-je-a-nah objects. But why would he?
You speak for him. What do you say?"

"We agree," murmured Red Paint.

128

Another unseasonably cold night hastened the yellowing
of the grasses and freed the last of the leaves from
their branches. The morning was creaky cold. Margaret
and Eight Minks wore bearskin robes to walk outside the

castle. Margaret's fears for Two Eagles contended with frustration over what she saw as childish obstinacy on his part.

Eight Minks discounted stubbornness. "It is our warriors' way to settle differences," she explained. "The way of all Iroquois. And to ask Burnt Eye to change any part of it would be a sign of weakness that would dishonor your husband."

"He won't even be able to defend himself."

"He may surprise you. In the war he fought with wounds many times, some very painful. Death standing so close angered him, gave him strength. That is so with many, something in them rises in their hearts making them fight like maddened wolves. Fear, pride, hatred of their enemy—who can say what it is?"

Margaret scoffed quietly. And yet, Eight Minks' eyes didn't show worry about him. Did she actually think he had a chance or was she being fatalistic?

"His wound is no better today," said Margaret.

"It is hard to tell. The healing starts within. The only way he can know is by his strength slowly returning."

"Isn't there something you can give him for pain?"

"I can remind him, but he knows: You do not let pain into your mind. That way you cannot feel it."

Margaret sighed. "Would that it were so."

She plucked a sprig of grass and glanced skyward. "Why is Burnt Eye coming all this way?"

"He wants all of us to see Two Eagles lose. And he will be bringing as many of his own people as will come to see him win. He thinks."

"I should have cut his miserable throat when I had the chance."

"And you think you would have gotten out of there alive?"

"We've got to find a way to delay it until he's healed. In four days, the condition he's in, he won't last sixty seconds. What can we do?"

"Nothing. Whatever we tried, everyone would look upon as interfering in something that is not our affair. And even if we could, do you think that would please Two Eagles? He would never forgive you." She smiled thinly. "I know ... *men*."

129

The moon reappeared as a sickle, a sight that sliced Margaret's heart. Two Eagles slept beside her. But form the moment she lay down, she could not even close her eyes. When dawn silently reddened the heavens, heralding a beautiful day, she examined his wound, confirmed that at least the infection had been arrested and, leaving him still asleep, dressed and went out to walk by herself and speculate on what midday would bring to them.

Why couldn't one of his friends fight in his place? Splitting Moon could step in and cut down Burnt Eye like a rotten tree. But the obstacle to every solution she came up with was: His face, honor, manhood must not be blemished.

"Damn him!"

"Damn him!" a voice repeated behind her.

He had followed her out of the longhouse. He smiled. "It will be over soon."

"Idiots, the two of you!"

"The sun will be halfway down the sky and he will lie dead in the dust and we will begin our life. That is what we both want. It is what my óyaron says. It will be."

"Let me see you raise your arm."

He eyed the wound. "I need to save my strength."

"You can't even raise it."

"I can!" he snapped. "I will hold his knife and return it to him blade first! And watch him drop and die, and retrieve my knife. Now no more talk about it. No more!"

"Don't shout at me!"

He stood looking at her. The breeze stirred his feather in his scalp lock and ruffled the fringes of his trousers. He seemed to have grown six inches, this giant, this fine husband whom she adored with all her strength. But in her mind she saw him instead lying mortally wounded, Burnt Eye standing over him grinning, dropping the blood-smeared knife. She turned from him, moving toward the main gate.

He did not follow her, did not call after her.

The Mohawks arrived before midmorning. It appeared as if all Onekahoncka had mobilized behind their chief. Sight of him strutting brazenly angered her. Hole Face and Splitting Moon agreed on a bare patch of ground as suitable for the cockfight. Margaret had come to call it that to herself, that was what it amounted to. She was seventeen when she attended a cockfight in London. The fight ended with the death of one cock, the winner emerging bloodied and half-dead itself. By far the most revolting spectacle she had ever witnessed.

This would be a cockfight, with knives in place of talons, and blood spilling to delight the audience, a fight to the death. And when it was over, home she would go to England. She'd find some way to get back. Living here without him would be out of the question.

Eight Minks came up beside her, forcing a smile, and patted her arm reassuringly.

"How is he?" Margaret asked.

"You have not seen him?"

"Not since we got up. I couldn't bear looking at him. I've been avoiding him since. It doesn't make me look very loyal, does it? It's just that it sickens me when I know he's doomed. Did you look at his wound today?"

"He would not let me."

"Obstinate jackass!"

The two combatants were coming through the crowd from opposite directions. They wore breechclouts and were barefoot. And to her shock their left arms were firmly strapped to their sides.

"Oh my God . . ." she murmured.

"They must fight only with their right hands," murmured Eight Minks. "Burnt Eye demanded it. He set the rules."

"Of course."

She was tempted to leave, at least spare herself seeing him killed, but she held her ground. The crowd was buzzing excitedly. None of the Oneidas looked downcast, none of his friends seemed to share her fear that he hadn't a chance. Now Hole Face and Splitting Moon entered the arena, preceding the contenders, each one carrying a knife on a square of deerskin, as if to present gifts to a king. Burnt Eye followed Hole Face, strutting like a rooster into the open space. Two Eagles followed Splitting Moon. He looked exhausted, his shoulders sagged. The crowd roared jubilantly. Her ears rang. She could almost see blood in the center of the dusty circle. It was the Colosseum in ancient Rome.

Once more she wanted to leave but did not, not with Eight Minks alongside. Two Eagles looked toward her, linking with her eyes. Drums thumped in unison behind the gathering. The seconds presented the combatants with their knives and withdrew. The drumming stopped abruptly, a loud voice sang a single long note. The fight began.

Two Eagles' arm was more stiff than sore; from, he realized, being immobilized for so long. He had wanted to challenge the pain and exercise his arm, loosen the dormant shoulder muscles and work life into his elbow and wrist joints, but Eight Minks insisted he rest his arm and not risk reopening his wound. The wound itself was covered. Burnt Eye would attack it first chance he got, slice through the protective pad.

They crouched face to face, right arms angled away from their sides, knives upward. Burnt Eye feinted, thrust. Two Eagles leaped back nimbly, retaliated lunging. His shoulder cracked loudly, bringing a smirk to the other's face. Very soon, even if Burnt Eye failed to reach it, the sudden jerky and wrenching movements would break the scab, bleeding would start, the pain would come. He would ignore it, feel nothing, concentrate on the fight, on the ugly, unblinking eye riveting him, glowing at the prospect of cutting him again and again, killing him slowly.

They sparred. With every lunge, Burnt Eye grunted like a wounded bear. No sound came from Two Eagles. The crowd too was silent, rapt at the spectacle, peering to see advantage on the part of one or the other, the edge that would signal superiority and the beginning of the end. Slowly they circled lunging, jabbing, narrowly missing, feeling each other out, studying reactions to thrusts coming from different angles, looking for signs of slow response, clumsiness, vulnerable spots.

Burnt Eye suddenly straightened and stood stock still grinning; and sliced the thongs binding his left arm to his side. Two Eagles did the same, wondering why he was changing his rule, in midfight.

He found out. Burnt Eye was ambidextrous, as strong, as agile, as accurate with left hand as right. Showing off, he began shifting his knife from one hand to the other flinging it rapidly between thrusts. Abruptly, Two Eagles felt he was facing two opponents. Now on the defensive, he dodged and danced, his breath coming harder, sweat drenching him, stinging his eyes.

Burnt Eye's upper body was extraordinarily powerful and despite the weight he carried he was surprisingly quick. His stumpy legs forced him to take shorter steps than Two Eagles and the Oneida outreached him by six inches but they were equal in agility and quickness.

But the Mohawk had one distinct weakness: his empty right socket. Instead of facing Two Eagles directly, he angled slightly right, giving his left eye a wider field. But this exposed his left side.

Crouching lower brought the taller Two Eagles' torso down level with his adversary's. Burnt Eye screamed, whirled, thrust. Two Eagles sucked in, the tip of the blade coming within an inch of his stomach, and whipped his knife to Burnt Eye's blind side, slicing the Mohawk's vulnerable ribs.

Burnt Eye roared, not in pain, for the tip had barely broken the skin, but in embarrassment; rage darkened his ugliness, turning the white scar running down his face as pink as his eyeless socket. Once more he whirled, this

time bringing up his right leg in a sharp kick to Two Eagles' left, knocking him to the ground on his side, on his
wounded arm. Over and over he rolled, to avoid the downward plunging knife. When he got clear and sprang to his
feet, he felt blood warming his arm down to his elbow.
Burnt Eye roared gleefully, resumed the attack.

Each had drawn blood. Up to now, the fight was
roughly even but the Mohawk was more aggressive. On
they battled, as the sun started down, the crowd still transfixed. Margaret clutched the front of her dress, her knuck-
les white, fear immobilizing her face. Into the third hour
Burnt Eye and Two Eagles fought, dust dancing around
them, swirled by the breeze.

Fatigue began gnawing at Two Eagles. If his wound escaped the Mohawk's knife, the power of his legs would be
first to desert him. Already they were becoming heavier,
slower. They would turn to stone, lock him in place, unable to elude the blade coming at him. The Mohawk did
not look tired. As the afternoon wore on he appeared to
gain strength, drawing it from his hatred.

Into the fourth hour they fought. Two Eagles' reserve of
strength was draining away faster now, deserting him,
leaving him to fight with his heart, with his love for
her. And somewhere in him finding the strength to kill this
ugly, grunting animal coming at him. Sight of her on the
sideline strengthened his will, charged his flagging muscles, revived his quickness. His wound had clotted but not
before too much blood blackened the ground in the small
circle that contained the battle. Burnt Eye's whirling attack
he found difficult to defend against. When the Mohawk
came out of his spin he might lunge, kick, duck, bring his
knife straight up or jump and bring it down, using either
hand.

Two Eagles' arms grew leaden. His biceps burned with
exhaustion. The eye noticed. The animal attacked furiously, intent on ending the conflict with a single swipe. Up
flashed his knife, straight for Two Eagles' heart. He pulled
back, but could not evade the tip which struck and drew

blood. Burnt Eye leered, roared, lunged again; again Two Eagles retreated, but tangled his feet.

Down he fell, down came the knife plunging deep into his side. Pain seared, his head whirled. Down sprang Burnt Eye, jerking out the knife. In falling, striking the ground hard, Two Eagles' knife had slipped from his grasp. He could not see where it landed. With both hands he gripped Burnt Eye's wrist, holding the blade inches from his face.

Two Eagles sucked in the dusty air, growled and rolled over with his attacker. Burnt Eye turned him over and again was on top, Two Eagles still gripping, locking his wrist. Once more, the blade inched downward. Releasing his left hand, groping desperately with his right to locate his knife, Two Eagles snatched up a handful of dust and flung it at his attacker.

Burnt Eye bellowed, straightened, dropping his knife, sending both hands to his face. Snatching up the knife, Two Eagles plunged it through the Mohawk's hand into his eye.

Into his brain. The crowd gasped. Burnt Eye shuddered and once more stiffened, the handle protruding from his hand, blood streaming down. Two Eagles pushed him off and got slowly up on all fours. By the time he was able to regain his feet, Burnt Eye had fallen and lay still. Bending, Two Eagles pulled out the knife and with his last strength held it high, for all to see. *His* knife, retrieved, signifying victory. The crowd, barely a third Oneida, roared approval. The Mohawks stared. Two Eagles teetered, dropped the knife, collapsed, sprawling across Burnt Eye's corpse. The Oneidas ran toward him. First to reach him was Margaret.

130

For four days Two Eagles lay in his chamber in riveting pain evidenced not by complaint but by his high fever

and sweating. Gradually, under care of Eight Minks and
Margaret, his wounds began to knit, his pain subsided.
Margaret sat by his bed bathing his gunshot wound and
applying a fresh bandage. His uninjured arm encircled
her neck, bringing her mouth down to his to kiss tenderly.

She pulled free. "No! I'm mad as blazes at you. You
will never ever ever ever fight anyone like that again.
Never!"

"Shhhh, how many times must you say it? I have no
brothers left to avenge."

"It's not funny." She softened her tone. "How's your
side?"

"No pain . . ."

"Onewachten."

"I am not lying. It itches, so I know it is healing. My
arm, too. I feel good. I will get up."

"No!"

"You cannot make me stay in bed."

"You're not getting up. Don't make me tie you down
and don't argue."

He grinned. "With you?"

"You must be starving."

"Neh."

She got up. "I'll get you something hot that'll stick to
your ribs. Don't you dare get up. That's an order."

She went out. He dozed.

Eight Minks came by, lifting the door covering, peering
in. "You look better, you have color. Where is she?" He
told her. "She is a good wife, Tékni-ska-je-a-nah. She
thinks only of you. I stood with her watching you fight.
She suffered through every minute. Every strike he made
she felt."

He grunted.

"Pay attention, you must not pick any more such fights;
with Maquens, with anyone. No more red days, no more
roaming about looking for trouble. Put aside your restless-
ness, stay home, be a good husband, a good father."

Again, he grunted.

Eight Minks smiled. "Make her happy, Tékni-ska-je-a-nah, as she will make you, your Englishwoman, your woman who fell from the sky."

"From the sky, yes. Into a tree, into our lives, into my heart."

═══ **EPILOGUE** ═══

Following the disclosure of proof of Pierre's involvement in the death of Little Cloud, Governor Frontenac pocketed the two incriminating buttons, dismissed his visitors and dispatched the guard to summon the captain. Pierre was not in his quarters. He was in town in his rented room with his new paramour, with whom he had spent every night since Margaret's departure.

Charged with murder, he was tried, found guilty and sentenced to ten years' imprisonment. He was placed in the cell earlier occupied by Two Eagles.

Fourteen months later, on the twenty-sixth of November 1698, following a brief illness, Governor Frontenac died and was deeply mourned by all of New France. One of the first acts of his successor, Governor Decallières, was to commute the remainder of the prisoner's sentence. Pierre was dishonorably discharged and returned to France in disgrace. Within seven months his father died of natural causes and he inherited the family estate. From that time on, he lived a life of ease and luxury. He never married.

In 1701, four years after the Massowaganine fire that terminated negotiations between the Iroquoian Confederacy and the French and their allies, a peace treaty was signed. In those four years of relative calm between the two sides, Margaret Addison gave birth to a son. He was named Canyewa Tawyne—Little Otter. His English name was Benjamin, for his grandfather.

Ataentsic's child.

"amor vincit omnia et nos cedamus amori"

AUTHOR'S NOTE

The author extends grateful thanks to her husband, Alan, for his tireless and exhaustive research into the Oneida and Mohawk tribes of the period. Available useful material was disappointingly meager. Many early authors of the Iroquois rivaled Parson Weems in the wealth of their misinformation and false inductive reasoning. Others merely copied earlier writers, repeating their errors. Unfortunately, the best scholars offered for research information, which, although accurate and well documented, proved of little value in the realm of fiction.

The spelling of virtually all Iroquoian words is disputable. Few scholarly sources agree on the spelling of place names in particular.

This is the case because the tribal languages were oral and only written when white men transcribed them.

—BARBARA RIEFE
Boca Raton, Florida

THE BEST OF FORGE

☐ 53441-7   CAT ON A BLUE MONDAY $4.99
            Carole Nelson Douglas   Canada $5.99

☐ 53538-3   CITY OF WIDOWS $4.99
            Loren Estleman   Canada $5.99

☐ 51092-5   THE CUTTING HOURS $4.99
            Julia Grice   Canada $5.99

☐ 55043-9   FALSE PROMISES $5.99
            Ralph Arnote   Canada $6.99

☐ 52074-2   GRASS KINGDOM $5.99
            Jory Sherman   Canada $6.99

☐ 51703-2   IRENE'S LAST WALTZ $4.99
            Carole Nelson Douglas   Canada $5.99
